JACKSON

DISCARD

 sourcebooks
casablan

Published by Sourcebooks Casablanca, an imprint of Sourcebooks
P.O. Box 4410, Naperville, Illinois 60567-4410
(630) 961-3900
sourcebooks.com

Printed and bound in Canada.
MBP 10 9 8 7 6 5 4 3 2 1

To my late grandparents, Mr. and Mrs. James and Doris Davidson, thank you for instilling all those down-home values in this Brooklyn girl's heart. Thank you for teaching me that family, whether born or made, is a source of strength, and to nurture and serve it is an honorable gift.

To Damon, because forever and always, it has, is, and will be you.

Chapter 1

"AJA MARIE EVERETT, YOU'D BETTER GET YOUR HIND PARTS down here before this food you had me cook gets cold."

Had her cook? Aja rolled her eyes from the safety of her bedroom. Once finished getting dressed, she rushed into the kitchen to the stove and placed a gentle kiss on her aunt's cheek. "Morning, Auntie. Smells like heaven in here." Aja pulled a mug from the cabinet and poured herself a cup of coffee before sitting at the eat-in counter.

As she sipped, Aunt Jo placed a piping-hot bowl of creamy grits in front of Aja. She took a long sniff of the buttery scent wafting up at her and hummed in appreciation.

"I didn't make biscuits and sausage because you said you had to get an early start."

Aja waved a hand. "This is more than fine. The girls and I have a lot on our agenda this morning." That was especially true after yesterday's collapsed construction scaffold. The shock of how close she'd come to being injured, or worse, made her insides quake with cold. Determined to chase the chill away, she blew on the steaming spoonful of grits and slowly slurped them into her mouth. "I swear you make the best grits in Texas, Auntie." She let a satisfied moan slip, then tucked into the dish. She was halfway through her meal when she looked up and caught sight of the bright smile lighting up Jo's face.

"What are you smiling about?"

"You." The single word spoke volumes. Two years ago, Aja had run from the pain of her younger sister's death in Brooklyn and showed up on Jo's doorstep. It had taken three months of Jo's tender care for her to do more than shuffle from the bed to the couch. "Helping those girls has done you a world of good, hasn't it?"

"Sure has," Aja answered with a smile. "And if I'm going to continue to help them, I've got to get to my office—"

"You mean that old empty barn?"

Aja smiled at her aunt's sass. It was no wonder Aja never met a smart comment she didn't love. Sarcasm was a hereditary trait, it seemed.

"My temporary office. I need to make a few calls."

"I assume to the sheriff. Has he decided to do his job yet?"

Aja's spoon was midway to her mouth when her appetite soured. She placed the utensil back in the bowl and sat up straight. Fighting on a full stomach would do terrible things to her digestion, so she pushed the unfinished meal away and decided breakfast was over.

"I called him twice yesterday after the scaffolding came down. He said to make sure I wanted him to come out here, because if he does, chances are any investigation he opens will focus on the two people he believes most likely to be responsible—Seneca and Brooklyn."

Jo huffed and sucked her teeth before responding to Aja. "That no-count man is unbelievable."

Aja slumped her shoulders. "Unfortunately, I don't have a choice but to deal with him."

"You have a choice, Aja. You're just choosing to ignore it."

Aja pressed the first two fingers of her right hand to her temple and rubbed. She was about to close her eyes to give in to the soothing comfort, but the sight of her aunt fiddling with the frayed edge of a dish towel made her focus sharpen instead. Josephine Henry was the epitome of calm and collected. The only time she wasn't was when she was up to no good.

"What did you do, Aunt Jo?"

By now she was nearly tearing the poor towel to shreds. "I called Ricky."

"Really, Aunt Jo?" Aja threw up her hands in defeat. "After I specifically asked you not to?"

"He can help. If the sheriff won't do his job, Ricky can make him."

As a Hays County sitting judge, he could. Aja didn't doubt that. But having her uncle involved meant him coming in and taking over. Aja couldn't deal with that.

"You know how your brother is. He's gonna make it worse, Aunt Jo."

"Chile, somebody seems bent on hurting, maybe even killing you. It don't get much worse than that."

"Auntie," Aja moaned.

"He'll fix it, chile. You'll see."

Aja stood and walked around to her aunt. She wrapped her arms around Jo and reveled in the peace one only knew when they were surrounded by love. She may not agree with her aunt's method of handling things, but she knew her actions came from a good place.

Headed for her office, Aja stepped out onto her front porch. She closed her eyes and breathed in as much of the sweet country air as she could, then opened them again. The deep-green and earthy-brown hues covering the expanse of her land were breathtaking. Restoration Ranch, or the idea of it, had helped Aja heal when the loss of her sister made her survival in this world questionable. It would soon be finished. She wouldn't let anyone keep that dream from becoming reality.

"Hey, Boss."

A year of rebuilding and it was still strange to hear someone call her "boss." Aja turned her head and watched the two women as they approached.

Brooklyn Osborn had short, pixie-cut cropped dark curls and deep-brown skin with glowing honey undertones. She was a tall, fit Black woman with her lean, tight muscles on display in her A-line T-shirt and fitted jeans. The serious lines of her face were in stark contrast to the woman walking beside her—Seneca Daniels. Like Brooklyn, Seneca was a thirtysomething Black woman. But that was where their similarities ended. Seneca was average height with a curvy build and reddish-brown skin that seemed to radiate in the Texas heat. Where Brooklyn's steps were even and methodical, Seneca waved an excited arm as she made her way from the side of the house to the front steps and climbed to greet Aja.

"What's got her so excited this early in the morning?" Aja posed the question to Brooklyn, knowing she'd get a direct answer. She didn't mind Seneca's round-the-mulberry-bush method of story-telling, but with her shortage of time and Seneca practically vibrating with excitement as she took her place next to Aja, Brooklyn's straight, no-chaser reporting style was definitely the way to go.

"You know it doesn't take much to excite her. But she honestly has reason to be excited today. Let her tell you."

This was true. Seneca was the bright spot of seemingly unending joy in their makeshift family. As long as she smiled, there was always hope.

Aja smiled at Seneca and gave her a reluctant wave of her hand. "G'on and tell me," she huffed, feigning lack of interest, knowing full well the sight of Seneca clapping her hands together in excitement pretty much made it impossible to be disinterested at this point. "I don't have all day."

Seneca continued to smile as warmth radiated off her and reached out to tug at the remnants of Aja's somber mood. "While I was working on updates on some external terminals"—she took a deep breath and shared a conspiratorial glance with Brooklyn before she continued—"that contractor in Austin you contacted sent in a bid. It's under budget, and they can start the job in the next two weeks."

Aja squealed as equal parts of relief and joy spread through her. Seneca's announcement was a much-needed bit of good news.

After Earl, their previous contractor, quit in the wake of the ranch's latest life-threatening accident, Aja worried she wouldn't be able to keep to schedule if it took too long to find his replacement. But Seneca, in her usual don't-sweat-it fashion, had curated a list of contractors in the surrounding area for Aja to send queries to last night.

Aja grabbed Seneca's and Brooklyn's hands, and they whooped and hollered in celebration. It didn't matter that the new contractor hadn't begun yet. Aja's dream of Restoration Ranch becoming a road to rehabilitation was no longer on pause.

"Oh my goodness," Aja huffed. "When I sent out those blanket queries last night, I never thought we'd get a response this soon. If this crew can get started in the next couple of weeks, once we vet them, we can still open by the start of travel season."

Aja pulled the other women in for a celebratory hug before she pulled back and attempted to gather herself again. She needed to focus and stay on task. There was still a lot of work to do.

"Boss? You okay?"

Aja massaged the back of her neck, trying to take it all in. "I'm fine. Just..." She took a deep breath and let her lungs slowly expel it. "It's really gonna happen, ladies. My dream hasn't crumbled with that scaffold."

With a wide grin plastered across her face, Seneca declared, "There was never any doubt."

Maybe not for them, but Aja couldn't fix her lips to tell that lie, so she quietly smiled instead as they headed toward the front door. "Go get something to eat. We've got a busy day ahead."

The ladies headed inside and Aja leaned on the railing, letting the good news sink in. Hope filled the center of her chest and spread through her body like the rays of the Texas sun chasing away the shadows. "It's gonna happen."

With renewed faith that everything might turn out okay, she walked through the pasture of green grass with a little swing in her hips. Good news certainly could change the outlook of your day.

"Boss...boss!"

She stopped, turning to find Brooklyn running toward her. Her long legs and easy gait ate up the ground between them in a flash. "You left your phone in the kitchen."

Aja patted her back pockets, realizing Brooklyn was right. "Thank you, doll. It would've been hard to make all the calls I need from the barn with no landlines out there yet." She took the phone and slid it into her pocket before turning away. "Don't take all day in that kitchen—we got work to do. We'll be holed up in the barn until lunch."

As she walked away, Brooklyn called, "You're turning into a hard-ass tyrant. It's too pretty outside to be cooped up in the barn all day."

Aja kept walking but tossed over her shoulder, "Just for that, we'll work through lunch in the barn. How's that for a tyrant?"

She stopped for a brief second to see the scowl she knew Brooklyn was probably wearing when the sound of breaking glass pulled her attention away. Aja stepped forward when she felt the ground rumble beneath her and a loud boom cracked the air, making her eardrums vibrate painfully. Before she could cover her ears, a blast of pressure knocked her off her feet.

She fought to orient herself while the smell of burning wood and smoke assaulted her. Her chest tightened with fear as she struggled to breathe through the soot-tinged air. She couldn't tell up from down, and no matter how hard she tried to stand, her legs wouldn't work.

You gotta get up, Aja.

She tried to summon her strength and lift her head. When she moved no more than an inch from the ground, sharp pain sliced at the top of her forehead, forcing her to press her head into the cool grass, searching for relief.

The gray-black clouds of smoke hovering over her were getting fuzzy, and the only thing she could hear was ringing in her ears. Her senses were overwhelmed with panic, and she was pretty certain she was about to pass out soon.

"Boss? Boss?"

The sound of a voice vibrating in and out of focus—loud then soft, close then far, with a disorienting echo clanging around in her head— made it hard to tell who was speaking.

"Hold on. I got you."

Strong hands hooked themselves under Aja's arms and pulled. The dirt and rocks hidden among the blades of grass scraped against the backs of her thighs and calves through the heavy denim of her jeans. When the movement stopped, she could see sunlight breaking through the billows of black smoke, and the air didn't smell as strongly of acrid and dense dust and ash.

A fuzzy shadow edged into her line of vision. The closer it came, the sharper the image appeared, and soon Brooklyn's cynical face was filling her sight.

"Boss," she called. "With the barn in flames, I kinda think your plans of us working all day in there are shot to shit."

Aja blinked slowly as the pins and needles of numbness prickled her extremities, marking the return of feeling in her body. "Yeah, Brooklyn." Aja's voice cracked halfway through the woman's name. "I think you might be right." She tried to take a deep breath in, but her lungs protested and she coughed, making the pain in her head throb harder. "But"—she coughed again—"I think there's something much worse than the barn burning down."

"What?" Brooklyn asked.

Aja took a slow breath, determined not to let it disintegrate into a coughing fit. "I think Aunt Jo is right. Someone might really be trying to kill me."

Chapter 2

JACKSON DEAN MADE HIS WAY INSIDE THE TEXAS RANGERS' headquarters and headed straight for his office. It was early in the morning, and he wanted nothing more than to still be in his bed. Unfortunately, a call from his boss, Major Hargrove, had put the kibosh on that plan.

He twisted the knob and switched on the light, waiting a moment for his eyes to adjust to the brightness flooding the room. He remembered how happy he had been to get an office of his own. The room was nothing much to speak of. A typical windowless space in a government building made of white concrete walls and filled with metal furniture. But no matter how bland it was, he was still proud to have his name etched on the door because it came with his promotion to team leader eight years ago.

Today, it looked almost exactly the same as it had when he'd first been given the keys. But at the moment, when sleep hadn't completely let loose its grip on him, boundless pride wasn't the emotion he was experiencing. No, it was more like annoyance and frustration grating on his nerves at having to come in early after working in the field late last night.

He dropped his bag on a nearby chair and headed straight

for the coffee maker on top of a metal filing cabinet. Fresh, frequent, and plentiful caffeine would be the only thing to keep him from getting an insubordination write-up in his personnel file, so he opened a couple of bottled waters and poured them into the machine.

A tap on his door grabbed his attention. He glanced up from it, rested his eyes on the yet-to-start-dripping coffee machine, and groaned.

"Someone must want me to get a write-up."

Another tap and he pushed away from the filing cabinet and opened the door.

"Morning, Jackson." Major Hargrove didn't wait to be invited in. He just assumed the open door was all the invitation he needed. "Thanks for coming so quickly."

"I'm still half-asleep," Jackson groaned as he stepped away from the door and made it back to his coffeepot.

"At least you had the chance to go to sleep. I've been up for about twenty-four hours, since I got this call just before I was about to head home yesterday."

Jackson stared through narrowed slits. Hargrove didn't play with his time. He stayed when necessary, but he was obsessed with him and his Rangers having a clear work-life balance. Nothing kept him from punching out at six in the evening unless there was a real emergency. "You made it sound like it was life or death that I come in at"—he raised his left wrist, pretending to read the wide-faced watch there—"ass o'clock in the morning. What's going on, Major?"

His boss slid a file on Jackson's desk and took the seat in front of it, waiting patiently for Jackson to fill the mug he'd grabbed the second the alarm on the machine told him his brew was ready.

"You're not gonna put any milk or sugar in the rotgut?"

"No, sir," Jackson replied, sitting down and taking a long, slow sip. "I like it the way it is: strong and black, just like me."

He took another sip before opening the file. The first thing that caught his attention was the picture of a woman in a fitted designer dress. Not that he knew fashion from foam rubber, but with the way the black material hugged her full curves, he was certain it had been made or at least tailored just for her.

"I'm not gonna be ready to read this without at least another cup. Just give me the highlights. Who is she?"

His boss crossed an ankle over his knee and tilted his head. "She's the niece of a friend. A judge in Hill Country. Her property has been vandalized, and the judge needs someone to look into it."

Jackson felt his brow inching higher toward his hairline. Something about the way Major Hargrove said "someone" scratched at his bullshit meter.

"What do the locals have to say about it?"

Hargrove lifted an open palm before letting his hand fall back to his knee. "Not a thing. There's some bad blood between the local sheriff's department and Ms. Everett."

Jackson shifted in his seat. The coffee plus his boss's preliminary recount was starting to sketch an outline to this tale of a spoiled judge's niece using her uncle's connections to get what she wanted.

"Anyway, the judge wants to make sure this is taken seriously. Especially since the vandalism has escalated from fence posts and a scaffold being knocked down to her barn being burned to the ground yesterday."

Jackson sat up straighter. "Anyone hurt?"

"Minor cuts and bruises on Ms. Everett. Her uncle called me while she was being seen at the hospital. Asked me to get her a protective detail and send a team out to investigate."

"She pointing fingers at anyone?"

Hargrove stood up and tapped on top of the beautiful woman's picture. "Don't know. But you can ask when she gets here. I assigned Jennings and Gleason to her protective detail overnight. They're bringing her in first thing this morning so she can swear out a statement. Get your team together and figure this thing out." He walked toward the door confident his orders would be followed. And they would be. Jackson might give his boss shit, but he always got the job done.

He looked at the picture of one Ms. Aja Everett again. He ran his finger slowly over the high cheekbones that turned her eyes into barely opened slits as her wide grin smiled back at him. "Why would anyone want to harm you?"

━━━━━━━━━━━━━

"So what's the plan for this case?"

Jackson glared at Colton Adams over the rim of his coffee cup. It was still early—pitch-black-sky early—and Jackson hadn't slept enough to keep a civil tongue in his head where Colton was concerned.

"We need to figure out who's trying to hurt Aja Everett." He summarized the events as he knew them for his team.

Colton stretched out in his chair facing Jackson's desk, crossing his legs and appearing the picture of comfort. "What do we know about the victim?"

"Her uncle is a friend of Hargrove's. He gave me the highlight notes her uncle supplied." Jackson pulled a file off his desk and handed it to Colton. "But he's her uncle, so I'm running a thorough background check of my own. Only a few details came in yet. The rest will be forthcoming."

Colton scanned through the information before returning his attention to Jackson. "The file says she's got two employees who did time. You looking at them for this?"

"I'm lookin' at everyone. A bold son of a bitch tried to blow up a woman on her own land yesterday. I'm looking at anyone who had motive and opportunity. Including the ex-cons she's got working for her. They are potential victims and suspects. It's up to us to figure out which."

"With only the three of us?" That question came from Storm Cordero. He was the newest member of their group. Team-centered, always there to offer help, and eager to learn, Storm had quickly become the glue that held this set together. He was also the buffer that kept two bristly personalities like Jackson and Colton from sparking to the point of combustion.

"I tried to get more manpower"—Jackson sipped another mouthful of his coffee before continuing—"but that's a no-go. We'll have Blaze Gleason and Kade Jennings here at the office to follow leads, get warrants, and interview the townsfolk. Since yesterday, they've been out on protection detail with the victim. They should be bringing her in for an official statement in an hour. So that leaves the three of us on the ground at the ranch."

Colton and Storm nodded in unison.

"Good, consider yourselves briefed," Jackson said. "Let's get this investigation underway." He sent up a silent prayer for quick resolution of this case while his colleagues filed out of his office. He flipped the file Colton had left on his desk and stared at the happy image of the confident woman in the picture. The idea of that beautiful smile slipping off her face because of fear weighed on him.

Maybe it was that he'd assumed her complaint wasn't a valid one the moment he discovered she was a VIP. Maybe it was the news that her property had been destroyed and she'd narrowly missed the danger. Or maybe it was the realization he didn't believe the fearless woman full of life in that photograph should ever deserve to be afraid to walk on her land. Whatever it was, Jackson was determined to keep her safe. The best way for him to do that was to put himself between Aja Everett and whoever was after her.

Aja sat in the back seat of the large, black SUV and focused on the scenery rushing by on the highway. The landscape was slowly turning from dirt road to paved city expressways as the vehicle ate up miles beneath its tires. By her count, they had another sixty minutes remaining of the ninety-minute trip from her small town of Fresh Springs to the big city of Austin.

Her ringing phone caught her notice, drawing her back into her unpleasant reality. She took a breath, recognizing the ringtone and dreading the conversation she knew she'd be forced to have.

"Morning, Uncle Ricky." She fought to keep her voice level and light, hoping to avoid her uncle's intense protective streak.

"Morning, Aja. Did you reach Austin yet?"

"No, sir. We're about an hour out."

"Major Hargrove tells me he's putting his best man on this. So you just g'on in there, tell 'im what's happening, and let him find out who's responsible for all this trouble on the ranch."

She pressed back into the soft cushion of the seat, letting her head fall against the headrest for support.

"Uncle Ricky. I already know who's responsible for the vandalism on the ranch."

"Hmmm," he harrumphed. "We both have our theories about that."

"Brooklyn and Seneca had nothing to do with this."

"That remains to be seen." She could hear his frustration level climbing, and she knew there were only a few moments left before he started hollering over the line. " All we do know is someone caused a fiery explosion at your barn yesterday. When your life is in the balance, everyone is a suspect, including the two ex-convicts you have living out there with you."

"Uncle Ricky—"

"You could've been killed." Aja swallowed the protest on her tongue and let her uncle's words sink in. He wasn't wrong. If her employee hadn't called her name before she reached the barn, Aja would've been inside when the electric wiring ignited the kerosene lamps and her barn went up in a loud burst of flames. "Dammit, Aja! Why are you so stubborn?"

"Uncle Ricky, I'm fine. Yes, my barn was destroyed, but the only thing that happened to me was a cut on my head that didn't even need stitches."

"I wouldn't care if the only thing you got was a broken nail. You are not setting foot back on that ranch, Aja. Not until Mat gets those ex-convicts off your property and you are unenrolled from that Pathways program."

The stiffness in her uncle's voice, coupled with the mention of Seneca and Brooklyn's parole officer Mat Ryan, made her head throb. She called this her uncle's "judge voice." He'd spent so many years using it to call people to order that he foolishly believed she'd fall in line when he used it on her too. "You know I won't agree to anything like that. I can't leave Aunt Jo and my employees to fend for themselves on the ranch."

"No," he replied. "I don't want my sister in harm's way, either, so I already moved Jo to my house. It's a gated community with round-the-clock security. She'll be fine, and so will you once you're under my roof too."

She tried to shake her head, but it throbbed from the movement, so she rubbed her temple instead. "Uncle Ricky. You're doing way too much. I don't want all this."

"You may not want it, but it's what's happening. I'm only waiting for Mat to figure out what to do with the parolees you're harboring before I send someone out there to close the ranch down."

She pulled the phone from her ear and glared at it for a long moment. "No, Uncle Ricky," she hollered, and she immediately regretted raising her voice when the Rangers each glanced back at her. She quieted her voice before resuming her conversation. "I'm not gonna let you close my ranch down."

His lack of immediate response told her he was gearing up for a fight. If she knew her uncle, he was squinting over his glasses, trying to put the fear that only southern elders managed to instill into their young'uns into her, even though they were on the phone. He was good, but she was better. She managed a similar glare of her own, slowly tilting her head to keep the achy stiffness from yesterday's drama from settling in again. "Uncle Ricky, you were the one who told me to fight for what I believed in. I believe in these women. I believe in the Pathways program. Why can't you support my decision to help them rebuild their lives?"

"Aja, you're my niece. My only niece." His voice cracked.

Aja swallowed, trying to shove down the grief that was suddenly clawing at her. God, she still missed her sister.

Yesterday morning before all hell broke loose, she'd been proud of her ability to move on these last two years. But in moments like this, when she had to deal with her grief—and her uncle's too—Aja felt like she was right back at the start of her own personal hell.

She took a deep breath, trying to desperately quiet the sad thoughts swirling in her head. "Uncle Ricky, you've called in the Texas Rangers against my will. I'll go along with them investigating the vandalism because obviously things have gotten out of hand. But I am not shutting my ranch down, and I'm not abandoning Seneca and Brooklyn when they've done nothing to deserve it. My house, my rules. Isn't that what you always say to me when I set foot into your place?"

Aja saw the Ranger in the passenger seat sneaking a sideways glance at her. She'd deal with him when this was over. Right now, she needed to get her uncle off her back.

"All right, Aja. As long as you let the Rangers do their job, I'll back off. But if there's any more trouble, I don't wanna hear a damn thing other than the sound of your boots headed out of that place. You understand me?"

"Yessuh."

She ended the call and focused her attention on the Ranger who was still trying to hide the smirk on his face.

"Is there something you need to say, Ranger...Gleason is it?"

He shook his head. "No, ma'am."

"You sure? The expression on your face seems to say otherwise."

He shook his head again. "No, just thinking that my boss, Ranger Dean, ain't ready for you."

She shifted in her seat, crossing her arms as she leveled a pointed stare at him. "No man ever is."

And she doubted this Ranger Dean would be an exception to that rule. Ever since her uncle had called the Rangers in last night, she'd surmised they, like her uncle, would never look further than the obvious suspects Seneca and Brooklyn seemed. But that was all right. Aja always had a plan. She hadn't been one of the most successful trial attorneys in New York for nothing. Her gift was always being able to outstrategize her opponents.

This Texas Ranger wouldn't be any different as far as she was concerned. She wanted this case solved, but not at her ladies' expense. To avoid that, she'd simply have to get Ranger Dean off their scent with the same steps she used to win over unforgiving juries.

Step one: Humanize the defendants. Step two: Provide an alternate version of the crime. Step three: Create a reasonable doubt the defendants could ever have committed the crime. Step four (the most important step of all): Smile and turn those that would condemn you into your advocates. Make your enemy do the fighting for you.

A calm stillness spread over her and she returned to staring out the window. Brooklyn and Seneca were counting on her. She'd done this before with great success; there was no reason Aja could

see that it shouldn't work now when her success was more important than adding another mark in her win column.

A smile crept onto her lips as her plan solidified. Aja had the
perfect strategy and her secret weapon was tucked away safely in
the cargo area of the SUV.

I won't let you down, ladies.

Chapter 3

JACKSON TRIED TO KEEP HIS MIND EMPTY AS HE WAITED IN HIS office for Gleason and Jennings to arrive with Aja Everett. It was a common practice of his, mellowing enough to push distractions out of his head before the start of a case. But every time he attempted to do it, the image of the confident woman striking a model's pose with her hip jutted out and her hands on her waist popped into his head.

Jackson caught himself groaning and was thankful Colton and Storm had left him alone. The idea of having to explain to his coworkers why he was so distracted had no appeal.

He glanced down at the open case file on his desk and thumped his finger on top of it. The three of them at the ranch weren't nearly enough to investigate as many angles as they needed to, but they'd been in tighter spots, and they worked well together. With Gleason and Jennings backing them up at headquarters, hopefully there would be a quick and effective end to all this. Because if the way he couldn't take his eyes off the sumptuous beauty's photo was any sign, spending time with Aja Everett was bound to be a problem for him.

A tap on his door drew his attention as Colton leaned in.

"Gleason and Jennings are in the parking lot with Ms. Everett. You want me to put her in one of the interrogation rooms?"

Jackson shook his head. She was the niece of a sitting judge and the victim of a serious crime. Putting her in an interrogation room could be misconstrued in all sorts of ways. That was grief he didn't need. "No, bring her in here."

Colton tapped on his phone's screen. When he was done, he opened the door wide and he and Storm walked in. "Message sent. They'll come directly here."

Another knock on the door, and Jennings stepped inside, greeting Jackson and their colleagues while holding the door open and jerking a thumb behind him. Jackson blinked, and suddenly Aja Everett was filling his doorway in the flesh.

And what lovely flesh it was. She wore a red blouse with a black fitted suit vest and matching black slacks that hung like a second skin on her. No way she pulled that outfit off any rack, the way the material seemed to lovingly hold each of her curves. It was a power suit, battle armor for the powerful attorney the preliminary background check he'd run said she was.

"Morning, Ranger Dean." A bright smile graced her lips. "May I come inside?"

Jackson was caught off guard by the greeting. Her outfit, the stacked platform heels that peeked out from the hem of her pants, even the bloodred matte lipstick she wore told him firmly she was poised to attack. Her easy smile seemed out of place.

"Please, call me Jackson." He ushered her into the room, then pointed to Colton and Storm seated at the conference table. "These are the rest of my team members, Colton Adams and Storm Cordero." She waved at each of them before looking at Jackson. "Can I offer you a cup of coffee before we begin?"

"From a federal building?" She shook her head. "I care about my health more than that. In fact, I brought my own coffee and snacks too." She raised her hand in a graceful wave and pointed toward the door. Like magic, Gleason appeared at the door pushing a cart with a large thermal coffee dispenser and two large insulated food bags.

Jackson closed his eyes and took a deep breath. He moaned as his stomach protested that breakfast so far had been one and a half cups of bad black coffee.

He opened his eyes, and his chest tightened as he took in the sight of her again. She looked even more tempting standing in front of him now than she had in the picture in her file.

She unzipped the food bags and pulled out two large pans of what looked and smelled like the best cinnamon rolls he would ever have in his life. When she was finished setting up the food and made disposable cutlery and flatware appear out of thin air, she returned to Jackson and his men with a broad, welcoming smile.

"You didn't need to go through this kind of trouble, Ms. Everett."

She lifted her shoulders, dismissing his comment. "My mama taught me to never show up anywhere empty handed. It's bad manners."

He chuckled. Aja might be a New Yorker, but her southern sensibilities were definitely showing.

"Now that that's settled, I hope you gentlemen don't mind something sweet, hot, and sticky for breakfast."

Jackson closed his eyes again as he tried to control his breathing. He'd hoped for short and simple. But this woman standing in the middle of his office, looking the picture of a poised, dominant professional mixed with a touch of down-home goodness, was as complicated a start to this case as Jackson could imagine.

A two-dimensional Aja Everett in a photo, Jackson could deal with. But this tempting stranger, smiling as she offered him something sweet, hot, and sticky, would not be easy at all.

"So what brought you out to Fresh Springs, all the way from New York?"

You mean besides the world caving in on me and attempting to swallow me whole?

Aja gave a sweeping pass to the three remaining Rangers at the table before focusing on Jackson. The two men who'd watched her all night grabbed a few rolls and some coffee before taking their leave.

Gleason and Jennings hadn't invaded her space. They'd worked diligently to stay out of her way. But the way Jackson's gaze burned into her gave Aja the feeling he wouldn't leave her in peace as his colleagues had.

Aja placed a practiced smile on her face before answering. "My aunt Jo needed help with the ranch. My mom used to send me—" Aja stopped herself before she could finish. She grabbed the fork resting on her plate and cut a healthy piece of the cinnamon roll. She shoved it into her mouth and chewed until she could feel the jitters in her stomach subside. "She used to send me down here every summer when school was out. With so many fond memories, it wasn't that difficult a choice to say yes when Aunt Jo called."

Aja put down her fork and reached for the disposable coffee cup sitting in front of her plate. She needed another moment to get her nerves together, and eating and drinking would allow her that without raising suspicion. She was firm in that belief until her eyes met Jackson's and she felt a chill spill down her spine.

"So it was your aunt's idea to turn this place into an ex-convicts' paradise?"

Aja bit the inside of her lip to make certain the tongue-lashing she was struggling to swallow wouldn't escape into the air.

"Jackson, the women who work on my ranch are more than parolees. Yes, they made choices in the past that led them down an unfortunate road, but that doesn't define who they are."

"You sure about that?"

She gave him a terse look, wondering if the asshole he was displaying was for her benefit or if this was his natural disposition.

She was about to give him a piece of her mind when he took a sip from his coffee cup, leaving an errant drop on his bottom lip that he summarily collected with a single swipe of his long, pink tongue. The world somehow slowed down as she watched with envy.

She closed her eyes to retreat from one tempting image when her brain decided to conjure up the picture of him standing in front of his desk when she arrived.

He was tall with tight, low-cropped dark curls at the top of his head and a full, neatly trimmed beard whose lines looked as if someone had carved them into his face. She wondered if his beard would prickle to the touch, like sharp wire against delicate skin, or if it would tickle and entice, inviting someone to stroke it. Her fingers itched to find out. That beard was a statement, a promise a person was in for a rough ride and they would like it.

Her mind's eye took the scenic journey down the length of him. Dark-brown eyes stared back at her. She'd swear she'd seen a spark of interest in them when she'd stepped inside this room. The deep brown skin on his face and neck and the loving way the fabric of his shirt and slacks outlined the solid build of his body made her blood run hot. He was beautiful and strong. A proud Black man who exuded confidence with each breath he drew.

"Ms Everett!"

The use of her formal name cleared some of the haze clouding her brain. She focused on the voice; it was deep, but not as full as Jackson's. She followed the sound until she was staring at Storm Cordero.

He was Latinx, slightly shorter than Jackson, but not by much. His build was broad and wide, his corded muscles filling out the plain white shirt he wore. With a head full of midnight curls and a smile that said he liked trouble more than he should, Aja could see how women could easily fall for a man like that. But other than good looks worth a passing acknowledgment, nothing about him spoke to her or pulled at her the way the dark, brooding vibes his boss was giving off from the other side of the table did.

Storm's face, bright with amusement, and dark eyes shining with laughter said he knew she wasn't paying attention. She was busted.

A quick glance around the table told her Colton and, thankfully, Jackson were engaged in eating and not looking directly at her. But Storm knew she was watching his boss like a starving woman watched a fine cut of steak.

"I'm sorry, could you repeat yourself, please?"

The side of Storm's mouth tilted in a lopsided grin and he replied. "Sure. I asked how Ms. Daniels and Ms. Osborn were chosen for this program. Did you select them yourself, or was it a random lottery? What criteria were used to determine they'd be suitable candidates for this Pathways program you mentioned?"

Storm's questions were still centered on Seneca and Brooklyn, but they didn't sound as accusatory coming from him as they did Jackson.

"I volunteered at the state penitentiary shortly after I arrived in Fresh Springs. I instantly saw that all the women in that horrible place weren't the monsters the world makes them out to be. I wanted to help. The Pathways program is a way for me to do that. Seneca and Brooklyn were two of the top candidates who fit the program's requirements. They each were model prisoners. They'd both been granted recent paroles with two years or fewer left on their sentences. They also had to have a marketable skill they could use to assist with the restoration of the ranch."

"What specific skills do they have?" The deep rumblings of Jackson's voice made her feel both intrigued and anxious at the same time. She glared at him briefly before answering.

"Seneca is a former IT network director. She knows how to

build computer networks, which is essential for a resort business. Everything from booking the cabins to payments to communication between the staff is all done digitally. If we don't have a proper network set up, we can't make money.

"Brooklyn is an architect. She's responsible for renovating the existing cabin structures and creating designs for new buildings I want erected on the property. She'll work closely with the construction crew I've hired to turn this dusty plot of land into something tourists will pay good money to stay at."

Jackson pushed his now-empty plate away from him and picked up the pen and paper he'd rested beside it. "And you can afford to fund such a major project on a lawyer's salary?" He hadn't bothered to look in her direction. Instead, he gripped a pen between his fingers and kept his hand hovering over his notepad as he awaited her responses.

Prick.

That wasn't the lone insult she could think to appropriately describe Jackson. From where Aja sat, he was rude, dismissive, and didn't appear at all capable of thinking beyond the obvious. Why her uncle believed he would be an answer to Aja's troubles was beyond her. But when he lifted his eyes from his all-important notepad and allowed the weight of his stare to pour over her, Aja was certain of one thing. Bending him to her will might not be as easy as she'd believed.

In the depths of his dark eyes she saw a flash of power that rivaled her own, and as she watched his eyes fall from her face and down the not-so-subtle line of her cleavage, Aja felt a wave of trepidation pulse through her. Wanting him she could handle. Him being unable to keep his eyes off her ample bosom wasn't anything she couldn't manage either. But seeing the way need blazed in his eyes every time he watched her gave Aja pause. Because that fire called to her in ways that would make it so easy for her to surrender to him.

Aja pulled her eyes away from his face, needing a moment to get herself together and get back to the plan at hand. She needed to be more strategic in her handling of the man sitting directly across the table from her. Otherwise she was figuratively and possibly literally screwed.

Chapter 4

"I'm not your average lawyer, Jackson."

I'm pretty certain nothing about you is average.

Jackson bit the inside of his jaw to keep from speaking those words and tried to think of monotonous things—like office inventory requisition forms and doing payroll for his unit—to cool his blood.

He hazarded another glance at her and knew in that instant he'd lost the battle to keep his mind focused on this case. The table hid half of her, but her curves were still on full display in the V-neck of her fitted blouse and vest.

Jackson had never cared much about a woman being well-endowed or not. The truth: since his marriage crashed and burned, beyond physical companionship, he merely required a woman be unattached and not looking for anything more than a liaison or two to sate baser needs.

But sitting here trying his best to keep his mind from wondering what was beyond the first buttons of her blouse and vest took considerably more effort than it should.

"I'm afraid that's not a real answer to my question, Aja."

When she still didn't answer, he put down his pen and crossed his arms. "Ms. Everett? How exactly can you afford this as an unemployed lawyer?"

"I was the managing partner of my law firm in New York. We weren't a small-time operation. We specialized in what I like to call 'celebrity criminal law.' All the celebrities you see getting into major trouble on all the gossip news shows, my firm was usually responsible for getting them off with little to no legal ramifications. Our clients paid us very well for our services. As managing partner, I received the biggest slice of the profit pie. I have more than enough liquid cash to build this resort. And even if it goes belly up, my investments will keep me nice and comfy until I close my eyes to this world."

Jackson picked his pen up and scribbled a few lines on his notepad. "So you're paying the ex-convicts a fair wage?"

"Market value," she answered. "So no, neither of them would have reason to retaliate against me for making them work for a pittance. I treat my workers well. Their employment and compensation packages are competitive with their education and work experience, minus the cost of room and board, since housing comes with the job. My people have no reason to do this, Jackson. So can we stop focusing on them and look for the real culprit?"

"What if you're wrong? What if your little social experiment has gone belly up and the very people you're protecting are the ones responsible for damaging your property and terrorizing and nearly killing you?"

He knew he'd crossed a line the moment the words left his lips. He saw a spark of anger flash in her eyes before she stood and collected her used dish and coffee cup from the table. Her movements were aggressive and quick, and he worried the innocent paper products might pay the price for his words.

"Aja—"

She held up a finger to interrupt him. "I don't like repeating myself, Ranger Dean. However, since it seems you didn't get the message earlier, I'll reiterate it now. My uncle's idea of help was to send you and your men. I wasn't on board with that. But I'm willing to put my dislike aside and work with you to keep my people and my property safe. However, if you can't let go of your bias long enough to seek the truth, then you may as well stop wasting both our time."

She didn't turn away from him as she spoke. No, Aja leaned in, bringing her face and the controlled fury he could see bubbling beneath the surface of the calm veneer she wore closer to him. "The Rangers are our last hope. The sheriff will lock Seneca and Brooklyn up for the mere crime of being parolees in his town. He has made it abundantly clear he doesn't want them in Fresh Springs. So if you and your men are here simply to pile on, I can tell you I've officially had enough. You can close this case, and I'll tell my uncle I asked you to do so. There'll be no repercussions for you."

She turned and started zipping up the now-empty food insulation bags on the cart. A quick glance to either side of him found hard set eyes glaring at him.

He'd been working long enough with these men to catalog their disapproval of his behavior without them needing to say a word.

He pointed toward the door and whispered, "Give us a minute," before he stood from the table. Colton and Storm followed suit, walking through his office doorway and closing the door behind him with an intentional click. Jackson cleared the rest of the table before facing her.

"Aja, I didn't mean to offend you."

"I'm a big girl, Jackson. I'm not worried about you offending me. I'm worried about protecting Seneca and Brooklyn from being sent back to prison based on nothing more than their past convictions. Prior bad acts aren't allowed in a court of law for a reason. They shouldn't be used as an excuse to make a collar either."

"Agreed," he proceeded. "But I can't ignore their pasts either. I have to look at all the evidence, Aja. And usually, no matter how much people would like to believe otherwise, it's those with access to victims that perpetrate crimes against them."

She was wiping down the surface of the coffee carafe with a furious circular motion. He couldn't say what made him reach out to her and place a stilling hand at the top of her shoulder, applying slight pressure to encourage her to stop her machinations with the disposable napkins. But whatever it was, when she stopped and leaned into his touch instead of pulling away from him, a weight lifted off his chest.

"Aja." His voice was raspier than usual, rough like he'd just awoken. It sounded weird to his own ears. "I can't promise you I won't look into Seneca and Brooklyn. What I can promise is that I will run a fair investigation and look at all parties that make reasonable suspects. So why don't you stop assaulting that carafe and come sit and tell me who you think might be responsible for your troubles."

She turned to face him. There was a gleam of something bright in her eyes, and the joy of seeing it there made him want to curl his lips into a wide grin. What the hell was it about this woman that made him want to do silly things like smile when he saw hope dancing in her eyes?

Jackson knew he'd regret giving in to the delight swirling around the bottom of his belly right then. "Is that agreeable, Counselor?"

She smiled back and Jackson felt an invisible band squeeze around his heart. He decided right there that she should always have that look of hope and anticipation painted across the soft lines of her face. It felt so good that he'd put it there, and he was certain he'd give near anything to see it remain.

"Yes, Jackson." The breathy way his name rolled off her tongue and slid through her lips made his blood simmer. She stepped closer to him and widened her crimson smile. "That's completely agreeable."

And in that moment when her smile felt like pure temptation, Jackson knew one thing: he was in trouble.

Chapter 5

"ELI BENNETT." SHE PULLED HER FEATURES INTO TIGHT LINES as if she'd tasted something bitter. "He's sort of the unofficial mayor there. His money and influence have garnered him the loyalty of our neighbors."

A light knock on the door pulled their attention away from their conversation. Storm's face peeked through the small opening with a lifted brow, silently asking if it was okay to enter. Jackson waved him in, grateful it was considerate Storm at the door instead of bullish Colton.

As his men filed in and sat around the table again, he watched Aja with careful attention. He'd never seen her in a courtroom, but the way she handled him made him think twice about taking her on. The fire she'd directed at him as she defended her two wards made him think she must have been a formidable opponent across the aisle. And there was something about the light trigger she had on her mouth that made him wonder what it would be like to be on the receiving end of all that passion for reasons that had nothing to do with being cursed out.

"Okay, so you think Bennett is the culprit. Why? What's he done to make you think he could be capable of something like this?"

She smoothed her hands out flat on the table in front of her. "I mentioned before that Aunt Jo needed help with the ranch. It wasn't merely physical labor she needed. The ranch's finances were in trouble. I inherited the ranch from my mother five years ago. I wasn't really in the best frame of mind after losing my mom, so I let Aunt Jo handle everything where the ranch was concerned. In her worry over my grief, she failed to inform me the taxes were in arrears. She tried to handle it all on her own, but she couldn't. We were in danger of losing everything.

"Eli Bennett offered to buy the ranch, and when she refused to sell, because she couldn't actually sell it without my knowledge, he used his influence to get his cronies in the local government to deny her extensions on the back taxes. When I finally discovered what was going on, I came down here, paid the taxes, and took the ranch off the auction block."

Jackson continued to write things down on his notepad. "Why does Bennett want your spread bad enough to make you and your ranch his special project? Is there oil on the land?"

"No, there's no oil. The land borders the main road that travels down the middle of town. That same road, which starts at the tip of my property line, is also an inlet onto Interstate 35. As a tourist attraction, that's perfect placement. We're about ninety minutes from Austin in one direction, and three hours from the border of Mexico in the other. My presumption is Eli saw the earning potential. It's that, or he simply can't stand to lose to a woman. Knowing him, it's probably a little of both."

"Is there anyone else you can think of? I know you said you pay Seneca and Brooklyn well. What about day laborers? Do you have them? If you do, any problems with them?"

She shook her head. "It isn't a ranch in the traditional sense. We don't have livestock so that cuts down on a significant need for ranch staff. We hire out the landscaping and turn the grass shavings into straw for the stables. Seneca, Brooklyn, and I take turns caring for the horses and their habitat. As we get closer to open-ing, I'll hire hospitality staff, but other than the construction crew coming to build more structures for us, there really isn't a need for many day laborers."

"Okay, so let's go back to you and your past. You were a lawyer in New York. Leave any disgruntled clients behind?" Considering the tongue-lashing she'd just given him, it wasn't hard to imagine that mouth of hers got her into more trouble with someone else.

She shook her head before sharing a weak smile with him. "Most of the time, I worked my magic and the world never knew their favorite celebrity was in legal trouble at all. If it went as far as court, I got them off with a slap on the wrist. My clients were very happy with my services."

She took another deep breath, her shoulders lifting slightly as if the weight of his line of questioning was physically wearing her down.

"The only person who stands to gain anything by me leaving my place is Eli. He's more than capable of stooping to strong-arm tactics to get me to leave."

Jackson finished up his notes. "Have you told Seneca and Brooklyn about the investigation yet?"

"I haven't had time to tell them anything. Between being seen at the hospital and leaving at first light to travel to your head-quarters, I haven't had time to talk to either of them."

He pointed a finger in her direction. "That's good. Here's how it's going to work. Colton, Storm, and I are going to arrive on the ranch tomorrow posing as ranch hands."

Her brows pinched as his meaning became clear. "You mean you want this to be an undercover investigation? I don't think that's such a good idea."

"Why not?"

"Because combined, Seneca and Brooklyn have spent more than a decade in state prison. I think they can spot law enforce-ment before I could."

She was probably right. But it didn't change the fact that they needed this operation to be concealed.

"So tell them we're both ranch hands and extra security. Tell them we're all ex-military if they clue in to something more going on." It was a reasonable explanation, and it was the truth. They'd each served in the military before becoming Rangers. Hopefully, it would be enough to throw anyone being too nosy off the scent of their true reason for being on the ranch.

Colton shook his head as he spoke. "We're completely screwing the chain of usual command by coming in there without the invitation of local law enforcement. Things can get really ugly between us and them if we go in there without their knowledge."

"But Sheriff Hastings doesn't want the case."

"He may not want it"—Jackson picked up where Colton had left off—"but having the Rangers come in and make him look bad probably isn't on his list of things to do either. Locals can be very territorial. It's a hassle we don't need."

Storm gave her a compassionate glance before adding, "Not to mention, your people will probably be more cooperative if they aren't aware there's an active investigation going on."

She shook her head and folded her arms. "I don't like this, Jackson. I'd be lying to my people. Keeping their trust is important to me. This isn't what I imagined when my uncle brought you in."

"You may not like it, but it's the only way I'm willing to go in. I don't have enough men to manage this case as is. I'm not going to add the extra pressure of walking into a potentially hostile situation with ex-convicts and the local law. It's a potential risk for *my* people I'm not willing to take. I do it my way, or we walk."

The heavy sound of the breath she blew out clued him in that she still wasn't thrilled with his mandate. She extended her hand, and when he took it in his own, she offered him a firm shake.

"Okay, we'll do it your way. How will this work?"

"Colton, Storm, and I will arrive tomorrow morning. While we handle things covertly on your ranch, Jennings and Gleason will handle the official, visible parts of the investigation. They'll run down leads, do background checks, question suspects, get warrants if necessary."

"All right." She stood, smoothing her hands over her pants before shoving them in her pockets. "I need to get back to the ranch to set things up for your arrival and prepare Seneca and Brooklyn."

"Gleason and Jennings are waiting downstairs for you. Storm and Colton will walk you down and help you with the cart. Thank you again for the rolls and the coffee."

She stood there, obviously troubled about their conversation but somehow resolute. Her strength was a visible thing. But the burden of it and how she bore that load on her rigid shoulders made his need to help her more profound.

His men walked out first, taking the cart with them, and she walked toward his door to follow them. She stopped, turned to look at Jackson once more, and then disappeared down the hall.

When he could no longer see her, he closed his door and leaned against it, looking up at the ceiling. "Please let this be over quickly," he whispered. It was a prayer, because something told him that Aja Everett was more of a threat than any imagined foe he could face.

"Ranger Gleason, would you mind taking the next exit? I need to stop off to the pharmacy before we return to the ranch." She'd ignored her doctor's order last night to take Tylenol every eight hours to stave off the aches associated with her fall during the blast and resulting fire. After sitting in a car for ninety minutes each way and dealing with Ranger Jackson Dean, she needed either a painkiller or a good stiff drink.

How can someone be that fine and infuriating at the same time?

Ranger Gleason pulled over, then Ranger Jennings got out and opened the door for her. She thanked him for the hand he offered her as she stepped out of the big vehicle. He let her walk far enough ahead of him that she couldn't feel him breathing down her neck. But no matter how much distance he put between them, she'd never shake the discomfort of having someone watch her every move. Even when it was for her own protection.

She'd made it to the outer pharmacy doors when a blur of blond hair rushed past her, nearly knocking her down. She felt herself falling when a set of hands wrapped around her arms and kept her steady.

"I'm sorry. You all right, Ms. Aja?"

Aja blinked twice to get her bearings before staring into familiar blue eyes.

"Taylor Sullivan?" Out of the corner of her eye, Aja saw the Ranger approaching them. She gave a small shake of her head, and he stopped in his tracks. She returned her attention to the young man helping her steady herself. "Where are you headed in such a rush? You nearly knocked me down."

The young man stepped to the side of the entrance to keep from blocking the door, and Aja followed him. "I'm sorry, ma'am."

She cocked her eyebrow. "What did I tell you about that 'ma'am' stuff? I'm not old enough to be anybody's ma'am. Ms. Aja, Ms. Everett, or even plain old Aja will do fine."

His tanned face turned bright scarlet, and his cheeks lifted into an embarrassed grin that tugged at the soft spot reserved for him in Aja's heart. He'd been born the summer she'd finished law school. She'd come down to visit with her family and discovered the Sullivans had a beautiful new baby boy. In a town as small as Fresh Springs, every new birth was a town-wide celebration, and Taylor's had been no different.

She'd spent her entire summer helping out the Sullivans and babysitting Taylor whenever the new parents needed a break. They thought she was helping them. For her, it was about snuggling with that happy infant and taking advantage of all that wonderful baby scent she got to inhale whenever she was near him. Although her work in New York kept her away for most of the year, whenever she made it back to Fresh Springs, she always made time for the sweet cherub who followed her around like an energetic puppy. Now, that tiny baby was a tall, cornfed sixteen-year-old who towered over her, and Aja was suddenly feeling all of her thirty-nine years.

He's going to be a beauty of a man when he finally matures into adulthood. How is that possible? Where has the time gone?

"I'm real sorry, Ms. Aja. Trying to mind my manners, is all."

He had the same crooked grin from the day he was born, and for the second time today, she ached for a simpler time.

"Well, you can stand there and be sorry, or you can come on and hug my neck. I've missed you, boy."

God, had she. After seeing him every day for a full summer, rekindling their connection that started the day Earl Sullivan let her hold him for the first time, it was strange not having him waiting in her kitchen for one of Aunt Jo's hearty meals. The truth was in the two days he'd been gone, it nearly broke her heart that Earl refused to let Taylor come back to the ranch. Sure, with all hell breaking lose on Restoration, she understood. But that didn't mean it felt good.

Taylor leaned down wrapping himself around her, swaying from side to side the way they always did when they greeted each other. He let her take her fill and when he felt her pull away, he stepped back, like the polite little gentleman she'd always knew he'd be.

"Where you going in such a rush?"

"Pete's Hardware," he answered. "My shift starts in thirty minutes. Trying to always be on time like you told me."

Aja's smile grew. Her baby really was becoming a man. "Well, since you were rushing to get to work, I guess I can't be mad at our little collision then, can I?"

The young man bit his lip and tried to keep from meeting her eyes. "Just trying to do my part. Dad says a man's got to pull his weight."

"Your dad's a real good person, Taylor. Don't ever forget that."

Taylor smiled again and ran a nervous hand through his wheat-colored locks as he spoke. "He said the same thing about you when he heard what happened at the ranch. Might not be worth much, but he was really sorry he had to quit work on you and leave you without a contractor and crew."

Aja understood Taylor's hesitance to relay his father's remorse for her situation. "I don't blame him." She cleared her throat to try to keep the sadness from settling in her voice. Who could blame a man for trying to protect his people the same as she was trying to protect hers?

A slight movement in her peripheral vision brought her attention back to the Ranger waiting on her at the edge of the sidewalk.

"I'd better let you get on your way."

Taylor dipped his head before pulling the door open for her so she could step inside the pharmacy. "I'm glad you didn't get hurt, Ms. Aja. I know someone destroyed your barn and all, but I'm really happy nothing happened to you in the middle of that craziness."

Aja's heart swelled slightly. This teenager had lasered in on the important detail that Aja was letting her anger make her forget— she was alive and it could've been so much worse.

"Thank you, Taylor. Please tell your dad I said hi when you see him next."

An enthusiastic smile and the brightness in his eyes revealed that slight bit of boyhood still left in him. She wished she could be that carefree and hopeful again. But too much had happened between sixteen and thirty-nine to make her ignore the fear that she was on the wrong end of an hourglass with only a few grains of sand remaining until her time was up.

Chapter 6

The sound of familiar female voices and footsteps on the back porch pulled Aja's attention from her coffee cup to the back door. She'd been dreading this moment since she woke up. Now that it was here, she wasn't feeling any better about it.

The door opened and Brooklyn, followed by Seneca, walked into the kitchen and stood on the opposite side of the counter from Aja.

"As I live and breathe, Sen. It appears Aja Everett really hasn't been a figment of our imaginations." Brooklyn crossed her arms and lifted her brow. "Wouldn't know it, though, considering we ain't heard nothing from her since the barn exploded, like, two days ago?" She gave Aja a wink. "No big, though. Not like we were supposed to give a damn about her well-being anyway."

Aja shook her head and smiled. Sure, she could get upset at the more than slightly disrespectful tone coloring Brooklyn's words, but it didn't really make sense to. First, Brooklyn was right. Aja's presence had been extremely scarce on the ranch. Yeah, she'd had to visit the hospital and then the Rangers' headquarters all the way in Austin, but that didn't mean she shouldn't have called or texted to keep them from worrying. Second, Brooklyn was like the bold, sometimes cynical town she was named after; she was going to let you know what was on her mind whether you wanted to hear it or r.ot. Third, Aja's guilt over the lie she was about tell wouldn't let her chastise her employee for her impertinence.

Instead, Aja raised her hands in mock surrender and smiled. "I know I've been absent and unreachable since the explosion. But I've been terribly busy taking some necessary measures to both stop these dangerous pranks someone keeps playing on us and keep us on track with the overhaul of this ranch."

When she wasn't more forthcoming, Seneca was right on cue with her usual talent for breaking the tension in a room. She waved her hand as if she were ushering in an opportunity for Aja to respond. "Like?"

"Like solidifying start dates with the new construction company and hiring some new ranch hands."

Aja grabbed her coffee cup and kept her eyes on its contents. Standing in a courtroom, leading strangers to contemplate her version of the truth was easy. Standing in front of people she cared about, knowingly lying to them wasn't something Aja thought she could do with a straight face.

"Ranch hands?" Brooklyn asked "We suddenly get a shipment of livestock I didn't know anything about?"

"No, but even with the ranch as a resort, I was always going to need to hire more staff. The vandalism upped my timetable. They'll be working as ranch hands but each of them will be taking on security duties as well."

"Security?" Seneca repeated. "Damn, I guess things are getting worse if you're bringing in rent-a-cops."

"They're not rental police officers. They're ranch hands. They each have a military background and understand keeping vandals off the property will be part of their duties."

Aja waited to see their reactions. Seneca was usually a bit more easygoing than Brooklyn. But honestly, Aja didn't think either of them would be happy about this new situation.

"You know what, Boss," Brooklyn began. "I think it's about time you got security on the ranch. Seneca and I have been talking about that since we found out the scaffolding was cut."

"Yeah," Seneca added. "We definitely are on board with that. We wanna be safe, but we also don't want the law to have any excuses to come up here giving us grief. If someone gets hurt, Sheriff Hastings is coming straight for us."

Aja cringed at the mention of the sheriff's name and the recognizable concern passing between Brooklyn and Seneca. They shouldn't have to fear him for the simple fact that they'd done time. She was about to state that when the front doorbell rang. "That'll be them. Stick around for a minute so we can discuss living quarters and general ranch stuff."

She excused herself and headed for the front door, hoping the ladies stayed in the kitchen. Her nerves were making her stomach jittery, and she needed the brief moments alone before she had to let Jackson and his men into her world.

She plastered on her professional smile and opened the door, greeting first Colton, then Storm, and finally Jackson as they filed into the foyer.

They made an impressive human wall standing next to one another, blocking the view of the hall that led to the kitchen. Each of them tall, bulky, and imposing with all their focus on her.

"Morning, gentleman. You're right on time. The ladies and I were discussing your arrival. Please follow me." Storm stepped to the side and made an opening for her to walk through. She led them into the kitchen and stopped once she reached the eat-in counter that sat in the middle of the room.

"Seneca and Brooklyn," Aja began. "This is Jackson, Colton, and Storm." She cleared her throat as she turned slightly to look at the three men standing behind her. "Jackson is our new foreman, and Colton and Storm are ranch hands."

There was silence as the two women assessed the men and

then shared a knowing look between them. The pause was nearing that awkward stage when Seneca turned away from Brooklyn and extended her hand to Jackson. "Welcome to Restoration Ranch, where everyone gets a second chance. I'm Seneca, and this is Brooklyn."

Seneca released Jackson's hand and shook Colton's and Storm's. Everyone in the room waited for Brooklyn to offer her hand, but she kept to her post at the counter, giving a two-fingered wave to them instead.

"You day laborers or permanent?" Brooklyn said.

Jackson chuckled at Brooklyn's directness, and it eased the tension in the quiet room, bringing a friendly smile to Aja's own face. If Brooklyn weren't an ex-convict he was investigating, Aja could see Jackson and Brooklyn possibly being friends. They were both surly as hell and mistrustful of anyone they didn't know. And Brooklyn was playing right to type by getting straight to the point, abandoning the niceties of polite society to get the information she wanted.

"More like temporary while Ms. Everett sees how we work out," Storm answered, putting enough drawl in his voice to make himself sound as friendly and country as any cowboy who'd stepped foot on this land.

"Ms. Everett was about to explain the accommodations to us before you came in," Brooklyn added.

All eyes fell on Aja, and she glared at Brooklyn, giving her a silent warning across the counter. "Ladies, because the two working staff cabins are all we have available, I will have to ask you to move in together. The men can use the other cabin."

"What about the third man?" Seneca asked. "They're two-bedroom cabins with a queen-sized bed in each bedroom. Is the third man sleeping on the couch?"

Aja closed her eyes and pinched the bridge of her nose as she whispered, "Dammit." In all her planning, she hadn't considered that. She was certain she could find a cot somewhere in one of their storage rooms but eliminated that as a reasonable solution. It was uncomfortable and more than a night on it would ruin anyone's back.

"Jackson?" His deep-brown eyes were sharp as he focused all his attention on her at the call of his name. She cleared her throat, trying to decide if it was his penetrating scrutiny or merely the stress of this entire situation that had her so rattled. "Since you and I will need to stay in close contact to discuss ranch matters, it's probably best if you took my guest room upstairs. This way, neither of us has to go far to have our morning meetings."

"Sounds like a plan to me," he answered.

She turned back to the ladies, trying to keep her cool veneer in place. "Good. Seneca and Brooklyn, decide which of you is moving, then start packing so Colton and Storm can get settled."

Jackson turned to his colleagues, pointing between them. "Colton and Storm, please help the ladies move their things over when they're ready."

The men gave a collective nod, and when Seneca and Brooklyn waved and stepped toward and through the back door, Storm and Colton followed behind them.

Quiet filled the room. The air crackled with electricity. Aja could feel it tickling the hairs on the back of her neck, making her rethink sleeping in the same house with Jackson. She wasn't threatened by him. Everything from his wide stance to his strong shoulders and his determined glare made Jackson a poster boy for security. But she was beginning to notice being in his presence somehow made her uneasy. Enough so that for the briefest moment, she wondered if him sleeping on that old, rickety cot in the cabin was a safer bet for her.

If he were really her foreman, the sleeping arrangements would make sense. There'd be a ton of things they'd need to discuss every morning before the workday began. But standing here, feeling out of sorts and awkward in his presence, Aja wasn't certain this was a good idea.

Deciding she needed to put on her big-girl pants and do a bit of adulting, she walked from the security of the counter and waved a hand at Jackson. With a steady voice, she said, "Follow me and I'll show you to your bed."

———————

Aja took a sip of her second cup of coffee while she thought about the visiting cowboy upstairs. She glanced down at her trembling fingers and regretted her compulsion for more caffeine in her system. "Get it together, girl. He's simply a cowboy doing what your uncle told him to do. No need to let his presence rattle you."

The pep talk sounded good to her ears and her head. But somehow she didn't feel the usual comfort her self-affirmations brought. She took another sip from her cup and savored the sweet, creamy taste.

"You ready to show me around your spread?"

She took another swallow of her coffee and kept the smart retort that threatened to slip through her lips. Her uncle had made certain neither of them had a choice in this, so reminding Jackson she hadn't wanted him on her property in the first place wouldn't help them get on with their day.

"Sure. It's best if we go on horseback. You ride?"

"Is water wet?"

She gave him an okay sign and took one last swallow of her drink before pouring the rest in the sink and leading him to the back door. "The stable is within walking distance of the house."

"I assume horseback riding will be one of the activities you offer to your guests."

"Yeah. That along with good food, a spa, and rustic lodging will hopefully draw people into the resort."

They walked through the back door and followed a path alongside a garden bed for a few moments. The structure they came upon looked very much like the barn that had burned down two days ago. A twinge of regret tightened around Aja's chest, and she dragged a long, heavy breath in through her nose. Losing the structure wouldn't delay her plans for the ranch, but the memories of carefree summers spent in that barn made the loss meaningful in ways dollars and cents would never express.

She turned around to usher Jackson inside and met the wide grin on his face. His lips were full, the corners curling as he looked around. "I take it you've spent some time in horse stables before?" she asked.

His wide shoulders moved with each easy chuckle that slipped from his lips.

"Yeah." He took in a deep breath through his nose, and his grin spread wider, showing a full mouth of bright teeth. "Nothing like the familiar smell of hay mixed with animal musk. I mucked stalls before and after school at my next-door neighbor's place in junior high and high school. It wasn't easy work, but the pay was good, and I got to ride any horse I wanted as a work perk."

Aja shook her head, biting her bottom lip to keep the smile she felt tugging at the corners of her mouth from blooming. She loved riding horses, always had. But she didn't think she could ever look at mucking stalls with the same fondness Jackson seemed to display.

"Well, I hope you find mucking stalls as rewarding a job now as you did then." She walked to the end of the row of stalls until she found the two she was looking for. "I'm sure the residents will appreciate your experience." A chestnut-colored quarter horse pushed her muzzle into Aja's waiting hand and neighed excitedly at Aja's gentle touch. "Hey, Pride. I've brought a friend to visit." Never taking her eyes off the beautiful creature in front of her, she called over her shoulder, "Jackson, this is Dru's Pride. She's a sweet girl who loves a good run. Introduce yourself, and we'll take her and Shadow out for a little exercise."

She walked over to the next stall to greet her personal horse. No one rode Shadow but her. Not because she didn't allow it, but because the quarter horse had decided a long time ago that Aja was his human and wouldn't permit anyone else on his back. She stood for a moment, marveling at the strong creature. A proud, long neck, strong legs, and a shiny black coat made Shadow a horse any owner would be proud to possess. But it was his loyalty to Aja that made him more than a pet. No, Shadow was a trusted friend. A valued member of her small family.

"Morning, Shadow. Miss me?" The horse bobbed his long neck up and down, giving the appearance of a nod.

"Did you train him to do that?"

"No." She laughed. "He loves me. It's a given he misses me when I'm not around." She returned her attention to the horse and gave his neck a few quick strokes before she waved her hand for Jackson to follow and stepped inside the tack room. She turned around to see if he'd followed her lead and slammed into a solid wall of broad, muscular chest.

Slightly disoriented by Jackson's nearness, she stepped back before getting her footing. She felt herself falling until strong hands wrapped around her waist, keeping her upright. Goose bumps pebbled the skin on her arms at the firm press of his hands on her hips.

The sure way he held her against him, like he was always supposed to have a handful of her beneath his touch, made her tremble with a strange mix of apprehension and need. When she finally found the nerve to look up into his shining, dark-brown eyes, he gave her a playful wink and a smile that did little to dispel the nerves swirling in the bottom of her belly. "Looks like Shadow isn't the only one you can trust to keep you from falling 'round here."

Aja swallowed hard, trying to move the ball of tension sitting in the middle of her throat. *Trust* wasn't the word she was thinking of right now. Nothing about the way he held her tightly against him made her trust him. But worse, the way her body instinctively wanted to press closer to his heat made her trust herself even less.

———————

Jackson rode alongside Aja as she showed him her land, taking in the endless hills of vivid green grass bending to the slight breeze. It was early September. The scorching temperatures of August were giving way to eighty- and seventy-degree days. But soon winter would roll in, bringing chilly sixty- and fifty-degree temperatures, and it would hamper the ability to build on this land. Colder temperatures would make riding on horseback a little less pleasurable than it was now too.

Aja led them over a ridge to where a small hovel of a house sat. Its worn wooden planks desperately needed attention. Jackson was certain no one had lived there for at least half a century. Even out in these backwoods, building codes had to be adhered to. The house's deep lean to the left wouldn't pass the most basic building inspection.

The building was old. A fact that was reinforced as they dismounted and walked closer to it. The loud wail of the brittle wooden porch steps made Jackson skeptical the planks would hold his weight. He lifted a questioning brow as Aja watched him take careful steps to where she was standing outside the front door. "You sure this is safe?"

"Safe enough," she answered. The cavalier tone of her voice didn't bolster his confidence. But if she were willing to take the risk, he reasoned he could too.

"What is this place?"

"It's the original homestead from when my family first

purchased this land at the end of the nineteenth century." He watched her run a light hand over a brittle wooden plank on the doorway. Her smooth, brown features settled into a soft, gentle smile, something too delicate to touch for fear of destroying its beauty. Something so powerful he had to fight the growing need in his chest to reach out and trace it with his fingertips. "Slavery was introduced to Texas in 1821 when Stephen F. Austin promised white settlers eighty acres of land for every enslaved person they brought with them."

Jackson knew how the frontier of Texas was settled. It wasn't something taught in public schools. But his father had insisted Jackson and his brother know where they came from and take pride in the history of their ancestors.

"During that migration," she continued, "six generations ago, my great-great-great-great-grandfather Scipio was brought to Texas as one of the enslaved. He wasn't more than a year old when he arrived here.

"He was probably near forty when the Civil War began. Up until that point, he thought he'd live and die in chains on this plantation. But once Texas joined the Confederacy, and his master left to join the Confederate ranks, he escaped and fled to Galveston to help with the Union naval blockade."

She stepped toward the door and motioned for him to follow behind her. He wasn't certain what to expect. If the front porch and the exterior were in such disrepair, he was sure the interior hadn't fared much better. But when he stepped through the door, he was pleasantly surprised to see a simple one-room space filled with covered furniture and a beautiful brick fireplace that looked like it might have been the center attraction for those who called this place home.

It was daylight outside, but the windows were covered, so Aja turned on a small kerosene lamp on the mantel to bring a soft glow of light into the room.

"The Union didn't allow Blacks, whether they were enslaved or free, to join the army at the start of the war. But Scipio was a blacksmith, so the commander allowed him to work shoeing horses and making and repairing weapons. It was the first time he realized something originally intended for bad could be used for good. He'd been taught his trade to fashion horseshoes, weapons, and other ironworks for his master to keep him enslaved. Now, he was using it to fight for his freedom."

Jackson felt a chill pass through him as he thought of the pain and dehumanization Scipio and so many others like him would've experienced. He could feel the pain of that trauma as if it were a living thing cutting through the fibers of his flesh until it rooted itself in his soul.

"During the four years of that war, he saved every penny he made in Galveston." He could see a smile blooming on her full lips and stepped closer just to get a better view. "He was there on Juneteenth when Union soldiers read Major General Gordon Granger's order upholding and enforcing Lincoln's Proclamation. So as a free man, he returned to this land and found it in disrepair. Bless all the angels in heaven that his wife and children hadn't been sold off or worse. They were still enslaved on the ranch. Scipio informed them and the widow owner that they were now free.

"Family lore has it he told the widow she could keep the land and he would take his family and leave her broke with nothing, or she could leave the land and have his money. What he offered her was a small fortune for the deed. She turned over the deed quickly. He renamed it Restoration Ranch because the land that was once his condemnation to a brutal life became his redemption. When the former owner cleared out, Scipio tore down all the old structures. This one was the first one he built as the owner. He made it his home."

Jackson noted the gleam of pride in her eye as she spoke of her ancestor. More than a century had passed since Scipio Henry had courageously secured this land for his family. Jackson couldn't even imagine the strength it must have taken to endure fighting through the bonds of enslavement to freedom to make sure his people would always have something of their own. But watching his descendant six generations later as she told this story, Jackson understood where Aja's unshakable resolve came from.

"For over a hundred years, this land has passed from parent to child. After my aunt and uncle, I'm the last direct descendent of Scipio. I'm the last one left to carry on Scipio's legacy of restoring and rebuilding the land and our family's name. It's why I jumped at the chance to participate in Pathways. I knew Scipio and all my ancestors leading up to him would agree with my choice to help people like Seneca and Brooklyn. It's why you've got to stop whoever's trying to destroy it, and me. If they succeed, there will be no one left to carry on the legacy, and everything Scipio sacrificed for will be gone."

Watching Aja caress this old shack like it were a palace as she recounted her family's history eased something in Jackson he couldn't quite identify. Why should he care that she took pride in where she came from? She was someone he'd been tasked to work with, nothing more. But knowing her past somehow made her seem planted in the land. Not merely an owner on paper but someone whose roots were deeply sewn into the fabric of the landscape.

Jackson walked his sight from the top of Aja's braided hair down the deep, full curves of her body, to her work-boot-covered feet and back. She was confident and vibrant, qualities any man would be attracted to. But in that moment, he recognized Aja was more than her attractive parts. She was a woman committed to her family, loyal to the ancestors she'd never met.

In his experience, people weren't made like this. Not anymore. They didn't remain true to ideals and morals such as loyalty. It was all about individual success and happiness. Getting ahead the best way you could without worrying about anyone else. And yet here she was, a big, beautiful, and bright light, a beacon shining on him, showing him a better way, a better model of what he'd ached for all his life.

His silence must have pulled her out of her musings, because she turned to him, sharing a genuine smile, chipping away at his exterior. And as he stood there marveling in her glory, the singular thought to cross his mind was: *Why couldn't I have met you first?*

Chapter 7

JACKSON KNOCKED TWICE AND WAITED FOR ONE OF HIS MEN to answer the door. Colton answered. Once Jackson was across the threshold and heard the lock click in place behind him, Colton jutted his chin in his direction. "You finished your date with the boss lady?"

Jackson gave the open room a single glance, spotting Storm sipping what looked to be a glass of juice on the nearby sofa. "I'm assuming you both took a look around already." He knew Colton would've stopped him at the door if neither he nor Storm had swept for any obvious audio or video equipment in use in the cabin. But there was never any harm in double-checking his facts.

Both Colton and Storm answered yes, so Jackson moved over to the sofa where Storm was sitting, pulled a map of Restoration Ranch out of his back pocket, and unfolded it until it covered the coffee table he was leaning over.

Colton sat in a recliner adjacent to the sofa. "It's not polite to answer a question with a question. I asked you about your time with the boss lady."

Jackson ran a hand over his close-cropped dark curls and scratched his head. "Date? It was more like an exercise in frustration. I don't understand how someone with all those fancy degrees can be so uneducated about safety. This ranch is basically a series of open gates for anyone who wants to trespass."

"What we looking at, Jackson?" Storm asked.

"Too much access." Jackson sat on the couch, the agitation over his discovery still resting between his tense shoulders. "Most of the perimeter has an expansive wooded area that pretty much keeps it safe from the outside." He tapped the three sections he'd marked with bright-red ink with his finger. "But these three spots are a real problem."

Colton leaned in to get a better look at the map. "They don't look all that close to each other either."

"That's part of the problem. There's three of us, and these three access points are miles and miles apart. There's no way we can keep this under control without some surveillance equipment. I'm not simply talking about something we can use to watch suspects. There's literally no security on this property at all. Who lives like that?"

Storm shifted on the sofa. "There are still people who believe there's no crime in the South, no need to lock their doors at night. We know better."

Jackson had seen too much ugliness in these parts to trust the good nature of people so completely. He wasn't paranoid. He didn't see threats everywhere he turned, but he had sense enough to take basic precautions out here in these hills. He didn't understand why Aja hadn't.

"I'm on my way back to the main house to figure out some solutions to this. Until we can get something set up, we will have to do security rounds ourselves. We'll each take turns on watch out there at night until I can come up with a better solution. Hopefully Ms. Everett will be agreeable to whatever I propose."

Colton belted a hearty whip of laughter into the air. "I don't see the lady rancher being agreeable to too much of anything when it comes to you. You seem to know exactly what to say to insert your foot in your mouth when talking to her."

Jackson couldn't deny it. "Since you've got jokes, Colt, you'll be first up for guard duty tonight. Better get your nap in now. Your shift starts at zero hundred. You can report back to the main house at oh six hundred."

Colton's hard blue eyes sparked with fire and Jackson smirked in satisfaction. They might have been friends for years, but no one knew how to piss Colton off better than Jackson. A fact he was most proud of now.

He folded the map back up and handed it to Colton. "I've got an extra one in my truck. I'll see you two tomorrow."

———————————

Aja checked on the pot roast in the oven. When she placed the large roasting pan on top of the range, she questioned her sanity for making such a massive roast. Sure, Jackson was tall, broad, and built like a lumberjack. But that didn't mean he ate like one too.

She picked up a serving spoon and basted the brown specimen of roasted perfection with a healthy amount of drippings from the pan. "Too late to worry about the portions now. Whatever we don't finish tonight, I'll serve as leftovers for lunch tomorrow."

"Aja, I wanted to talk to you about—"

She turned toward Jackson as he stepped into the kitchen from the back door. He closed his eyes and inhaled a long, deep breath through his nose. "God in heaven, that smells good. What is it?"

She was too busy staring at the hungry need etched into his face to answer him immediately. But when he called her name, she quickly snapped out of the brief fog. "Pot roast, mashed potatoes, and Aunt Jo's honey carrots."

His approval shone in the wide smile that graced his full lips. "Do I have time to wash up before dinner?"

"Yeah, the roast needs to rest for a few minutes before it's served. You've got plenty of time." She turned back to basting the roast with a vengeance, hoping her fixation would keep her from thinking about the titillating things Jackson could do with soap, water, and a washcloth upstairs in the shower.

She waited until she heard his footsteps above her head in his bedroom to scold herself. "What the hell is wrong with you? He's not the first good-looking man you've ever eaten a meal with." She'd spent a good portion of her adulthood around attractive, wealthy, powerful men who wore tailored clothes that fit their carved bodies with precision. Why did a Texas Ranger with dusty jeans and boots make her mouth water and her mind wander to places it had no business going?

Too afraid of where her own line of questioning would lead, she took the coward's way out and set the table instead.

When she was done, she turned around to rinse her hands in the sink as the loud creak of the back stairs filled the air, signaling Jackson's descent. "You can get started while I slice up the rest of the roast for leftovers."

"You spent all this time cooking, and you're not even going to eat while the food is hot? That doesn't seem fair."

She turned around to answer him, but again, her words wouldn't flow. He stood in between two chairs at the counter, his chest covered in a fitted black cotton T-shirt. She wasn't certain if it was designed to stretch so tightly across the expanse of his upper body or purely a result of Jackson stuffing all that hard, corded muscle under the fabric. Whichever the case, he looked tastier than the meal she'd prepared. If there were anything that was unfair, it was the temptation the image of this man covered in simple cotton stoked inside her.

"Aja, please do that later. Eat with me?"

She watched him pull out the chair next to him and pat the back, motioning for her to sit.

Suspicion filled her senses like bad cologne at a mall perfume shop. Her eyes narrowed into small slits, and she folded her arms as she glared at him. Maybe he had a get-into-your-enemy's-good-graces plan too.

"What's wrong?"

His brow furrowed as he looked back and forth before settling his vision on her. "I'm not sure what you mean."

"You're being too nice. I've known you less than thirty-six hours. You haven't been all that kind during that time. Why are you being so considerate now?"

He laughed, an honest chuckle that rumbled in the air, easing the suspicion pulling at the edge of her thoughts. He threw his hands up in surrender, broadening his smile as he looked at her with those maple-colored eyes, making her wish she could be the one giving up instead. "I thought I was supposed to be the mistrustful one. I'm the law-enforcement agent."

She shook her head. "I'm from Brooklyn. We're mistrustful by nature. I'm also a lawyer. Suspicion is part of the training. So come on with it. What are you really up to, Jackson Dean?"

He put his hand down and held the edge of the counter in front of him. "Nothing bad, but I would like you to eat with me. It'll give us a chance to discuss some important things about your ranch's security."

She relaxed, walking around the counter and taking the seat he'd pulled out for her. "Next time, don't bury the lede. You could've simply said you wanted to talk."

"Yeah, but it was way too much fun watching you go into bullshit-radar mode."

She gave him as much side-eye as she could muster and went about placing food on her plate. When she finished, she was about to grab her napkin when she saw Jackson bow his head. She followed in kind, smiling as he said a simple blessing over the food. *Hmmm. A man who pulls out chairs for women and says grace? If he wasn't such an asshole most of the time, he might actually be a nice guy. Forgive me, Lord. But you know it's true.*

"So what did you want to talk about?"

He was midchew when she spoke, holding up his finger as the muscles in his jaw flexed with each movement. "This is really good. I mean, it tastes like you maybe know a little more about country cooking than your New York City pedigree suggests."

"I could always take it away if it's not to your liking." She stretched her hand out as if she would take his plate. "I think we've got some peanut butter and jelly around if that's more to your tastes."

He blocked her hand by placing his thick forearm on the counter. "Touch my food and you'll draw back a nub." Aja laughed, pulling her hand back. He took a few more bites, washing them down with a healthy chug of the sweet tea in his frosted mug before he grabbed his napkin to wipe his mouth. "Honestly, the food's great. I haven't had a roast this tender in a while. Thanks for going through all the trouble."

"No trouble." She took a sip from her mug. "Cooking and baking are stress relievers for me. Whenever a case was giving me trouble back in New York, I'd stay up all night cooking or baking, or both, until I worked the problem out in my head. Our associates loved it whenever I was working on something problematic. They knew the food would always end up in the staff kitchen."

"These attacks on the ranch really have you worried, don't they?"

She blew out a weary breath. "Until someone burned down the barn, I thought it was about running us off the land, not physically harming us. Even the tampering with the scaffold… I thought someone was simply attempting to stop us from working on the ranch. Now, I'm not so sure. Not knowing is the stressful part."

"I think I have a way to take care of some of that worry for you."

"How?"

He reached for his frosted mug, allowing his finger to glide around the lip of the cup. "I want to take a few measures to improve the security on the ranch."

"What does that mean exactly?"

He moved his mostly empty plate to the side and turned to face her. "On the tour, I spotted at least three access points where anyone who wanted to enter the ranch undetected could. I think you need to get better, electrified fencing to keep people out. I also think you need to add surveillance cameras all around the property. This place is enormous; there's no way any one team can monitor it completely. Having cameras will give you eyes all around the ranch."

She took a deep breath and leaned back into her chair. "I'm not opposed to any of the things you've mentioned. I know, as a proprietor, I must have cameras somewhere on the property anyway. But right now, while we're still closed, it seems almost voyeuristic. I don't want to compromise Seneca's and Brooklyn's privacy."

"This isn't about their privacy, Aja."

She understood why he didn't see it that way. When you'd never had your freedom taken from you, it was hard to see why someone wouldn't want to be watched constantly. "For nearly ten years, Seneca and Brooklyn have lived in cages, having their every move monitored by a camera or an authority figure. I promised them they wouldn't have to live like that here."

"Integrity is very important to you, isn't it?" He cocked his head to the side as if he were trying to gauge her answer simply by watching her.

"I know most people think lawyers are inherent liars, and the truth is, I'm not all that certain I disagree with that notion. But I try to be as honest as I can. My word is all I really have in this world. Breaking it always costs me something valuable."

"Is your integrity worth more than their lives? Could you carry the burden of knowing you could've protected them but didn't act in time?"

Her heart rate sped up, each beat a heavy thud in her chest. She closed her eyes, taking deliberate breaths to calm down. *He doesn't know. He couldn't.* A few more breaths and reminders, and she got her pulse under control.

"No," she murmured. "I don't want to be responsible for anyone getting hurt. How do you suggest I handle this? Eli Bennett has everyone in this town running scared; getting local help is almost impossible. You'll have to find someone out of Fresh Springs to do it like I did with this second contractor. It's the only way I could get a replacement construction crew out here in time."

"Why do you think the town is scared of Bennett?" Jackson asked. Concern marred his smooth features, and her fingers twitched to touch them. Determined to keep her actions appropriate, even if her thoughts weren't, she tapped her fingers on the counter instead.

"The town hasn't done anything against us specifically—not anything actionable anyway. They just never seem to be available for service when it comes to Restoration Ranch. Contractors, landscapers, hell, even takeout. There's never anyone in the area when we call. Except for Earl, I always have to go outside the town for skilled labor. I can't prove it, but either an entire town is scared of my money, or maybe they're scared of someone who doesn't want them to take it."

He scratched at his beard as he took in what she'd said. "You think Eli is threatening them?"

"He's sleazy enough that I wouldn't put something like that past him," she replied.

"Well, Jennings and Gleason are going to his ranch tomorrow to talk to him. We don't have enough to bring him in for official questioning, but we can show up on his doorstep and see if he'll talk to us."

She waved a dismissive hand in the air, hoping to get off the topic of Eli. She'd had a lovely meal. There was no need to sour her stomach talking about that piece of filth.

"Back to my security. How do you plan to get someone out here big enough to handle my problems and not blow your cover?"

"I know someone," he answered. "My dad's security firm handles emergency jobs like this all the time. Your contractors are coming in soon; they could work in conjunction, get everything up and running in a quick and efficient fashion. If you're all right with me calling my father, that is."

He sat next to her, eyes wide with expectation, waiting for her to agree. All it took was her softly whispered "Okay" for him to pull his phone from his back pocket and connect the call. One simple gesture to begin the process of securing the property and for her to break another promise to the people she'd pledged her friendship to.

While he talked on the phone, Aja slid away from the counter and stood at a nearby window, looking out into the darkness on the other side of the glass pane. Was it her destiny to hurt the people she wished to love and protect? Would she never know the peace of being able to keep her promises and keep those she cared about safe at the same time? Because to date, she'd never managed to do both simultaneously.

Chapter 8

"WE CAN MAKE IT OUT THERE FIRST THING IN THE MORNING. Are you sure this woman understands..."

Jackson's attention drifted from the voice coming through his phone to the woman standing in front of the kitchen window. Her shoulders drooped like she was weary, exhausted from carrying the twin invisible weights perched there.

"Jackson, did you hear what I said, boy?"

The sharp ring in his father's voice pulled his attention from the sad picture Aja made and back to his phone. "I'm here. She owns a ranch in Hill Country; I think she can handle whatever this will cost. First thing in the morning should be fine for a consult."

"All right. Kip and I will see you at nine."

"See you then."

Jackson ended the call and slid his phone back into his pocket. He cleared his throat, hoping the sound would draw Aja's attention away from the darkness outside. "They'll be out at the start of business tomorrow to speak with you and gets pictures of your land."

"That's fine." The soft utterance dissipated into the air. Her usual voice, as he knew it, was full and rich. Like her presence, it resonated across a room, pulling everyone in, forcing them to focus on her whether or not they wanted to. But the way she stood so still, shutting the world out with her silence—it didn't feel right. Not to mention, the unexpected meekness in her voice made him ache, and not in a pleasurable way. *This is all wrong.*

He rubbed a hand over his face. She was still standing there, weighed down by her worries with her hands wrapped around each upper arm as she held herself.

This wasn't fear. This was vulnerability. There was something almost breakable about her as she stared out into the night. And as he watched her literally fold into herself, the need to protect her scratched at him from somewhere deep inside.

Protecting those around him wasn't a foreign concept to Jackson. He was a lawman, someone sworn to protect the public. But what Aja stirred in him wasn't anything like his trained reaction to professional situations. No, this ran deeper. It was rougher, calling to a baser need in him.

This thing clawing at him from the inside tested his will. It made him stand rooted to the floor. It made him clench his fists to keep from reaching out for her. He let a long, frustrated breath escape. He was literally battling against himself, trying not to answer the burning desire her vulnerability sparked in him. And for the life of him, he couldn't understand why.

He walked over to her, placing a tentative hand on her shoulder. There was no reason to touch her, other than he thought it would make her feel better. Second-guessing himself, he withdrew but the gentle press of her hand stopped him.

She barely touched him; a minor twitch of his wrist, and her hand would be dislodged. But he stayed, tightened his grip on her shoulder, letting them both know he wasn't going anywhere.

"I can see you beating yourself up over this. No one will invade their privacy. Not much anyway. There'll be no surveillance devices in their private dwellings. This is all to protect your business from harm and liability. As the proprietor, you must make this ranch safe."

"I know. But it feels wrong not to inform them of it beforehand."

"You can blame it on me if it makes you feel better. No one else has to know."

"I would know," she whispered.

She turned around to face him. He glanced at her shoulder where their hands still mingled even with the change in position and thought how right that idea seemed. The two of them tangled together, touching everywhere at the same time.

"It's bad enough I'm keeping the truth of who you are and why you're here from them. I can't add this on top of it. I'll tell them I've decided to add cameras to the property. I may as well. It's not like they won't notice them as they go up."

"You can't tell them about the cameras. They won't notice them; they'll be hidden. The fencing and the added security personnel they'll notice, but we need the cameras to be kept quiet."

"You still suspect them?"

"This is standard protocol, Aja. It's not about suspecting them. It's about keeping everyone on this ranch safe."

She breathed a heavy sigh, the weight of this new burden clearly becoming increasingly difficult to carry. "I don't like lying to them, Jackson. This is their home too."

"Integrity being so important to you, I know this can't be easy, Aja. I don't think I've ever met anyone who believed in the truth as much as I do. Going against your instincts must be playing havoc with your mind right now."

She dropped her eyes as if they were too heavy to keep his gaze. The image of her downcast lids in the soft light of the kitchen with her long ebony lashes sweeping the apples of her cheeks nearly broke him. Her beauty and sadness were tied together in an intricate pattern of twists and swirls, making it impossible to see where one ended and the other began.

The sight of her like this unnerved him; it made him reach for her. He pulled his hand from her shoulder and cupped the side of her face.

He took a moment to consider her, to contemplate how many ways this decision would come back to bite them both on the ass, and while his mind screamed for him to get away, her tongue swept across her full bottom lip and he was lost.

Suddenly, he needed to know what her bare flesh would feel like pressed against his, or how that wicked mouth of hers would taste when he tangled his tongue with hers. He groaned before leaning down and joining their lips together.

The kiss was fleeting, over in a matter of seconds. But the way heat surged through his veins and seeped into his flesh made his body burn from the inside out.

He wanted to reach down and steal another, but the way she looked at him, her dark eyes bright with wonder and a mix of something he didn't quite recognize gave him pause. "I'm sorry, I shouldn't ha—"

"I'm not." She placed a firm hand behind his neck and pulled him forward. Her movements were adept and intentional. Her lips pressed against his without the slightest bit of concern or reservation. She wanted to taste him. Her kisses, demanding, tempting, and filled with fire, made it impossible for him to let common sense intervene.

He pulled her closer into his embrace, their bodies touching while their mouths feasted on each other. His fingers delighted in the softness of her plush curves. A desperate moan escaped his lips, and he could feel his body tightening behind the godforsaken constraint of his denim zipper. If the fire between them didn't consume him, his jeans would probably injure him for life.

That thought alone should've been enough to douse his burning arousal, but it didn't. Knowing Aja tasted like sweetness and spice—like a deep, rich cognac aged to perfection, potent and smooth at the same time—kept him bound to her. He wanted more.

He slid his hand down from her waist until he had a handful of her ass in his palm. If Jackson Dean wasn't an ass man before, he certainly was now. Wide and firm and yet still soft, even through the stiff material of her jeans, it molded perfectly to the shape of his palm.

Stop this now, Dean, before you have her spread over the floor. Have more respect for her than that.

He gentled their kiss, moving his mouth from hers, placing sweet pecks on her chin, each of her cheeks, and then her forehead. She burrowed the side of her face into his chest like she was seeking warmth and comfort, and his need to hold her, and hold on to her, burned deeper than before.

Then, he'd simply guessed at how good it would feel to touch her. Now that he knew something as simple as her kiss could send him up in flames, he wasn't certain he could willingly walk away.

Standing in her kitchen with their bodies wrapped around each other, Jackson wasn't sure of the tactful way to disengage from a woman who had effectively set his soul on fire with merely the touch of her lips. He didn't dwell too much on either because he saw something move in the shadows outside.

He didn't want to alarm Aja, so he gave her a light squeeze and whispered in her ear, "Do you get any animals close to the house?"

She cleared her throat and looked up at him. "No. Closer to the edge of the property, but never near the occupied buildings."

He glanced briefly out the window and saw what appeared to be the shape of a man crouching near the side of the porch. He kept her in his arms, not wanting to tip his hand to whoever it was lurking in the bushes, and whispered again, "I'm gonna check on things. Lock the door behind me. If I'm not back in ten minutes, call Colton and Storm to come to the house."

He could see the worry in her furrowed brow and the tight lines around her mouth. He gave her a quick peck before he released her. "Do what I ask, please."

She silently stepped aside while he grabbed the shotgun he'd placed in the broom closet behind the door when she told him to settle in and get comfortable. Grateful that she was cooperating, he stepped through the doorway, closing it behind him and waiting until he heard the click of the lock turning before he crossed the porch and headed in the direction of where he saw the shadow moving.

He padded through the grass with his weapon held at the ready, the mounted flashlight atop the barrel lighting his way. He watched the large bush on the side of the porch move and aimed the barrel where the leaves fluttered, using the mounted flashlight at the weapon's front end to cut through the thick night.

"Unless you walk on four legs, you'd better ease on outta that bush. Hands up where I can see them." The motion shuffling the leaves stopped. Jackson pumped his weapon to let whoever was in those bushes know he meant business. "You either come out, or I shoot."

"P-please, don't shoot."

Jackson moved the gun slightly to the left, focusing the flashlight's beam on where he saw the shrubbery parting. "Let me see those hands!" The person shoved their hands through the leaves, palm side up with their fingers spread wide.

First, his hands were visible, then one leg at a time, finally followed by his head and torso. Jackson saw dark, shoulder-length wavy hair. The man was either white or Latinx—from this distance and with the poor lighting in the backyard, he couldn't tell which yet. He was slim and nearly four or five inches shorter than Jackson's six feet, two inches, and he seemed to be appropriately frightened by Jackson's threat to fire.

"Pl-please, don't shoot! I'm supposed to be here. If you'd let me reach in my back pocket—"

"Not on your life. Make your way up the steps to the porch and get on your knees." The man followed his instructions. "Lay prostrate, then slowly toss whatever you wanted to show me behind you."

He did as instructed, tossing a wallet behind him. "My name is Mat Ryan; Ms. Everett invited here me. Sh-she is expecting me."

"If she invited you, then what were you doing sneaking around like some prowler in her bushes?"

"I dropped my phone."

Jackson was about to ask another question when he heard the click of the lock and saw Aja opening the door. "Aja, go back inside until I know it's safe."

"Jackson, put the gun away!" She dashed in front of him, kneeling on the floor to help the stranger up.

"Aja, what are you doing?" Jackson lowered the barrel of the gun and fought to keep himself from snatching her up by her neck. What kind of crazy game was she playing at?

"Hopefully, I'm keeping you from killing this harmless soul." Once she and the stranger were standing, they both faced Jackson. "Jackson Dean, my new foreman, please meet Mat Ryan, Brooklyn and Seneca's parole officer."

Chapter 9

Aja placed a warm cup of tea in front of Mat as he sat shivering at the kitchen table. A quick glance at the digital thermostat on the wall told her the poor man's body wasn't shaking because it was cold, so she assumed the big Texas Ranger sitting across the room terrified him.

Aja squinted her eyes and gave the best scowl she could to Jackson. He was leaning against the counter with wide, bulging arms folded across his chest while he mean-mugged poor Mat. An angry curled lip and a low growl slipping between clenched teeth were all that was missing from the menacing picture.

She put her hand on her hip and tilted her head to the side, doing her best imitation of Aunt Jo's I'm-not-too-pleased-with-you-right-now look. But Jackson didn't seem to care about her displeasure. The only thing his sharp features appeared concerned with was scaring Mat to death.

"Tell me again how you ended up creeping around in the backyard at this hour of the night."

"Jackson—"

He held up his fingers, silencing her in her own damn kitchen. *Who the hell does he think he is? This is my house.* She was about to tell him the same when she heard her uncle's voice sounding off inside her head. *"Do what he says, Aja. Don't give him any trouble."*

She folded her own arms and continued to glare at the belligerent Ranger standing across the room.

"I was supposed to meet with Ms. Everett and her charges yesterday morning for a home-and-community meeting for Ms. Daniels and Ms. Osborn. She rescheduled for this evening. Appointments that ran over delayed my arrival. I called Ms. Everett to reschedule, but she told me to come no matter what the hour. I had my phone in my hand as I walked from my visit with Ms. Daniels and Ms. Osborn at their residence. It slipped through my fingers and landed in the bushes. I was attempting to retrieve it when you found me."

Aja smoothed a comforting hand over Mat's shoulder, hoping to soothe the anxiety Jackson was causing the man. "I can verify everything Mat says, and I'm sure Seneca and Brooklyn will too. He's not trespassing, simply clumsy."

If Jackson knew Mat like she did, he would understand how typically Mat this story really was. Over the year he'd visited Restoration to check on Seneca and Brooklyn, he was always tripping over one thing or another, especially if Brooklyn was around. Seeing her always seemed to make his clumsiness worse. If something could cause him to break his neck, he'd make contact with it in the most awkward way. It was honestly a miracle the man hadn't broken or sprained something while conducting his check-ins with her workers.

Aja ignored Jackson's semipermanent frown and softened her features as she looked at Mat. "Please forgive Jackson. He's doing his best to prove he's the best foreman ever hired. Don't let him worry you."

Mat gave her a trembling smile and took a sip of his tea. When he finished, he looked up at her. His smile read a little less panicked and closer to his standard level of everyday nervous instead.

"My visits with Ms. Daniels and Ms. Osborn went well. I need you to sign the review forms I emailed to you, and I'll be out of your hair."

She snapped her fingers, remembering where she'd placed them, and walked over to the small cove in the kitchen where she dropped mail, bills, or anything important when she entered the house. She looked in a pile marked Outgoing, flipping through a few pages until she found the packet of forms she was looking for.

"Here you go." She handed the forms to Mat. He folded them, grabbed the wallet sitting on the table that Jackson had demanded when Mat was facedown on the floor, and offered her a shaky smile, one filled with more fear than warmth.

"It's getting late, Ms. Everett. I don't want to outstay my welcome. I'll call you if there's anything more I need."

Aja glanced back at Jackson, mustering as much cold as she could in her sharp glare before she turned back to an already retreating Mat. "Mat, please call me Aja. You're welcome to stay for another cup of tea. There's even a slice of pineapple coconut cake if you give me a second to cut it."

Mat shifted his eyes from her to somewhat beyond her shoulder before he shook his head. She didn't have to guess what or who had captured his attention. "I really must go. Thank you for your hospitality. I'll call you soon."

A few quick steps and he was at the door, twisting the knob back and forth until he could finally get it open. Before she could raise her hand to wave goodbye, Mat closed the door behind him with a sound thud and disappeared into the night.

She turned on her heels slowly until she faced Jackson. "You could've at least apologized to the man."

"For what, exactly?"

"Treating him like a criminal without cause."

Jackson shook his head, dismissing her claim. "Not how I see it. He was sneaking around your property at night. Any fool would know that's the easiest way to end up on the wrong end of a rifle in these parts. I don't trust him."

She threw up her hands and walked toward the stairs. "You are paranoid. Mat is harmless."

"Mat could be a serial killer for all you know. Just because a man appears meek and mild doesn't make him a saint."

Aja waved her hand and rolled her eyes. Arguing with this man would take more energy than she had to spare. Rather than allow him to pluck her nerves anymore, she decided going up to her room was the best solution to end this debate with no bloodshed.

"So." The deep rumble of his voice halted her steps. "Is there really pineapple coconut cake, or were you telling Mat that to make him feel better?"

"Are you really asking me for cake right now?"

He held his hands out wide. "What? I like pineapple coconut cake."

The beginnings of a headache throbbed behind her eyes. She pressed stiff fingers against her temples, trying to relieve the dull, stabbing pain twisting the muscles of her neck and eyes tighter with the passing of each moment.

"Lord have mercy! You cannot be asking me for cake as if we're two regular acquaintances retiring for the night. I have worked with that man for a year. He's been nothing but supportive to the women who work for me. He's helping them change their lives. And tonight you possibly destroyed all the work, all the goodwill we've all strived to create. Yes, there's pineapple coconut cake. It's damn good cake too. But I will not reward bad behavior. So as far as you're concerned, no, there's no cake."

"I was trying to protect you, Aja."

She shook her head, a stupid move considering the dull ache throbbing inside it. "Jackson, going out there and subduing him was you protecting me, but the overbearing ogre thing you had going on afterward had nothing to do with that. He was obviously not a threat then. Yet you were practically growling at him."

She was still trying to figure out what that was about. Every time she showed Mat any kindness, Jackson's mood seem to sour further. It was odd considering there was usually some professional respect between law-enforcement officers. But his speech along with his body language made it clear Mat was an unwelcome guest.

She waited for him to admit his mistake. Any reasonable person would have. But seeing him intimidate poor Mat that way rubbed her patience raw like an ill-fitting shoe against the back of her ankle.

It was painful, something she couldn't ignore, and watching that sweet man cower in fear as Jackson behaved so badly made her blood boil with unspoken rage.

Doing his job was fine, but bullying wasn't. And if he treated Mat that way, a man with no negative marks on his record, how far would he go with people like Seneca and Brooklyn? Women whose pasts were checkered, who were judged harshly by their mistakes.

She'd made a terrible mistake by kissing this man. Letting her guard down again in front of him was something she could ill afford. Not if she wanted to protect Seneca and Brooklyn from being on the receiving end of his brand of hard judgment.

Chapter 10

JACKSON STOOD BEHIND THE GUEST BEDROOM DOOR WITH HIS hands planted on his waist, contemplating his next move. He'd fucked up big time. After a rough night's sleep, attempting to figure out how things had gone from the cozy warmth of their kiss to the chilly end of their night, he worried about what awaited him on the other side of the door.

If Mat hadn't shown up when he did, things might've continued down another path, a path that led him to pineapple coconut cake and, if he were lucky, more satisfying treats than Aja's baked goods.

Jackson shook his head. He didn't regret securing the scene last night until he was certain Mat wasn't a threat. But Aja was right—the way he'd gone out of his way to let Mat know he wasn't welcome crossed a line. He wasn't even certain why the sight of the slight man all hunched over at Aja's kitchen table, accepting her tea and hospitality, made him so goddamned mad.

All he knew was he wasn't able to let go of the fire that seemed to burn inside him with red, angry flames licking at his soul as he watched her rub Mat's shoulder.

It was comfort. Logically he understood that. But a few seconds before Mat interrupted them, Jackson had been exercising his own form of comfort with Aja. And he didn't know if he was conflating the two, but the idea that she could comfort Mat the same way Jackson sought to soothe her made him lose his fool mind.

"No sense putting this off. Time to go downstairs and man up."

He turned the knob and took the back stairs to the kitchen. If Aja was anywhere in this house at this hour of the morning, she'd be there.

The rich aroma of fresh coffee was the first thing his sleep-deprived brain noticed, followed by the savory scents of various breakfast meats.

God, this woman knows the key to a Texas boy's heart.

He found her standing at the stovetop. From his vantage point, he couldn't tell what she was cooking, but the inviting aroma tickled his nose and made his mouth water. "Smells great in here."

She didn't turn around. Simply offered him a quick "Morning" as she continued monitoring the sizzling pans in front of her.

He caught a glimpse of the spread already taking up residence on the counter. There were chafing dishes marked Bacon, Sausage, Salmon Cakes, Grits, Oatmeal, Eggs, and Fruit, accompanied by a large bowl filled with yogurt cups on ice.

"Morning," he responded. "Looks like you're expecting an army."

She offered him a wide grin and the sight of it relaxed the knot sitting in the pit of his stomach, untwisting it one complicated loop after another. *Maybe I haven't screwed things up as badly as I thought.*

"With you and your men added to our ranks, and your dad's security consultation firm coming, I figured variety and volume were called for. You or your men didn't mention any food restrictions. In case any of you are vegan or lactose intolerant, I used soy milk in the oatmeal and plant butter in the grits. I put everything in separate chafing dishes with designated serving utensils on the off chance any of you might have food allergies. I can whip up some avocado toast, too, if any of you want it."

She wasn't wrong about the volume part. She didn't know it yet, but his brother, Kip, ate like he had a hole in his stomach.

"All the chafing dishes have food in them except the one for the eggs. I'll start those after I finish this last batch of bacon. Get a plate and help yourself."

By the time he reached the middle of the buffet, she walked around the counter carrying the largest skillet he'd ever seen piled high with fluffy eggs. He rested his plate on the counter and opened the empty chafing dish for her.

"Thanks," she muttered. "I appreciate the help." She glanced up at him and gave him that sweet smile again where her long lashes fanned across high cheekbones, and her full lips curved into a most tempting bow that made need twist inside him.

"I take it by your pleasant mood this morning I'm no longer in the doghouse?"

"It's a new day, Jackson. With each sunrise, there's a new chance to get things right. That's what Restoration Ranch is about. Everyone deserves a chance to make things right—even you."

"Does that mean I get my slice of pineapple coconut cake today?"

She laughed and threw a dish towel at him. He caught it before it connected with his face. The playful way the glint of danger danced across her eyes called to him like metal to lightning, inevitable as if there was no way he could walk away. "That means you get another chance to earn a slice of pineapple coconut cake. Let's hope you don't lose the privilege again."

"Speaking of privilege, I abused mine last night. I crossed a line when I kissed you. I'm very sorry for taking advantage."

The smile spilled from her face as she squinted at him, and that somehow made her look more captivating than she already did. She stepped closer and he could smell something sweet, like a decadent frosted treat that wafted up in the air, pulling him nearer.

"You apologized barely a minute ago for being an asshole. Don't continue with the same dickish behavior."

He wasn't sure how to respond to her. Was she chastising him or consoling him?

"Jackson." Her voice was soft, but it was strong, filled with certainty and confidence. "I didn't feel taken advantage of. In fact, I seem to remember telling you last night I wasn't sorry about it. If you have some protocol that forbids you from kissing me, that's fine. Because I can understand needing to follow the rules. But if you're doing it out of some misguided sense of decency, then please spare yourself the trouble. I wanted that kiss as much as you did."

He swallowed, partly because hearing in her voice how much she'd wanted his lips on hers set his blood on fire, and partly because his mouth was so dry from surprise that he couldn't speak. He cleared his throat quickly before focusing on her again.

"I don't want to overstep, Aja. Your uncle didn't send me here to maul you."

"No, he sent you here to help me. And the comfort of physical affection was what I needed then. You have nothing to worry about. It was a kiss. Nothing more."

The edges of her mouth lifted into that wide, welcoming smile of hers, and a heavy weight lifted off Jackson, one he hadn't been aware he was carrying. Relief caressing him like strong but comforting fingers across his skin, Jackson wondered, and not for the first time, how different his life might have been if he'd met this woman before his life had shattered into tiny splintering pieces.

He didn't know if he could manage not to piss her off again, especially when he seemed to be so good at doing it. But the hope blooming inside his chest at the possibility of keeping that perfect smile on her face spread all the way out to his limbs and made him ache with everything he had to please her.

The hum of morning conversation filled the kitchen, and a familiar swell of joy bubbled up inside Aja. Six people sat at her table volleying friendly chatter back and forth between each bite of food.

The scene tickled something deep inside her. Before her relationship with her sister turned into something dark and sinister, and before work consumed her world, there was joy. Back then, she was a happy little girl surround by a family with no cares in the world.

That place, that person was a forgotten wonder to her. But as the sun streamed into the open room, filling it with light, and she looked around at the six of them sitting, eating, and talking together, Aja's heart danced a little.

She sat next to Jackson, sneaking a peek at him, and wondered why eating with him, his men, and her ladies made her feel so nostalgic.

This moment somehow tapped into the treasured memories of days gone by. Back then, the ranch would be filled with loads of her Henry kin. Aunties, uncles, and cousins once, twice, and thrice removed filling every available nook and cranny of this property and every structure on it until it was full to bursting.

Every morning, all the adults would eat in the kitchen, and her mother, Aunt Jo, and Uncle Ricky, and the rest of their brothers and sisters, would sit around this table and eat while the children sat in the living room on the floor. Everyone balancing their plates on their knees as they huddled around the television. It was loud and chaotic, but everything about those moments made Aja grin over her raised cup of coffee.

"Penny for your thoughts."

She shook her head. "Thinking about my family."

Jackson leaned in closer. His words were a whispered rumble. "You have a big one?"

A familiar pang of loss tried to push its way into her good mood as Aja thought about the loved ones she'd lost in the Henry clan. "I used to." She moved her coffee cup in a slow circle, watching the creamy liquid inside swirl about. "My mother was the oldest of eight. She raised her sisters and brothers on this ranch. Aunt Jo and Uncle Ricky are the last living of the eight Henry siblings. Since my mom passed, few of the extended family comes around anymore." She looked around the kitchen, then leaned in again to whisper to him. "Today reminded me these walls were built to be filled with people."

He tapped his finger on the table next to her hand, then looked at her, his eyes full of concern as he spoke. "You ready to tell them about the security upgrades?"

His question poured over her like iced water on a wintry New York day. It stung, spreading a chill through her that made her insides quake.

Might as well get it over with now, Aja.

"Everyone…" She waited for the chatter to slowly abate before she continued. "Shortly I plan to take a meeting with a security consultant. After the last attack on the ranch, I've concluded we need to protect ourselves a little better around here."

"You buying more firearms for you and Ms. Jo?"

Aja shook her head at Brooklyn. She was never comfortable around firearms. Growing up in the heart of Brownsville, she saw what happened when the wrong people had access to weapons. She kept a rifle in the house to scare off wandering animals with a warning shot in the air. But other than that, she hoped to never have to aim the weapon at another living, breathing thing.

"No, I'm hiring a security company to add stronger fencing around the perimeter of my property line and security guards to man some of the open access points."

Brooklyn sat up straighter in her chair, placing her hands flat against the table on either side of her plate. "You bringing in guards to watch your property or to watch us?"

Aja couldn't say Brooklyn's response to her announcement shocked her. Like the city she was named for, she was brash, direct with no filter. She said what she meant, no time for games or pleasantries.

"This isn't about you and Seneca, Brooklyn. It's about keeping the ranch secure, keeping all of us safe, and keeping our future resort guests safe. If the ranch is unprotected, I'm opening myself up to liability."

She kept her eyes focused on Seneca and Brooklyn, who were staring at each other. Unspoken messages passed between the two women, and Aja knew they'd talk about this when they went back in their cabin.

Seneca reached across the table and touched her fingertips to Aja's. That and the usual bright grin she wore were a comforting balm to her raw soul. "It's your land and your business, Boss. Do what you think is best."

Brooklyn shoveled another forkful of food into her mouth, looking unbothered by the conversation in the least. "That fire situation could've been much worse than it was. Protect yourself."

It wasn't Seneca's sentimental way of expression. Brooklyn didn't have time for reassuring smiles and small affectionate touches. Her agreement that protective measures needed to be taken was enough for Aja to stop punishing herself a little. And with enough sins in her past to fill a heavy trunk, she welcomed anything that would lighten her guilty load even the slightest bit.

Aja clapped her hands together, then pointed in their direction. "If you ladies could finish up and get started on your morning chores, I'd like to have a brief meeting with our new hires before they settle into their day. Oh, and if you're taking any to-go plates with you, make sure to leave some for the security crew. They'll be here shortly."

With little fanfare, Brooklyn and Seneca picked up their dishes, rinsed them out in the sink, and placed them in the dishwasher. A quick wave goodbye and they were out the back door and walking into the field.

Aja walked to the kitchen island and pulled a file from a drawer. "This is a list-slash-schedule of all the chores we do around here. Jackson, as the foreman, you can change this around however you like." He didn't speak, so she continued. "If you have questions about anything, the ladies can help you out. Seneca has the patience of a saint. Brooklyn, not so much. So don't get on her nerves."

Storm laughed. "If we can put up with Colt's grouchiness, Brooklyn should be a sweetheart."

Colton may be an old cuss at heart, but she doubted he had anything on the chip Brooklyn wore on her shoulder like an additional appendage. Aja tipped her head in his direction. "Don't say I didn't warn you."

Storm and Colton stood from the table, emptied their plates, and walked toward the back door. Colton pulled on his Stetson and tipped it in her direction before addressing Jackson. "Come find us when you need to, Jackson."

Jackson replied with a two-fingered salute and waited for the door to close behind his men before he covered Aja's hand with his.

It was a simple gesture, but it was filled with complications she didn't want to think about right now. In this moment, she wanted to focus on how warm his skin felt when it covered hers, or how it made her nerves zip with electricity.

"You handled that well."

"I'm glad it went okay. I consider this place their home. I don't want them to feel violated here."

He gave her hand another squeeze. "I promise everything will be fine." His words felt heavy and purposeful, as if he'd considered their weight before using them, placing them on the scale to make certain their impact would pull down her defenses and make her trust him more.

This is a bad idea, girl. You need to get away from this man right now.

As the sound of the doorbell severed their connection, Jackson removed his hand and stood. "Time for you to meet my father and my brother."

He walked off toward the front door, and she sat there shaking her head and then looked up at the ceiling. "Please, Lord," she whispered, "don't let them be anywhere near as fine as he is. If they are, I can't be held responsible for my actions."

Chapter 11

JACKSON FOLLOWED AJA, HIS FATHER, AND HIS BROTHER BACK into the house after they'd returned from assessing the access points he was concerned about. Aja led them into the great room of the homestead.

"Your land is beautiful, Ms. Everett. I imagine you're quite proud of it," Jacob said.

Jackson watched a proud smile spread across Aja's face. As if she were both agreeing with and thanking his father at the same time. She did that a lot when she talked about her land or the people who worked on it.

And why do I know that?

The easy answer was that he was an investigator. Someone trained to take notice of the small things people did to track behavior. But the honest truth was that Jackson watched Aja all the time.

He furrowed his brow as he thought about how creepy that admission sounded in his head. He wasn't stalking her, but he was noticing certain things about her he didn't think she'd realized she'd revealed.

Breakfast was a perfect example of her letting her guard down.

She sat watching the people she'd cooked for enjoy her meal. While she played with the spoon in her bowl of grits, she smiled, uncaring if anyone saw, open, enjoying the buzz of life happening around her.

"Please, call me Aja, Mr. Dean." She swept her hand in the air, pointing to one of the sofas for her guests to sit down. "Can I offer you gentlemen anything to eat or drink?"

His brother and father shook their heads. "No, dear," his father replied. "I'm still full after that morning spread you were kind enough to offer us when we arrived. If possible, we'd like to look around the house to go over some spaces that could be problematic if ignored." He turned to Jackson's brother, Kip. "Son, you mind going upstairs to look around? I can start down here."

"Sure, Daddy," Kip answered and looked to Aja for permission to go upstairs.

She steadied her shoulders. This was obviously still difficult for her. But somehow she didn't let that stop her.

She wore her determination to keep her ranch safe etched into the furrowed lines of her brow and the stiff set of her back and shoulders. The sight of her preparing for battle, her fierceness shrouding her like a warrior goddess's battle cry, unfurled a tangible need in Jackson's chest.

When Aja and Kip disappeared from the great room and he could hear their footsteps taking them up the stairs, his father turned around and said, "She sure is nice. Ain't she?"

Jackson called up the memory of Aja exiting through the doorway into the hall a few seconds earlier. If "nice" were a euphemism for sexy, spirited, dedicated, and confident, then yeah, Aja Everett was as nice as they came.

The familiar heavy chuckle that fell from his father's mouth, making the man's shoulders and torso jiggle like a bowl of gelatin right out of the fridge, pulled Jackson's eyes from Aja's disappearing form.

"What's so funny, old man?"

"I got your 'old man' all right. No matter my age, I'm still young enough to tan your hide."

Jackson laughed. He didn't doubt Jacob's words at all. Jackson and Kip matched their father in height and brawn. The retired sheriff back in Jackson's hometown, Jacob Dean still kept himself in good shape. According to him, he needed to be ready to knock some sense into his foolhardy boys if they ever became too wily.

But since Jackson could remember few times when Jacob had needed to use more than his rich bass to corral his rowdy boys or more than a stern look to make them think twice about crossing a line, Jackson knew his father's threat was nothing more than Jacob's personal brand of Texas bravado.

"However long in the tooth I am, I'm not too old to recognize my son making eyes at the pretty lady who's upstairs with your brother right now."

Jackson turned around to face his father, tension spreading through his body as quickly as confusion seeded his mind. "What's that supposed to mean?"

"I don't believe I stuttered. You haven't taken your eyes off Ms. Everett since we arrived."

"She's a beautiful woman," Jackson explained calmly, hoping his father wouldn't see through his need to deflect. "Any man would take more than a second glance at her."

"But you're not just any man, Jackson. That you're giving her more than one look tells me there's something further to this than an investigation."

Jackson shook his head, not sure who he was trying to convince. Yeah, there was something there, something about the way Aja carried herself that made him want things he shouldn't. But history had spent too many years beating it into his head that beyond the superficial, entanglements with women only led to devastation in his life.

"Your Ms. Everett is a good woman."

"I've known her for a handful of days. She's not *my* Ms. Anything. And you've spent even less time in her presence to know if she's a good woman or not."

His father walked to the other side of the room, sat, and leaned back against the sofa, crossing a boot-covered ankle over his knee as he glared at Jackson. "She may be from Brooklyn, but she's tied to this here land. She takes pride in it. You can see it whenever she talks about. While we were out canvassing her acres, it was obvious this place is in her blood. And if she loves the land, the way she feels about the people she's helping is more of credit to her character than anything else. That is a good woman, Jackson. It wouldn't do to let her pass you by. Certainly not because of your past."

Jackson placed his hands on his belted waist, his tense shoulders hiking up near his ears. He didn't doubt there were good women in the world. He simply doubted one would ever fit into his life.

How many times did a man need to make the same mistake before he learned his lesson and changed his ways? He might be drawn to Aja, might even be curious enough to dip his toe in that particular pool, but diving right in off the highest board wasn't in Jackson's plans.

"As far as I remember it, Lana wasn't the only one who taught me women shouldn't be trusted. Margie was the first to drive that lesson home."

"Your mother—"

"Margie." Jackson hadn't thought of her as a mother since they day she told ten-year-old Jackson to watch his five-year-old brother while she went to the market for an afternoon milk run. His father found him hours later, standing at the door, waiting for her after Jacob's shift ended at the sheriff's office.

Jacob took a slow breath before rising from his perch on the sofa. He walked over to Jackson, his steps careful and his gaze steady, before placing a strong hand on his shoulder. "Yes, Margie left, and Lana put you through hell. But, Son, don't let them be the reason you don't let anybody else in."

Jacob's words made logical sense. But they did little to reassure him.

"If you really believed that, why haven't you let anyone else in? Why didn't you remarry?"

Jackson watched as Jacob's eyes widened, and an odd combination of sadness and surprise filled his deep-brown eyes.

"Daddy, I'm sorry. My mouth gets away from me sometimes."

Jacob squeezed Jackson's shoulder, the motion more comforting than punitive. "I didn't remarry or let you boys meet every woman I kept time with after Margie left, because I didn't think it right. I didn't want the two of you getting attached if things didn't work out. You being unaware of it doesn't mean I never found someone else to love."

Jackson canted his head to the side and stared at his father. He cataloged the tiny twinkle of a spark in his father's eyes and wondered what he was seeing.

A few seconds more of the wheels in his head spinning, and the answer was painted in a clear vision across his father's face. *He's happy?* "You're seeing someone, aren't you?"

Jacob dropped his hand and walked to the window, staring out as if it held the answer to all the important questions in life. "I've been seeing someone for the last twenty-five years. We both had reason to keep things between us. But now, those reasons make little sense anymore. I love her. I want to marry her."

"Do I at least get to meet her?"

"Do you really want to?"

Jackson wanted to be hurt, offended by the question his father posed. But deep down he knew he couldn't. After Lana, he'd spent the last eight years avoiding being part of anyone else's happiness.

He ran his fingers over the tense muscles in his neck and

rubbed. When his father turned from the window, he wore a deep glow that shone from the inside outward. At that moment, all the anger caged in Jackson's chest dissipated into a gentle calm. It spilled from his heart, through his great vessels, and buried itself deep within his bones. "I'd be honored to meet her if you want me to."

A crooked grin softened his father's features, casting a rejuvenating glow on his aging skin. "I'd like that very much. But you know what I'd like even more?"

"What's that, Daddy?"

"For you to find someone to love you the way my lady friend loves me. You need that, Jackson. Don't wait 'til you're my age to realize it. And looking at how that young lady smiles at you when you speak, I'd say she's probably the right person to teach you how nice caring about someone can be."

Jackson didn't have a lot of time to think about all his father had shared with him. He could hear his brother's and Aja's footsteps overhead, headed back to the staircase. Within moments, the sultry tones of her voice became more pronounced as she walked down the hall, coming ever closer to the great room.

She stepped inside the room, and he watched her face blossom into a bright canvas of rose-tinted, silky brown skin. A familiar mixture of anticipation and nervousness tumbled through him.

When their eyes met again, Jackson knew one thing. He might not be able to let himself have what his father had found, but maybe there was something between him and Aja Everett that he wanted to explore. There were two things he needed to consider, however. Would he let it happen? And would it be such a bad thing if he did?

Chapter 12

Jackson waved at the disappearing SUV as it moved toward the front gates of the property.

He watched as his brother turned the vehicle to the right onto the main road until it was no longer in his sight. With Aja having an afternoon meeting with her employees, Jackson headed straight for Colton and Storm's bunkhouse for a check-in of his own.

A few moments later, he tapped on their door and waited for Storm to let him in.

"How did it go?"

"Good," Jackson responded as he stepped inside and closed the door behind him. He followed Storm back into the kitchen where Colton sat sipping a glass of iced water. "She seemed agreeable to the suggestions Jacob and Kip made."

Storm pulled a glass from the cabinet and pressed it to the ice maker/water filter compartment in the freezer door of the double-sided fridge. "When does their crew return to install the security system?"

"Jacob promised to expedite everything because of Aja's situation. But for a property this size, it will still take a few days to get all the equipment she needs in his inventory. The only answer is to keep a close watch until Jacob and Kip can do their thing."

Storm returned to the counter, handing Jackson the cold beverage and waiting for him to continue after he emptied the glass.

"You two have anything to report? See anything strange during your rounds?"

Colton sat at the counter, running a single fingertip in a circular pattern, then shook his head. "It's been quiet so far. Nothing at the access points we're concerned about last night or today. Seneca's been locked up in her office all day on her computer. I've passed by several times; she's always where she's supposed to be, tapping away on those keys."

Jackson folded his arms. "How much do you know about computers? You think you could get in there undetected and figure out what she's working on?"

Colton pulled his fingers through his thick, straight hair. "I don't know. I know a few things about computers from my days in the army, but if Seneca is knowledgeable enough to build a computer network for a resort, she'd figure out someone was trying to spy on her pretty quickly. I'll see what I can do, though."

Jackson agreed that was the best chance they had of getting any info. Seneca presented as a sweet and upbeat person who made mornings look easy with her unending perkiness. But that didn't mean she wasn't up to no good. The most notorious criminals often hid in plain sight. Possibly a closer look into her digital tracks would offer information to help their investigation.

"Can't say tailing Brooklyn was any more informative, Boss. She's all over the ranch. But she's the architect. She needs to be mobile to survey the land to design structures for Aja." Storm crossed his arms, something the good-natured Ranger did when he was mulling over case information. "I can't tell if she's up to anything yet. She's constantly on the go and doesn't slow down long enough to let the grass grow under her feet."

Still at square one, Jackson set the glass on the counter and hooked his thumbs into his denims. "Stay on them both. If either of them is up to something, they'll eventually slip up."

"Are we gonna look into Bennett?"

Jackson shook his head in response to Storm's question. "Not yet. We don't have probable cause to officially tail him. But we can see what dirt we can find on him on the internet. It's not a thorough background check, but it could at least point us in the right direction of where we should be looking. Also, Jennings and Gleason should have tracked him down by now to have an unofficial chat. Check in with them to see if they contacted him and what Bennett had to say if they did." Jackson headed toward the door.

"What are you going to do while Storm and I are doing all that?"

Jackson turned around to face Colton, scratching the back of his head as his thoughts came together. "I will try to talk to Aja again, see if she can think of anything from her past in New York that might shine a light on all this."

"You think she's hiding something?"

Jackson tugged his bottom lip between his teeth as he thought. "She seems truthful. I know for certain her being scared isn't an act. I'm thinking she may have overlooked something. Maybe if I can get it out of her, we can figure out who we're dealing with."

Jackson waved and stepped on the porch, closing the door behind him. He pondered Storm's question and his answer came up the same. She wore her integrity like he wore that five-point Texas star, proud in the open for everyone to see.

He'd know if she were lying, especially after the way she felt in his arms when she was pressed so close to him that he could feel her heart beat strong and steady against his chest.

His daddy was right. Aja wasn't Margie or Lana. She didn't think about herself. She put her people first. She protected those she cared for. She didn't abandon them like Margie or lie about all the important things—crucial things that could mean life or death—the way Lana did either. Anyone who would put themselves in harm's way to secure someone else's future was stand-up in Jackson's book.

As he made his way to the stables to take care of the chores he'd missed during the security consultation, all he could wonder was who would try to hurt someone like Aja. Why would someone want to destroy a person who worked to make things better for others?

Jackson's muscles burned by the time he returned to the main house. A half day of backbreaking work in the stables had produced a good enough workout that he was covered in a sheen of sweat.

It was well past dinnertime now, and his stomach protested missing one of Aja's meals. As he climbed the steps to the back porch, he toyed with the idea of heading straight for the fridge and cleaning up later. But as he caught a whiff of the barnyard special scent he was wearing, he bypassed the empty kitchen and headed toward his guest room for a hot shower instead.

A few moments of washing the outside off, and his fatigue turned into a mellow relaxation. He was tired, sure, but not tired enough to want to go to sleep yet. A pair of sweatpants, an A-line T-shirt, and a comfy pair of thick socks, and Jackson was headed down to the kitchen to scavenge in the fridge.

The kitchen was still quiet when he returned. Maybe Aja had gone to sleep. Disappointment sank like a weight in the bottom of his stomach. He realized that maybe dinner wasn't all he'd missed. Perhaps he should add Aja's presence to that list too.

Her smart banter, the way she always had an answer for

everything he threw at her. He even missed the way she made him justify everything, never accepting his word as truth but making him prove it.

Too afraid to think about the reason behind his disappointment at eating alone, Jackson opened the fridge and found a plate covered in aluminum foil with a note on top.

> *Jackson, if you're hungry after mucking out stalls, here's a roast beef sandwich on my special French loaf bread. If you look on the counter, you'll find a batch of my homemade potato chips in a baggie with your name on it too.*
>
> *Enjoy,*
> *A.*

He stared at the note and the neat curly loops of her handwriting, and the disappointment that tried to settle inside him dissipated, a new warmth permeating his bones.

He smiled and pulled the plate and a bottle of Coke from the fridge and picked up his bag of chips from the counter.

He settled in the great room, turning on the television, making sure the volume wasn't loud enough to disturb his sleeping host. He set his bounty on the coffee table and dug in.

He alternated between chewing, flipping channels, and taking a swig of his carbonated beverage until he found a syndicated episode of *Star Trek: The Next Generation*. He didn't care what anyone had to say, Patrick Stewart was the best captain who sat on the deck of the *Enterprise*.

His phone vibrated in his pocket, and a new text from his brother flashed across the screen.

Kip: Overnighted equipment for the Restoration Ranch job. We'll be able to start in two–three days.

Jackson: Good. Question: Daddy with you?

Kip: No. Why?

Jackson: What's this about him getting married?

Kip: 🙂 🙂 👃

Jackson: If you pay so little attention to him, I can see now
    how you let him get caught up.

Kip: Let? Last I checked, he was growner than both of us
    put together.

Jackson: Growner is not a word. Who is she?

Kip: If you came 'round on a regular, you'd know.

Jackson: Is she nice? Are you okay with this?

Kip took a moment to answer and Jackson worried during the
silence. What if this woman was terrible for his father? What if she
hurt him?

Kip: She makes him smile, J. After everything he's been
    through, he deserves to smile. That's all I'm interested
    in.

Frustrated with his brother's nonanswer, Jackson took another
sip of his drink and texted again.

Jackson: You're an asshole. Give me a straight answer.

Kip: I'm told I take after my big brother. If you wanna know
    about Daddy's lady friend, bring ya ass home.

Jackson: 👆

Kip: 💋

He smiled as he put the phone back in his pocket. Kip might
get on his last nerve, but he still loved him. Not to mention, he was
right. Jackson needed to spend more time with his family.

Jackson popped the last chip in his mouth when he recognized familiar footsteps heading toward the great room. He looked up and found Aja leaning against the doorway. "Ready for a snack?"

A snack? She was standing there with her head wrapped in a black satin scarf, her face free of any makeup, her torso covered in a fitted gray tank, and pink sweatpants that looked more lounge worthy than workout appropriate—fitted to accent her thick thighs and the deep curves of her hips. Good God. A snack? Yeah, he wanted one. But only if she were on the dessert menu.

She walked into the room with her hands behind her back, grinning like she held the sweetest secret. She stepped in front of him. If she was waiting for him to speak, she'd wait a mighty long time, because watching her in her natural, comfortable glory stole his breath and made speech impossible.

She pulled a dessert plate from behind her back that boasted a thick and tall slice of pineapple coconut cake. He struggled for a moment, trying to pull his sight from the tempting way the swell of her breasts called to him from under the thin material of the tank. He closed his eyes and released a low, long sound that was a strange symphony of lust and frustration coming together in a unique blend.

"Wow, you really weren't kidding when you said you loved this kind of cake."

Cake? Oh, yeah. There's cake too, he reminded himself. Focus on the cake, Dean. It's the only treat you can have that won't complicate the hell out of your life.

"I do. But I thought you said I had to earn it."

She handed him the plate, followed by a fork and a napkin she appeared to pull out of thin air. The truth was, she could've been wearing them for all he could remember. Once he'd caught sight of her looking like the perfect mix of comfort and sexy, he hadn't focused on anything other than her.

His brain was oblivious to anything except the way her curves were making his blood rush and his heart beat in an erratic rhythm.

God, this felt so good and bad at the same time. Was it possible to send a perfectly healthy man into cardiac arrest from sexual arousal and frustration?

"You earned it. You helped me see why the security upgrades were necessary. You also got your dad to clear his schedule for this consultation. Not to mention the discount. There's no way your father's charging me market value for this."

"That's probably because of the new lady friend he's been seeing. He's giddy enough to be talking marriage. Maybe he missed a decimal point because his head was in the clouds."

"Cynical much?"

He sliced the fork into the moist cake and shoveled a large piece into his mouth. It was a fusion of sweet and tart, of flaky coconut shavings and chunky pieces of juicy pineapple, and when the rich, soft yellow cake balanced all the flavors together, Jackson felt the satisfaction down deep in his soul.

"About this cake? Not even a little. About people and love? Pretty much all the time. He's too old to get lost in the foolishness of love. To let someone make him believe in fairy tales."

He made it halfway through the dessert before regretting that his Coke wasn't a tall glass of milk, but enjoying it just the same. He turned to find her staring at him. Watching him as if she were trying to figure out the secret to some great mystery.

"What? I have cake on my face?"

She said nothing, tilting her head to the side as she continued to watch him. She took a deep breath, closing her eyes and breaking their connection for a moment. "Why does your father have to be a fool for wanting to share his love with someone else? Maybe it's not about love and passion at his age. Perhaps it's about companionship and comfort. Maybe at this stage of his life, that's something worth having."

Maybe it was—Jackson couldn't truly say. He'd had girlfriends before Lana. Nothing too serious, but significant enough he missed them when those relationships came to their amicable end. But with Lana, he'd poured every ounce of his being into loving her, and it wasn't enough.

"Are you worried about your dad remarrying, or are you a mama's boy who doesn't want his dad with anyone else?"

If that wasn't the most laughable thing he'd ever heard. Jackson was fiercely loyal, especially to his father and brother. Margie, on the other hand, could get as much of his attention as a drop of water in an ocean. As far as it concerned him, she was a useless human being taking up resources on the earth.

"Considering my mother walked out on us when I was a boy, I doubt that's the case."

"Jackson, I'm so sorry. I never imagined…"

He interrupted her by picking up his cake and slicing off another piece. This cake had brought him more pleasure in the five minutes since she'd brought it to him than his five-year marriage or his selfish mother ever had. No sense in dwelling on the past when the present was so much more inviting.

"Are you gonna eat some of this with me?" He held up the healthy chunk on the fork and balanced it as he moved it in her direction, hoping it would be enough of a distraction she'd drop the subject.

She shook her head. "No, indulging in that kind of decadence this late is a bad thing for me."

He held the fork in front of her mouth, trying to tempt her, but she politely declined again. "Please don't tell me you're one of these women who can't enjoy a piece of cake because she's worried about her figure? You're gorgeous."

A soft chuckle left her lips as a spark of something bright flashed in her eyes. "You're right. I am. Me not wanting cake this late in the night has nothing to do with me keeping my fabulous figure."

She waved a hand down the length of her sexy lady lumps for

emphasis, making it hard for him to chew and swallow his cake without choking.

"I'm happy in my size-sixteen skin. And that's not me hating on my size-two sistren, but if God intended for us all to be the same, he wouldn't have made us different. My desirability is not at all tied to my dress size, so there's nothing to watch."

On that he could agree. He was sitting in front of her eating one of the most decadent desserts he'd ever tasted, and yet hunger still ravaged his body with a need that contorted his insides into impossible positions.

"So if you're not watching your girlish figure, why won't you indulge with me?"

She raised her eyebrow as if silently asking if he'd meant his words to sound as provocative as they had. The truth lay somewhere in the middle.

He liked the flash of interest he saw turning her chocolate-brown eyes to a warm amber. He also didn't miss the delicious way her knowing smile spread across her thick, full lips.

It was an invitation to keep the double-entendre game going as far as it concerned him. But even with their heightened wordplay, the fact was the cake was good.

"If I give in to something that sweet this time of night, it would keep me up all evening long." She leaned closer to him, and his pulse sped up. His body responding to her nearness, his length already thickening under the soft material of his sweats. She glanced down, noting his delicate predicament, and her mouth curled into the perfect bow as her smile widened. "As much as I want it"—she looked up, her voice dropped to her lower register, the sultry sound pulling him closer to her without conscious effort on his part—"and believe me I do, tomorrow is an early workday."

His fingers tightened on the fork, and he figured he'd best put the plate and the cutlery down before he mutilated himself accidentally. He quickly made sure the plate, the fork, and the remains of his cake didn't end up on the floor. When he turned around, his eyes locked with hers.

She slid her hand from its perch on her lap and reached for his face, wiping a thumb across his mouth. "You had a bit of icing there."

She went to pull her thumb away, and he couldn't quite explain what happened next. His tongue darted out of its own volition, because there was no way in hell he told it to do that. It curled around her digit, licking the icing from her fingertip as if it were the secret ingredient to life. And with that one move, something changed in the air.

"If we were in court, I'd submit this as evidence to my claim I'm more than confident I can turn a man's head."

"If we were in court, we'd both be held in contempt for what I'm about to do."

Chapter 13

AJA HAD WALKED INTO THIS ROOM OFFERING JACKSON A sweet treat as a reward for his kindness. Now, the way he stared at her—as if she were the only thing in the world that could bring him satisfaction—made it clear her cake wasn't the lone sugary delight on his mind.

He grabbed hold of her hand as she tried to lower it from his mouth. "Are you okay with this, Aja? Is this what you want?"

She was sitting so close to him that she could smell the scent of cake on his breath. If he didn't recognize she was all in, he wasn't as good an investigator as he believed. But then the strong grip he had on her hand gentled. He slid his digits down and made soft circles where his finger met her racing pulse, as if he were trying to coax an answer from her.

Understanding fell over her like a delicate mist tickling her senses. He wasn't unsure of her desire for him; he was giving her the opportunity to decide how tonight would end.

God, can you be any more sexy than you are in this moment?

"I want this, Jackson. Do you?"

It was a question she needed to ask. The weight of his powerful gaze on her, the way he breathed as though it was a struggle to focus on their burning connection and fill his lungs with air, the way his manhood hung heavy and full against his clothed thigh were all indicators he wanted her. But the way he wore integrity like it was imbedded in his DNA would mean crossing this line could be painful for him.

This wasn't smart. Her conscience echoed the same. *It sure ain't. But we both know that won't stop you from jumping on this fine-ass man who's holding you like you're something precious.*

He didn't respond, a fact that made the first kernels of disappointment crackle in her chest. She took a deep breath and pulled away from him slowly. No need to make a big deal of it if he wasn't willing to risk complicating their already tenuous connection.

"Don't." His proclamation was a whispered command that made every nerve ending tingle with need.

"But you didn't answer."

He laced his finger with hers and kissed the back of her hand with a barely there press of his lips. "I'm where I want to be, Aja. My only concern is that you're all right."

Spending so many years as a lawyer made Aja decent at reading people. On any other man, there was no way she would believe this was anything more than a calculated ploy to get her out of her pretty La Perla panties. But the struggle to be good while wanting nothing more than to indulge in his need was painted across every straining muscle in his body.

"No pun intended, but literally and figuratively, I'm a big girl. How are you going to hurt me?"

"I've watched you these last few days. You're a fighter, someone who champions the downtrodden. You're rebuilding Restoration for more than profit. You want its people to prosper, not you. A person who gives that much of themselves deserves every happiness. You deserve a man who will give you forever. I'm not built for that, Aja. And if that's what you're looking for, this won't work."

She gave the fingers still entangled with hers a playful squeeze.

"Who says I'm looking for forever? I'm thirty-nine years old, Jackson. I've had plenty of chances to settle down and build the perfect picture of domestic bliss. But I haven't because it's never been what I wanted. Like I said earlier. Sometimes physical connection is simply about feeling good. Beyond that, I have no further expectation of this moment. So now that we've cleared the air, Jackson Dean, are you down?"

"Hell yeah." He sealed his mouth against hers, pressing her backward into the sofa cushions as he devoured her mouth. Last night's kiss had been about discovery. Tonight, as he nibbled at her bottom lip until she opened to him and gave him the opportunity to slip his tongue inside her mouth, was all about conquering her. And with the way her untouched clit vibrated with need, she was all for this man climbing to the top of Mount Aja and posting his flag.

He tasted of sweetness and desire, a heady mix that made her mind fuzzy with want and her body instinctively buck under his, searching for contact.

"Steady, sweetheart. I promise I'll make it better." This wasn't Aja's first romp with a prime piece of meat like Jackson. But the simple way he spoke to her had her thighs shaking and her opening dripping wet without the benefit of at least a simple stroke.

He settled himself between her legs, the sweet pressure of his body touching all the right spots. Dammit, he hadn't even gotten her naked and the feel of him against her brought her so close to the brink of satisfaction, she could hardly think.

"You do not understand how much I've dreamt about being right here like this with you."

Oh yes, she could. That had pretty much been her favorite pastime since she'd laid eyes on him.

He slid his hand from her thigh to her hip, until it reached the hem of her tank. When his rough callused fingertips caressed the sensitive flesh there, a tremor of desire shook loose any doubts she might've held about crossing this line with him. Not that there were many. Well, she knew he still suspected her ladies, but she told herself she could handle that. What else could she say?

If she'd been thinking about anything other than how good his body would feel on hers, there was no way she could let this happen. But it had been so long since her soul had felt anything but the crushing despair and guilt that seemed to walk with her every moment of the day and follow her into her dreams. Like a relentless stalker, those twin emotions hid in the shadows, making certain she always knew they were around, even if she couldn't see them.

Tonight, though, while his hand crept up the soft flesh of her side, lifting the hem of her tank with each measured inch he gained until her shirt was above her breasts and his fingers were cupping the aching weight of her flesh in his palm—as his hips began simultaneously rocking his heavy length through her covered slit—the only thing Aja thought about was how fast they could get naked and end this torture.

He must have sensed her desperation, or perhaps the heavy musk of her arousal clued him in to how much she needed relief, because he took her exposed nipple into his mouth, scraping it gently with his teeth, then soothing it with his tongue until it peaked into a turgid pebble. When she shivered, he made certain to do the same with its twin and drove her need a few more notches up the drive-Aja-crazy-with-your-hands-and-mouth meter.

She was so out of her mind with desire, so overwhelmed by the heightened sensation of his skin on hers, that by the time he repositioned his body to the side and dipped his head to reclaim her mouth, she was in danger of peaking before he even touched her sex.

She broke the kiss, gasping for air as she moaned, "Close."

"Shhh, darlin'. I'll give you what you need."

He slipped his hand beneath the waistband of her sweatpants in a slow but steady motion. The anticipation almost broke her, but she refused to give in to that ache to fall into release before he delivered what he promised. And when she felt his thick digits slide between her slick folds, it was like a match set to gasoline— explosive, dangerous, and too brilliant to turn completely away from.

He rubbed slow, firm circles around her clitoris until her hips chased his fingers' rhythm. The pressure built until his touch was almost painful. And when his ministrations made her muscles clamp down with blessed tension and the beginnings of her orgasm spread from the tiny bundle of nerves his thumb rotated over, he pushed two fingers into the wet depths of her opening, and her body exploded in spasms that racked her entire being, stealing her ability to draw life-giving air.

She grabbed his upper arm, needing something strong to anchor her to the couch, otherwise, the convulsions taking over her body would land her in an unsexy heap on the floor.

"That's it, baby. Ride it out."

God, why did he have to say that? Why couldn't he simply let her enjoy her destruction? But he didn't. He kept whispering sweet nothings in her ear while his fingers played her like an instrument, and her pleasure peaked again, sending her into another frenzied fit of spasms, screams, and pleasure she could easily overdose on.

When the last tremor of satisfaction traveled through her body, he removed his soaked fingers from her quivering body and held them to her lips. A wicked snap of mischief flashed in his eyes before he painted her mouth with her release, then kissed her. He used his tongue to lick softly inside her mouth, letting her savor the delicious mix of her on him.

She could sample her flavor anytime. But with the spice of Jackson added to it, it was a powerful substance, one she would more than likely crave like an addict going through withdrawal. She didn't care though. She could not concern herself with how problematic walking away from this would be when this was over. She'd been foolish enough to think a night of Jackson Dean would be enough. But if a man could make you come like a geyser from a kiss or two and a few strokes of his finger, chances were one night would never be enough.

She pushed her hand between them, cupping him through his sweats, smiling at the girth and length, and licking her lips in anticipation of watching it stand tall when she pulled it free of its cotton prison. "Let me return the favor."

He smiled down at her, dropping a quick peck on her mouth. "Yes, ma'am," he chuckled. "I fully intend to."

He hooked a thumb in the waistband of his sweatpants and pulled down enough that she got a glorious glimpse of his stretched, domed cap. Her mouth watered. As she was about to push his hand away to get to her bounty, the chimes of a phone ringing cut through the air.

His body tensed alongside hers, and not in a good way. He shifted in an awkward rocking motion until he was sitting upright, pulling his phone from his pocket. One look at the flashing screen and his head dropped.

Disappointment fluttered in her belly. She really wanted to see how many licks it took to get to the cream inside his chocolate pop. But the strained lines of frustration marring his features didn't give her hope for that happening right now. "I gotta take this. It's the office." When her bottom lip poked out, he gave it a quick kiss and a nibble. "Go to your room and wait for me. This should only take a sec."

She pouted for a second more and stood on noodle-like legs, adjusting her clothes, then left the room. A quick glance over her shoulder and the sight of him righting his clothes made her the tiniest bit sad. Whatever the hell his office wanted at this hour of the night, it had better be important. Because knowing what that man's manhood felt like as she slid it inside her mouth was something Aja desperately needed to experience before the rooster crowed.

Chapter 14

JACKSON JABBED HIS PHONE'S DANCING ACCEPT BUTTON WITH more force than necessary to answer Kade Jennings's call.

"Whatever this is about, it better be important." He knew Jennings didn't deserve to be growled at like an angry animal, but having the image of Aja coming on his fingers forever burned into his memory, Jackson didn't want to entertain much of anything that would keep him from discovering more of her secrets.

"Did I wake you, Boss? I hear life on a ranch is tough."

"Something like that." He cleared his throat, trying hard to remove all traces of the lust running through every cell of his body. *Professionalism, Jackson. Try to at least act like you remember what that is.* "What do you need, Jennings?"

"Gleason and I spent the day interviewing the townspeople of Fresh Springs. Ms. Everett isn't imagining things when she says the townies don't support her and her people much."

Jackson straightened on the couch. "Any of it seem more serious than townie chatter, like they'd try to actually hurt her?"

Jennings let out a long whistle. "Honestly, they seem more afraid to talk to us about the ranch than anything else. We didn't get wind of any kind of malicious behavior, though. Everyone we mentioned it to seemed to be looking over their shoulder for some invisible boogeyman to jump out at them. Can't say for sure what's going on, but something's got this entire town spooked about Aja, her people, and that ranch."

Jackson scratched his head in frustration. Would it be too much for a lead to pop up and save him the complication of mixing his business with Aja's pleasure? He knew the answer to that question. Of course it would be. Cases were never solved in such a brisk way. Only on television could a case be solved in an hour. If *Walker: Texas Ranger* were anything like his actual job, this situation at the ranch would've been finished two days ago. But because this was real life, Jackson was walking a close line that could end badly for all of them if shit went sideways.

"Anyone have anything to say about Eli Bennett?"

Jennings blew out another long breath. "Same reaction. Too afraid to say anything about him. We tried to meet the man at his office, but his secretary said he was too busy to meet with us. Without any tangible evidence, we can't really force the issue. We're still in town at the local hotel. We're gonna head to his spread first thing in the morning and try to get an audience with him before he leaves."

Jackson chewed on his bottom lip and tried to think of any angles he could've missed. He wasn't getting anything from the normal channels, and Aja's safety was in question as long as this mess continued to play out.

"Keep digging, Jennings. This lowlife is out there somewhere. We need to track him down."

He hung up the phone and headed toward Aja's room. If he couldn't bring her closure on this matter, he'd at least bring her comfort in this moment. Like she said, sometimes comfort was the best you could do in any situation.

He made it halfway up the stairs before something niggling in the back of his mind kept pulling at him. A beautiful woman waited on him upstairs, so why was he stuck with one foot planted on the step? *Maybe if you weren't so eager to play naked footsie with Aja, you might remember to do a routine perimeter check around the house.*

"Shit. How the hell did I forget that?" *You know exactly how.*

Jackson grumbled for the angel on his shoulder to shut the hell up and went about the business of checking all the doors and windows on the first floor, making sure all the locks were in place and the house was safe.

He dragged himself up the stairs. Their lack of progress on the case and his absentmindedness about the security check still bothered him, but he was determined to keep his disappointment to himself.

Aja didn't need to know any of this. Despite his recent lapse in judgment, the Rangers were doing everything they could to protect her. *What if that isn't enough? Could you live with her getting hurt on your watch?*

He stood in the middle of the hall and looked back and forth between her bedroom door and his. If he walked into her room, he'd never be able to stop himself until he was buried deep inside her. If he crossed her threshold, he wouldn't be able to protect her because he'd be too busy satisfying her.

He couldn't do this. No matter how much he wanted to.

He went inside his room and closed the door before he could talk himself out of doing what was right. The way he'd succumbed to his desires in the great room didn't leave him much hope he could control himself in Aja's bedroom.

He sat at the side of the bed as he'd done the previous night, checking his firearm in case he needed to use it. He had several stashed throughout the house and the ranch to get to at a moment's notice. When he was satisfied the gun was prepped, he slipped it inside its hip holster and put it back inside the nightstand drawer.

The guns weren't the singular security measure he'd taken. He'd even acquired Aja's permission and made three sets of bump keys for his team to gain access to the house in the event of an emergency. Safeguarding Aja's home had been the first thing on his agenda. Even if the ranch's defenses were lax—or better phrased, nonexistent—where she slept needed to be safe. There was no compromise about that. Earlier he'd been thinking like a lawman; tonight, he'd been thinking as a simple man. No more. Not until the bastard trying to harm Aja was apprehended.

Jackson heard a *thump* in the hall that pulled his attention to his closed door. He knew what Aja's footsteps sounded like by now, and that wasn't them. He grabbed his holstered weapon, attaching it to the waistband of his pants in the small of his back before he sent off a quick text to Colton and Storm.

> Possible B&E. Need backup. Perp possibly in 2nd floor Master. Going in. Enter through rear.

Text sent, he stepped easily across his room. His hand on his automatic pistol, he cracked the door open, using the tiny slit to check the hall. When he was reasonably certain it was clear, he eased the door back and walked across the hall to Aja's bedroom. He leaned in for a beat, listening for any signs that this was merely his overactive lawman's imagination at work, when he heard the telltale sound of glass breaking. Satisfied that his instincts were correct, he stepped back far enough to kick the door open.

Time moved in slow motion as he assessed the scene. The room was dark with only the light from the hall spilling in from the doorway. He could make out the broken glass and wood panels on the balcony door, as well as the two figures—one Aja's, lying on her back in her bed fighting, with a stranger crouched on top of her with his hands around her neck.

Jackson aimed his weapon, but with Aja and the intruder entangled in the dark, he couldn't risk taking a shot. Instead, he holstered his weapon, then took a running dive for the bed, knocking the assailant down on the floor where they tussled for purchase on top of glass shards and wood splinters. He'd bear a few nicks and scratches from this scrimmage for sure, but he couldn't pay attention to that now. He hadn't heard Aja make a sound since he'd barged in; he needed to make certain she wasn't hurt.

He used his bulk to swing them around so he straddled the struggling body beneath his. Jackson landed two punches to the mask-covered face and was about to level a third when the assailant swung his arm wide. At first, Jackson thought the man threw a bad punch. But the biting sting of glass cutting through his upper arm assured him that the intruder's aim was spot-on.

He released his hold, and the masked man seized the opportunity to push Jackson off him and scurry through the broken balcony doors. "Dammit!"

Jackson heard footsteps bounding up the stairs. It was probably his backup, but until he could hear Colton's loud baritone asking for his twenty, he wouldn't be caught off guard. "I'm in the master bedroom."

His two men came in with guns drawn until they laid eyes on Jackson. Colton came to assist Jackson with his arm while Storm headed for Aja's bed. She was still and quiet, which didn't correlate with the scene. She should be yelling her head off right now in fear or shock. Quiet wasn't right. Fear spilled down Jackson's spine in cold, hard waves that made him flinch as he watched Storm place two fingers against the side of her neck to check for a pulse.

"It's strong and steady. She's alive but passed out."

Relief spread through Jackson like air-conditioning on a hot Texas day. It tingled the top layer of his skin until it permeated his cells and he could feel the heat receding into nothingness.

He pushed past Colton and moved Storm out of the way until he sat beside Aja. He placed a gentle hand on her cheek and had to fight not to press his lips to hers. "Contact the sheriff and get an ambulance out here, then check around the perimeter. When it's safe, tell Seneca and Brooklyn to make sure their doors and windows are locked and that they don't come out until one of us says it's safe."

The lack of movement yanked his attention from Aja's still form. "Why are you still standing here?"

Colton stepped forward. "Are we certain it wasn't one of them?"

Jackson shook his head. "That was a man I was tousling with." He stared at Aja's sleeping face and stroked his thumb across a raised, reddened spot on her cheek. That hadn't been there thirty minutes ago when he'd had her on the couch in his arms. Then she'd been happy and satisfied as he stroked her to release. Now, she was still and hurt, and Jackson wanted to break something or someone for daring to harm her.

His heart rate picked up as anger pulsed through him. He'd left her alone because he thought their connection had compromised his ability to protect her. It wasn't lost on him that this attack might never have happened if he'd gone to her like he'd originally planned instead of letting his fears get the better of him. Would he ever get this right?

"With all that's been happening on this ranch, I don't believe this was a random break-in. I'd bet my badge this is our perp. If I hadn't heard him, he'd have killed her." He jerked his thumb toward the doorway. "Get some help in here now. I'll sit with her."

His men moved quickly and dispersed from the room. When he and Aja were alone, Jackson slid down next to her so he could touch her the way he needed to, desperate to feel her heat against him as proof she was still here for him to hold and keep close. He'd process later why he wanted those things. But right now, all he cared about was ensuring that Aja was safe.

"Aja, baby. I need you to open your eyes for me." She still didn't move, so he pressed his lips to her temple, thankful she was warm to the touch. "Aja, girl. Come on, let me see those beautiful brown eyes." When she remained unresponsive, panic swelled in his chest. What if he hadn't gotten to her in time? What if she couldn't wake up?

"Aja." He applied firm, hard pressure to her shoulder. Not enough to hurt her, but certainly enough to cause her discomfort and wake her. The muscles in her face flinched, but he kept pressing on her shoulder. Responding to pain wasn't enough. He needed her awake and alert. Her eyes fluttered, and he released the breath he'd been holding. "Aja?"

She moaned softly. "Can you please stop squeezing my shoulder?" He lightened the pressure as soon as she spoke. Her words were a little jumbled, but he could make out what she was saying. "I don't need a new set of handprint bruises to match the ones I probably have on my neck."

Feisty, even though she still seemed a little groggy. Jackson sent up a quick prayer of thanks. If she'd walked away from this with anything other than a few bruises, he didn't know what he would've done. "Do you remember what happened?"

She sat up slowly with his help. "Yeah. I went to the bathroom to freshen up. I lay down on the bed to wait for you, and I must've dozed off. Because the next thing I knew, he was bursting through the balcony door and jumping on top of me."

"Did he say anything? Give you a reason why he came?" Most sick bastards liked to hear themselves talk. He was hoping this guy would follow suit and leave them some information they could use.

She took a deep breath, rubbing her neck slowly. "Yes. He kept saying 'die' repeatedly until I passed out."

Jackson's anger pushed against the calm veneer he tried to keep in place for her. She'd experienced a traumatic event. The last thing she needed was him blowing his top, acting like the brute who'd put his hands on her. "Did you recognize his voice?"

She shook her head. "It was like a rough whisper, angry enough for me to hear, but still too low for me to recognize." She shuddered, the vibration rumbling beneath the palm he used to cup her cheek. "It could've been anyone, Jackson." She looked up at him, her eyes sparkling with the sheen of unshed tears and the distinct smell of fear wafting off her skin. "Anyone."

She closed her eyes and wet tracks slid down the sides of her face. Something snapped inside him like a brittle branch underfoot. He used the back of his hand to swipe the fat drops away. Then he pulled her into his embrace and let her burrow into his chest. He rubbed soothing circles on her back and didn't speak until the pronounced shaking of her shoulders quieted to soft hiccups.

"You're safe, Aja. Whoever this bastard is and whatever he wants with you, he didn't win. That is the last time I'll let him get to you. I promise."

There was a knock at the door and she stiffened in his arms, lifting her face from his chest before looking toward the door.

"Jackson?" He focused on the door to see Storm peeking his head inside the room. "The sheriff is on his way. Colt and I want to take some pictures of the scene for our report before the locals come trampling through."

Aja moaned, settling her head back against Jackson's chest. "Please tell them not to come. I want to stay here with you until this is over."

What he wouldn't give for that to be possible. But it wasn't. The sheriff and his team needed to canvass this scene, and he needed to check it out first before they made it up the stairs.

"Aja, come on. You passed out. Please, humor me. Let the EMTs examine you. Not to mention, we really need to get in here and get pictures for our reports. If this sheriff is as bad as you say he is, I don't trust him not to fuck up this crime scene."

He gave her one final squeeze, and it seemed to be enough to get her to cooperate. She sat up, rubbing her exposed arms, folding in on herself as if she were trying not to be seen. She was clothed, but after having someone invade her personal space like this, he understood if she wanted to be covered, protected by as many layers as possible to keep the outside world from getting in. "You have a robe or a sweatshirt you want me to grab for you before the boys come in?"

"On the back of my bathroom door."

He rushed to her bathroom and grabbed the gray cotton garment from the lone hook on the back of the door and hurried back to his perch on her bed. He held it open for her, and she wrapped it around herself with quick hands. "You ready for them to come in?"

"Yeah."

He waved Colton and Storm into the room. Colton carried what Jackson recognized to be their forensics bag. They couldn't do a full canvas of the room because local law enforcement would notice. Or at least they should. If they noticed professionals had been there before them, then their cover would be blown.

But for now, they could get some pictures. While Aja recounted the attack to Storm, Colton took pictures of the surrounding scene. And Jackson took on the most important role of all. He held Aja's hand while she relived it, stroking her knuckles while she spoke, encouraging her to continue. He didn't care in the least that his men were there to witness it. Aja needed him, and that was all that mattered. He'd deal with the significance of that realization later. Right now, he needed to focus on her.

Chapter 15

AJA KNEW FROM THE MOMENT JACKSON MENTIONED THE local sheriff that things would get worse. She'd been assaulted in her own home, and now she had to deal with the likes of this asshole sitting across from her. Sheriff Leroy Hastings was a tall, lanky man with orange-brown hair that always seemed in need of a haircut. Whenever he removed his hat, he'd undoubtedly have to brush his unruly mop out of his eyes.

He'd walked in her front door thirty minutes ago wearing an ill-fitting sheriff's department uniform hanging off his beanstalk form, like a child in his older brother's hand-me-down suit.

If the way he looks in that too-big uniform isn't a metaphor for the piss-poor job he's doing as the sheriff, I don't know what is. Why is this man even in my face right now?

He sat before he was offered a seat. No sign of the grace and manners of a southern gentleman. Instead, he sat facing her with his legs manspread like some kind of barnyard animal. With no notepad or writing instrument, he cleared his throat.

"You wanna tell me what happened, Ms. Everett?"

His voice was heavy with impatience, as if her being attacked were inconveniencing him somehow. Aja sat up straighter in her chair, determined to make this man see her annoyance.

"I was attacked in my bedroom. I went to sleep and awoke to a stranger on top of me, trying to strangle me."

His eyes finally connected with hers. His mouth tilted in a small, lecherous grin. "Do you make a habit of entertaining strange men in your bedroom?"

She heard Jackson slam his hand against the kitchen counter and take a heavy step toward where she and the sheriff were sitting at the table. She held her hand up to stop him. The last thing she needed was her "employee" getting arrested for assaulting the sheriff.

"Whether I do or don't isn't the point, Sheriff. Are you somehow insinuating that I brought this act of violence on myself?"

The man dropped his eyes to his thigh, refusing to bring his gaze back to hers. "Sometimes women don't realize the signals they give off. Perhaps this man thought you wanted him to do this."

She narrowed her eyes and forced him to look at her. "I don't know what kind of sick games you play with women in their beds, but if I want a man to put his hands on me, I have the fortitude and the vocabulary to express that. This had nothing to do with a late-night rendezvous gone wrong. This person entered my home uninvited with the intention of killing me. Now, are you going to sit here wasting my time asking nonsensical questions, or are you going to be useful?"

Aja wasn't having any of this son of a bitch's victim-blaming nonsense, and she sure as shit wouldn't let him off easy. Someone had come into her home and put their hands on her. That was not acceptable.

"I'm not sure what you want me to do about this, Ms. Everett. You said yourself, you didn't see his face or recognize anything about him. How do you expect me to find him?"

Jackson moved from his post leaning against the counter. The way tight lines pulled his smooth brown features into a flat expression showed he wasn't too thrilled with the sheriff either. She shook her head again, silently begging Jackson to stay where he was. She'd deal with Hastings. She'd dealt with plenty of men in her tenure as an attorney. Hastings was chump change compared to them.

"I expect you to do your job, Sheriff. Or isn't protecting a tax-paying, voting member of this community part of your job?" He flinched at the question and was poised to respond, but she held up her finger to cut him off. "You may not like me or the people I have working here, but I don't have a bit of a problem using my resources as a high-powered attorney, or nepotism as the niece of a sitting county judge, to out you as an unprofessional and negligent asshole. Trust me, Sheriff. No one is better at shit-stirring than me, and I know too many mainstream media outlets that would love a story like this. You want to take that chance?"

Hastings narrowed his eyes into slits and stuck his tongue in his cheek as if he were attempting to keep it otherwise occupied so he couldn't speak.

Good. Because I'm done playing with you.

"We're a small operation, Ms. Everett. I don't have the capacity to investigate this the way it should be." His shoulders slumped, and he rubbed the back of his neck as if the muscles there were too fatigued to hold up his head. "I'm gonna have to call in the Texas Rangers for this."

She folded her arms and leaned back. "I guess you'd better make that call then."

Hastings dropped his eyes before standing. He leveled a cursory glance at Jackson, and when the response was the flexing of his large muscles, Hastings made a quick beeline for the exit, closing the door soundly after himself.

"I really wish you would've let me handle that guy."

Aja held up a hand, stopping Jackson. "Jackson, you can't fight my battles with Hastings for me. If I let you, the moment you leave, everything will fall to the status quo."

She glanced over at him, her chest full of sadness and her throat tight with regret. He would leave. That was a fact. And when he did, he'd take the incredible sensation of safety and desire with him. *Don't get used to it, Aja. It's not here to stay.*

"I have worked harder than most people to push through the bullshit people lob at you when you're a woman, especially a Black woman. I'm not about to let this son of a bitch think he can handle me with a few threats. Him shirking his responsibilities to protect me, my workers, and this ranch stops today."

She was serious. This place was where she went to heal and where she wanted others to heal. She couldn't let this go any longer.

"If Hastings reports this to the Rangers, how will it impact your investigation? Will they be able to get a team out here to examine the scene?"

He pushed off the counter, taking the seat next to her at the kitchen table. He leaned in, placing his hands on the outer portion of her thigh, giving it a reassuring squeeze. "It won't impact us. They'll get the request in Austin and put it in the system. I'll let Austin know we're running an undercover investigation, and no details should be disclosed to the sheriff other than they'll send someone out when they can."

A weight lifted from her chest. This entire business was wearing on her nerves. And with the amount of stress she'd carried for the last eighteen months, she didn't think there was much left to fray. "What about evidence? How long can my room go unprocessed?"

"It won't. We already started some preliminary measures. Now, we'll do a full canvass. We came prepared for this."

She squared her shoulders and looked him directly in the eye. "Good, because I'm tired of walking in the dark. I need to know who this bastard is."

She stood and walked to the broom closet, pulling out a spray bottle of household cleanser and a fresh pack of nonabrasive scrubbing pads. She knew the kitchen was spotless. She didn't go to bed unless it gleamed like a bald man's shiny head. But as she sprayed the counter with cleanser and scrubbed like her life depended on it, she felt her anger bubble over and spill from her in the form of fat, abundant tears. She was so busy scrubbing the nonexistent stain that she didn't hear Jackson move from across the room. She didn't notice he was standing behind her until his heat enveloped her and his hand was resting on top of hers, stilling it, as he took the nonabrasive pad out of her hand.

"You're gonna wear a hole in the counter if you keep that up. Don't let Hastings upset you like this. There's no reason to be afraid or to let him bring you to tears."

Aja whipped around, bracing her hands against the counter, looking into his eyes. "Afraid? I'm not afraid, Jackson. I'm mad." She threw the scouring pad down on the counter and slammed her hand against it with a solid thud.

She was ready to allow her anger to consume her when she noted the smile tugging at the corners of Jackson's mouth. It drew her attention to how perfectly full and plump his bottom lip was. She might be pissed off, but she didn't think there was a level of mad she could reach where she didn't want to nibble on it. "Why is this funny to you?"

"Oh, I'm not laughing at you. I'm feeling sorry for that poor fool Hastings. Because if he could see all the fire in your eyes right now, he'd be terrified."

Her anger receded enough for a brief chuckle to escape her lips. "I want this over. I want my life back. I want to feel safe on my land again. I want to lie in my bed expecting the handsome man I fancy to make love to me and not worry that some creeper will show up instead."

Jackson's hand moved from her forearm to her upper arm, rubbing a comforting stroke there before he tugged her into his embrace. He held on to her, much like he had a couple of hours ago after rescuing her. There was something soothing about the way he held her, as if his arms and chest formed their own kind of paradise made especially for her. *Good Lord! What is it about this man?*

"You'll get your life back, Aja. And I will champion you every step of the way. My job is to keep you safe." He leaned back, staring into her eyes. His eyes were dark, but there were still sparks of something hot and dangerous that flickered in them like an open fire. "If that means staying at your side every minute of the day, I'll make that happen."

Her skin tingled with that promise, electricity sizzling as it jumped from one nerve ending to another. How could the promise of safety be so sexy? Her nipples pebbled underneath her tank top and robe. Even with two layers of clothing, they were so sensitive that she was certain she might embarrass herself if she didn't extricate herself from his embrace.

"I believe you, Jackson." She did. Everything from the way he held her to the way his gaze poured over her told her he wouldn't let harm come to her. Hell, even the way he'd charged in during her attack, literally launching his body at her perpetrator to protect her, was proof he would give everything to make certain she was taken care of. And never remembering a time in her life where she didn't have to fight for someone else, having a man like Jackson swear his protection to her and mean it made her stomach twist in knots and her heart flutter. This man was getting under her skin. *Tell the truth. Shame the devil. You know he's beyond getting. He's already there.*

The sting of unshed tears burned her eyes. There were too many emotions tumbling around inside her. Fear, exhaustion, anger, and desire all swirling together, each attempting to dominate. Which did she give into? Which would make the pressure in her chest ease a little so she could breathe through the obstruction of pain and anxiety? "I know you'll protect me," she whispered. "I just want to forget for a few moments. That's all."

"Aja?" It was a plea and a question rolled into one. With one word, he was asking her if she recognized the consequences and begging her to decide all at once. "It's late. Or early, depending on your perspective. We should try to get some rest before the day calls."

"I'm aware of the time, Jackson."

He shook his head, stepping away from her as he rubbed at the back of his neck. "I'm trying to do the right thing here. This isn't what you need."

She should probably agree with him and let this go. But she couldn't. She couldn't let something else be decided for her because someone else had wreaked havoc in her life. She'd lived through that once before, and she wouldn't allow it to happen again. "You're wrong, Jackson. This is exactly what I need. It's what I want." She moved into his personal space, pressing closer to him as she looked up into his eyes. She could see the battle he was waging between his desire and his willpower unfolding in the depths of his deep-brown eyes. He wanted this too. "The question is: Are you going to give it to me?"

He swallowed and his Adam's apple bobbed as the muscles in his throat tightened and released. The hum of desperation vibrated around him like the ambient heat of a powerful motor, making the air around them thick and heavy with aching want. But when he continued to stand there, his only movements his heaving chest and the open-close motion of his hands, she decided his will was more powerful than anything she stirred in him. She stepped back but was quickly pulled back against him by his large hands now gripping her shoulders.

"I will always give you exactly what you need."

Chapter 16

"THIS ISN'T EXACTLY WHAT I HAD IN MIND WHEN YOU SAID you would give me everything I needed."

Aja lay on her side with her eyes narrowed into slits as she watched Jackson pull the large, plush comforter over her and tuck her into bed. When he was done, he walked around the expanse of the bed and climbed in beside her, on top of the covers. She was about to comment on the number of layers between them and how much it displeased her when he placed his arm around her waist and tugged her closer to him.

"I know it's not. But it's what you need."

She'd followed him into the guest room expecting they'd tear each other's clothes off and get naked and sweaty within minutes of entering the room. Instead, she was frustrated and swaddled in a blanket like some oversized baby.

"Jackson—"

"I watched someone put their hands around your neck tonight. If you won't do this for you, do it for me. Humor me. I need to know you're safe."

The fight building inside her deflated, and she settled in his arms. She hadn't thought about how tonight affected him. If she were honest with herself, she hadn't thought about how it impacted her either—and if she could help it, she wouldn't.

She snuggled closer to Jackson, allowing the rest of her anger and disappointment to bleed away. Their current huddle in the middle of the bed might not have been what she'd pictured when she'd demanded he make love to her in the kitchen, but it had its benefits.

The easy way her body relaxed into his, as if his arms were something familiar and safe…she could definitely count this as a perk.

"You didn't need me taking advantage of you."

"It's not taking advantage when I gave consent."

"It is when my conscience tells me to decide with more than my little head. You're a grown woman, and I'm sure you know how to communicate what you want. But mauling you after you've experienced something like this doesn't sit well with me. You can call me old-fashioned, but I believe in taking a little more care with the women I'm intimate with."

She took a deep breath, letting the last vestiges of her anger slip away as the deep rumble of his voice rippled against her back. "You're such a Boy Scout."

"A cowboy," he corrected as he tightened his arm around her waist. He moved his hand to her hip and rubbed slow circles there as slumber called to her. She yawned, and he laughed before dropping a gentle kiss to the back of her head. "Go to sleep."

"Yes, Ranger."

———

A knock on the back door pulled Jackson out of his thoughts. He took a sip of his coffee before resting it on the kitchen counter and answering the door for Colton and Storm.

"Morning, Boss. How's Ms. Everett?"

Jackson acknowledged Storm's question, directing him and Colton to the kitchen counter. "She's still upstairs."

"She must be worn out after last night. She doesn't strike me as the sleep-in-late sort." Storm's observation was spot-on.

"More than even she realized. She was still sleeping when I—" He stopped before he could finish the "left her in bed" sitting on the tip of his tongue. Deciding quickly his men didn't need to know that, he took another sip of his coffee, then finished with "checked in on her a little while ago." *Good save.* "When she wakes, I might try to convince her to speak with the crisis counselor we work with, depending on her mood." He pointed to Colton. "Are Seneca and Brooklyn aware of what happened?"

Colton shook his head. "We were watching a movie in their cabin when you texted. We told them the ranch was on lockdown due to a security drill."

"Did they buy it?"

Colton scratched his temple. "They didn't seem disturbed by it. The main house is far enough away that they didn't hear the disturbance. Hell, if it weren't for you texting us for backup, we wouldn't have known either. This damn place is big."

Storm agreed. "The shady-ass sheriff didn't have his lights and sirens on either, so it's unlikely the two know anything about it. Unless they were part of it."

Jackson scratched the day-old stubble on his chin. "That doesn't seem likely. It was definitely a man I tussled with last night. Plus, like you said, they were watching a movie with you when it occurred. That doesn't mean neither of them set it up, but it makes little sense. Aja is probably the only person in the world who gives a damn about them. Why sabotage the good thing they've got going on?"

"People do all sorts of stupid stuff for any number of reasons." Colton's response, although surly, was true. People did things for reasons that made sense to them alone. However, the pieces weren't fitting here.

It was looking more and more like Aja was right. Perhaps Brooklyn and Seneca were victims of this situation too. "How far are you in processing Aja's room?"

Colton folded his arms, pointing briefly at Storm. "We finished a good bit of it before the sheriff arrived. We'll finish the balcony and the surrounding area near the bottom of the attached staircase this morning. Without daylight, it was too dark to process the scene completely and go unnoticed by Seneca and Brooklyn. We did find a footprint while we were out there. We grabbed a couple of flashlights and made a cast. We also found this."

Colton pulled a small evidence bag from his pocket and handed it to Jackson. When he unfolded the bag, there was a slender piece of gold inside the plastic. It appeared to be part of a women's bracelet with the words "Mañana no está—" on it.

"'Tomorrow isn't' what? Do we know what this means? Any sayings that use these words?"

Both Colton and Storm shook their heads. Although Storm was fluent and literate in Spanish, both Colton and Jackson understood enough to get by in a rudimentary conversation.

Storm held his hand out and waited for Jackson to place the evidence bag in his palm. "Granted the Latinx community is vast and differs across the globe, but nothing jumps out at me from this phrase. It could mean anything. And since we don't have the other half, we might never know what it means."

"Okay," Jackson answered. "I'm gonna pull Gleason and Jennings in to take over the forensics. I'll have them come pick up everything. I need them to get on that ASAP. We don't want to lose any evidence."

Both men looked at each other and then stared at Jackson. "Then what will we be doing?" Storm asked.

"Over the next few days, this ranch will be buzzing with people we don't know. I called my brother and father as soon as I got up. They weren't supposed to come out for another few days, but they'll speed up the timetable on Aja's security installation to tomorrow. Besides them, the construction crew starts then too."

"We don't have enough men to watch all those people."

Storm was right. There were only three of them. Attempting to stake out so many people at once wouldn't be possible in their small number.

"No, that's why the cameras are going up first tomorrow. We need eyes. They won't be able to secure the entire ranch tomorrow, but they'll work together with the construction crew to seal off the three problematic access points we're worried about."

Storm raised a finger to interrupt. "If we're putting in wireless cameras, won't we have to get network access from Seneca? You really want someone we think could be involved with this case to have access to our security?"

"No," Jackson answered. "My father's loaning us one of his surveillance vans. It's a plain white van, and he'll have it outfitted to look like one of the construction crew's vehicles. It has a private server that's masked and undetectable. There's no need for Seneca to know about any of this."

"So what's the plan for today?"

Jackson could feel the corner of his mouth lifting into a smile. That was Colton—direct and to the point.

"I'm gonna stick close to Aja. Wherever she goes, I'll follow. I want eyes on her until we can get the security equipment and protocols implemented. You two will be on patrol duty most of the day. Until those cameras go live tomorrow, we have to keep an eye on those three access points. It's not perfect, but it's all we have until the equipment is up and running."

"What about the front gate?" Again, the military man in Colton was thinking three steps ahead.

"My father is adding a security detail to the front gate and sending extra men to help you two keep eyes on those access points. No one gets in without credentials or prior authorization."

Storm stepped closer before asking, "Who's on that list?"

"Badges, emergency personnel, and the people living here. Either Aja or one of us needs to clear anyone else." Storm and Colton looked at him, then each other, then back at Jackson again. "What?"

Storm leaned back as if he needed to create a little distance between Jackson and himself. "What about the parole officer, Mat Ryan? Doesn't he visit the ranch to meet with Seneca and Brooklyn? Doesn't he have to meet with Ms. Everett as their employer?"

A knot tightened in Jackson's stomach at the mention of that man's name. Yeah, all the points Storm made were correct. However, despite the man's official role on the ranch, Jackson couldn't shake the idea he needed to keep Mat as far away from Aja as possible.

He was being an asshole. He knew that. The man was a law-enforcement officer. That fact alone should've garnered him Jackson's professional respect and courtesy. But every time he thought of how cozy the man seemed with Aja, it made his ire spike. No, there was no way he would give that spineless son of a bitch open access to Aja and her ranch. He could call first like everyone else.

"We gotta keep this thing tight," Jackson answered. "If that means Mat has to conduct his meetings off the ranch now, so be it."

Storm raised a finger again. "How do you think Ms. Everett will react to that?"

Like hot grease in a skillet—volatile and dangerous if not handled correctly. "She probably won't like it. But we have little choice. There's three of us. We have to minimize how many people are on these damn acres. Otherwise, we're inviting trouble."

His men shared a conspiratorial glance between them before agreeing with him. Jackson relaxed slightly. As of now, his cover as an impartial lawman was intact. As long as no one else figured out the real reason he didn't want Mat Ryan on the ranch, he was good.

Storm slapped Colton on his shoulder. "Let's get back to the cabin and pack a lunch and supplies so we can brave it out there on the prairie." Colton grunted in reply, and they both shuffled out of the door, ready to execute their assigned tasks.

All that was left was for Jackson to tackle his work. Everything in him ached to return to the guest room and wrap Aja in his arms again. But her safety was more important than his desires. As long as he remembered that, everything should be fine.

Chapter 17

THE QUIET YET INSISTENT TAPPING IN THE DISTANCE PULLED Aja from a restful sleep. She stirred, stretched, and ran her hand against the cool spot where she expected to find Jackson lying next to her.

"Morning, Aja. You up yet?"

"Yeah, come in." She pulled herself up against the headboard and reached for the alarm clock on the nightstand to make sure she was reading the time correctly. "I think 'morning' is a euphemism in this case. It's nearly noon."

"You had a rough night. You deserve to sleep in." He pushed the clock aside and made room for the tray he was carrying. Toast, a small dish with butter and strawberry preserves, a bowl of fruit, a small cup of yogurt, a small glass of apple juice, and a cup of coffee greeted her.

She smiled at his offering. "That's some variety you've got there, sir."

He pointed at the tray before shoving his hands in his front pockets. "I wasn't sure if your throat would be too sore to swallow, so I brought a few things to see what you could tolerate."

She swallowed, testing to see if there was any soreness from her ordeal last night. "My neck and shoulders are tender, but my throat is fine. I don't think I'll have a problem eating. Thank you for being so thoughtful."

She looked at the time again and cringed. She hadn't slept in this late in a long time. There was no way her charges wouldn't be aware what was going on with her absence.

"Considering I wasn't there to make breakfast, I assume Seneca and Brooklyn know?"

"After yesterday's 'security drill,' I told Storm and Colton to tell them the kitchen would be closed down for the rest of the day." She opened her mouth to protest, but he held up his hand to stop her. "It's for the best, Aja. Gleason and Jennings were here this morning picking up the collected evidence and to question Eli Bennett. They used your attack as an excuse to get in the door."

"What did he have to say?"

Jackson answered on an audible huff. "A whole bunch of nothing."

She swatted at the air. "I'm not surprised. He's sleazy, not stupid. Eli's too slippery to let you catch him that way."

He slid his hands into his pockets, backing away slowly toward the door. "I'll leave you alone to eat. I'll come back later to take the tray. If you need anything, I'll be milling about the house all day."

"You don't have to go. In fact, I'd love it if you spared me a minute."

He stopped, then retraced his steps back to her bedside, sitting in the spot she patted next to her. "Thank you for showing better sense than I did last night. I don't know what I was thinking by coming on to you in the middle of my kitchen."

It wasn't her finest moment, that was for certain. Aja had never had to beg a man for his company. Despite being a plus-size woman who'd grown up in a society that told her big girls weren't desirable and should be "grateful" for whatever attention they received from would-be suitors, Aja never, absolutely never, subscribed to that notion. According to Chaka Khan and Whitney Houston, she was every woman, which in her mind meant every man should treasure her fabulousness.

But last night, her need to reclaim control over her life, her house, her sense of safety, had demanded she lose herself in something that would help her forget, if only for a moment. "I'm sorry for my behavior."

He took her hand, bringing it to his lips and placing a gentle kiss across her knuckles. "Please don't forget that before your attack, we were on your couch engaged in some heavy petting I wholeheartedly wanted to lead to sex. The idea of making love to you was no hardship. I wanted what you were offering, but it wasn't the right time."

He rubbed the spot he'd kissed with the pad of his thumb before looking at her. "If we ever get back to that moment—and I hope like hell we do— I want it to be because it's what we both want, not because we're running from something. I'm a proud man, Aja. My ego couldn't take it if anything but your desire for me landed you in my arms."

She couldn't help the warmth that spread through her, touching all the cold parts she thought were immune to the slick talk from a handsome man. *What is it about this man that makes me feel so safe, even in my weakness?*

"Understood, but I still apologize."

"You have nothing to apologize for. Focus on resting. If you need me for anything, holler and I'll be here."

He tried to stand, but she put her hand on his thigh. "I actually do have something I need your help with."

"What is it?"

"Give me a few minutes to get dressed and meet me downstairs."

He let his eyes pass over her as if he were trying to gauge whether she'd finally lost her damn mind. "What are you up to, Aja?"

She held up her hands. "I promise, it's nothing that's gonna make you have to draw your weapon."

He watched her carefully for another brief moment, then held his hands up in surrender. "All right then. I'm in."

———————

"I do not get paid enough for this." Jackson cringed as he mixed what he thought amounted to floury slime. "Are you sure this is gonna end up being edible? It feels disgusting." He tried to pull his hand free of the gooey white mess clinging to his fingers, but the more he pulled, the more it seemed to stick to his skin.

"It will be edible once you add some more flour in there. You've got too much butter and water. That's why it keeps falling apart and sticking to you like that. Here, let me."

She stepped closer to him, leaning over his arm slightly as she poured flour into the large mixing bowl. "Don't you need measuring cups or something?" he asked.

She pulled away from him, grimacing as if he'd struck her with the back of a mixing spoon. "Real cooks don't need measurements. We eyeball it and season to taste. Don't insult the lessons my grandmothers, mama, aunties, and all the ancestors have handed down to me through the generations by asking about some measuring cups. Now move on outta my way and let me save these pastries."

He lifted his ashen hands and grabbed a hand towel to clean off the pastry mix. He grabbed two glasses from the cabinet with one hand and milk from the fridge with the other and filled them to the brim before resting them on the counter.

"All right, taskmaster. Take a break and have some milk and cookies with me."

She finished mixing the contents to her satisfaction and tore off a piece of plastic wrap, carefully laying it over the top of the bowl. "I told you I'm making those as treats for the crews arriving tomorrow. If you keep eating them, there won't be any left."

He snatched a snickerdoodle and hummed his appreciation when the rich flavors of butter, sugar, and cinnamon came together in his mouth. "Don't take this the wrong way." He chewed the rest of the cookie in his hand. "Your cooking is amazing, but the way you bake would make a man sell his soul to the devil for a taste. Did your aunt Jo teach you how to bake like this?"

There was a distant look in her eye, a mix of sadness and happiness that spoke of good memories past. "No, my mother taught me. My dad was in the army, and every time he was deployed, I'd turn into a worrying little ball of anxiety. To keep me calm, my mother taught me how to make his favorites. Its monotony is an assurance of sorts. It will always be here, always be like this. After last night, I needed that."

Jackson sipped at the sweating glass of milk in front of him as everything clicked together in his mind. This was her way of reclaiming her normal, of working through her attack. He'd never seen anyone use baking as therapy before, but if the outcome was Aja could process what happened to her, he was all for it.

"Is it working now?"

She circled the rim of her glass before offering him a thoughtful smile. "Part of the charm of this ranch is me helping the people I care about to find a little happy while they're here. If a sweet treat takes them out of their revolving hells for a moment and gives them a chance to feel safe, treasured, taken care of, then all this work is worth it."

She finished her cookies and drank half her glass of milk, then she got back to work, kneading dough, working out every inch of the sadness and apprehension that weighed her down. It sparked something in him, something that made him get up, put the evidence of his snack away, and get back to work at her side. If she was doing this to work through the hell she'd experienced last night, he wanted to do everything he could to be helpful and supportive of her process.

He stood next to her, stilled her working hands, and added flour to the countertop to facilitate her kneading. He couldn't do this work for her, but he could make it easier, and for the rest of the day, that was exactly what he did. He worked by her side, creating something sweet and pretty out of something tasteless and messy. And at the end of their day, when he was tired and covered in flour and sugar, because he couldn't seem to pour either without getting it all over himself, he watched the worry lines etched into her face disappear, and he knew it was all worth it.

Chapter 18

JACKSON SAT ON THE EDGE OF THE QUEEN-SIZE BED IN THE guest room, exhausted after their day of baking. Who knew mixing, kneading, and frosting could be such hard work.

It was hard but rewarding. Especially after watching the way Aja's body relaxed by the end of the day. The tension wasn't completely gone, but she didn't look like she was scared, waiting to see what jumped out from around the corner at her.

A creak pulled him out of his musings, and he caught sight of Aja leaning against the doorjamb. Her face was fresh, clear of the flour dust he'd more than likely been responsible for with all his clumsy handling of the ingredients. She wore an A-line tank again, this time coupled with a pair of lady boxer shorts that landed at the tops of her thighs. He took in the image, his eyes feasting on the sight of her lush flesh. If a big ass was his first weakness when it came to women, thick thighs ran a close second, and everything in him wanted to know what those thighs felt like wrapped tightly around his waist.

His gaze traveled upward until it landed on her face again. She was smiling, really smiling the way she had when she'd brought him a slice of cake in the great room.

"What are you up to?"

She glanced at him through hooded lids. "Who says I have to be up to something? I was thinking how good it was for me to spend the day laughing at your expense. I thought I should reward buffoonery of that caliber." She stepped inside the room, the hypnotic sway of her hips and thighs lulling him into a daze. When she stopped in front of him, she held out a cookie on a napkin. "There was an extra oatmeal raisin cookie left all by its lonesome, so I figured you'd enjoy it." Her smile widened as she extended her hand closer to him. "Don't you want a taste of my cookie, Ranger?"

He bit his lip, trying his damnedest to remember exactly why he was there. "Wanting your cookie isn't the problem, and you know that. I'm trying to look out for you, Aja. What you went through—"

"I've spent a hell of a lot of time reliving past hurts and traumas. I refuse to do it anymore. Restoration Ranch is all about rebuilding, renewing, and finding a safe space. That bastard tried to take that from me last night. But I won't let him do it. I won't let him take the thing that's made me feel the safest since I returned to this land."

His heart pounded as he listened to her, need pulsing through his vessels in hard, thumping beats. Strong, resilient, tougher than the strongest steel, this woman tore through his defenses and common sense the way nothing else had. "What is it, Aja? What's the thing that's made you feel the safest?"

He took the cookie out of her hand and rested it on the nightstand. He spread his thighs and pulled her between them, keeping a firm grip at her waist. She closed her eyes, lost in the sensual rhythm of his touch, leaning into him as she spoke. "You, Jackson. I always feel safe with you."

Good Lord, she knew the right words to say to pull him over the edge. But he couldn't let her do this without letting her know what she was getting into. "Aja, I'm not the relationship type. This could go sideways if we both aren't on the same page. There's a lot to risk. I can give you today, but tomorrow isn't on the agenda."

Panic commingled with anticipation sat in his chest like a large boulder perched precariously at the top of a hill. Any moment, it could tip over, its momentum and heft generating enough power and speed to crush him. She could say no. It was well within her rights, and he would never think to sway her decision for his benefit. But knowing his admission could remove this opportunity to share something this special with her made his heart race a few beats faster than normal.

He wanted this. He wanted the privilege of knowing her body as intimately as he understood his own. If she changed her mind, he'd accept it. But damn if he didn't want the chance to be with Aja in this bed with nothing separating them.

She widened her smile. "Then we'd better use the time we have. The cover of night is burning, Ranger."

Why wasn't he a better man?

The question kept gnawing at him as he pulled Aja down onto the bed with him, lips locked together and hands moving frantically against whichever body part they could reach. If he were a better man, he'd spend more time at home with his family. If he were a better man, he'd have seen through Lana's lies and stopped her from destroying so many lives, the least of which the one they'd built together. If he were a better man, he wouldn't be ripping Aja's clothes off her like some addict chasing his next hit.

No, if Jackson were a better man, he would never have allowed Aja to cross the imaginary line between the professional and the personal. But he wasn't a better man, and since he'd decided he had a reservation in one of the devil's hottest dwelling spaces a long time ago, he figured he'd better enjoy whatever pleasure was left to him before he closed his eyes to this earth.

They were both shaking by the time they were naked, and Jackson pulled Aja on top of him. The feel of her heat pressed against his when she straddled him made lust unfurl in his belly, snaking its tentacles up, twisting itself around his insides as he fought himself to keep from thrusting up. That was all it would take—a simple movement of his hips and he could be buried inside her, flesh to flesh with nothing between them.

Tormented with the need to join with her body, he sat up, kissing her, demanding entrance to her mouth. If he couldn't feel her complete warmth one way, he'd taste it instead. A muted relief spread through his body as his tongue touched hers. She tasted of heat and fire and need, and he feasted on the offering like a starving man uncertain of where his next meal would come from.

He was lost in the feel of her hips rocking back and forth on him, begging for him to answer in kind. He pulled his lips away from her tempting mouth, nibbling at her full bottom lip, promising himself he'd find out what it looked like spread around his girth before the sun rose. He turned them around, switching their positions so she was now beneath him, strewn across the rumpled fabric of bed linens, looking like the perfect mix of beauty and want.

He slid a finger between her wet folds and smiled as her hips chased his touch with each swivel. He gave in and allowed her the prize she sought, letting his finger slip into her entrance. "So wet for me," he whispered as he watched her close her eyes and fall under the spell of his rhythmic strokes. When he removed his hand from her opening, she mewled an almost anguished sound that made him ache to fulfill her vocalized need. "Sweetie, I've got to get a condom, or neither one of us is getting what we want tonight."

"Hurry" was her only answer. He walked quickly to the chest of drawers against the opposite wall. As he searched through the folds of his wallet, silently despairing he wouldn't find a condom while simultaneously hoping he wouldn't, he held his breath. Not having a condom would be the exact thing he needed to give him an excuse to stop and think about why this was all kinds of fucked up. But as his finger grazed the top of the foil packet tucked away behind his billfold, Jackson knew he wouldn't be engaging in any thoughts that would stop this. He had the means, the motivation, and Aja lying on his bed with her fingers disappearing in and out of her wet pussy as she waited for him, moaned for him to hurry. This was the opportunity he'd been waiting for since their first meeting.

Yeah, he was going to hell with gasoline drawers on, and he didn't feel the least bit bad about it. At least not in this moment anyway. He crawled back to her, his mouth watering as he watched her fingers disappear again. How he could be both envious and enthralled at the same time was beyond him, but as much as each dip of those digits made fire lick at his skin, the need to be inside her burned through him like hot knives against bared flesh.

"God, woman, are you trying to kill me?"

He stroked himself once, letting out a long hiss. He was so ready. He hadn't touched her yet and his body was trembling on the edge. It wouldn't take much for him to lose control. One more stroke and he was certain he could reach release if he sat here between her legs watching her pleasure herself, teasing her way toward her own orgasm.

He could watch her play in her pretty cunt all day. He moaned. It was loud, deep, and long, and he didn't care if anyone heard it for miles. It was becoming his predicted response to what the old folks would call her sassiness. He called it confidence, though, because that was what it was. She was sure of herself. Sure she belonged in her own skin, certain that the man she was allowing into her space would appreciate her the way she did herself. She was certain life held something for her, and with a little hard work, she'd somehow tap into it. To understand one's self like that was a gift. One he used to believe he possessed himself. But as of late, as he spent more time with Aja, he wondered if he'd been substituting work competence for life confidence.

There was a difference. It was subtle, but it was still there.

He leaned into the kiss before his subconscious could remind him what a bad idea this was. Yeah, that was actual truth, but it didn't mean Jackson would attempt to resist this any longer.

His lips covered hers, hard and firm, a display of his intent. He didn't want her to think their joining was born out of her ability to convince him. He'd wanted Aja since the first moment she'd walked into his office, and her knowing was important enough to him that he devoured her mouth, pouring all his need and desires into that one kiss.

He couldn't promise her tomorrow. But here and now, he could show her how much her choosing to share herself with him meant. He didn't take it lightly, and if he were honest, it wasn't merely about the physical pleasure he knew being with her would bring him. There was something in the way she melted under his touch, the way she moaned, like he was vital to her existence in this moment, that tripped the circuits in his brain and made his desire for her feel more like an essential life element than simply something his baser self wanted to indulge in for a little fun.

He moved down to the curve of her neck, alternating between kissing and biting as he made his journey to her shoulders, then down until his mouth was covering a large brown nipple. He gave it a gentle lick, and she placed an insisting hand on the back of his head, giving it a firm press. "I won't break, Ranger. Delicate doesn't really do it for me. I need a man to be deliberate and purposeful in his actions. I'm giving you permission to take what you want."

He shivered, his arousal cranking up from interested to nearly painful. God, a woman who knew what she wanted—and apparently held no qualms about sharing that with her partner—was so refreshing.

Her decisiveness wasn't only a quick guide to getting her off. No, it was an aphrodisiac that set Jackson's blood on fire and made his desire to have Aja squirming beneath him in pleasure burn like kerosene-soaked paper.

"God, woman. I'm doing everything I can to make this last, and you're pouring gas on the flames by letting slick words fall off your tongue like that."

Her body stiffened beneath his, drawing his vision to her face. Aja's eyes were wild with excitement as she took in the sight of him. "Who said anything about making this last, Ranger? Foreplay was downstairs on my couch. I need the main event right now." Her voice was deep and raw, as if every word was a struggle to produce, and watching her wrestle with the want shining in her bright eyes made his dick so hard, he feared he'd hurt himself.

He crawled up her body, the predator in him slightly disappointed he wouldn't get to play longer. But when he joined his lips to hers and let his weight sink on top of her, the only thing his body cared about was how soon he'd get to slide his aching flesh inside her.

He broke their kiss, his head a little dizzy with need as he pulled away from her. "Have it your way, darlin'. I had this entire seduction planned. But if hot 'n ready is what you want, I can oblige."

"It is" was her only answer. "Jackson?" The slow drawl of his name pulled him out of his trance and brought his eyes to her face again.

When he saw how slick her fingers were from playing in her folds, how easily they slid around that beautiful nub, how deep they slipped inside her opening with no obstruction, he released the light grip he had on his dick and covered his length with the condom.

"Close." She forced the word through clenched teeth on a short, choppy breath, and the fire in his blood flared. His cock twitched, a physical plea to put them all out of their misery. Unable to hold back any longer, he positioned himself at her entrance, rubbing his stretched tip against her opening. Even with the layer of latex between them, overwhelming sensation rippled through him.

Aja was right; this wouldn't last. He pushed inside at a painfully slow pace, fighting the instinct to bottom out until he was balls-deep inside her. She canted her hips, silently asking for more. The desperation circling in the depths of her hickory-brown eyes clutched at him, called to him to answer with the relief of unity. He responded. A long growl climbed from the pit of his stomach up through his chest and out of his mouth as he pushed forward, spearing her depths one glorious inch at a time until he was buried inside her to the hilt.

God, she wasn't lying about being close. As soon as he was fully seated, the snug grip of her cunt on his cock became impossibly tight, choking him, milking him, as the first waves of her climax crested.

"Dammit, Aja." He hooked his arm under her knee, giving himself more room to work and deepening the angle while planting his other hand near her head for leverage. Fighting the instinct to let the electric sensations that covered his skin consume him, to join her in bliss, he snapped his hips until he found a rhythm that would satisfy her but not drive him to completion.

He plowed into her, delighting in the ravenous sounds coming from her as she met him stroke for stroke, falling into her pleasure headfirst with no regret or hesitation.

"That's it, sugah. Take what you need." His encouragement, coupled with the deep, hard strokes he rendered, drew louder moans from her. He marveled in the beauty of both her and her orgasm. Each was powerful, demanding, striking in ways that made a man want to sit and watch with an unobstructed view of her strength and allure for much longer than one night.

When her spasms subsided, he leaned down to press gentle kisses to her cheek and lips, to draw her back to him as the fog of bliss cleared. Her hands slid up the length of his back, pulling him to her, wrapping him in her embrace like a warm blanket to chase away the cold. She held on to him like he was treasured, necessary, and once again, he was reminded of what this woman's superpower was. Her ability to make a person feel worthy was intoxicating, and right now, he almost felt like he deserved to be here with her, sharing her body. She was a goddess, and he was a lowly mortal who shouldn't dare to raise his eyes to glimpse even the smallest vision of her. But in the glow of her satisfaction, he felt invited, beckoned, as if this was where he was supposed to be all along.

The gravity of that realization washed over him like a deluge of desire and fear mixed together, and he couldn't figure out for the life of him if this was good or bad for him. Instead of thinking about it further, he gave himself over to the pleasure her tightness around his cock offered him.

He forged deeper, wanting the delight of her spasming walls to bring him to oblivion. In the bliss of release, the perils of crossing ethical lines wouldn't be present, and his past and the terrible lapses in judgment he'd had with women wouldn't dog him like the incredible failure he was.

No, their joining was nirvana, a blissful place where nothing but pleasure existed. He'd think about the consequences of his actions later. In the twilight, that strange hour where day and night met in perfect unison with no end or beginning to either, Jackson would let himself think about nothing but the delicious heat of her cunt wrapped around him and the godlike feeling of pride that slipped through his bloodstream every time she called his name and begged him for more.

This time, when she placed a firm two-handed grip on his ass as she tumbled over the precipice of climax again, he allowed the viselike hold of her walls to pull him into the free fall of pleasure. And when his muscles burned as he struggled to reach satisfaction, and he gave every remaining bit of strength he possessed to his thrusts, he heard her whisper, "Baby, please. Give it to me."

It was as if the softness of her words took control of his body. His rhythm faltered as his heart pounded in his ears. His balls inched up and his climax spiraled around the base of his spine. He struggled to hold on, but he made the mistake of glancing down at the wicked smile that curved the corners of her luscious mouth into something sinful and dirty in the best of ways, and he lost his control.

Like a brittle twig, his will snapped and his climax soared up the length of his cock, so powerful that his arms struggled for purchase to keep from crushing her. Her hands slid up the globes of his ass to his shoulders where she gave him a gentle press, telling him it was okay to let go. He fell gracelessly into her arms as every muscle of his body tightened, his release tearing everything from him.

He buried his face in the curve of her neck, fighting for every bit of oxygen his greedy lungs could snatch from the air, and he realized something more dangerous than any criminal he'd ever faced. He never wanted this moment to end.

Chapter 19

AJA TURNED TO HER SIDE AND GAVE IN TO THE FULL BODY stretch her achy limbs demanded. She instantly came up against the hard wall of a man's body. Her smile bloomed as she realized Jackson was still in bed beside her. When he'd wrapped her in his arms a few hours ago and demanded she go to sleep, she hadn't been sure he would still be there when she woke up.

He tightened his grip on her and pulled her against him until their bodies touched at almost every point. "Morning," he whispered as he nuzzled into her neck, giving her a sweet kiss there that made her skin prickle with excitement. "You feeling okay?"

She savored his nearness, too afraid to move for fear of ruining the coziness of the moment. "Are you searching for compliments, Ranger?"

"No, I'm trying to make sure my moment of selfishness didn't cause you more harm than good."

The worry in his voice made her uneasy. "Jackson, if you're going to ruin this by bringing up my attack, I'm going back to sleep."

"This isn't something to joke about, Aja. A day of baking and a night with me won't erase what happened."

She grabbed the pillow next to her and hugged it tight. "I know. Is it so bad I don't want this to become the focus of my life?" He rubbed his hand up and down her shoulder, generating a much-needed warmth. "I don't want to think about this, Jackson. All I want to focus on is how great last night was."

"Aja—"

"I guess that means it wasn't that great for you if all you can focus on is the attack?"

He pulled at her shoulder, coaxing her to turn around. He rested on his back and pulled her in to his side, using his finger at her chin to lift her gaze to his. "You are the sexiest woman I've had the pleasure of spending time with. I would be out of my mind not to treasure every moment of bliss you gifted me with. I could never dismiss or forget what we did, Aja."

Relief bled through her body as she let his words soak in. Knowing they shared the same perspective on their time together eased the tightness building in her chest.

"But even though it's important to me, I can't be blind to how you might not be ready for all this. Maybe talking to someone might help."

"You mean like a therapist?"

"Yeah." He reached over to the nightstand, picking up his phone and tapping on the screen. "I just sent you a text with the number of a friend of mine who works with us in Austin. She's a counselor. She helps survivors work through their experiences."

She smiled, slightly overwhelmed by his concern and his persistence but comforted too. "Thank you for trying to look after me. I promise you I'm fine." When he raised his brow, she laughed. "I promise, if anything changes, I'll reach out to her." He shared a smile with her and the easy mood she'd awoken with slowly returned. "Thank you for comforting me last night."

He tightened his arms around her. "If you want to see it as comfort, fine. But being with you was all about indulgence for me." He pressed a kiss to the top of her head and squeezed her with his strong arms again. "We'd best get up and get dressed. We have a lot of work ahead of us today."

She gave in to his embrace before rolling over onto her back. He slipped from the bed, moving around the room to pull clothes from the chest of drawers. He left the room with a handful of folded items, leaving her to wallow in the warm spot he'd left on the bed next to her.

Yeah, it was time to get up and get back into the normal flow of things. But before she did, she would lie here for a few more moments and enjoy the scent of him on the sheets.

Jackson stood in front the coffee maker, sifting through recent events in his head. He'd slept with Aja—a euphemism for screwed like bunnies until their bodies demanded sleep. He'd found one more condom in his duffel, and they wasted no time putting it to good use.

Note to self: Pick up more condoms or you're gonna be in trouble. Other note to self: If you think not having a condom at your disposal in this scenario is the potential threat and not the fact that you screwed— and apparently are planning to screw again—a principal in your case, then you're worse off than you realized.

Jackson sighed into his cup of coffee. As much as he should, he couldn't bring himself to feel bad about spending the night with Aja. Oh, he knew he should regret it. But he felt no remorse over giving in to the thing he'd wanted since he first laid eyes on her.

He didn't know what to do with that. He should care; he should be ashamed for giving in to his need repeatedly. But as he remembered the taste of her flesh, the sensation of her coming as she rode him, all he could find within him was the renewed need to experience it all again.

Aja fiddled with the bandanna tied around her neck. With most of
her wardrobe still sealed behind the police tape on her bedroom
door, she was lucky to find enough clothing in her laundry room
to piece an outfit together. Finding a bandanna she would usually
wear on her head that actually matched the outfit she'd scavenged
meant an angel was smiling somewhere near her.

She looked in the mirror hanging on the back of the guest
bedroom door and assessed her appearance. With her hair down
and the scarf artfully tied to rest comfortably inside the collar
of her shirt, the bruised flesh on her neck was camouflaged. She
looked like her normal self, even if everything about her world had
upended so much over a short amount of time.

The sabotage on her ranch, the attack, it all felt so separate,
so foreign. She could hardly reconcile herself with those terrible
memories.

"Get it together, Aja. Fake it 'til you make it. As long as you
act like yourself, no one will be the wiser. Not Jackson, and not
anyone else."

She stood in front of the mirror for a moment and thought
about the counselor's contact information sitting on her phone.

"There's no time for that, Aja. There are too many things and
too many people you need to worry about right now. You'll be
fine."

Aja tugged at the bandanna one last time and decided it was as
good as it would get. Playing in the mirror wouldn't make it any
better, so she should at least get downstairs and get her day started.

She made her way to the kitchen, took one look at the large
empty space, and decided she was too tired to pull out the usual
stops for breakfast. They were closer to the midday meal anyhow,
so a large breakfast made little sense in her estimation.

She made herself a quick bowl of oatmeal, sprinkled a few

raisins and cranberries for garnish, and poured herself a large cup of coffee. Breakfast was done.

She sat at the counter, savoring the first spoonful. Aunt Jo was right; all you needed was a hot meal to chase the cold away. *Is that what chased the cold away for you last night?*

Determined not to give the issue any more thought, Aja made it halfway through her meal and poured herself another cup of coffee. By the time she was sipping her second cup, she heard the familiar voices of Seneca and Brooklyn nearing her back door.

She walked to the door and leaned casually against the door-jamb, trying to exude as much normalcy as possible. *If only normal was something I remembered how to be.*

"Morning, ladies. How y'all doing?" Aja stood there forcing a wide smile on her face, attempting not to look strange—or worse, suspicious—in front of the two women climbing the few short stairs up her back porch.

Seneca and Brooklyn looked at her, then each other, a puzzling expression passing between them. "Morning?" Brooklyn asked as she stepped through the threshold. "You're about six hours late on that one. The newbies met us in the stables this morning to tell us you'd be skipping our morning meeting and breakfast. Everything okay? This is the second day in a row you've been MIA."

Aja chose that moment to walk back inside the house and sit in front of her coffee again. "With all that's been going on, I needed a day off to veg and bake. You know how I get. Everything is fine. The security and construction crews are starting today. I needed to get a few things organized this morning before they arrived. We can have our daily meeting after lunch."

Aja tried to smile and felt her lips tremor slightly as she pulled them into the false grin. Too afraid she'd give herself away, she dropped her gaze to the cooling oatmeal and picked up a spoonful. She busied herself with the act of eating the rest of it and hoped that would be enough to satisfy the two women standing in front of her.

"All right. We'll get back to it then." Brooklyn's apparent acceptance loosened the uncomfortable tightness in Aja's limbs. Lying to her workers—no, her *friends*—was something she'd never wanted. But right now, it couldn't be helped. "We came to check in, but I also needed the final blueprints for the construction foreman. You have them?"

Aja pulled her eyes from her bowl and turned her head to the right. "Yeah, they're on top of the desk in the corner over there."

Brooklyn didn't move. Instead, both her and Seneca's mouths hung open in shock. "What's wrong?"

"The fuck, Aja. What happened to your neck?"

"Shit." The curse slipped from Aja's lips as she realized her carefully tied bandanna had slipped when she turned her head, exposing her very bruised neck to Seneca and Brooklyn. "I promise, it's better than it looks."

She fumbled with the piece of cloth, trying to ignore their reactions.

"Aja," Brooklyn continued. She could hear the reprimand in the stern way Brooklyn spoke her name. "Your neck looks like someone tried to choke the life out of you. Now unless you've got an asphyxiation fetish you didn't tell us about, you get bruises like that one way. What the hell happened? And before you come at us with that bullshit security drill nonsense the newbies threw at us two days ago, know we're not leaving until we get the truth."

Aja looked from one to the other, hoping she could find less scrutiny in Seneca's eyes than Brooklyn's. No such luck. Seneca's critical glare collided with Aja's, and she knew she'd have to come clean.

"An intruder came into the house night before last. He attacked me."

"Attacked you how?"

Aja could see familiar ghosts from Brooklyn's past coloring her question. She slid her hand across the counter and placed it atop Brooklyn's, hoping to offer some kind of comfort to her. "He tried to choke me. I think he meant to kill me. At least that's what it felt like. But Jackson interrupted him before he could finish the job."

Brooklyn laced her fingers through Aja's and squeezed. "Thank God." Brooklyn let out a loud, ragged breath before looking at Aja again. "Why would you try to hide this from us?"

"Brooklyn—" Aja tried to interrupt her. She could see the steam building up to what would be an explosive tirade.

"Didn't you think we'd notice?" Brooklyn continued, her pitch climbing a half note higher than her last.

"Brooklyn, please—" Aja started but was cut off again.

"Why are you so damn calm about this? Like this was some irrelevant thing that slipped your mind."

"Brooklyn!" Aja screamed as she slammed her closed fists on the counter. She shut her eyes and counted backward from ten in her head. Allowing the silence to bleed some of her frustration out before she spoke again.

"I'm sorry," Aja whispered. "I didn't mean to lose my temper, and I didn't mean to keep you out of the loop. I need to process this my own way."

"By pretending it didn't happen?" Seneca asked.

Aja shook her head. "No, by handling it the best way I know how." She opened her eyes, slowly dragging her eyes up to meet theirs. "I don't have the time or the luxury to fall apart right now, Seneca. My land, my people, and my life are being threatened. I'll lose everything that means anything to me if I crumble now."

Brooklyn stood quietly as she watched Aja. "Aja, you have been good to us. You gave us a place to call home when no one else would. We're more than the people who work for you. We're family. And when you fuck with my family, you fuck with me."

Aja knew Brooklyn wasn't lying. She took family seriously—all one had to do was read her rap sheet to know that was true. But it was the sullen look dripping off the usually bubbly Seneca's face that almost broke Aja.

"I didn't mean to hurt either of you. I simply wanted to protect you from—"

"From what?" Brooklyn barked. "From knowing you were put in danger because of us?"

"Brooklyn," Aja countered. "This is not your fault."

"The hell it isn't." Brooklyn's chest heaved as her anger became visible in the tight lines of her face. "This is a direct result of us being here. If you weren't trying to help us, this wouldn't have happened. We're not worth all this trouble."

The slight tremble in Brooklyn's voice cut across Aja's heart like a surgical blade. It was precise, clean, but so deep, Aja's entire being shuddered against the pain.

Aja opened both her hands and turned them up on the counter. She waited for each of them to place a hand on top of hers, and when they did, she closed her palms, holding onto them as tightly as she could without causing them discomfort.

"The day you two came here, I promised I would allow no one to shame you because of your pasts. You've done the work, your debt to society is nearly paid, and I won't allow anyone to make you feel undeserving of the benefits of your labor here. You two have earned the right to live beyond your yesterdays. You are worth more to me than anything on this ranch. I can handle what anyone has to throw at me. I chose to have you here. That's not a decision I'll ever regret. No matter what happens. Are we clear on that?"

The two women looked at each other and then peered at Aja, nodding slowly in unison. The pitiful looks on their faces had her heart in tatters. This was exactly what Aja had attempted to avoid.

She gave their hands one final squeeze before releasing them. "I am fine. Jackson came to my rescue. He heard the commotion and stopped the attack. The attacker got away, but he was at least able to save me from any real harm."

"What does the sheriff have to say about all of this?"

Aja broke eye contact, circling her finger on the cool marble of the counter as she spoke. "The usual. He'll look into it but can't make any promises." As the two of them took a collective breath, Aja lifted her hands in surrender. "Don't worry about the sheriff. I'm taking precautions of my own. The security company will secure the ranch. It'll be harder to get in here than Fort Knox. Get back to work. Everything will be fine. Trust me."

She put on her finest smile, reassuring them as best she could. When they finally relented and headed for the door, she let a long sigh spill past her lips. If only she could believe the guarantees she'd given them, Aja's day would be made.

Chapter 20

AJA SAT AT THE DESK IN HER KITCHEN, TRYING TO FOCUS ON the numbers in front of her. Unable to concentrate, she gave up trying to get any work done and decided a midday break was in order. A quick trip to the fridge and she poured sweet tea into frosty mugs before she headed out to the front porch where Jackson was now pacing back and forth.

"You think you can stop wearing a hole in the wood on my porch long enough to have a drink?"

"Yessum."

She handed him a mug and took a seat on the porch swing. She patted the cushion next to her and waited for him to sit. "How are you?"

He turned to her with furrowed brows. "How am I? I think I should be the one asking you that question. Your entire life is being upended for this investigation."

"It's true." She took a sip of her drink and let the familiar flavor soothe her before she continued. "My life is filled with chaos right now. But I can't stop being me because some lunatic has it out for me." She waved a dismissive hand before meeting his eyes again. "Anyway, you seemed tense. If you're going to be shadowing me all day, I can't have you looking like a bomb slowly ticking toward detonation. I figured it would be easier to offer you some sweet tea and ask you what's going on instead."

The intensity of his glare was a palpable thing that slid down the length of her before returning and settling on her face. "You knew I was purposely sticking close?"

"Wasn't hard to figure out." She took a sip of her sweet tea. "Aside from when you took your truck to the back forty this morning, you've been either in or around the house all day. Smart money says if I actually needed to get work done outside the house today, you'd be walking in the fields right beside me."

"I'd say that's a fair assumption."

Aja laughed and nudged his arm with her shoulder. "What's going on?"

"This person who's after you, his aggression is escalating. He started off with things that could almost be considered harmless pranks. He went from that to trying to burn down your barn with you nearly in it. And when that didn't work, he tried to kill you with his bare hands. I want him caught and you safe. But we're shorthanded. I'd usually connect with local law enforcement on a case like this to increase our chances at a successful outcome. But Hastings is negligent, almost criminally so."

Cold flooded her nerve endings, making her shiver, and she put down her cup on a nearby end table. He wasn't pulling any punches. Part of her was glad about that. But the very human part of her that worried about her mortality bristled at how tenuous this entire situation was.

"Any word from forensics?"

He shook his head. "It's way too early for that. Jennings and Gleason picked up the evidence we collected yesterday before you woke up. We collected prints, but since he wore gloves, they'll probably belong to you or someone that has usual access to your room. We're hoping there was some transfer of DNA between him and you during the struggle. All the swabs we took from you are being processed now. But until then, we only have the bracelet we found. If we can get a hit on where it was made or sold, we might use that to generate a suspect list."

"Bracelet?"

Jackson pulled his phone from his pocket and flipped through the screen until he found what he was looking for. He handed her the phone, and she examined the picture of a broken bracelet plate in an evidence bag.

"Do you recognize that?"

She shook her head. It was a small gold plate, the words "Mañana no está—" on it. "No, I've never seen it before." She handed him the phone. "Do you think it belonged to the attacker?"

"No way of knowing. We won't know anything until we can get the forensics back. Until then, we're fighting in the dark, Aja. I don't know who is after you, and I don't know which direction to look."

She was about to ask more questions when Jackson's phone lit up in his hand. "Dean. What does he want? Hold on." He pulled the phone away from his ear and tapped the mute icon on the screen, then turned to her. "Eli Bennett is at your front gates. He says he wants to come speak with you. You up for seeing him?"

She calculated all the things he'd said to her as she pieced together the unsaid things in his question. "You put security at my front gates?"

Jackson leaned over, bracing his elbows on his thighs. "I had my father add plans for a security booth. Once it's completed, you can hire security of your own. Until then, there's a patrol car at the gates being manned by two of my father's employees who have a background in protection details."

He tapped his finger on the screen a few times again. She looked up when her own phone vibrated. "I sent you the numbers of the men sitting at the gates, in the event you need to leave them instructions of some kind."

She didn't check the text. Not then. She was too busy attempting to process that she needed to live under lock and key now. A prisoner on her own land.

"Outside of a short list of people, no one is allowed to enter without prior authorization. If they show up unannounced, security has to contact one of us for clearance."

There was something about the way he said the words *short list* that made her brain cells twitch. "Who's on that list? How d'you cultivate it to begin with?"

"It's based on necessity. There are a handful of people that need unobstructed access to you and the ranch. Your aunt and uncle, Brooklyn and Seneca, and me and my men. Other than that, everyone else needs to make an appointment."

"And what about Mat Ryan?" She watched his lips tighten into a flat line at the mention of the man's name and shook her head. "You cannot bar him from the ranch. He is Brooklyn and Seneca's parole officer. He needs access to them."

Jackson frowned, dismissing her displeasure. "So they can't go into town and have their meetings with him there?"

"This is a small town where everyone knows everyone else's business. Why would I subject them to the humiliation of walking into Mat's office in the middle of the town square? People can be cruel, Jackson. Sometimes without meaning to. If I can spare them that embarrassment by having him meet them here, that's what I'll do."

"I understand all that. But it doesn't change my mind about how this needs to play out. This person will come for you again, Aja. The best way I can protect you on a place this size is to limit the number of people who have access to you."

"He's harmless."

"Good." Jackson lifted his brow. "He'll remain that way with scheduled appointments like the rest of the population."

She opened her mouth to respond, but he lifted a finger to stop her and unmuted his phone. "Send him up."

She waited a beat for him to end the call before she spoke. "After finding this out, I don't think I'm in the mood to talk to Eli after all."

"Aja, you know my men have tried to pin him down for an interview. They even used your assault to force some face time with this guy. We've got nothing. Without probable cause, I can't force Bennett to talk to us. This may be my best chance to get anything usable out of him without the presence of his high-priced attorneys."

She gently pulled the inside of her cheek between her teeth to keep her cool. She knew he was attempting to protect her, and everything he'd implemented made more than a little sense in their current situation. But considering his previous reaction to Mat, she wasn't at all certain Jackson wasn't penalizing the parole officer for some unseen crime that had nothing to do with the attacks on the ranch.

"There's got to be another way, Jackson."

He shook his head. "Bennett's smart. If he is involved, no way in hell he was gonna tell two Rangers that. But he might slip up in front of his rival and her foreman."

Juggling her annoyance with Jackson over Mat pressed her patience. Trying to add Eli Bennett to her overworked tolerance was probably not the best thing. But again, her hand was forced by circumstances she had no control of. And that realization was setting her anger off more than Jackson's behavior.

By the time she'd cooled down enough to speak instead of yell, she saw Eli Bennett's large blacked-out truck barreling up the road toward her house.

"We'll discuss this issue with Mat later." Aja watched Jackson bristle at her edict. *Good, he knows I mean business.* "I don't have the energy to deal with you and this joker at the same time."

She saw the dismissive cut of his eyes in her direction and leveled an equally contemptuous one at him in return. She was willing to follow his lead regarding this investigation, but she couldn't allow him to do anything that would force Mat Ryan to make life difficult for her Pathways participants.

When the truck stopped in her circular driveway, she stood and braced a hand against Jackson's arm when he attempted to follow. She was grateful that he easily agreed, sitting back against the swing without argument. She wasn't lying about her dwindling energy levels. Too much had happened in the span of a few days, and having to deal with Eli Bennett's unsavory ass would probably drain what little strength she had left and require a nap afterward.

Eli's lean and diminutive body jumped down from the monster truck, and Aja fought to keep the smile off her face. He was barely taller than her petite stature, but everything he owned had to be larger than life. His truck, his house, his land, all of it had to be bigger and better than everyone else's. Even the ridiculous ten-gallon hat he insisted on wearing that made him look like a cartoon character purposely drawn out of proportion for the comedic benefits.

Aja leaned a hip against the porch railing and crossed her arms. Before Eli could place his boot on the bottom step of her porch, she stopped him in his tracks with a cool greeting. "What can I do for you, Eli?"

"Howdy, Ms. Everett. I heard about the trouble you had two nights ago. I wanted to come by and see for myself that you were all right."

More like see if the job was done or not. "How did you hear about my supposed 'trouble,' Eli?"

"A couple of Texas Rangers stopped by my spread yesterday asking me about it. Like I'd know anything about something terrible like that. Everyone on my land is a law-abiding citizen. I told them they might want to ask the women who worked for you, seeing as they're known for running with the criminal element."

She said nothing, simply continued to bite the inside of her cheek and waited for him to go on.

"Are you all right? You don't look much the worse for wear for someone who was assaulted." He pulled his large cowboy hat off his head and held it against his chest as if that made this obvious act seem more sincere. "But to be neighborly, I thought it would be best for me to come in and check on you. Is there anything I can do?"

"Everything's fine here. I have it under control."

Eli attempted to place his foot on the first step, but Aja pushed off the railing she was leaning against, making her stance wide and placing her hands on her hips for effect. Eli moved his foot back to the dirt where it belonged, and a satisfied ripple of electricity buzzed in her chest. He'd gotten her "You're not welcome" message loud and clear.

"Aja, we're neighbors. We should look out for each other. This place is too big for a little lady like yourself to handle. The rough terrain of a ranch is no place for a gentlewoman. Let me help. My bid to buy the land still stands. You could take my very generous offer and live comfortably back in the city. You don't need to do this. You've got nothing to prove."

"I know I don't." She owned the land free and clear. She didn't need to prove a damn thing to anyone. That wasn't what this was about. Unfortunately, someone as money-hungry and small-minded as Eli Bennett would never understand that. He would always see a woman's need to thrive and succeed as just a silly little tantrum to prove something to a man. "This is my land and it will remain so. I've told you before, I'm not interested in selling it."

Aja watched as the feigned concern dripped from Eli's face and was replaced by the nasty curl of his top lip. "It's not safe for you, Aja. A wise woman would accept my generous offer."

"Doesn't matter how many times you offer or whether you serve it up with honey or vinegar, my answer will always be the same. No."

He watched her for a moment, then moved his gaze over to

a still-sitting Jackson and back to Aja. "Well, you certainly seem determined. I hope your stubborn pride doesn't end up costing you something you can't replace."

The creak of the swing behind her told her Jackson was up on his feet. Before he could take a step toward them, she held up a finger to stop him. "Good day, Eli. If you know what's good for you, you'll get off my land now."

He took a moment to take in the scene, and more than likely Jackson's imposing frame, before he put on his hat and turned toward his vehicle. A few seconds later, he was tearing up the road, kicking up dust as he headed toward the front gates.

The heavy press of Jackson's hand against her shoulder was reassuring, helping Aja relax slightly as she watched Eli's truck disappear down the road. "I dislike that man, Aja."

A derisive chuckle shook her shoulders. "Join the club."

Chapter 21

JACKSON SAT AT THE KITCHEN COUNTER DOODLING ON A notepad as he watched Aja carefully layering what looked to be lasagna ingredients into an extra-long casserole dish.

"Jackson," she huffed. "When you said you would watch my every move, I didn't think you meant literally. I'm placing pasta, cheese, and meat sauce on top of each other. Surely there's something else you can do to secure my safety that doesn't include this."

"Maybe I find your culinary skills interesting."

"You ain't slick, and you're not off the hook either. I'm still mad at you about barring Mat from the ranch."

He stiffened, preparing himself for battle. "Are we really gonna fight again about this?"

"Yeah, we are," she continued. "But not right now. I firmly believe that fighting while you're preparing food spoils the meal."

"Just another reason I love watching you cook. You take so much care when you do it. It's like watching the creation of art."

She waved a dismissive hand. "I'm hardly an artist or a chef. I don't know the difference between julienne cut and a paper cut. I'm simply repeating the same steps that have been passed down from generation to generation in my family."

Jackson laughed. "That may be. But your cooking is still better than most, so I'm not the least bit bored watching you. Besides, you always seem so content when you're doing it."

She placed the ladle full of meat sauce carefully in a nearby pot as she stared at him. "Is that your way of saying you think this cooking thing is women's work? You do know most cooking schools are filled with male students?"

He chuckled. "My daddy didn't raise no fool. I'm not stupid enough to let something like that slip out of my mouth. I wasn't assigning a gender role. I happen to have been raised by a single father who insisted my brother and I contribute to the family upkeep by cooking and cleaning."

She raised a skeptical brow, and a loud ball of laughter swelled in his chest, pressing against his insides until Jackson set it free into the air. "I swear it's the truth."

"So you've had me sweating over a stove for you when you knew how to cook all along?"

He pointed an accusing finger at her. "Now, Counselor, you can't blame me for that. You never asked if I could cook. You simply shoved a plate in my face."

She threw a nearby hand towel at him. "Watch it there. Your chauvinistic tendencies are showing, cowboy."

He caught the towel and waved it in surrender. He laughed again, this time in a silent but deep chuckle that made his entire body shake. When he caught his breath, he marveled at how easily laughter seemed to come when he was in her presence.

Maybe that was why he liked being around her so much. She made him laugh. *That ain't the only reason, and you know it.* "I really wasn't trying to be a chauvinist. I was simply observing that you seem relaxed, as if you forget about all the real-world hardships when you're cooking. I've been told I do the same when I draw."

"Draw? That's what you've been over there doing? I thought you were doodling on the notepad."

He was slightly surprised himself that he was drawing. The desire to put more than a few uninspired lines on the page hadn't filled him in a long time. "Yeah, I haven't done it in a while. But watching you doing something that made you that content inspired me to do the same."

A bright smile spread across her face. "May I see?"

He was hesitant. He hadn't shared his art with anyone since the world was pulled from under him. Sharing this with Aja, even after the intimacy of sex, felt like he was stepping further over the line than he should.

"You don't have to if you don't want to. I was just curious."

He put his pencil down and slid the notepad toward her. She grabbed a nearby towel before carefully picking up the notepad as if it contained a masterpiece instead of the doodling of a bored Ranger.

"Jackson." She whispered his name like it was a prayer. "Is this how you see me?"

He swallowed uncomfortably. The last thing he wanted to do was offend her with his untrained drawing. "It's a hobby. I told you, I haven't done it in a long time. It's not very good."

He reached over to take the notepad, and she pulled it away from his grasp. "A hobby? This is beautiful. If I hadn't been here to watch you draw it, I never would've believed this is me."

"Why not?"

"Because the way the lines flow and converge on the page gives off an angelic, ethereal quality I'm not sure I possess in real life."

Jackson tilted his head as he let his eyes slide slowly down her frame. She was dressed in a pair of fitted jeans and another one of those V-necked women's T-shirts that exposed enough of her cleavage to make him want to lean in and see where that sexy dark-brown line between the swell of her breasts led. Her tiny braids were piled high on the top of her head in some sort of messy bun. But instead of looking haphazard, it drew his eyes to her face and neck, giving her a more regal glow. She wasn't simply angelic; she was the queen of all angels as far as he was concerned.

"Aja, I don't lie. My job doesn't always allow me to be as truthful as I'd like to be. But in real life, I don't lie. Lies destroy. They corrode." He took the drawing from her and ran his fingers slowly across it, hoping some of her depicted glow would somehow jump off the page and chase away the cold shadows of his past. "The truth is important to me. So if this drawing makes you see yourself as angelic and ethereal, it's because beauty is in the eye of the beholder. Besides, I've never been that imaginative when it comes to drawing. I just draw what I see."

She was quiet for a moment. He couldn't tell where her thoughts were going, only that she was piecing something together behind those deep-brown eyes. In the short few days he'd spent with her, he'd come to realize her intellect, her ability to puzzle things together until she had a working explanation in her head, was one of her greatest superpowers. Well, that and her ability to both bless and curse you with her tongue.

"You're so talented. Why don't you do this more often?"

A long sigh slipped from his lips as he slid down in his chair. "My ex-wife didn't much care for the garage full of sketch pads and art supplies I stored over the years. She said it was a silly hobby I was too old to indulge in."

Her brows furrowed, and the need to run his fingers across those creases and smooth them out almost overwhelmed him. "That seems unsupportive. No wonder she's your ex." Her eyes widened, and she placed her hand over her mouth. "I'm sorry. I had no right to pass judgment like that. I never want to be someone who villainizes the woman who came before her."

Jackson shook his head. "Making a truthful assessment isn't the same as passing judgment. Lana had good qualities. When things were going well, she was fun and generous. She effortlessly managed to be a bright spot wherever she went. But when things were

bad, she changed into another person. That Lana wasn't supportive. Not of things she didn't feel there was a tangible benefit to
anyway. You'd think her lack of support might have made me walk,
but no, it wasn't. I left because—" He searched for the words to
express as much of the truth as he could. No one wanted to bare
their scars to the world, but after proclaiming himself to be a pur-
veyor of truth, it felt wrong somehow not giving Aja exactly that.
"She's my ex-wife because she lied to me, and those lies ended up
killing someone."

He glanced up to witness the quiet shock written across her
face. Jackson wasn't surprised she didn't know about it. What was
big news in a small hick town rarely made it on the mainstream
wire. The anonymity of a small town in the South was the only
thing that had saved his career after Lana's unthinkable crime.

The light brush of Aja's palm on top of his registered somewhere in the back of his mind, and he looked down to see her
holding his hand carefully, as if he needed a delicate touch.

"Jackson?"

She didn't have to ask the actual question for him to understand her meaning.

"About thirteen years ago, I married the mayor's daughter back
in my small hometown. Lana was a party girl. I'd always known
that. Hell, everybody in town knew that. But as an adult, I wasn't
aware that the wild partying had turned into something much
more ugly and uncontrollable than her silly high-school antics.
After college, I did a stint in the military. By the time I came home
for good, I figured she'd grown up like the rest of our peers. But I
was wrong."

He took a deep breath and cleared his throat, trying hard not
to sound like the victim in this scenario. Because no matter how
bad things got for him, he was still here, still alive. That wasn't true
for the real victim in this story. "Apparently her father threatened
to cut her off if she didn't get herself together. That meant no

foolishness in public—she had to settle down, or he would snatch away everything his power and local celebrity offered her. Forever a daddy's girl, she figured out how to play him and still do exactly what she wanted. And when we dated, she learned to play me the same way.

"Lana was an alcoholic, and even though I lay next to her most nights, I never knew it. By the time I figured something was off, she'd been so deep into her addiction, there was no way she could get out of it on her own.

"I tried to support her the best way I knew how. I put her into rehab, threatened to leave her if she didn't give the program a serious try."

Aja squeezed his hand, letting him know she was there for him, and the easy way she comforted him both soothed and stirred something deeper he wasn't willing to acknowledge at that moment. "I'm guessing you sending her to rehab and threatening her to straighten up didn't work."

He shook his head. He'd hoped like hell it would, but none of it helped. "No. She smiled and made me and her daddy believe she was doing her best to get a handle on her problem. But the truth was, Lana hadn't cleaned up her act. Instead, she learned to get smarter about when and where she drank and whose company she kept while doing it."

"Jackson, addicts are very good at hiding in plain sight. Until someone is ready to address their problems, there isn't enough outside motivation in the world to make them stop. They have to do the work for themselves."

Again, she was right. But in his own arrogance, he'd believed he could pull Lana out of darkness with tough love and support. But it hadn't worked. Nothing he did worked.

"What happened, Jackson?"

"We'd been arguing all week about something or other. It's strange—as important as the subject seemed then, I can't remember for the life of me what we were actually fighting about. All I remember is telling her I got called out on assignment and I wouldn't be home that night. Somehow that bit of information escalated whatever else was going on. From what I can gather, because Lana never remembered, she went on a bender and decided she would give me a piece of her mind face-to-face."

He laced his fingers through Aja's, somehow needing an anchor to the present while his past sought to draw him into pain and guilt. "Halfway there, she drove the wrong way up a highway exit and slammed into another car. It was a young family. Parents and a toddler. The parents were pretty banged up. The little one died on impact."

"My God." She let go of his hand only to walk around the counter and stand next to him. Once she reached his side, she burrowed her way under his arm and wrapped him in her tight embrace, reinforcing the invisible cracks that were spreading through his foundation.

"Her blood alcohol content was more than double the legal limit. Even her daddy couldn't get her out of the trouble she'd landed in, landed us all in."

"You mean the legal and civil liabilities that come along with something like this?"

She was sharp, Jackson had to give her that. "Lana had two previous DWIs that her father paid the fines for quietly and kept her records buried. But with her killing a child, even her daddy couldn't get her out of that unscathed. She was sentenced to twenty years and must serve at least half that before she's eligible for parole. She was also fined ten thousand dollars. And that was just the legal penalties. The family sued us and was awarded a hefty sum in damages."

She looked up at him, her eyes wide, filled with compassion as she calculated her own conclusions. "You lost everything, didn't you?"

He pulled her in tighter to him, kissing her on her forehead. The connection calmed the familiar anger and guilt that whipped around inside him like the raging waves of a stormy sea. "No, that young family lost everything." Even through all his pain, he still realized nothing compared to the loss of that little one's life. "I walked away with the clothes on my back and my job. And the only thing that kept me employed was that I hadn't attempted to cover up Lana's issues with my badge. Her father didn't fare so well in that regard. He was removed from office when an investigation revealed he'd used his position to get her lighter sentences for her past transgressions."

"Jackson, I'm so sorry."

He held her closer. The feel of her pressed so tightly against him was reassuring, keeping the shadows of the past away. Who would've thought Jackson Dean, the big, burly Texas Ranger, needed someone to make him feel safe? *God, this is all kinds of wrong.* It was true. *He* should provide comfort, not her. But then he realized comfort was what Aja was all about. She'd said as much to him several times since they'd met. She was here to make things better for the people around her. And damn if he didn't feel lucky to fall even on the margins of her proximity. Because being with her felt damn good, even when it shouldn't.

Chapter 22

Aja remained in the kitchen thinking about Jackson after he'd shared his past with her. He'd been called away to one of the access points to help with something security related a few moments before. But even in his absence, she could still feel the heaviness of his confession.

She shook her head as she sat at the counter, in the very seat Jackson had recently vacated, and thought more on their conversation. It all made sense now, why he always seemed to walk the straight and narrow, why he seemed so torn between wanting her and doing his due diligence. Why he insisted he didn't do relationships, and why even though they'd slept together, he still seemed to keep some distance between them.

During the most difficult time of his life, his job was all he had. And Aja'd been so angry and wrapped up in her own needs, she'd practically begged him to forget about his oath and focus on what she needed instead.

She closed her eyes and pinched the bridge of her nose. "You really are a piece of work, Aja. Didn't your past teach you the cost of your selfishness yet?" The image of her sister's face formed behind her closed lids, and regret, cold and heavy, spun tight around her chest. "Doing what you want has already ruined one life. You can't add Jackson to that list too."

She stood and walked over to a nearby desk off the edge of the kitchen and sat down. She pulled out her phone and opened a browser for her favorite online catalog. At first, the inconvenience of not having a major store within walking distance of her home had been a pain. But now, with one- or two-day shipping available, she didn't miss going into the stores at all.

She was running low on planning supplies, and that was a problem she needed to rectify immediately. In the day of digital calendars, you'd think the paper planner was obsolete. But Aja was a visual learner who needed to see things and write them and rewrite them to commit them to memory. So although her planning sessions were about decompression and getting to play with pretty stickers, they were also about keeping her life and business in order.

Today, after Jackson had removed the police tape from her room so the construction crew could assess the damage inside, Aja had walked in and pulled her planner from her nightstand.

She'd tried to sit on her bed as was her custom, but flashes of her struggle against her attacker filled her mind. So she collected her things, brought them down to this desk, and decided she'd organize the rest of her week when she found a moment.

Now was that moment, but instead of thinking about appointment stickers and color themes for her weekly spread, thoughts of a guilt-ridden Ranger and the terrible ordeal he'd found himself in the middle of filled her head. Jackson had made the same mistake Aja had made with her sister all those years ago. Thinking you could save people from themselves was the quickest road to despair she knew. A lesson he still seemed to be in the throes of.

"Jackson." Just the thought of him made her sigh his name like a besotted schoolgirl. He was strong, determined, a little insufferable, but mostly committed to doing the right thing. And now she understood why. That stick she'd presumed was shoved up his ass was actually a reasonable reaction to a horrific experience.

Aja knew exactly what that pain felt like when your entire existence was being threatened by someone who was supposed to love you. She didn't wish that on anyone, especially not the horrible guilt of a lost life that Jackson wore like a cloak.

God, he could use some happiness.

Aja was about to go to her online cart and check out when an idea formed, pulling a wide grin on her lips. "And I know just how to bring him some."

———————

Jackson was searching for the foreman of the construction crew when he found the man standing at one of the building sites on the ranch, talking to Brooklyn. There were five different structures covered with large construction tarps that looked like this one. Foundation poured, beams and framework erected, wiring done, but still an empty shell of what a building should be. Aja had mentioned that the previous construction crew from town had stopped work when they realized the scaffolding was sabotaged. Fortunately, the man had lost his nerve after he'd erected the building frames. Otherwise, Aja's goal of opening by travel season wouldn't be possible.

"Thanks for the clarification on your designs, Ms. Osborn. Once we're finished assisting the security crew, we'll get right on these."

Brooklyn wiped her forehead with the back of her hand. "You sure we can still make our deadline?"

The man hooked a thumb in his belt loop and tapped his fingers on his thigh. "Barring any terrible weather, we should be able to make it. The previous crew left you in the lurch, but by our inspections, the work is solid. Insulation, adding Sheetrock, laying tile, and adding the fixtures are definitely doable in your timeline.

Your boss hired five of my crews, one for each structure, to make sure the work was done in a timely fashion. It ain't cheap, but it's damn efficient."

Brooklyn didn't smile, simply gave the foreman a handshake and went back to looking at her designs spread across the tailgate of one of the ranch's pickups.

"Mr. Tracey?" Jackson waved the roll of papers he held in his hand as he walked closer to them. "My father said you needed these." The man offered Jackson one hand to shake while he accepted the roll of papers with the other.

"Yeah, he wants me to add a planter to Ms. Everett's balcony that can conceal some of his hardware. I just needed the specifics so we can build it accordingly." Mr. Tracey tipped his hat to both Brooklyn and Jackson and made his way back to his truck.

Jackson stood there watching the foreman leave before he turned his attention to Brooklyn. Still focused on the blueprints in front of her, she was seemingly unbothered by Jackson's presence.

"You needed something?"

Jackson couldn't help the tickle of amusement that pulled his lips into a small grin. Brooklyn Osborn was a straight shooter from what Jackson could tell from the few moments they'd been in each other's presence. She didn't have a lot of words. But when she spoke, she wasn't wasting them on things like small talk either.

"No. You're on top of things with the construction crew. Aja will be happy if things stay on schedule."

"Well, that is my job. She hired me to design her ranch, and making sure the construction crew stays on task is part of that." She never took her eyes off the designs before her; she simply kept marking things as if Jackson weren't there. "Anything else?"

"No," he answered quickly. "Just making sure things are running smoothly. It's my job."

As he walked away, she spoke again. "You take it seriously, don't you?"

He stopped, turning his head toward her to find her sight lasered in on him. "My job as the foreman? Yeah, I do."

"Thank God you were there when she was attacked. I don't want to think about what would've happened if you weren't."

He didn't either. If he'd been a moment too late, all could've been lost. "Fortunately, I was. Aja is fine."

"Because of you."

He lowered his lids; there was no sense in denying what they both knew.

"Aja's too good a person for this shit. She won't let us go. She keeps fighting for us. I just… I don't want her to suffer because of me and Seneca. Few people in the world would care about someone like me."

She tore her gaze from his and looked up toward the open sky as though it held the key to life itself until she'd blinked away whatever spark of emotion he'd seen flash across her brown eyes. "You keep doing your job, Foreman. Keep looking out for her. She won't do it for herself."

She rolled up her blueprints, closed the tailgate, and climbed in the truck and drove away, leaving Jackson standing in the middle of the grassy knoll with nothing but wall-less buildings behind him.

Brooklyn's words replayed in his mind, an eerie chill passing from one nerve to another as he recalled each of them. Fear gripped him. Everything he'd seen of Aja and her crusade to save Brooklyn and Seneca from this faceless foe made Brooklyn's words resound inside his hollow chest as truth. Aja wouldn't save herself, so he'd have to.

Chapter 23

Aja felt her phone vibrate in her back pocket as she chopped salad fixings and placed them in a decorative pattern inside the oversize bowl in front of her. She put the knife down and wiped her hands quickly on a nearby hand towel before she retrieved her phone. She smiled as Mat Ryan's name flashed across her screen. "Mat, how are you this late afternoon?"

"Good. But I'm more concerned about you. It's all over town that the sheriff was at your house night before last. Is everything all right? Did something happen with Brooklyn and Seneca?"

Aja bit her lip to keep from cursing the Fresh Springs gossip mill. "Everything is fine, Mat. Brooklyn and Seneca are great. We had a minor disturbance on the ranch that had nothing to do with the ladies. We handled it, and the sheriff came to take a routine report and left shortly after."

"Are you sure? If the women are posing a threat, we can revisit moving them."

Aja took a deep breath. This was exactly what she was afraid of. She didn't want Brooklyn and Seneca displaced or, worse, sent back to prison because of some faceless phantom who'd decided terrorizing her land and her people would be fun.

"Mat, I do not want the women moved. They are doing an excellent job here. They're thriving. We've gotten another construction crew to finish what the last crew started. The permits are in place, the sites are already cleared, the foundations laid, and my materials are already here. They can have the work finished in about four months. Four months, Mat. That's all it will take to realize all of our hard work. Don't take that away by removing Brooklyn and Seneca from the ranch now. They need this win as much as I do."

He was quiet for a moment. So quiet, Aja pulled the phone from her ear to make certain the call was still connected. "Aja, you make a compelling argument. But as their parole officer, my job isn't only to make sure they're following all the rules but also that they're in an environment that isn't filled with criminal activity. There's been so much going on. Not to mention, you've added three live-in workers on your ranch without telling me."

She rubbed her temple, trying her best to hold on to her temper. "The terms of my contract with Pathways mentioned nothing about clearing my personnel with you. Although I am happy to take part, I still have a business to run that has nothing to do with the state or this program."

She heard him clear his throat. She was fond of Mat and treated him with respect because it made things easier for her workers. But the ranch was hers, and if she needed to remind him of that, she had no problem doing so.

"Forgive me," he said. "I didn't mean to suggest it was a requirement. We've had a wonderful working relationship until now. I'm just a little concerned about your workers. Especially that Jackson fellow. He seems rather disagreeable."

Ain't that the truth. "Let me worry about Jackson. He won't be a problem. Please, don't pull the women."

"Well, it will be evening soon, but I still need to come over today and visit with Brooklyn and Seneca because of the recent police activity. It was my intention to get out earlier in the day, but I've been swamped in my office. Depending on what they have to say, I'll make my decision based on that."

"I'm sure it will all be fine," she replied. "When you're done, drop by the main house for dinner. If you have to work so late, you might as well get a meal out of it, right?"

"Certainly. Thanks for the offer. I'll see you this evening."

Aja ended the call and returned her phone to her back pocket before she could throw it across the room. That damn Jackson and his bullish ways had Mat ready to pull the plug on all the work her employees had done. "Not on my watch."

After a few cleansing breaths, she retrieved her phone and dialed one of the numbers Jackson had given her for the men watching her front gate. After the first ring, the call connected. "Hello."

"Hello, this is Aja Everett, the owner of Restoration Ranch. Is this Mr."—she paused long enough to switch back to the text Jackson had sent, scouring for a name—"Pruitt?"

"Yes, ma'am. How can I help you?"

"I'm expecting a visitor. His name is Mr. Mat Ryan. Mr. Ryan has an open invitation. Please add him to your security clearance list."

"Certainly, ma'am."

"Thanks for your help. Have a nice day."

She disconnected the call while walking toward the door, grabbing her hat from a nearby coatrack. She had a few more hours of daylight before it would be time for dinner. Since the rest of this day had gone to crap, she might as well find something productive to do beyond these walls. Otherwise, she might find herself tempted to shake some sense into the lawman invading her life.

She stepped outside and saw strangers still traipsing across her land. She'd had about enough of this situation she was in; the last thing she wanted was to engage with more people who were a direct response to the mayhem in her world.

She walked toward the woodshed. There was a slight chill in the air. At this late hour of the afternoon, that spoke of temperature dips in their future. Their woodshed was full, waiting for the winter months to approach, and natural gas would supply most of their heating needs anyway. But having extra kindling around during a power outage brought on by a random storm was always a plus. So she walked inside the shed to retrieve her ax and gloves, then went back outside to the wide tree stump they used for chopping.

She pulled the tarp back on the pile of logs and grabbed one, standing it in the stump's middle and picturing Jackson's face on it. She pulled her ax back and let it fly in an overhead swing, splitting the log clean in two. The sound of the wood cracking sent relief sparking through her. Eager to feel more of it, she repeated the steps until her skin prickled with the sheen of sweat from her labor, and she no longer desired to split Jackson's head open like a melon.

"You're either cold as hell or mad as hell the way you're swinging that ax. Which is it?"

Aja turned around to find Colton leaning against her woodshed with a corner of his mouth slightly turned up into a grin. "Isn't the point of working with your hands getting to burn through a little natural aggression in a positive way?"

"I guess," he hedged. "But I sure wouldn't want to be the person you were imagining every time you swung that ax. You're scary good with that thing."

She laughed, and he joined her, and she felt better. The wood chopping had helped her, but the giggling she was doing at the moment almost made her forget what she was mad about in the first place. Almost.

"Let me guess, the big, bad sulking Ranger that's been barking orders all day at everyone is getting on your nerves too?"

"He has been extra barky today, hasn't he?"

Colton chuckled. "He's been all over Storm and me."

"Then I'm certain he wouldn't want you slacking off here with me." She paused and glared at Colton for a moment. "Or did he send you out here to babysit me?"

Colton cocked his head to the side. "Kinda. He relieved me for a long overdue break. He asked that I check in on you while I was headed back in this direction." He moved closer to her, clearing off the shards left from her chopping, and sat on the stump. "I know Jackson can be a bit much sometimes, but he really is trying to protect you. And if he's being such a pain in the ass that he's got a delicate flower like you out here chopping wood like it's an Olympic sport, it's only because he's worried."

"You're saying that because he's your friend."

Colton shook his head. "No, I'm saying it because it's true. The situation you've found yourself in isn't a good one. Jackson is doing everything he knows to keep you safe. So keep that in mind while you're plotting his murder."

Colton tipped his hat and headed back toward the cabin he shared with Storm. The man had said maybe five words to her since the Rangers showed up on the ranch. But his insight into her dilemma with Jackson was profound. Jackson was taking his job seriously. She honestly should let him do it. But she couldn't. Not when it meant jeopardizing Brooklyn and Seneca and all the work they'd put into rebuilding their lives.

"You're gonna be pissed about my decision, Ranger. But you'll have to deal with it."

Chapter 24

AFTER SLIDING THE LASAGNA TRAYS INTO THE OVEN, AJA SAT down again to catch up on balancing the ranch's books. The physical work of chopping wood had burned some of the frustration and restlessness she was carrying out of her system. Her mind was finally clear enough to make sense of the numbers in front of her.

They were in good standing. Even with the added expense of hiring a larger construction crew to get the work done in half the time. Good, quick work was what they needed to get these cabins up and ready for inspections before the upcoming travel season.

As she wrote the last digit in her balance column, she heard a knock on the front door. She looked at her watch before whispering, "You're a little early, Mat." She opened the door ready to greet the parole officer but found her uncle and aunt standing on the other side.

"Aunt Jo, Uncle Ricky." She grabbed them into a collective hug. "What are you doing here?"

"Well, last I checked, I lived here, chile. We knocked 'cause we didn't want to scare you none with all that's been going on." Her aunt Jo kissed her on the ball of her cheek and motioned for Aja to step aside and let her in.

"We wanted to check on you." Her uncle followed behind her aunt. "Jackson called to tell me about the attack. Why did I have to hear it from him to find out what was going on, Aja? You're my niece. It should've come from you."

Aja was caught in that strange place of being an adult while trying to remain respectful to her elders when they were getting on her nerves. She started counting backward from ten in her head and clenched her teeth to keep from letting something she would regret later slip out of her mouth. Her aunt must have seen the tight set of her jaw as a sign of Aja's struggle, because she waved a dismissive hand at her uncle.

"Leave this chile alone, Ricky. She called me. You were in court all day, and I didn't want to leave a message like that with your clerk. Jackson got to you 'fore I could. All that's important is she's all right."

Her aunt's reprimand took some of the air out of her uncle's displeasure. His shoulders dropped a little and his eyes softened as he looked at her.

"Are you all right?" He touched a comforting hand to Aja's arm, and any remaining anger she had slipped away.

"Other than a few bruises, I'm fine. Jackson found me in time."

"And you didn't want me to bring him in on this case. Thank God I had more sense than to listen to your foolishness."

Aja tried to remember her overprotective uncle loved her. His need to keep her safe went deeper than his irksome insistence on bringing in the Rangers to investigate. She might not have liked it, but in this case, his pushiness had saved her life.

"I'm grateful Jackson was here, Uncle Ricky. But that doesn't change the problem he poses for my workers. Until the attack, he was convinced they caused my troubles. But even if he believes me, his presence is interfering with their lives."

Aunt Jo crossed her arms against her chest as she settled into the couch. "How so? It's not like he can send them back to prison without cause. You just said he doesn't suspect them any longer."

"He doesn't. At least I don't think he does since he keeps referring to the attacker as a he. But Jackson is freaked about the attack. He's upping the security on the ranch. I'm sure you saw the guards posted at the front gate." They both nodded. "That was all him."

"Good," her uncle chimed in, shaking a pointed finger to reinforce his approval. "You were gonna have to secure this place anyway before you opened. It should've been the first thing on your to-do list when you came down here."

"Uncle Ricky. Aunt Jo lived out here for years with no fancy security system."

"Your aunt also had a bunch of ranch hands living on the property. There's safety in numbers, Aja. Now it's just the two of you—"

"Women? Is that what you were going to say?"

Her uncle took a deep breath and shook his head. "No. I was going to say it's just the two of you together." The lines of his face softened into that tender expression he always used with her as a child, and Aja's heart constricted a little from the force of the love that kindness had gifted her with over the years. "Aja, me wanting to keep you safe has nothing to do with you being a woman. You and your aunt aren't the first women to run this place. Your mama, our mother, our great-grandmother all ran the ranch without the help of a man. I know you can do this. My only concern here is your safety."

"I'm sorry, Uncle Ricky. I understand. Things have been a little tense around here." Another knock on the door caught her attention. "It's probably Mat. I'd better answer that."

Aja stood and walked to the door, pulling her shoulders back, getting ready for the battle she knew Mat's presence in her home would bring.

She opened the door to a smiling Mat, his glasses pushed high on the bridge of his nose and his smile wide across his face. "Hi, Aja. You ready for our visit?"

As ready as I'll ever be. "Sure, come on in. Dinner will be on the table in a few minutes."

Chapter 25

Jackson walked into the house tired, filthy, and satisfied with the progress made in securing the ranch. The three access points were fenced off and the security cameras were up. There was still a mountain of work left to do, but at least they'd accomplished the day's task.

Jackson leaned against the back door for a moment, trying to shake the fatigue in his bones. Running around on the land to check the progress of the crews had taken more energy than he'd had to give. A shower and one of Aja's delicious meals would be the perfect way to end this frantic day.

The sound of laughter coming from the great room made him push off the door and head down the hall to see what all the ruckus was. He smiled when he found Aja sitting on the couch, her head thrown back in laughter. It was a shocking sight. Not that he hadn't seen her smile in his short time on the ranch. But the only time he'd seen her this relaxed had been those fleeting moments when she'd allowed him to touch her body.

His eyes traveled down the length of her seated form until he saw a hand on her knee. Jackson felt his tired muscles tensing and immediately chastised himself. *She isn't yours. She doesn't belong to you.* Yeah, he could tell himself that, but somehow it didn't stop the flame of anger from swelling in the pit of his belly.

He tracked the hand back to its owner and clenched his jaw so tightly, he thought he might have damaged something. There, sitting cozy next to Aja, touching Aja, was Mat Ryan. *Son of a bitch.*

Jackson's hands curled into tight fists on their own as he swallowed the hard pill sitting in the middle of his dry throat. He wanted to fight, and he might have given in to that barbaric desire if he hadn't glimpsed movement to the right of the room.

He blinked, trying his best to clear his vision. He saw Judge Henry sitting with a woman who, if Jackson's assessment of their shared almond-shaped eyes and high, round cheeks was accurate, must be Aja's aunt Jo, sitting and laughing at something Jackson had missed.

Jackson heard his name in the distance and returned his attention to Aja. She was smiling, but her eyes seemed to question him as they darted back and forth, as if she were scanning him for answers. "Jackson, is everything all right?"

"Everything's fine." His answer was direct, absent any of the familiarity they'd come to share. "Wanted to give you an update on the work that went on today. Could I pull you away from your *company* for a few moments?"

Aja must have caught his meaning because he saw the brief tick in her jaw before she painted a polite smile on her face. "Sure. Excuse me, everyone. This won't take but a moment."

She stood and walked into the hall, gesturing for him to follow her with the wave of her hand. She headed toward the kitchen in the back of the house, but Jackson lightly touched her shoulder, shaking his head when she turned around to look at him. "Upstairs, please."

"Why, are you afraid you won't be able to keep your voice down in my kitchen?"

"Exactly."

She rolled her eyes so hard, Jackson had to wonder if she was on the verge of popping something vital. By the looks of it, she was as displeased with him as he was with her. When they made it upstairs, she went to open the door on her own, and he reached over her, moving her hand out of the way and opening the door instead. She might be pissed with him, and he with her, but there was no need to forget his home training.

In the center of the guest room with her arms folded over her chest, she worked her hard stare into a full-on glare. He motioned for her to take a seat, but she continued to stand there, staring at him. Her beautiful eyes were bright, the fire of her anger transforming them from their rich, soothing brown into something like a dazzling chocolate opal. His body responded to that fire, and he was this close to forgetting why he'd brought her upstairs in the first place. *Focus, Jackson.*

If he weren't so mad at her, his mouth would be hitched in a grin. She was sexy, even when she was being as hardheaded as his daddy's old mule. But now wasn't the time for smiles or for satisfying the need simmering beneath his skin.

No, now was the time to lay down the law. The problem was, Aja knew the law better than most, and Jackson knew from the sharp set of her jaw that she was ready to tell him to go straight to hell before he'd even started the conversation. *No sense in dragging this out. Let's get to it.*

"What do you have me up here for, Jackson?"

"Aja, don't play dumb. It doesn't suit you. You know damn well why I asked you to come up here. Why is Mat sitting in your house?"

"I don't think that's a question that requires answering. I explained his presence in my home the first day you arrived here."

"Aja, I asked you to limit his access to the ranch. He could be the person who had his hands wrapped around your neck two nights ago."

She shook her head and waved a dismissive hand in the air.

"You know damn well your problem with Mat has shit to do with my attack and everything to do with your jealousy."

The truth of her accusation struck him in the gut, and it was all he could do to keep from folding over at the center. "I'm not jealous."

She lifted a skeptical brow and pointed a finger at him. "That's bullshit. Every time he gets anywhere near me, you act the ass. I watched you watching him touch me—a platonic, meaningless touch, by the way. I'm surprised you didn't melt the man into a bubbling puddle of goo with the angry laser beams you were directing at him."

She was right again, but damn if he would concede that fact right now. He needed to get the conversation back under control. His control.

"It didn't look all that platonic from where I was standing."

She huffed, as if she were trying to keep her blood pressure down. By the exhausted sound she made, he didn't think it was working, though.

"That man has no interest in me. I'm not the one he's sweet on—Brooklyn is."

Jackson's mouth hung open. "He's dealing with Brooklyn?"

Aja shook her head. "I didn't say anything about him seeing Brooklyn. I said he's attracted to her. He helped Brooklyn a lot when she got out. I think they both developed a bit of a crush on each other as a result. But Mat wouldn't cross the line with her as long as she was his parolee."

"And you believe him?"

"Yeah," she answered. "He used to have separate meetings with Seneca and Brooklyn. But shortly after Brooklyn started living and working here, he stopped their individual visits. He never allows himself to be alone with her. He really is a decent guy who's just trying to do the right thing."

Jackson stood with his arms crossed and lips pushed out into a petulant pout. "Maybe. But I still don't like him touching you."

She waved her finger in front of his face until she was certain she had his attention. She hadn't needed to do that because Aja always had his attention, even when she didn't know it.

"Newsflash, Jackson—you are the one who said we couldn't have a relationship. I would've gladly made it more. Hell, as good as we were together, I would've considered making it last beyond your time here on Restoration. But that's not what you said you wanted. All you offered was a night. And since I'm not about begging a man to give me his time, that's all I accepted.

"You were clear on your boundaries, so let me be clear on mine. This is my home, my land, and my business. Mat plays an integral role in that as Seneca and Brooklyn's parole officer. You will respect my decision that he is allowed on the ranch. Just because I spent a night with you doesn't give you rein over my life."

"I don't get it." He threw his hands up in the air in frustration. "You will take on anyone, including the sheriff, to protect Seneca's and Brooklyn's rights, but you won't lift a finger to protect yourself. Why are they more important than you?"

Her shoulders drooped a little, as if some of the fight was leaving her. "Because sometimes you help people so you can live with yourself, so your own life can have meaning."

"Live with yourself? You were a lawyer for debutantes and celebrities. What could you have done that requires this kind of atonement?"

She looked down at the floor for a moment, shaking her head before she looked at him again. There was sadness there. Something so serious, it made goose bumps rise underneath his skin.

"I'm not perfect, Jackson. I've never claimed to be. And I hope that's not how you see me. We all have things in our past we're not proud of. I'm simply trying to be a better version of myself. And the best way I know to do that is to help people like Seneca and Brooklyn reestablish their lives."

He groaned, trying to hold his temper at her refusal to see her self the way he did. Aja might not think she was perfect. But in his eyes, aside from her stubborn streak, she was about as perfect as he'd come across.

"I know you want to help them. But let me tell you, as worthy as they are to live their lives in peace like the next person, you are the only one I care about saving. You are the one in immediate danger. Not them. So maybe I am a little possessive about you, more than I have the right to be. But I make no qualms about admitting you are all I care about in this scenario.

"Perhaps I can't give you a relationship, Aja. But that has no bearing on the way you've burrowed yourself under my skin, the way you've made your presence and well-being a priority. Even if I can't have you for my own, I'll be damned if I'll see anything happen to you. If you won't protect yourself, I must. And the only authority I need to protect you is my badge, and whatever this thing is that's been sitting inside my chest since the moment I laid eyes on you. I'll do what I have to in order to keep you safe."

She continued to stare at him, her vision roaming over his face, looking for something unspoken. If it was the truth, she wouldn't have to look far, because Jackson meant every word he'd said.

"Jackson," she huffed as she dropped her arms to her sides. "I don't know how you can be such an asshole one minute and so endearing the next."

He dared to let a smile cross his lips as he took slow steps toward her. He placed a careful hand on her cheek. They might have shared each other's bodies, but it was obvious he hadn't earned the right to touch her at will. Besides, knowing she wanted him, that she would allow him to enter her personal space, was so alluring. He lived for moments like this one, where she answered his request by burrowing into his touch. "It's part of my charm."

"It has to be." She stepped closer until she was pressed against him, pulling his hand from her face and wrapping it around her waist as she laid her head on his chest. "Otherwise, that cut I got on my head when the barn exploded did more damage than I realized. Because for some unexplainable reason, I keep wanting to end up in your arms."

He tightened his hold on her, reveling in the way her nearness soothed and excited him at the same time. What he wouldn't give to keep them like this all the time, secluded away from the outside world. They fit together perfectly when it was just them. When his job and her crusade to save everyone else weren't in the way, there was harmony between them. It was selfish of him, and he had no problems admitting that to himself or anyone else who would listen, but he wanted more of this. More of her.

He placed a kiss on the top of her head, and she looked up at him. The fire in her eyes had cooled to a sexy simmer instead of the angry blaze he'd witnessed before. He leaned down, taking the moment to press hungry lips to hers. When she responded with a languid moan, he deepened the kiss, licking at her full bottom lip, demanding entrance into her mouth.

Aja was no wilting flower. She met each demand with one of her own, and soon, instead of arguing like two fools, they were standing in the middle of the room, tongues tangling, fighting to taste as much of each other as possible.

He felt her pull away first and chased her mouth with his until she took a step away from him. "I would so love to see where this could go, but I've got lasagna coming out of the oven in"—she looked down at her watch, then back at him—"two minutes. And Cajun lasagna isn't a thing, so I have to save it from burning to a crisp. And also, you're filthy. I love a rugged cowboy as much as the next girl, but 'smelling like outside' is not as tantalizing an aroma as one might think."

He reached for her, and she dodged his hand by stepping to the side, barely out of his grip. "Are you telling me I stink?"

She tugged her bottom lip playfully between her teeth. "You said it."

"You could help me get clean."

"I could, but the lasagna would burn." She looked at him again, something wicked flaring in her eyes. "It would also violate that one-night rule you instituted. And I wouldn't want to contribute to you breaking your own rules."

He closed his eyes. Her words were as sharp as a slap across the face. "That was my rule, wasn't it?" He opened his eyes again to see the gleam of amusement brightening her features. She liked this. She wasn't the least bit concerned that her entertainment came at his expense.

"It certainly wasn't mine." She circled him, appraising him as she took her fill. "I'm all for indulging in the things I enjoy. Denying yourself the things that make you happy is masochistic, in my opinion. And masochism ain't my thing. Although since I met you, I can't lie and say the whole bondage thing hasn't crossed my mind. Imagining what you could do to a girl with your handcuffs has been entertaining, to say the least."

He groaned so loud, he was certain the people downstairs could hear it. "You are trying to kill me."

She smiled, then walked to the door. "No, Jackson. I'm trying to show you the opportunities that lie in front of you. All you have to do is take them. Now, clean up and get downstairs. I'll have a thick slice of lasagna served up for you when you get there."

She left him standing alone in the room, wondering what the hell had happened. He'd dragged her up here to bend her to his will. But instead of getting her to agree to keep Mat off the ranch, she had him rethinking the one-night moratorium he'd placed on their lovemaking. *Like you haven't been rethinking that stupid rule of yours since she let you slide inside her.*

He ran a hand through his tight curls and shook his head. Once again, the sexy lady lawyer had used her skills to turn the tables. And deep down, he wasn't so certain he was all that upset about it.

Chapter 26

JACKSON HAD NEVER BEEN SO HAPPY FOR A MEAL TO END. Sitting across from Mat, he found fighting to keep the scowl off his face harder than he'd thought. Even after Aja's declaration that the man had a thing for Brooklyn, the memory of his hand on Aja's knee didn't sit well with Jackson.

Quit it, Dean. You're only mad because you're being a possessive asshole.

It was the truth. He wouldn't lie to himself by saying it wasn't. Jackson was a brute for sure. But jealous and possessive weren't traits he usually exhibited. He didn't walk around marking his territory. But his inability to do so with Aja was making him suspicious of a man who wasn't even interested in her.

"Jackson, may I have a moment on the back porch?"

Jackson turned to see Aja's uncle standing at the counter. He followed the judge out the back door and looked around to make certain they were alone. Satisfied they were, Jackson waited for him to speak his peace.

"I see you've taken her safety seriously. There was security to greet us at the front gates. Is the entire ranch secure yet?"

"Not all of it." Jackson huffed. "This is a big place. It will take at least a week or more to get the ranch covered in weatherproof cameras. But the crews are working hard. I'm keeping an eye on Aja, and my men are watching the ladies that work for her."

"So you don't think it's them?"

Jackson couldn't definitively say what he thought. Other than them being ex-convicts, there wasn't a clear motive why Seneca or Brooklyn would terrorize Aja. "As of now, they're clean. My men were actually with them when Aja's attack occurred. We have no reason to believe the culprit is one of them."

The judge scratched at the back of his head. "What's the next step, Jackson?"

"We prepare and wait. He was bold enough to step into her room. He won't stay away after that. And when he returns, I'll make him wish he hadn't."

The judge slapped him on his shoulder and turned toward the door. "That's exactly why I placed you here. To make whoever did this pay."

The sound of footsteps and voices entering the kitchen filtered out onto the back porch, bringing their conversation to an immediate end. Jackson followed the judge back inside the kitchen where Mat stood next to Aja as she sliced healthy helpings of pineapple coconut cake and placed them on dessert plates on the counter.

"Mr. Dean." Jackson's gaze followed Mat's voice. "We didn't get much of a chance to chat at dinner. Aja tells us you're helping get the ranch ready for opening next spring."

Jackson allowed a long pause to linger in the air before responding. "It's my job to keep things running smoothly for Aja. It's why she hired me."

"How…um…how long have you been a ranch hand?"

Jackson squinted as he tried to figure out what Mat was after. The small talk was obvious and awkward. He'd never said more than a few words at a time to Jackson before now.

Probably because you're always silently threatening to do him bodily harm.

Aja must have worried that Jackson's inner asshole was about to show up, because she cut the last and largest slice of the cake, plating it and pushing it in front of Jackson.

Their eyes connected, and he could see the bright twinkle of mischief in her eyes. She was bribing him with cake. It was ridiculous—this woman actually thought a thick slice of the sweet confection could convince Jackson to play nicely with Mat.

He stared at Aja for a moment more and then down at the cake. He felt the decided tear in his armor when she slid a napkin with a fork on top of it next to his hand.

She was wicked. The teasing smile on her face was a clear indicator that Aja knew exactly what she was doing. He surrendered by picking up the fork and cutting into the moist layers of yellow cake, pineapple, meringue, and coconut. When he slid the fork into his mouth, they both knew he'd agreed to her terms. *Don't be an ass to Mat, and you can have as much cake as you want.*

Without drawing attention to herself, Aja stood next to him, politely bumping her shoulder into his. It was a simple, playful gesture, but it somehow felt right, like it was supposed to be this way. The two of them in cahoots, banding together, providing strength and comfort to each other, clicked inside him like lock to key.

Jackson didn't question why it felt so good to be near her, to have her touch him. He simply settled into it. Knowing he would have it for a limited time and that he could only have it in small doses while he was on her ranch, he decided right there to let himself enjoy it. So while they pressed their arms together like teenagers, hiding while still in plain sight, Jackson stared at Mat and spoke. "I've worked on farms and ranches since I was old enough to hold a shovel." It was the truth. And more importantly, it was all Mat needed to know about him.

"I'm glad Aja found qualified people to help get this place on track." The parole officer gave Jackson what looked like a nervous but friendly smile. "With all the progress Aja's reported, I've no doubt you'll have the ranch in working condition in no time."

Jackson gave Mat a polite smile that earned him a "friendly" brush of Aja's arm against his. Jackson stole a quick glance at her and delighted in the playful smile she was wearing. He was about to take another bite when he felt his phone vibrating in his pocket. He wiped his hand on his napkin and pulled it free.

Colton's number flashing on the screen made the sweet and tangy taste of the dessert on his lips turn sour. He'd texted both Colton and Storm that he would be in this ridiculous dinner and he wasn't to be disturbed unless it was an emergency. Neither of them would disobey that order without cause.

"I'm sorry, everyone. I need to take this." He made his way out of the kitchen, slightly beyond the back porch where he assumed he couldn't be easily overheard. "Hello."

"We've got a problem on the east bank. Cameras caught an intruder going into the original family homestead."

"Shit, that's the next section of the land the security crew is supposed to be working on. We thought the rough terrain and the depth of the creek wouldn't make it easily passable."

He rubbed the back of his neck where the muscles were tensing.

"Yeah, we're fortunate they at least got eyes set up nearby even if it's not fenced off yet. Otherwise, we wouldn't have known."

Jackson was never more grateful that his father was so anal and determined to do a job right. "Where are Seneca and Brooklyn?"

"They're with Storm. We were all having dinner when I checked the camera footage on my phone. He's gonna stay with them; me and the security detail are on our way to track whoever this is."

"Good. They're safe with Storm." Jackson took a moment to let the relief settle in his belly. If they were with him, that meant they weren't a part of this and were safely tucked away from the danger. Both scenarios helped his case and, more importantly, meant Aja wouldn't be hurt by the outcome.

"I also sent two of the security personnel to the house to keep watch over Aja in case you wanted to back me up."

Jackson saw one of the security guards coming up the back way and took his cue to leave. "I'll meet you there." He suddenly remembered the pride in Aja's face as she told him the history of her ancestor and the sacrifice of blood, sweat, and tears he put into this land. "Colton, whoever this is, don't let him destroy that old house. If you need to move in before I get there, don't fire any weapons if you can help it."

"Sure thing, Boss."

"Good," Jackson replied. "I'm on my way."

Jackson met one of the security guards halfway down the path. "Don't leave that back porch unless I tell you to. Tell your partner to do the same at the front."

A quick "Roger that" was all the confirmation Jackson waited for before he jumped into his truck at the end of the pathway, heading toward where the intruder was last seen. The only thing there would be the original homestead Aja's ancestor built. But for someone looking to hurt and harass Aja, demolishing the structure would definitely accomplish that.

He called Aja's cell phone and prayed she picked up. When she did, he didn't bother with a greeting. He simply said, "Keep everyone in the house. There's a guard on the front and back porches. Stay there until I get back."

"Jackson, what's going on?"

"I don't have time to explain, Aja. Promise me you won't leave the house until I return."

He heard her intake of breath over the phone and prepared himself for the argument to come. "Promise you'll be careful, Jackson."

Silence filled the line, and he thought for a moment she might have disconnected the call. But then he heard her call his name again, the last syllable spoken higher, as if she were asking a question, and he realized she was waiting for him to respond.

She's worried about me. He wasn't certain what to do with that revelation. Outside of his family, he'd never had that. Not even when he was married.

"I promise, Aja. I'll be careful." He disconnected the line and slowed down as he neared the original homestead, cutting the engine and the lights and letting the vehicle coast in neutral until he parked behind a thicket of brush in the back of the house. He pulled a pistol from his glove compartment, checked the amount of ammunition in it, and headed for the gathering group of men kneeling quietly behind the cover of trees.

He made his way over to where Colton leaned against a thick tree trunk. In a hushed tone, he asked, "We have eyes on the subject yet?"

"Yeah. He slipped into the house through an opened side window."

"Good. Let's flush him out. I want him alive, and I want as little damage done to that property as possible. It's important to Aja and her family. You have any tear gas on you?"

"I'm not SWAT—why would I have that on me?"

Jackson lifted a suspicious brow, and Colton rolled his eyes before reaching into the black duffel next to him and handing Jackson a metal canister.

"I hope you have a plan to explain why you're walking around with this in your report."

"Sure do: my superior asked me for it."

Jackson shook his head as he pulled a small flashlight from his back pocket and shone its light on the canister. It was a smoke grenade, not tear gas, and Jackson was happy about that. Neither they nor the security detail helping them had gas masks, and Jackson wasn't looking forward to his face and eyes burning.

He handed the canister back to Colton. "Get closer and toss it; your throwing arm is better than mine."

"My everything is better than yours, Dean."

"Including your ability to court trouble." He slapped Colton on the back and used hand signals to communicate to the men who were too far away to hear their whispered plan.

When everyone nodded, they all inched closer to the rickety structure. Jackson gave Colton the signal, and he ran toward the side of the house, throwing the lit smoke grenade inside and then returning to the safety of cover in the tree line.

Billows of smoke seeped from the opened window. Soon they saw the back door open, and through the cloud of smoke, a figure covered in black clothing emerged. The masked person fell through the opened door as he tried to get away from the smoke.

Jackson gave the go-ahead, and Colton and the rest of the men surrounded the intruder, pointing guns and flashlights at him and yelling for him to get on the ground.

The suspect raised his hands in surrender and carefully walked down the creaking back porch stairs, then fell to the ground on his knees. Jackson holstered his weapon and removed a set of zip-tie cuffs from his pocket. He shoved the suspect to the ground, pulled his arms behind his back, and secured them with the ties. Finally, he yanked the man to his feet, grabbing the ski mask covering his face.

Jackson stared into the face of a young white man, no more than twenty years old, closely scrutinizing his face and drawing a complete blank. "Now, who the fuck are you?"

Chapter 27

Aja paced back and forth in her kitchen, clutching her cell phone in her hand, waiting for it to ring. Nearly forty-five minutes had passed since Jackson called with his cryptic message. He'd been direct and abrupt, two things that weren't necessarily unusual about the Ranger. However, the sense of urgency in his message and his tone still made Aja tremble with unspoken fear.

Something was wrong, terribly wrong. She didn't need to read minds to know that. Something was happening on her land that was more than likely dangerous, and her instinct to protect those around her was reaching near-panic levels.

"If you don't stop pacing like that, you will wear a hole in the floor. Not to mention, you're making your aunt and uncle worry."

Aja looked up to see Mat standing in the kitchen doorway, leaning against the doorjamb. "I don't mean to, but I'm worried." She'd left her three guests in the great room to prevent them from seeing how concerned she was for Jackson's safety.

"Didn't you tell me you stress baked? I'm sure whatever's going on out there will be over by the time you whip up something fabulous in your oven."

"Not this time," she answered. Not with Jackson out in the darkness, possibly facing the person who'd attacked her.

Mat moved farther into the kitchen, sitting at the counter and sharing a friendly smile with her. "You really care about him, don't you?"

Mat's question was a reasonable one. She cared about Jackson. He'd come here to help her—that alone warranted her gratitude and concern. But as Mat's eyes darted back and forth as if he were trying to read her answer in the lines of her face and her body language, she knew her feelings for Jackson were more than mere gratitude.

You don't sleep with someone because you're grateful, Aja. No, she hadn't shared her body with Jackson because she was grateful to him. She'd crossed that line with him because she'd wanted him, because she'd connected to something inside him that bound her to him in indescribable ways.

"He's my employee. You know how I am about my people. Messing with them is like messing with me. This situation is dangerous. I don't want him to get hurt because of me."

"I know," he replied. "Your loyalty to the folks who work for you is legend around these parts. It's one of the reasons Brooklyn loves working here so much." Aja saw a far-off look fall across his face and she ached for him. She didn't think she'd be able to see Jackson as much as Mat saw Brooklyn and deny her attraction to him.

"When did she tell you that?"

"The last time I was here to see her and Seneca." His mouth bent into a sweet smile. It was something he did whenever he mentioned Brooklyn. "She said she hopes you let her stay beyond her parole. I think she's beginning to finally settle into her life here."

Aja was about to respond to Mat when the sound of the back door opening and closing pulled her attention from him. At the sight of Jackson filling the room—bold, strong, and unharmed beyond initial detection—she pulled away from Mat and headed directly for the subject of her thoughts.

"Jackson, you're all right." She didn't give Jackson a chance to answer. Instead, she launched herself at him, wrapping her arms around his middle, clinging to him with all the might she could muster, demanding a full-body hug in the middle of her kitchen floor without thought or concern for who could witness her actions.

She didn't care. Jackson was safe, and she wouldn't have to bear another mark on her conscience.

Before she could stop herself, tears flowed and her shoulders shook. Maybe it really was her relief he was all right. Maybe it was everything she'd endured since the sabotage and her attack finally crashing down around her. Whatever it was, she held on to him as tight as she could, pressing herself into his hard frame, rejoicing because he was still with her.

His arms encircled her in a warm cocoon. His hand stroking her head as he held her to chest, his heartbeat a strong and delightfully loud rhythm in her ear, he bent down and whispered, "It's over, darlin.'"

Those words made her hold him tighter. Through her tears and the melodious tune of his heart beating, Aja heard Jackson ask Mat to give them a minute.

For a brief second, she felt bad. She'd forgotten about the poor man as soon as Jackson stepped in the room. But that didn't last long. She couldn't do anything but focus on Jackson being back in her arms.

She assumed Mat had left because Jackson's lips brushed the top of her head, pouring his heat into her to dispel the cold chill of fear. "You don't have to worry anymore, Aja. We got him."

Her river of tears slowed enough to allow her an attempt at coherent speech. She pulled far enough out of his embrace to look up at him. "I wasn't concerned about it being over. I was worried about you. I knew something bad had happened, but I didn't know what. After what he did to me upstairs, I was so worried that he'd do worse to you."

He pressed a sweet kiss to her lips and stroked the side of her face with his thumb in slow, soothing movements. "I'm fine, really. This was probably the least dangerous takedown I've ever experienced. No one was hurt."

She dropped her shoulders and used the backs of her hands to wipe away the tearstains on her wet cheeks as she moved out of his embrace. "So it's really over?"

He smiled in response. He looked around the room again and curled a finger at her, silently asking her to step outside on the back porch with him. When the door closed behind them, he turned to her, speaking in hushed tones. "The danger is over. We've apprehended him, we'll take him in, and the courts will handle the rest. But first, I need you to follow me to Austin. You're gonna need to pick him out of a lineup and fill out some paperwork. I know it's a trek and it's already evening, but are you up for that?"

"Yeah," she answered. "Let me tell my aunt, uncle, and Mat we're headed out, and they can head on home."

She stepped closer to him and gave him another tight hug. When she was satisfied, she moved out of his embrace, walking toward the back door, but stopped halfway there. She turned around, heading back into his embrace, and squeezed him with all her might one more time as she whispered, "Thank you," into his chest.

———

Jackson watched as Aja walked through the back door and headed into the house. The band of swirling emotions pulled taut around his chest, restricting the flow of much-needed air.

The takedown had been simple. Not much drama or heightened

danger. Whoever it was in their custody had no weapons on him. If Jackson wasn't aware of all the menacing things the suspect had pulled on Aja's land, he probably would've characterized the young man as a harmless prankster. But even knowing that, seeing Aja's reaction, the way she clung to him for reaffirmation he was safe, made his insides tingle.

Something meaningful had happened in that moment, and he was both shocked and grateful to be experiencing it.

How he'd gone forty years without ever knowing what it felt like to be treasured, needed by another person, he didn't know. But in that moment, he understood Aja's concern was born out of something special, even if he couldn't put his finger on exactly what that was.

As Aja returned to the back porch, grabbing her keys and her handbag from a nearby table, he knew beyond any doubt that everything he wanted came in the glorious package of this intelligent, compassionate woman with the killer curves and a body made to satisfy him, who was smiling at him, asking, "Are you ready, Jackson?"

For the first time in what seemed like forever, he thought he might be.

Chapter 28

"HOW MUCH LONGER BEFORE THIS LINEUP BEGINS, Jackson?"

His heavy gaze fastened on Aja as she planted herself in front of the one-way mirror with her arms crossed and her fingers tapping on her forearm. He recognized this pose was a combination of frustration mixed with apprehension.

"The prosecutor just arrived. After your ID, he'll take your statement."

She gave him a hefty dose of side-eye before turning back to the one-way mirror. "I'm a lawyer, Jackson. I know how this works. What I'm asking is why is the process taking so long? It's been hours since we arrived. The prosecutor should've been en route when you first called this in. I'd like to get home before the cock crows."

"This ain't New York, darlin'. Things don't move that fast below the Mason-Dixon."

She dropped her hands to her hips and raised a sharp eyebrow. "Stop it. This is Austin, not some rural, one-pony town. I'm sure you all have videoconferencing capabilities. My property has been vandalized, I've been attacked, and two people I care about have been implicated in all this mess. I want it over now."

Her shoulders were pulled back into a sharp line. Even though she was speaking barely above a whisper, her chest was heaving, and Jackson could see the clear signs of anxiety taking control of her.

Aja didn't do scared; she did angry. And she was about ready to blow. He placed a careful hand on her shoulder. It was the most he could offer in this setting, surrounded by his colleagues and the constant reminder he was here to do a job, not involve himself with her. "It's gonna be all right. I promise."

"Don't patronize me. Don't treat me like I'm some hysterical woman."

"I wouldn't dare. You have a right to be angry, scared, and frustrated. This joker has been doing his best to harm you and people you care about. Frankly, I'd be worse if it were me and mine."

She took a breath, and some of the tension she was carrying receded.

"This will be over soon, and you'll be back on your ranch before you know it." He tightened the hand resting on her shoulder, aching to pull her into his arms and keep her cradled there, protected from the rest of the world.

She steadied herself and returned to her perch in front of the one-way mirror. He'd settled in to watching her again when a tap on the door pulled his focus, and as the prosecutor stepped inside the room, Jackson sent up a tiny prayer. Things were about to get started, and soon she'd be able to return to the safety of her home.

This time, it would be safe, and knowing that gave Jackson more relief than it should have. She was a case; she was work. He shouldn't feel this bone-deep reassurance that spread through him like the warmth of a fire on a cold night.

Jackson turned to face the prosecutor, a tall white man with a slender build, as he stepped into the room. John Ross had two recognizable characteristics. Except for inside the courtroom, he was never seen without a Stetson covering his head, and he always played to win. So if this young punk stood any chance of leniency, it had floated out the door as Ross walked through.

"Howdy, Ranger Dean." Ross extended his hand to Jackson.

Ross was every bit the quintessential cowboy. Big hat, big belt buckle, and Jackson was pretty sure if he lifted the man's pant legs, he'd find spurs attached to the backs of his boots.

Jackson shook Ross's offered hand. "Hey, Counselor. Thanks for making it in." Jackson pointed toward Aja. "This is the complainant, Ms. Aja Everett."

Ross extended his hand to Aja. "Ms. Everett, I'm John Ross. Thank you for your patience in this matter. I have your original statement. Do you feel it needs to be amended in any way?" Aja shook her head. "Good, then after the ID, I'll question the person we have in custody, and we'll try to get you home and out of here as quickly as possible."

"Where's the defense attorney?"

"The suspect hasn't requested a lawyer yet," Jackson answered. He could see tension lines furrowing her brow. "No worries. We'll Mirandize him again before we question him to make sure he knows his rights."

Aja agreed and returned her attention to Ross. "Thank you, Mr. Ross. I want this over. I have a life I need to get back to."

Ross tipped his hat to Jackson. "What say we get this started, Ranger?"

Jackson agreed. He pressed the speaker button on a nearby desk phone and said, "Send them in," before disconnecting the call.

They all turned toward the one-way mirror and watched in silence as each man filed into the room, one behind the other, standing against the wall, each holding a number in front of himself as they faced their darkened side of the same mirror.

Aja tensed, her body pulling itself straighter and tighter, bracing against the task before her.

The intruder wore a mask during the attack. She'd never seen him. Hopefully, there was something about the suspect she'd recognize, or it would be hard to pin her attack on him.

"Are you okay? There's no pressure." Jackson stepped closer to her, hoping to impart his concern through his nearness, since he couldn't show her in any other meaningful way in the prosecutor's presence. "Take your time and tell us if you recognize anything about them."

"Number Six, I know him."

Jackson and Ross looked at each other, and then Jackson pressed the button on the intercom positioned at the side of the mirror. "Number Six, please step forward."

The nerves in his stomach loosened. She recognized the same person he'd arrested tonight. He was hoping this would turn into a positive identification.

"Where do you recognize him from, Aja? Is he the man that attacked you?"

"His name is Taylor Sullivan. He's Earl Sullivan's son. He was part of the original contractor team that worked on my ranch before his father pulled them for unsafe working conditions. Aside from all that, he's a friend of my family. I've known him all his life. I used to babysit him, for God's sake. This has to be some mistake."

Jackson pulled a notepad from his back pocket and scribbled the information down. "Is he the man that attacked you?"

She held out a hand. "I never saw his face. I don't know." She looked back at Number Six and then turned back to Jackson. "That's not a man, though. That is a sixteen-year-old boy. He's a child."

"I'm afraid the law says he's an adult, ma'am. I intend to prosecute him as such."

Aja's glare was sharp enough to slice Ross in two. The man didn't know Aja like Jackson did. He didn't understand the warning signals. If Aja's fury reached the point where she had to cross her arms or place her hands on her hips—gestures he believed were a control tactic to keep her from smacking fire out of someone—John Ross was in trouble.

Aja took a deep breath, her fight for restraint obvious in the labored sound of her actively pushing air out of her lungs, and turned toward Jackson. "The smart move would be to get that boy some representation. If Mr. Ross does in fact prosecute Taylor as an adult, you don't want the charges kicked back by the jury simply because they don't believe he's capable of this type of menacing behavior since he's a kid."

Jackson had to admit to himself she was right. As much as he wanted to see justice done, finding out the person he'd put in cuffs was this young gave him pause.

"What about height and build, Ms. Everett? Does the individual you're identifying seem similar to your attacker?"

Again she shook her head. "I don't know. I was lying down, asleep in bed when he attacked me. When Ranger Dean entered the scene, the attacker was straddling me on the bed. The Ranger dove onto the bed to get him off me, and they fell to the floor. The attacker scrambled out the balcony on all fours. I never saw him standing up."

Jackson picked up the phone on a nearby desk and waited for Maureen, their floor receptionist, to answer. "Hey, Reenie, would you escort Ms. Everett from the lineup box to my office, please? Thanks."

A few seconds later, Maureen opened the door. Aja took a deep breath, her eyes filled with sorrow and disappointment. "I'm sorry I couldn't be of more help."

"You were more help than you believe. Wait for me. I'll meet you in my office soon."

She left the room, and Maureen closed the door with a quiet click, leaving Jackson and Ross alone.

"She a friend?"

Jackson ground his teeth together before he answered. "What do you mean?"

"You seem…invested in her. Like it's important to you she's okay."

Give that man a prize.

"I wish that for every person who's been the victim of a crime. Don't you?"

Ross watched him a moment longer, then placed his hands on his Texas-sized belt buckle. "I do," he answered. "I guess if we didn't, we should all be in a different line of work. Right?"

Jackson let the breath he was holding ease out through pursed lips. "Yeah, we should," he responded. "What do you think of that ID? Think it will hold up in court?"

"I've seen weaker IDs work. But I would like to see a bit more evidence to connect him to the assault. I can probably get him to agree to a deal based on what we have now. But if this goes to court, we will probably need more."

Jackson ran his fingers through his tight curls and headed toward the door. "All right, Counselor. Let me get him into an interrogation room so I can get you that more you're talking about."

Chapter 29

AJA'S PATIENCE WAS WEARING THIN. SHE'D GONE FROM SIT-
ting at the small table in Jackson's office and tapping her fingers
against the cool metal surface to pacing back and forth across the
room.

She didn't like this. Not one bit. She was all for people being
held accountable for their actions, but this was a child. A sixteen-
year-old boy who Aja knew personally. The image of Taylor standing in that lineup didn't mesh with the mild-mannered, sweet
young man who'd worked on her ranch for the better part of the
summer. Something wasn't right.

She'd been waiting to tell Jackson that, hoping she could per-
suade him to urge the prosecutor to show a little leniency or, at
the very least, wait until Taylor had a lawyer or parent present
before he questioned him. But she knew in her gut that John Ross
wouldn't give any such boon, and he was probably in there right
now, grilling that poor child.

A child who may have attacked you.

She shook against the bristle of doubt as it brushed its way
down her spine. Nothing about her interactions with Taylor had
ever showed he was capable of that kind of rage. She had to believe
this was some kind of mistake. She refused to believe the sweet

child she'd had such a special bond with all these years could turn out to be this kind of monster.

She had to do something, try to find out what was going on. She couldn't sit idly by again, watching another child get dragged into adult court because of her.

The first time she'd been eighteen and allowed her own naïveté to keep her mouth shut while events unfolded into irreversible consequences.

"I can't let the same thing happen to Taylor. At least not without all the facts."

Aja walked toward the door to Jackson's office and stepped into the hall. She headed down the same corridor the receptionist had used to bring her there nearly twenty minutes ago. She found a sign with the word *Interrogation* in bold letters and followed the arrow.

Jackson stood leaning against a wall while his attention was fixed to a one-way mirror. When she approached him and glanced inside the room, she saw Taylor sitting on one end of a small table with his handcuffed hands shackled to the top of the table in front of him. Colton sat directly across from the boy, and the prosecutor stood in the corner of the room watching the two.

Taylor was shaking, leaning back from the table as if he was preparing to be struck, and Colton was leaning across the table, yelling, the vessels in his neck and face popping beneath the surface of his flushed skin.

"What the hell is this?"

Jackson pointed to the one-way mirror. "Colton's playing bad cop. He's putting a little fear into the boy to get him to tell us the truth."

"Jackson, that is a child. Where is his lawyer?"

"Aja, why do you think it took so long for Ross to get here?" When she shrugged he answered his own question. "He was tying up loose ends. We may be country, but we ain't stupid. We know how to handle a case."

She flinched at his response and she could see regret shine in his eyes instantly. He inhaled slowly, she assumed to gather his patience before he continued.

"Taylor's parents have been notified of his arrest. He's been brought before a magistrate who read him his rights. He said he understood them. The judge signed a judicial waiver to have this case remanded to adult court. So as far as the law is concerned, he is not a child. Unless he asks for a lawyer, I'm not required to get him one."

"Please don't do this."

"He put his hands on you, Aja. I can't ignore that. What if I hadn't been there? What if he does this to someone else?"

She shook her head and tried to keep calm even though she was angry enough to throw a chair through the one-way mirror in front of them. "Allegedly, Jackson. He allegedly put his hands on me. We don't know that. We don't have enough evidence to support that right now. Please, don't ruin this child's future based on an assumption."

Jackson rubbed the back of his neck as he stepped away from her and looked up at the ceiling. When he looked at her again, his eyes were softer, filled with more worry than anger.

"What's going on here, Aja? Why are you trying to help him? We might not have enough proof to pin your attack on him, but you know we have him dead to rights on the vandalism. Why are you trying to save him?"

Because I couldn't save her.

It was the truth, a truth she could never speak aloud to Jackson, but the truth nonetheless. "I came from a place where if you were poor or working class, the legal system ate you up and spit you out. Taylor's father might own a construction business, but he's not swimming in cash. After Earl was forced to walk out on the renovations at the ranch, he took a big financial hit. He's a small-town local doing his best to feed his family and pay his workers enough to feed theirs. Paying for more than competent legal representation would bankrupt him."

"I'm trying to protect you, Aja. If you haven't forgotten, that's my job."

"Well, defending people and protecting them from the unfairness of the legal system is mine. As of right now, I'm asserting myself as Taylor Sullivan's attorney of record. If you don't allow me to speak with my client privately, I will have this entire division strung up by the balls. Do I make myself clear, Ranger?"

The lines of his face tightened, and his lips pulled into a flat line. "Don't do this, Aja. Don't sabotage your own case. Don't fight me."

"Are you going to let me speak to my client, or am I going to have to file a formal complaint with a judge, then call the press and tell them how your division is attempting to railroad a sixteen-year-old boy?"

The dark circles of his eyes flamed with fire as he stared at her. He didn't utter another word, simply banged his hand on the thick mirror, and then opened the interrogation room door.

When she stepped inside, she looked at Taylor and said, "Stop talking."

"Ms. Everett." John Ross stepped from his perch in the corner and walked toward her. "This isn't the place for you. I'm going to have to ask you to leave us to our interrogation of the suspect."

"Your suspect is my client. Clear the room, and turn off the speaker—I want to talk to him in private."

When Ross looked beyond her, she knew he was focusing on Jackson. "What the hell is going on here?"

"She's a lawyer, Ross, and she's taken young Mr. Sullivan on as a client."

John Ross stared her down. She could tell by the way his shoulders hunched up with his hands on his hips that he was a man who wasn't often challenged. Too bad for him that Aja had made a career of challenging the status quo.

"What the hell do you think you're doing? You can't come in here and sabotage your own case."

"I am the victim. I have every right to refuse to press charges against Taylor. So either you back off and let me represent him, or I'll drop the charges."

"I don't need you to take this case to a grand jury, Ms. Everett." If words were daggers, Ross's would've sliced her to pieces. "Even without you, I can still have him indicted."

"True," she responded. "But we both know your case won't go well at trial when the victim takes the stand for the defense."

Ross tried to stare her down, but when she folded her arms and tapped her foot in an I'll-wait stance, he threw his hands in the air.

"This is a fool move, Counselor. And if I can find the slightest precedent in Westlaw to stop you, I will."

With an arched brow and a confident smile, she responded, "By the time you do that, I'll already have him out of custody." She gave him a wink and a smile, putting her smugness on display. The resulting tight set of Ross's jaw was proof she'd already won this argument. But just for good measure, she restated her position so the surly prosecutor understood her assertion.

Tipping her head in Taylor's direction, she said, "From now until his father arrives with an attorney, I will be his attorney of record during this interrogation. I told you to get him a lawyer, and you didn't. So now his lawyer is me. Again, clear the room, gentlemen. I need to talk with my client."

Chapter 30

AJA STOOD ACROSS THE TABLE FROM A SEAT FULL OF trembling sixteen-year-old boy, and her blood boiled. She was angry. Angry with the men who'd been so eager to collar this child that they'd been willing to let him hang himself. She was angry at the justice system. More often than not, it treated kids—who did stupid things, as kids do—as adults who should know better. But most of all, she was angry that someone she'd trusted may have set out to harm her.

If she were her aunt Jo, she'd have taken off her shoe and tanned his hide for putting himself in this position. But since she didn't want to end up with an assault charge herself, she folded her arms and glared at the frightened young man.

"From the first moment I laid eyes on you, you became the nephew I'd always wanted. There's been nothing but love between the Henrys and the Sullivans for generations. When I wanted to rebuild my family's legacy, your father was the first and only name I thought of to help me do it. Earl was family. I wouldn't have to explain to him why this project was everything to me. And even when your father couldn't finish the work he'd begun because of unsafe working conditions, I never lost respect or love for him. I didn't even attempt to seek retribution in a civil case. So tell me, why would you do this? Why would you steal from your own father? Why would you create the situations that forced him to lose half the money he was supposed to make? Why would you deliberately try to hurt someone that loved you like blood?"

"It wasn't like that, Ms. Aja."

"It wasn't like that? That's your response to the trouble you've caused? Do you even know what you almost did tonight?"

The way his blue eyes darted back and forth in his head as he stared openly at her told her Taylor had no clue what his actions would have destroyed if he'd succeeded.

She leaned over him, much like the way her mama used to crowd in on her when she was in trouble. Aja figured if it worked to keep her on the straight and narrow, maybe it would do the same for Taylor.

"My great-great-great-great-granddaddy built that house with his own hands after toiling for the Union Army during the Civil War. He left the brutality of slavery on that land and returned four years later with his freedom and his dignity. He bought this land from the people who enslaved him and his kin and vowed that his blood would forever have a place in this world to call a home of their own. That's not just some old rickety building, Taylor. It's a mark of my legacy. A reminder of everything my people have endured and survived. It's a promise of what we can achieve if we keep trying and refuse to succumb to the pressures of the outside world. So whatever you have to say to me, it had better be damn good. Otherwise, I'm gonna let that prosecutor swallow you whole." She bared her teeth behind curled lips and spoke with her jaw clenched. "Do you understand me?"

The child was shivering now. "I can explain everything, Ms. Aja. I pr-promise. I just gotta know you're really here to help me."

His pleading blue eyes shimmered with unshed tears as they darted from side to side, scanning her face for the truth. The implication that he didn't automatically know he could trust her sliced her heart into fine shreds.

"Unlike the police, as an officer of the court, I'm not allowed to lie to you. If I've asserted myself as your lawyer during this interrogation, I have to perform on your behalf. If I don't, it can be used against me, and it can also be used as a means of getting you out of this mess you've made for yourself. Not to mention…"

She sat down on the table facing him, stretching a slow, nonthreatening hand out to him. As she laid it softly against his cheek, she longed for the days when doing this would make every hurt better for him. "You're my baby, Taylor," she huffed. "I'm mad as hell at you, and if we weren't sitting in a law-enforcement agency, I'd take a switch to your behind. But I'm not gonna let anyone harm you without going through me first. You understand?"

He closed his eyes, relief flowing like the streak of tears falling down his face, fast and unchecked. "Believe me, Ms. Aja. I never wanted any part of this, but I didn't have a choice."

She wiped away the wet tracks on his cheeks before continuing. "What do you mean?"

"Mr. Bennett said—"

Aja held a hand up as she sat across from Taylor. "Wait, Eli Bennett? Is that who you mean?"

He huffed frantic breaths in and out before blurting everything out in one headlong rush. "I'm so sorry, Ms. Aja. He made me do this."

Aja's heart beat fast and hard in her chest, knocking against her rib cage in pronounced thuds.

"Tell me everything."

Still handcuffed to the table, Taylor raised his arm in an awkward position to wipe the tears on his face away. Sitting here, watching uncertainty and anxiety paint the canvas of his face reinforced how much of a child he truly was.

If Eli Bennett has done anything to harm this boy, I swear I will end him.

"What happened, Taylor?"

"Ever since my me-maw got sick, my daddy's business hasn't been doing so well. He was paying for her cancer treatments out of pocket. At first, it wasn't so bad. But then he got underbid on a few projects, and there wasn't as much money coming in. So my mama took a housekeeping job at the Bennett ranch."

Aja's stomach roiled. She could already see where this story was headed, and she didn't like it.

"One day, Mr. Bennett saw me drop Mama off to work and asked how I planned to spend my day. I told him working with my daddy over at your ranch.

"I didn't think nothing of it then. But a few days later, when I dropped Mama off again, he asked to speak with me. He told me he had a job for me, one that would pay better than my summer gig with my daddy, and it would be less work." Taylor shook his head, then looked up to the ceiling as if he were reading his past through a new set of lenses, understanding things now that had escaped his comprehension then. "I should've known better than to listen to him. If I'd taken off, I wouldn't be in this mess, and you wouldn't have been hurt."

She was quiet. It was too soon for her to add her thoughts to the mix. Aja didn't want to disturb his flow. She needed every detail if she intended to use this account to get Taylor out of this predicament somehow and lay the blame where she was certain it rested—at Eli Bennett's feet.

"He told me he wanted me to push a few of your fence posts down as a joke. He said he was teaching you a valuable lesson about ranching. He said you didn't have any livestock, so no one would get hurt by a few posts being knocked down. I figured he was right and that it couldn't cause any harm because my dad would probably fix them anyway, so I agreed."

She let a long breath escape her, hoping it would ebb her frustration. "But that wasn't the last of it, was it? He came back with another task, and another task until you were burning down my barn and trying to strangle me in my bed?"

The boy shook his head furiously. "No, that wasn't me. I swear I didn't attack you." She watched him for a minute, then waved him on to continue his story. "When he demanded I cut the scaffolding, I told him no. He said he'd turn me in to the police, and he'd make it so my dad never got another job, and he'd fire my mom. I thought he was bluffing until my dad lost three bids back-to-back the following week. With no cash, we'd be on the streets, and my me-maw would die."

"So you went along with his plan and cut my scaffolding, burned down my barn, and tried to kill me?"

He shook his head again. "I cut the scaffolding after I knew my daddy's men were through with it. They were coming to take it down the same day. I didn't know you'd be under there taking more measurements. The barn was an accident. I went in there to damage some electrical work, but I heard Ms. Daniels screaming your name as she walked by, and I panicked. I accidentally stepped on some kerosene lamps, a spark from an exposed wire hit the spilled gas, and the fire got out of control so quickly, all I could do was run."

She watched him carefully. His eyes never wavered from hers. "Where were you the night of my attack? I need more than your word you weren't the one to attack me."

"I was with Mr. Pete at the hardware store. We had a late shipment come in, and he needed my help doing inventory and restocking. He keeps a camera running in the store. You can ask him to show you if you want."

She believed him. But she was still going to check it out. She'd get Pete on the phone before she left this room. But for now, she was satisfied Taylor was telling the truth.

A strange sense of relief washed over her. She wasn't thrilled with Taylor's admitted involvement in the vandalism on her ranch, but knowing he wasn't the one to attack her made her anger and frustration ease.

"I believe you, Taylor." The boy sighed big and loud, sliding down somewhat in his chair as he leaned back. "The problem is, without irrefutable proof, there's no way anything you told me gets you out of cuffs and Eli Bennett into them. Even without the assault charge, you could be looking at serious time for the vandalism."

"Would a video recording of him admitting he made me do this be proof enough?"

She sat up a little straighter in her chair. "It would be a hell of a bargaining chip if you had one."

Taylor shared a nervous smile, the corners of his mouth still anxiously trembling before he gave her his log-in information for a cloud account. She sat back and watched the video on her phone, a smile spreading across her face as she did. When it finished, she looked up at Taylor with a lifted brow. "Now this is a game changer—something I can use. Sit tight, Taylor, and watch me work."

"How did you let this happen, Dean?"

Jackson leaned against the wall and watched as Ross paced back and forth. "How did I let it happen? I'd like to see how you planned on stopping her. And honestly, I agree with her."

"So you want to let him go like that sentimental fool sitting in there, blowing a hole in this case, because he's sixteen?"

Jackson shook his head, keeping himself planted against the wall, unsure if he could ignore his instinct to snatch Ross up by his neck for talking about Aja like that in front of him. "No. If he did it, I want him to pay just like you. But I agree with what she said. If it comes out that we questioned him and got a confession without representation or a parent present, this entire scenario could blow up in our faces. Even though we're working inside the parameters of the law, the public won't see it that way. I don't want him to get off because we couldn't make it look good on paper."

Ross stopped pacing, staring at Jackson with a pointed glare that pissed him off more than intimidated him. "It doesn't matter anyway. Now that she has crossed this line, we'll never be able to get this in front of a jury. If the victim is defending him, this is all a waste of my damn time."

The door to the interrogation room opened and Aja peeked outside. "Gentlemen, all is not lost. Come inside. I believe my client has something to share with you that's going to makes us all smile."

Ross turned to Jackson, his brow furrowed in tight, straight lines as he silently questioned him. His response to the prosecutor was to shrug and follow Aja back into the room. If the confidence he saw in each sway of her hips was an indicator, he knew she was about to blow their minds. Because one thing he knew about Aja Everett was that she was a problem solver of the highest caliber. She always got the job done.

Chapter 31

"WELL, I'LL BE DAMNED. ELI BENNETT SHO' DOES PUT ON AN interesting show."

Aja's smile widened as she sat across the table from John Ross. This was exactly the reaction she wanted from the prosecutor.

"As you can see from the video, my client was being threatened and coerced by an adult. Now, putting my client in jail for these crimes might get you another notch in your win column, but we all know if you take Eli Bennett down, you'll get the acclaim that goes along with catching a big fish."

Ross whistled and wrote on the notepad placed in front of him. "You're right. It would definitely be something to see if we could pin this on Bennett." Ross scribbled some more on his notepad before making eye contact with Aja again. "All right, Counselor, I'll give you the immunity you're asking for. But only if your client agrees to testify against Bennett if this goes to court."

Aja narrowed her eyes. "You're gonna try to plead Bennett out?"

The prosecutor tilted his head as his eyes met Aja's. "Bennett is a big deal in Fresh Springs. The crimes were committed in Fresh Springs. More than likely, they'll be tried there too. If he fights this, he'll more than likely lose with this video. But that still doesn't mean he won't fight us. I'm about to put in a call to a friendly judge to get a warrant to search Bennett's accounts and his home. Hopefully, we can catch him off guard and get more to pin on him to use as leverage for a plea bargain. Does your client still have the money Bennett paid him?"

Aja tapped her pen on the table, then wrote down an address and slid it to Jackson. "My client says Bennett handed him the money himself. Maybe you can trace the bills back to Eli through the serial numbers once the Rangers retrieve them from that address."

Ross watched her again. The lawyer in her knew he was tallying up the ways in which she'd practically made his case for him. He wrote a few more lines on his notepad and stood, extending his hand to Aja. "You're not half bad at this lawyer thing, Ms. Everett. If you ever feel like working for the prosecution, look me up."

She stood and accepted the hand he offered, smiling as she answered, "Thanks, but this county couldn't afford me." She looked down at a wide-eyed Taylor and winked. "This was simply me helping out a friend." The boy smiled, relief smoothing out the worry lines previously carved into his young face. His ordeal wasn't over yet, not until they could put Eli Bennett behind bars where he belonged. But the immediate danger of him losing his freedom was over, and that was a win she was happy to claim.

Ross left the room, leaving Jackson, Taylor, and Aja remaining. She stole a brief glance at Jackson. There was something unrecognizable settling in his eyes.

He was probably trying to figure out how a person could manipulate a child like Taylor, or thinking about some other detail of the case. Because whatever he was thinking about it, she was certain it wasn't her. And she definitely didn't think he was feeling the looming sadness closing in on the margins of her heart.

No, that was reserved for her. Because as happy as she was that this craziness was about to be over, that Taylor would walk out of this building with his freedom, and that she and her people were safe again, a little corner of her heart ached the slightest bit in knowing Jackson would leave Restoration Ranch.

She cleared her throat, refusing to let her emotions get the better of her. She was a grown woman who'd walked into their one night of glorious sex with open eyes. It was never supposed to be more than it was, and she wouldn't let herself get all worked up like some clingy teenager who didn't know how to end things with a kiss and a smile. "Taylor, I'll wait here with you until your dad arrives with your new attorney."

"His dad arrived a few minutes ago. Reenie texted me."

Aja smoothed her hands against her braids, trying to control the awkward, nervous energy suddenly running through her. "Oh, good. That means you'll be out of here soon."

Jackson stepped on the other side of Taylor, leaning down and unlocking his handcuffs. "My associate Ranger Adams will be in with your paperwork and your dad, Taylor. Soon you'll be free to go."

The boy stood slowly, then in a rush of anxiety and relief, he threw his arms around Aja and hugged her so tight she knew he had to have rearranged some internal organs. "Thank you so much, Ms. Aja." She was about to tell him it was nothing when she felt tremors run through his body and heard his heavy, emotion-laden voice crack. "I'm sorry for what I did to you. Please forgive me."

She rubbed her hands up and down Taylor's back, soothing him as if he were a baby instead of the almost-man filling her arms. "The fault rests with Bennett, not you. He forced you into this. Not to mention, we've all needed a little forgiveness in our lives. Me especially. I'm simply paying it forward." She stepped out of his embrace, drying the tears on his face with a stroke of her thumbs. "Next time, if something like this happens to you, talk to someone. Your family loves you. They would never have let Bennett get away with this. Not for any reason."

There was a knock on the door, and Earl Sullivan stepped inside, followed by a brunette in a business suit. After a brief exchange on the events, Aja followed Jackson out of the interrogation room, leaving a grateful parent and child to wrap things up with their new attorney.

"You did a good thing in there."

Her lips curved seemingly of their own power whenever his velvet tones danced in her ears. She honestly needed to get a handle on that, or he would think she was some kind of grinning idiot. *If he doesn't already believe it.*

"I know I did. Glad you didn't fight me too much on it, or things would've gotten ugly."

Jackson held up his hands in surrender. "Fighting people is your thing, not mine. I'm glad you could help that boy. I was never comfortable railroading him, by the way. But I don't have a lot of control over Ross."

"Jackson, sooner or later, you will have to learn that there's a difference between the letter of the law and the spirit. Just because you can do something doesn't mean you should. That's not a judgment on you specifically, more on the system itself. People who are making ends meet or are poor, disenfranchised, or belong to marginalized communities don't have equal footing in the legal system."

Jackson let a derisive chuckle slip into the air. "This coming from a woman whose job it was to get her rich clients out of hot water with the law?"

"I worked with those rich clients so my firm could afford to take on double the pro-bono hours we were required to, and I donated my money and my time to legal clinics in areas of low socioeconomic status to give people a fighting chance in the system that often says they don't matter. There's no rule that says I can't like making money and help those in need at the same time. There's also no rule that says you can't bring people to justice and still help them at the same time. It's all about balance, Ranger Dean."

She waited for an angry reply; annoying him seemed to be her superpower, so it wouldn't surprise her if her words got a rise out of him. But instead of the defensive retort she was expecting, Jackson stepped closer to her and gave her a playful tap. "You're right. There's no reason I can't do both."

She stared at him. He still had that strange look of introspection mixed with speculation he'd had when they were in the interrogation room. She didn't understand what he was seeking the answers to, but whatever it was, there was something softer and less guarded about him. She was about to ask him what was going on when he pressed a gentle hand against her upper arm and said, "Let's get you back home."

———

Jackson took the scenic route back to Restoration Ranch, and he knew he was doing it on purpose. There was something about returning Aja to the ranch that felt final, like he was closing the door on an important moment in his life. He'd spent a handful of days with this woman and her land, and now the idea of never being there again with her was making him feel detached and lost.

He didn't want to think about why that was. Instead, he held on to the few remaining moments he had with her in the cab of his truck, wallowing in the quiet comfort of her presence for the last time.

Fighting the building desire to reach across the console and rest his hand on her thigh, he tightened his fingers around the steering wheel. Just because she'd allowed him to share her body once, that didn't give him the right to take such liberties now. Especially not when he'd insisted such intimacies could never happen between them again.

God, he was still kicking himself for that.

But watching her fight for the underdog at his headquarters, and now sitting here next to her when the case was essentially over, all he could think of was how foolish he'd been to push her away. Because somewhere just beneath the surface of his skin, he realized what his father had been trying to tell him. Aja Everett wasn't like any other woman he'd encountered, and he'd screwed up royally by not making her part of his life.

He pulled through the front gates of her ranch, and heaviness filled his chest. The band grew tighter as he neared the house, the discomfort of each breath a reminder he was about to give up something precious.

He brought the truck to a stop behind one of his father's security trucks parked in front of the house, then got out and walked around to her side of the truck to open her door. He knew she didn't need him to do that or hold her hand as she stepped down on the running boards, then onto the ground. It was all for him. An action that allowed him to take care of her one more time because after tonight, he wouldn't get the opportunity again.

He followed her to the bottom of the porch and stayed there as she walked up the steps. When Aja turned to see the security guard standing there, Jackson waved his hand and said, "You can return to your original post." The man acknowledged Jackson, then Aja, before making his way down the steps of the front porch and walking to the truck parked in front of Jackson's.

He'd hoped she'd keep walking once the security guard left, that she wouldn't notice he was no longer following her. That way, he wouldn't have to explain that if he stepped inside alone with her right now, he might never leave.

"You're not coming in?"

He shook his head. "Until I get the call that Bennett is in custody, I want to keep an eye out on the perimeter of the house. I can watch the security feed from my car. As tired as I am, I don't trust myself to do this from your comfy couch."

"Don't you need to be there for the arrest?"

"No, Colton sent me a text that the arrest warrant came through right after we left. Another team will handle the arrest. Bennett should be in custody soon."

She smiled, but it was weak, not like her usual that seemed to radiate light all around her.

"I guess your job is done, then?"

He slowly bobbed his head. "This part of the job is done. If this goes to court, I'll have to testify. But mostly, this portion of the investigation is over. The new focus will look into Bennett's affairs to see if he's been up to anything else, but as far as you're concerned, it's finished, Aja. Wrap-up will consist of my father completing the new security measures he's already started implementing and switching the cameras from our private network in the van to your network here on the ranch. You should probably give Seneca fair warning; he'll need to contact her about that."

He saw the tremble in her smile and the way she wrapped her arms around herself. She had a jacket on—the days still reached the sixties and seventies, but at night, the temperature could drop as low as the thirties. Watching the sadness fill her eyes made him guess her shivering had nothing to do with the chill in the air.

"You okay?" He ran up the stairs and reached out to comfort her, but she straightened her shoulders, plastering a weary smile on her face as if to reassure him everything was fine, even when he knew it wasn't.

"Would you wait here for a second? I have something I need to get."

"Sure."

She disappeared inside, and a few moments later, she reappeared with a gift-wrapped, medium-size square box in her arms.

"What's this?"

"It's something for you."

Nerves—no, excitement—hell, he couldn't tell which—were

making his stomach dance in a weird way. "Aja, I can't accept a gift from you for doing my job."

She huffed and rolled her eyes. "Forever the Boy Scout."

"You mean cowboy."

She rolled her eyes again. "Whatever. Listen, this isn't about your job. This is about all the things you did for me that weren't part of your job."

"Aja, giving me a gift for that is sort of like paying for services rendered. That's kind of illegal."

She moved over to a nearby porch table and set the box down before closing her eyes and pinching the bridge of her nose. "Saints alive, save me from this man's stupidity."

A hearty laugh bubbled up in his chest, making his shoulders shake. "What does a concrete princess like you know about that expression, 'Saints alive'?"

"I keep telling you, I may have been born and raised and even lived most of my life in Brooklyn, but my heart was always here on this ranch in Fresh Springs, Texas."

She smoothed her hand gently over the box, then looked up at him, the delight of the moment fighting to push her sadness to the fringes. "This isn't about your work or the sex, Jackson. This is about the important things you did while you were here. Comforting me after the attack, getting your dad and brother out here to set up my security, as well as the deep, deep discount I'm sure you convinced your dad to give me. All of it was beyond the call of duty. I appreciate all of it. I wanted to give you a little something to say thanks."

He stood there, staring at the beautiful lines and curves of her face, the dark eyes wide with sincerity, the genuine smile that spread the full lips of her mouth into a perfect bow, and he ached to touch her. But he knew if he started, he'd never stop, so he reached for the bow on top of the box instead.

She placed her hand on his, sending a jolt of electricity through his skin, the spark splitting, jumping from one nerve to the other, a charge of something bright and powerful taking over his senses. "Don't open it. Not yet anyway."

"You're giving me a gift you don't want me to open?"

She shook her head. "I'm giving you a gift I don't want you to open yet. This is called happy mail. It's usually a little something sent in the mail by a friend that will make you smile. You don't smile nearly enough. So I thought I'd send you some happy."

He stroked his thumb over hers. Whatever was in the box, he was sure it wouldn't make him as happy as standing out on the porch at night with their hands pressed together did. But the inviting smile on her face had him curious to know what its contents held.

"I want you to keep this box, and if you ever find yourself in a moment where you need a little happy, open it and think of me."

"I don't need a gift to remember you, Aja. I'm certain you're the most unforgettable woman I've ever met."

She shook her head. "Nonetheless, promise me, Jackson. Promise me you won't open this until you need some happy. You're a man of your word. I know if you make this promise, you'll do everything to keep it."

A silent, slow breath crawled up from his lungs and out into the air. "Aja, I'm no poster child for virtue. If I were, I never would've crossed the line with you, and I would have the decency to be remorseful about it. But I don't. I'm not the least bit sorry, and that right there is proof that my moral compass is on the fritz."

"You're human, Jackson. The kind of human that cares about the welfare of others. In my book, that makes you the best kind. So quit stalling and promise me, Ranger."

He matched the inviting smile on her face. "I promise." Her smile widened, and she handed the box over to him.

"Be happy, Ranger Dean. We all deserve a little happy."

He watched her saunter back inside the house as he fought the urge to follow her. He didn't know what was in the box, and he probably wouldn't be finding out anytime soon. But one thing he knew beyond certainty was that nothing inside that box had the power to make him as happy as the woman who'd given it to him.

Chapter 32

"I knew it was that no-good Yosemite Sam wannabe all along."

Aja looked over her steaming cup of coffee long enough to give Brooklyn a pointed glare. "I think anyone with a brain could've figured out it was Eli Bennett vandalizing the ranch. He's been after the land since I snatched it from the brink of auction."

Seneca pulled up next to Aja at the breakfast table and grabbed the tablet Brooklyn was reading the morning paper on. "At least he had the decency to confess. Paper says he took a deal. He pled guilty to all the charges—the intimidation, the vandalism, even your assault—in exchange for a reduced sentence. They gave him seven years and fines. Looks like you'll get your money back for the destroyed property."

Aja eased back in her chair. She wasn't worried about the money. And knowing the penal system, it would take forever for those funds to end up in her hands.

Brooklyn took the tablet out of Seneca's hand and scrolled until she found the section she was looking for. "I'm surprised they gave him that long considering how connected Bennett is.

I'm surprised they could find a judge outside of your uncle to sign off on this."

Brooklyn was right. Bennett owned most of Fresh Springs. But Aja was certain a particular Texas Ranger who she knew had a hand in the severity of the charges.

"I guess I have you two to thank for that. Because of my work with the Pathways program, the prosecutor upped the charges from a simple assault charge to a third-degree felony because I'm considered a government contractor."

"Well, I'm happy he's in custody." Seneca stirred the bowl of grits in front of her. "Whatever they had on him, it must have been serious, because no one could ever have made me believe Eli Bennett of all people would confess to his crimes."

Aja wouldn't have believed it either, except for the call she received from Jackson this morning. It was the first time she'd heard from him in a week since Taylor had implicated Eli.

His voice was still deep and rich, and her head spun at the mere sound of it. The call was brief, direct, detailing all the terms of Eli's deal. All that remained was for the man to allocute, and the case would officially be closed.

She was glad it was nearly over. But the realization that aside from Jackson dropping by at some point to pick up the few items he'd left, she'd likely have no interaction with him made it difficult for her to fully celebrate the news.

"Hey, you all right over there?"

Aja blinked until Brooklyn's face came into view. *God, the mere thought of him has me zoning out. Get it together, Aja.* "I'm fine. Long week, that's all. We have a lot of work to do."

"Yeah, especially since you sent our heavy lifters on some wild-goose chase looking for what again?"

Aja sipped her coffee instead of answering Seneca's question, hoping to delay the inevitable a little bit longer. "An equipment auction. I sent them to look at those giant mowers. Jackson thought mowing our own land and processing our own hay might be more cost-efficient for us. The auction and purchase process will probably last up to another week." There, she'd bought herself until the weekend before she had to come clean. Maybe that would be enough for her to put on her big-girl pants and tell Brooklyn and Seneca the truth.

"Is that what's had you looking so sad in the face for the last few days?"

Aja put down the cup of coffee, staring at Brooklyn across the table. "I'm not sure I follow. What do you mean?"

"I mean, every day since they caught that Sullivan boy on the property, you've been walking around looking like you lost something important."

She had. Even though Jackson was never hers to keep, his departure left a hole so wide, she wasn't sure if she'd ever be able to fill it.

"You know how much I hate to say these words, Boss. But Brooklyn is right. You're one of those whistle-while-you-work kind of people. But lately, you ain't doing so much whistling."

"No baking or cooking either," Brooklyn added. "I mean, I love grits as much as the next person. By the way, when is Aunt Jo coming back? If you won't feed us, Lord knows she will."

For the first time in what seemed liked forever, Aja smiled. "She'll be back this weekend, and I'll happily relinquish my duties as your personal chef."

Brooklyn's face lit up at Aja's news. "Good, and maybe some of her sweet bread will take your mind off missing your foreman so much."

Aja opened her mouth to speak, but nothing came out.

"Holy shit." Seneca's shocked whisper brought Aja back to her senses. "She was kidding. But you really do miss the foreman, don't you?"

Panicked, like an animal pressed into a corner, Aja looked for an exit out of this conversation. "I don't know what you're talking about." She picked up her mostly full bowl of grits and headed to the trash. If her aunt Jo were here, she'd be chastising Aja about her eyes being bigger than her belly and not wasting the food the good Lord blessed them with.

Her desire to not be wasteful notwithstanding, Aja's appetite was nonexistent. She scraped the bowl clean and headed for the sink, taking more time than necessary to rinse the dish out and place it in the dishwasher.

When she turned around, both Brooklyn and Seneca were standing at the opposite end of the counter, staring at her with accusing eyes.

"What's going on, Aja?"

Four years of college, three years of law school, and over thirteen years of arguing for her clients in legal matters, and the most sophisticated answer Aja could come up with was, "Huh?"

Her response sounded unconvincing to her too.

"If you can 'huh,' you can hear," Brooklyn said as she narrowed her lids into slits and folded her arms. A quick glance at Seneca standing by Brooklyn's side with arms folded, smiling at her well-timed verbal jab, was the nail in Aja's proverbial coffin. She was busted, and since Jackson had somehow screwed up her mental-verbal mojo, she couldn't think up a reasonable explanation fast enough to get them off her back.

"Jackson and I—"

"Totally smashed," Brooklyn interjected. She held out her hand, palm side up in front of Seneca. "Give me my money."

Seneca huffed, making an exaggerated show of reaching into her pocket and slapping what looked to be a twenty-dollar bill into Brooklyn's hand.

"Wait, you two bet on whether Jackson and I had sex?"

"Girl, please," Brooklyn countered. "That man was walking around here looking like a whole snack; you'd be crazy not to holler. Not to mention, as fine as that man is, and as dry as your social life has been, we've been praying and lighting candles that you would get a taste."

Aja pointed at both women. "And that is the end of this conversation."

"Ah, don't be that way, Boss."

Aja held up a pointed finger. "First of all, my sex life is none of your business. Second, I am not some wilting flower that needs a man in her life to blossom."

Seneca held up her hands in surrender. "No one's saying you *need* a man, Aja. You work so hard trying to get this place up and running, plus all the crap you've had to deal with while trying to protect us, so we wanted you to have a little fun. And I don't care what you say—climbing that brick wall of a man had to be fun as hell."

Aja tried to keep her annoyed face in place, but as usual, Seneca's colorful expressions had her smiling and shaking her head. "No comment."

Seneca playfully stomped her foot. "Ah, come on. I need details. Let me live vicariously through you."

Aja ignored her plea by taking another sip from her cup. "If you're so in need of that kind of entertainment, either let your fingers do the walking on the internet, or spend more time trying to find someone to have that kind of fun with."

"Ah, hello, this is Fresh Springs, Texas. There are no eligible bachelors here. Otherwise, I'd totally find someone to work the kinks out."

Aja shook her head. "I don't need that image in my head. How about we never have this conversation again, and you two can do what I pay you to do, instead of minding my business like it's your job?"

"Or," Seneca added, "we could continue to analyze your mood and figure out what's really been going on around here. I mean, I'm sure we could mow our own grass, but going away for over a week to an auction seems a bit much. Are Jackson and his men really at auction, or did you send them packing because things got too heavy between you and the foreman?"

She swallowed. It was an easy out, and she wasn't stupid enough to let it go. She'd already lost Jackson. No sense in losing her friends, nor her family, over a truth they need never know.

"It complicated things. It was one night, the night after the attack. Things got weird afterward, and we both decided him leaving was the best solution. His men were a package deal. They go where he does."

They both gave her a sympathetic look and headed toward the back door. Brooklyn stopped at the door and looked over her shoulder to address Aja again. "No worries, Aja. If it's any consolation, I think the foreman was just as taken with you. He's probably kicking himself for not finding a way to make it work. Anyone that spends a little time with you knows it don't get no better."

Aja wasn't certain she deserved that kind of praise, especially since she'd told them a flat-out lie regarding Jackson's disappearance. But Seneca's words, whether or not she was worthy of them, still sneaked beneath her skin and made it tingle with the warmth of the woman's kindness.

"Hey, we've been so busy talking about my personal life, we haven't discussed the details of your anniversary party."

The two women stopped, then stared at each other before simultaneously looking at Aja.

"You still plan on throwing this 'We've been out of jail a year' party?'"

Aja couldn't help but laugh at Brooklyn's description of the event.

"I promised the two of you we would celebrate every milestone. This definitely qualifies. I need to know what you want on the menu and if you have anyone to add to our usual guest list."

She grabbed a pen and notepad from the desk in the corner and waved them back to the counter. "Come on, ladies. Let's get these plans underway."

Jackson sat behind his desk, trying to shake the general funk he couldn't seem to get rid of. Of all days, today should've brought him a sense of professional pride. He'd sat in a courtroom galley, watching as Eli Bennett allocuted to the crimes he'd committed against Aja and Restoration Ranch.

The case was over, Aja was safe, and Eli Bennett was taken into custody immediately following his allocution. His team hadn't even had to work hard to get Bennett's confession. As soon as Gleason and Jennings presented him with the evidence against him, Bennett told his fancy mouthpiece to stop fighting and cut a deal. Everything was wrapped up in a nice, neat bow. Just the way he liked it. He should be thrilled. Yet looking around the courtroom and not seeing Aja there had somehow dampened his satisfaction of the way things concluded.

He stopped John Ross after the proceedings were over to ask where Aja was. She was the victim in all of this. She had a right to see justice done.

The prosecutor's mouth straightened into a flat line. "When I spoke to her yesterday, she said she'd seen enough allocutions to last her a lifetime. To call her if anything went wrong, but other than that, she was moving on."

Jackson's mood had tanked right then and there. Having her so easily moving on, especially without him, rankled something in him. Certain he wasn't fit to be in public spaces after that, he hurried to his office to find a sanctuary where he could do something monotonous like file paperwork and hopefully stay out of the path of people.

He was cracking open the first of a stack of files sitting on his desk when he heard a knock at his door.

"Come in."

A short man with a tall hat stepped into the room, and Jackson tensed up. It was his boss, Major Edward Hargrove.

"What's happened now?"

The major laughed, his shoulders shaking with each chuckle. "Why do you always assume I'm here to deliver bad news?"

"Because that's all you do." Jackson stood from his desk and offered the man his hand. "What can I do for you, sir?"

"I've been going over personnel files for HR's annual audit. It seems you've been slacking on taking your mandatory time off."

Jackson sat back down in his chair, tapping his fingers on the desk. "Oh, is that all? I'll sit down soon and schedule time off."

The major shook his head. "Nope. You've had four back-to-back undercover operations. The rules are very clear. You either take some time off, or I make you go sit with the department shrink to make sure you aren't a danger to yourself or others. Which do you prefer?"

Jackson ground his teeth. He didn't want to take any time off right now. Sitting at home with nothing but his thoughts of Aja would drive him up a wall.

Major Hargrove walked back to Jackson's door and tipped his hat. "Let me know your decision by the end of the day. Four weeks, or I make the appointment for you with the shrink."

Jackson sat for a moment, trying to get himself together before he picked up the phone on his desk. His fingers punched in the number by rote, and he waited until he heard a familiar "Hello" on the other end.

"Afternoon, Daddy."

"Hey, Son, to what do I owe the pleasure of a call from you in the middle of a workday?"

"Well, I was thinking I would come spend some time with you at the house. Can you put me up, or are you too busy with work right now?"

"As a matter of fact, I just finished the Everett job yesterday, so I have a few days on my hand before I have another install scheduled."

Relief bled through Jackson. If he couldn't work, at least he'd get to spend time with his family. "All right. I should be there by supper tonight."

"Great, I'll tell your brother. Love you, Son."

"Love you, Daddy."

His plans settled, Jackson stood and packed his things away in his bag. A few days at home with his family were what he needed to get his head right. Hopefully, four weeks would be enough to fix his heart too.

Chapter 33

"LOOK WHO THE CAT DRAGGED IN. IT'S THE PRODIGAL SON."

Jackson rolled his eyes and handed his brother one of his bags. "Either help me with one of these or move, Kip."

His brother grabbed the large duffel, reached for the shoulder bag, too, and ushered Jackson in. "Damn, how long you staying?"

Jackson pursed his lips. "Why, you got something better to do than hang with your big brother?"

Kip didn't even bat an eye. "Of course I do."

"And this is exactly why I should've been an only child."

His brother put Jackson's bags down by the stairs that led to the bedrooms and grabbed him in a bear hug. "You know you love me," Kip teased as he placed an exaggerated kiss on Jackson's cheek that made a loud smacking noise. "You wouldn't know what to do without me."

Jackson chuckled. Kip's antics might get on his nerves all the time, but he wouldn't trade his baby brother for all the money in the world.

They moved farther down the hall until they were standing in the middle of a wide, sunken living room. Jackson looked around, the old wood paneling on the walls making him smile. He'd bet those panels were older than his forty years.

He didn't mind them, though. His father had built this home with his bare hands, and every time Jackson stepped inside, comfort bled through him, each cell in his body soaking up the love and protection he couldn't get anywhere else except home.

"Daddy outside grilling?"

Kip jammed his hands into his pocket. "His big son is home. You know he's been looking for the perfect slice of animal carcass to throw on the coals since you called him."

Jackson noted the curled lip and general look of disgust on Kip's face. Just to needle him, Jackson rubbed his belly and moaned. "One of Daddy's steaks would hit the spot right now."

Kip made an audible gagging noise and grumbled something about caveman meat-eaters and walked from the living room through the kitchen and out onto the back porch with Jackson on his heels. "I don't know how you people can eat that stuff. It's so gross."

Jackson slapped a hand on Kip's shoulder and shook his head. "Is there anything sadder than a vegetarian Texan?"

Kip shrugged Jackson's hand off his shoulder. "Yeah, a carnivorous Texan dying of heart disease. Speaking of, when was the last time you had your cholesterol checked, Big Brother?"

Jackson groaned. He was due for a physical within the next month. Although he was certain he was fine, he didn't need that particular seed of doubt being planted so close to his next visit.

He spotted his father standing at his old smoker. The thing looked liked something out of a steampunk novel with all the smoke billowing out through the exhaust arm. His father had to be breaking all sorts of air pollution laws, but Jackson knew from experience that the taste of the barbecue coming out of the smoker would be well worth it.

Even his brother couldn't deny their father's ability on the grill. When Kip would have no part of their meat indulgence, their father learned delicious ways to cook vegetables on an open fire that had anyone with taste buds licking their chops.

"All right, old man," Jackson called out as he walked toward his father. "Don't you mess around and burn my steak."

Jacob closed the smoker and turned around with a big grin. He pointed his finger at Jackson in that loving no-nonsense way he always had about him. "I done told you 'bout calling me 'old man.' You ain't too old for me to tan your hide."

"You'd have to catch me first."

His father shook his head. "You know what comes with age, Jackson? Wisdom. I'm too smart to be out here chasing you. All I gotta do is wave a plate of this here barbecue in the air, and you'll come running to me."

Jackson winked and clapped his hand over his father's shoulder. "Never been truer words spoken, Daddy."

His father encircled him in his arms, and Jackson felt some of the tension in his shoulders drift away, as if someone were removing one iron brick at a time.

Perhaps this forced vacation was a blessing in disguise. Because standing in his father's embrace for all of two minutes did more to better his mood than any of the paperwork waiting for him back in the office. Maybe if he stayed long enough, he could cure himself of all that ailed him.

He was about to let that thought take further hold when he heard a distant knock coming from the back doorway.

"Sorry I'm late; these apple turnovers took a little longer than expected to finish."

Jackson looked over his shoulder to see a familiar face. "Mrs. Eames?" He hadn't seen his widowed neighbor in what seemed like years.

He watched her hug Kip after he took the platter of turnovers from her and then walked over to him and stretched out her arms wide. "Jackson Dean, it's so good to see you again."

He took a moment to marvel at her. She had to be in her sixties if not older, but the gleaming brown skin and the short pixie haircut concealed those years well. He didn't know what magic fairy dust she was sprinkling on herself, but she certainly had a fountain of youth somewhere if she still looked the same as when he was in high school.

He pulled her into his embrace and hugged her close to him. He smiled as the faint scent of candied melon teased his nose. Even her perfume hadn't changed in all this time.

When she stepped out of the circle of his arms, he stood there smiling and shaking his head. "Mrs. Eames, you still look amazing. What kind of sorcery are you using to still be looking like a beauty queen?"

She swatted her hand at him. "Chile, hush. I think that's what the young folks would call some of that Black girl magic. We get better with time."

"You certainly have."

She smiled and gave him a kiss on the cheek. "I'm so glad to see you again. Now, let me go over here and check on your daddy."

Jackson stepped aside and walked back over to the porch where Kip was sitting, sipping on a longneck. He pulled one out for himself, twisted the top, and took a large gulp. His eyes glanced over to Mrs. Eames and his father. There was something about the two of them together that registered as odd to him.

They'd always been friendly. Mrs. Eames often babysat Jackson and Kip when his dad had to work late when they were kids. She and her son, Holden, spent enough time at their house that Jackson owed a good bit of his culinary skill to her. So his father standing close to her and smiling shouldn't have tripped any alarms for him.

But the smiles they were sharing, the heated glances, and the familiar way she laid a hand on his father's upper arm seemed like a different kind of close in Jackson's eyes.

He looked at Kip sitting next to him, his eyes bright with amusement as if he knew a secret that Jackson was unaware of. "Am I seeing what I think I'm seeing?"

Kip glanced down at the sweating bottle in his hand before taking another sip of his beer. "Not sure I know what you're talking about."

Jackson looked on the other side of him again. This time, his daddy and Mrs. Eames were bumping shoulders and laughing at some private joke.

"The hell you don't, Kip. Is Mrs. Eames the 'lady friend' Daddy wants to marry?"

Kip slapped him on his back and gave him a conspiratorial smile. Jackson turned and watched his father and Mrs. Eames again and saw his father snake an arm around her waist and pull her to his side, pressing what looked to be a sweet kiss on the side of her cheek. The move still seemed like another friendly gesture, except his father never removed his hand from Mrs. Eames's waist. He kept it there, kept her there as if she was someone important. Someone he couldn't let get away.

"Dammit all to hell."

"Uh-uh. You will not ruin this for them. Those two are happy. And even if your cold heart can't find a use for love, they have. They are gonna announce their engagement tonight. And after all they've both done for the two of us, you are gonna smile and give them your blessing. You hear me, Brother?"

Jackson had a smart-ass comment waiting on the tip of his tongue. Who the hell did Kip think he was in the first place, trying to push him around? He was the older brother; it was his God-given right to be the bossy one. But when he turned around and saw the intense glare, Jackson realized Kip was serious.

"I don't want him to get hurt again," Jackson said. "Her either. She's been good to us. More of a mother than the one that ran out on us."

Kip's jaw relaxed, and he sat back into the cushions of his seat. "We don't get to make this decision for them, Jackson. It's on them. All we can do is support them."

Jackson hated this. Not the youthful giddiness he saw in the pair as they continued to talk and tease each other in front of his father's grill. Even he had to admit that was kind of nice. But he hated the worrisome hole he could feel boring into his gut, warning him to protect his father from being hurt again.

He sat back, stretching his legs out, trying to come to terms with the way his father's life would change, knowing there was nothing he could do to stop him or protect him. Because if Jackson could protect any man from allowing a woman to get under his skin, it would've been himself. And since he hadn't stopped thinking about Aja since he'd left her over a week ago, he figured he may as well sit back and do what his brother asked. If he couldn't allow his own happiness, no need to destroy everyone else's.

Jackson sat on the back porch with a hot cup of coffee and a heavy blanket draped over his shoulders to chase away the morning chill. It was still early, but that had never stopped him from coming out here before dawn.

He'd spent countless moments like this one in his past. Staring up at the moon for the answers the brightness of day would never bring.

When his mother left and after his marriage fell apart and his life crumbled around him, he'd stood in this very spot night after night until he could sleep without seeing the carnage of crushed metal and glass that his wife and her drinking had left behind.

And now, when his head and heart were confused by thoughts of Aja mixed in with his worries about his father's future, Jackson was here again.

He glanced down at the box he'd pulled from his truck before he'd settled in this sacred spot. *Open it when you need a little happy.* A quiet snicker escaped his lips. "Now would be a time for some of that."

He put his coffee cup to the side and stood, walking toward the door to turn on the porch light. Once it was on, he rushed back to his station on the stairs.

He lifted the lid on the top. When he looked inside, there was a folded note atop the tissue paper concealing the contents of the box.

He gently removed it as if it were something precious, protecting it from any harm. He carefully opened it to see Aja's neat and curvy cursive across the page.

Dear Jackson,

There was something so beautiful about watching you create your art in front of me. I've never seen a man look more at peace or more natural as when I watched you put pencil to paper. I still have your rendering of me put away for safekeeping. I thought I would have it made into a larger piece to display in the great room. But then I realized I didn't want to share the small piece of you that you allowed me to see with anyone else.

My wish for you is that you should always look as serene as you did that day, sitting at my kitchen table, doodling on a paper. Whatever troubles find you today, may you lose them in a moment of your own creativity.

Be happy.
—A

Jackson let his thumb trace over the last word of the letter, so touched by Aja's words he almost forgot to open his gift. He folded the note, placing it inside the lid next to him, and peeled back the tissue paper inside the box.

The breath caught in his chest when he realized what was inside. There was a high-quality charcoal pencil set and three sketchbooks of varying sizes all filled with textured, toned tan paper inside.

He opened the medium-size book, his hand shaking as he slid his fingertips across the blank canvas, and marveled at Aja's ability to always know how to take care of the people around her.

He didn't know how she knew this was exactly what he needed— the feeling of the pad in his left hand and the weight of the pencil in his right were more soothing than any balm he'd ever had.

He sketched on the dimly lit porch. He didn't need a subject in front of him, his muse guiding his hand with each instinctive stroke. A few moments in and he already recognized the soft shape of her eyes and the gentle slant of her chin. His pencil whirled over the paper until a face that was unmistakably Aja's stared back him.

He'd spent years with his wife, and she'd never been able to appreciate his need to let his thoughts wander while paper and pencil took him to places and people he'd never seen. Yet in a matter of days, Aja had seen through to the very center of him, and if her thoughtful gift was any sign, she didn't have a problem with what she saw.

"I never could understand your fixation with the night sky." His father's deep baritone cut through the chill and wrapped around him like the warmth of an open fire. "Even after I bought you that telescope and put it on a tripod by your bedroom window, it still wasn't enough to keep your butt inside the house at night. I'd still find you curled up in a blanket on that chair. What troubles you this morning, Son?"

Jackson lifted his head to greet his father, hoping the smile he fashioned would ease the worry he saw settled in the man's eyes. "It's early. You should be sleeping."

"I'm a father. When my children suffer, so do I. Are you really this bothered by my engagement to Sophie?"

Jackson let his head hang, glancing back at the rough sketch in his hand. What kind of son would he be to cause his father so much distress? "Daddy, I never said I had a problem with you and Mrs. Eames."

"You didn't have to. Your silence said plenty. I knew you wouldn't be thrilled about me marrying again, given how I know you feel about relationships. But I didn't think you'd be so bothered you couldn't sleep through the night."

"I'm not." Jackson laughed at the disbelief on his father's face. "I swear I'm not, Daddy. I've got a lot on my mind."

His father made a show of groaning as he took his time to sit on the steps next to Jackson. "Something or someone?"

Jackson didn't bother to hide behind the excuse that was waiting on his tongue. Instead, he handed his father the sketch he'd been working on.

"That's a beautiful likeness of Ms. Everett. I'm sure this will be right nice when you're finished with it. What kind of trouble could this lovely young lady cause you?"

Jackson glanced briefly at his father, then dropped his eyes back on the page.

"Oh, that kind of trouble," his father answered, patting Jackson on the leg as he spoke.

"Daddy, how did you know when you were ready to let go of everything you believed to be true about yourself?"

"When it became more important to hold on to Sophie than it was my past."

Jackson took the sketch pad from his father, darkening another layer of lines, wondering if he'd come to the point where something, someone, was more important than his pain.

Chapter 34

"Aja Marie Everett, you'd better get your hind parts down here before this food you had me cook gets cold."

Aja stood behind the bedroom door and huffed. Aunt Jo was once again bellowing her name from the bottom of the kitchen stairs, threatening her over food Aja hadn't asked her to cook.

"Everything's back to normal." Well, almost normal. She still couldn't bring herself to sleep in her old bedroom. She didn't know if it was because of the attack or if it was because she missed Jackson so much that she needed to be in the room where they shared their one night together. Either way, sleeping in one room while all her belongings were in another made getting ready in the morning a little hectic.

"Aja, you hear me calling you, gal?"

"Yessum." Aja opened the door and called out. "On my way down now."

She sped down the hall and took quick steps until she was in the kitchen. "Mmm, Aunt Jo, you have this kitchen smelling good. What's on the menu?" She walked over to her aunt and kissed her cheek.

"If you're lucky"—her aunt tipped her head to the right—"he

is." Aja followed the direction Jo indicated, and her knees nearly buckled when she saw Jackson Dean sitting at the breakfast table near the back window.

Aja turned to him, slowly walking toward the table as her stomach twisted in knots. Nearly two weeks had passed since they'd last spoken.

She took a deep breath and took the seat he pulled out for her. As they sat, her aunt placed two full plates in front of them, disappeared for a moment, and returned with a pitcher of orange juice and two glasses. "I'll be at my cabin doing a few loads of clothes if you need me."

"Yessum," Aja replied. With a wink and a smile, Aunt Jo made her way down the hall and out the front door.

Jackson poured a glass of juice and slid it across the table for her. "Thanks," Aja said. "Not that I mind you dropping by, but what brings you this way?"

"Well, I've been having a rough couple of days, so I opened your gift."

Aja tried to curb the enthusiasm bubbling inside her. But lost the battle as the edges of her mouth curled into a smile. "Did you like what was inside?"

He dropped his gaze, and when he lifted it again, there was a spark of excitement in their depths. "I loved it, Aja. I don't think anyone has ever given me a more thoughtful gift. I just—"

She held up her hand. "If you're trying to tell me you can't accept the pencils and pads I gave you, forget it. I refuse to take them back. And—"

"I have no intention of giving them back. I already used them." He pulled one of the sketch pads she'd given him from the seat on the opposite side of him and handed it to her.

She opened it to another drawing of her. This one was more detailed than the other he'd created in this very room, and it took her breath away how he captured her likeness and her emotion as well.

"Shortly after I read your note, I sketched this." He pointed to the drawing in her hand. "I kept thinking about what you said about being happy. And I realized the only time I seem to be happy is when I'm near you or drawing pictures of you."

Aja's heart beat faster. Was this happening to her?

He reached across the table and covered her hand with his, his warmth sending shocks of excitement buzzing through her.

"So I figured if I was going to listen to you and find the thing that makes me happy, I should probably start by coming to the source."

Her trembling lips curved into a nervous smile. "I don't know what any of this means, Jackson. What are you trying to say?"

He laughed and stood, pulling her to her feet with him. "I think the old folks call it courting. But if you need me to translate, in my very clumsy way, I'm trying to ask if you'd allow me the privilege of your company. Would you let me take you out on a date?"

Aja folded her arms, trying to contain her giddiness. She cleared her throat, amazed at how a small offering from one man could bring her such joy. "All right, Ranger. I'm game if you are. But are you sure you can handle me?"

He pulled her into his arms, cupping her cheek and leaning in close. "I can handle anything you've got."

———

"Okay, we're in Austin. We headed to Dirty Sixth?"

Jackson parked his truck before turning to her with a smile and shaking his head. Sixth Street was famous for its seemingly endless row of bars. If you were looking to tie one on in a loud, crowded place, you'd have your pick there.

Not that he hadn't been a patron a time or two. He'd certainly had his fair share of fun over the years. But he wanted tonight to be different, special. It was a chance for him to show Aja some of the gems tourists often missed.

He went to reach for the handle on his door and saw Aja doing the same. "Now, I don't know about those jokers in New York, but us country boys don't let women open their own doors. You've been in a car with me before; you should know that."

The sharp intake of her breath coupled with the high arch of her lifted brow was all the warning she gave him. "Let?" She released a long sigh before she continued. "First, 'let' implies that I need your permission. My case is officially over, and any deference I showed you before will not spill over into us getting to know each other personally.

"Second, I am perfectly capable of opening my own door. I am not fragile or broken; there is no logical reason why I should sit here and wait for you to walk around this monster truck of yours and open my door."

His smile widened as he stared at her. The very thing that frustrated the hell out of him while working her case was also the thing that turned him on. She was fearless and didn't back down from anyone, and after seeing her wield her lawyerly powers in that interrogation room, he figured she must be a marvel to watch in an actual courtroom.

"Aja, I wasn't insinuating you were helpless. Everything I've known about you tells me you're one of the strongest people I know. I don't want to open doors for you because I think you're this breakable thing—I do it because it's just one of the ways for me to show my appreciation for a wonderful person like you choosing to spend your time with me. Not to mention, holding doors open for people is the courteous thing to do. And you know us southern boys are all about good manners."

She stared at him as if she were attempting to gauge the veracity of his explanation. "You are so infuriating."

"Pot, meet kettle."

"We have to be some kind of insane to do this."

He laughed hard and loud at that one. "Baby, you ain't ever

lied." They were both so headstrong and determined to have their
own way, it would be interesting to see how they kept from slitting
each other's throats. But as her gloss-covered lips bent into a sultry
smile and her shoulders quaked with laughter, he knew whatever
minefields they had to navigate to get closer to each other would
be worth it.

"So now that you know I'm not being a chauvinistic pig, would
you allow me the honor of opening your door for you?"

"Absolutely."

He opened his door, quickly walking around the back of the
vehicle to get to her side. He pulled the handle, offering her his
hand as she placed one booted foot onto the running board and
then on the ground.

He bit his lip, for fear of saying something stupid as he took a
long glance at her. She wore a short red sweater dress that put every
one of her luscious curves on display, paired with black, over-the-
knee stiletto boots that made her petite legs look so much longer
than they had any right to be. Whoever lied and said full-figured
women weren't the sexiest thing on earth had never had the pleasure of meeting Aja Everett.

At the moment, he wasn't upset that society was stupid; it gave
him more of an opportunity to have her all to himself. *More for me.*

They walked around the corner until they were on South
Congress Avenue, in the middle of what appeared to be a small
street festival. People were walking the street while vendors
enticed pedestrians over to their shops with cocktails and appetizers, all to the sound of loud, rhythmic music.

"What is all this, Jackson?"

"It's called First Thursday. On the first Thursday of every
month, shop owners put on this sort of block party. People come,
they drink and eat, enjoy the music, and do a little shopping too. I
thought it would be a nice way for you to get reacquainted with the
area since so much of your time is dedicated to the ranch."

She laced her fingers through his and gave them a squeeze. "You're taking a woman whose idea of recreational time is a day on Fifth Ave shopping on your first date? You're either the bravest man I know or the least smart."

He pulled her hand up to his mouth and placed a light kiss on the back. "Probably a little of both."

She winked at him and pulled him in the crowd's direction. "Well, come on then, Ranger. Let's get this party started."

———————

Jackson retrieved wet paper towels from his kitchen and offered Aja one. "I still cannot believe you got us Franklin Barbecue take-out without us having to set up a tent on that line."

He was glad she was impressed. People waited hours in line to get inside that place just to order. Getting a table to eat in was nearly impossible without securing a reservation six months in advance. With good reason too. Eating their food was a spiritual experience.

"I was there one night last year to pick up an order for an office potluck when two patrons who'd had a little too much fun on Dirty Sixth got a little rowdy. I handled the situation, got them out of there without too much fuss, and the owner was grateful. Told me anytime I wanted something, call him personally, and he'd make certain I'd never have to wait in line again."

She finished wiping her hands and mouth, then took another sip of her beer. "I guess that Texas Ranger badge really does come with some perks."

"I swear, it's the only one I've ever taken advantage of."

She lifted her hands and laughed. "Hey, no judgments from me. Barbecue that good is worth bending some rules for. And techni-cally, if you're still paying for the food, it's not a bribe."

He winked and gave her a playful "No comment" before

removing their dishes from the table to his kitchen counter. He scraped the remains of their meal into the trash.

"You want me to help with cleanup? It's the least I can do after you took me shopping, showed me some of downtown Austin's culture, and fed me grilled meat I didn't have to cook myself."

"I've got the cleanup, but you can come keep me company while I wash the dishes."

She grabbed their beer bottles and met him at the sink, placing his on the butcher block surface as she leaned in to the counter, swirling her own bottle around in tight circles.

"Thank you for tonight. I didn't realize how much I needed a night out."

"When was the last time you did anything but work?"

She took a sip and the impish grin she wore as she swallowed told him she knew she looked damn sexy doing it. "You criticizing my work ethic, Ranger?"

"No, commiserating with it. I don't take nearly as much time off as I should. That's how I ended up on forced leave for four weeks."

She placed her beverage on the counter and looked up to the ceiling, shaking her head. "We're a sad pair, aren't we? We have everything in life we could need, and yet all either of us seems to find joy in is work."

He shut off the faucet, picked up a towel to dry his hands, and faced her. "Hopefully we'll help each other change that."

There was a spark in her eye. It was intense and consuming. She stepped closer to him, her hands sliding up the front of his white button-down shirt, playing with the collar as she tilted her mouth toward his.

"You don't have to do this. I didn't bring you back here to coerce you into sleeping with me."

"I know I don't have to do this, and I didn't think you did." Her words were intentional, as if she were educating him instead of him reassuring her. "I gotta tell you, this almost pathological need of yours to make me feel safe is the sexiest thing about you."

He was no prince when it came to romance. But he never wanted his partners to feel somehow pressured into being with him. Maybe it was his overinflated ego, maybe it was the constant insistence of his father that he always ask before he assumed when it came to sex, but whatever it was, he needed more than anything to know Aja's desire to be with him was as desperate as his.

"Really? I think my charm is way sexier than anything else I've got going for me."

She shook her head. "You mean your bull-in-a-glass-factory charm? No, not so much. I'm more intrigued by your struggle to balance your obligations versus your desires. Watching you watching me, trying your best to be the gentleman your father raised you to be, that was the height of foreplay."

Listening to her talk about foreplay made heat spread through his body. He could easily have blamed the electric buzz on the alcohol he'd consumed. But no amount of beer had ever made him feel as alive and aware as the thought of Aja Everett in his arms.

"Now that we have that settled, can we get to the part where we're both naked and happy? Because that would be a big, beautiful bow on top of this amazing gift of a night you've given me. What do you say, Ranger?"

He said nothing; he couldn't. This woman who was bold and forthright almost every moment he'd spent with her stole his ability to think and process language. The dynamic way her mind worked seemed to have more control over him than the siren's call of her body. God, when did words become so sexy to him?

He knew the exact answer to that. It was the moment she'd cursed him out when he'd arrived on her ranch. He'd thought it was annoyance. Now he saw it for what it was—an aphrodisiac.

All those verbal battles they'd had before were foreplay, a means of ramping up the desire that flowed so easily between them. And now, as he stood with her pressed against him in his kitchen, no restrictions from his job standing in the way of him delighting in this undeniable chemistry they shared, Jackson didn't want words between them. He wanted nothing between them. Not the clothes they wore and divested themselves of as he led them into his bedroom. Not the hang-ups about love and intimacy that had plagued him for more years than he could count, and most of all, not the hurt he'd been holding on to for so long he almost didn't know how to let it go.

He reached down, opening his nightstand drawer and removing a condom. The thin aluminum packet felt so heavy in his hand.

"Hey, everything okay?"

He pulled her into his arms, unsure of how to answer that question but needing to try anyway. "I have never in my life wanted to forgo using a condom as badly as I do right now."

"Jackson—"

He saw the concern on her face. Playing fast and loose with condoms came at a huge cost. He'd never knowingly endanger either of them like that.

"I'm not suggesting we don't use it. I'm saying for the first time, I don't want to. Does that make sense?"

She nodded. "Yes. It simply means if that's something we wish to explore, we've got to set up some ground rules first."

She took the condom out of his hand and opened it, then wrapped her hand around his hardened length and slowly slid it down. "But that is a conversation for another time. The only thing I want to discuss right now is how long it will take for you to join your beautiful body with mine."

"Woman, the things you say. I finally can have you without feeling like I'm committing a punishable offense, and you want me to rush straight through it?"

"You are absolutely correct."

She stood on tiptoe, pressing her lips against his, and whatever retort he had was lost in the sweet taste of her. It was such a heady flavor, the sweet and tangy spice of the barbecue they'd eaten mixed with the citrus flavor of the IPA they'd imbibed, and his senses were on overload.

He broke away from the kiss, placing sweet pecks along her jawline and down the curve of her neck, quietly savoring the tiny shivers underneath the skin there, wondering how he'd gotten so lucky to share her body again.

She shivered. Her skin was warm to the touch, and his apartment comfortably climate-controlled. Those were shivers of need, and it made his cock throb every time he felt those tiny tremors beneath the press of his lips.

"If that's the way you truly feel about it, take what you want."

He sat on the bed, his feet still planted on the floor. His fingers laced with hers, he drew her near until she straddled him. She leaned down, her eyes bright with arousal, her breath deep and steady. Her long braids fell over her shoulders, and he pushed them back behind her ears, needing to see all of her as they connected again.

The sight of her, the feel of her against him made his blood rush through his vessels, leaving him dizzy with need. Like a drug spreading through him, lighting him ablaze from the inside out, she called to something buried so deep inside Jackson, he hadn't realized it existed.

It reached beyond the disappointment of his broken marriage. It went further than his mother abandoning him. It dug so deep inside him, filling in all the empty spaces that had left him so cold and empty all these years.

He didn't know how she did it. He didn't understand what manner of magic she possessed to crack open his chest and find all his hidden spaces without him knowing it. But as her hand gripped him and she slid herself down his corded shaft, drawing him into her center, he willingly submitted to her power.

Where was his fighting instinct? Where was the thing that told him to never yield? Because with each swivel of her hips, Jackson was losing himself, and what was most unnerving about it all was that he didn't seem to care.

"What have you done to me?"

"Does it really matter?"

She was right. It didn't. With each snap of her hips, she was bringing him closer and closer to the end his desire sought.

Her muscles clenched him, their rhythm unpredictable as she neared her climax. He wasn't far behind. The impulse to let go and drop over into satisfaction with her chased him like a relentless foe, demanding that he surrender and give in.

Determined she would be satisfied first, he slowed her motions with a firm hand pressed into her lower back and the other wrapped around her neck, pulling her toward him, latching his mouth to hers, kissing her until his chest was tight with the need to breathe.

He sat up, cradling her in his lap, holding her as she wrapped her legs around his back. When she encircled her arms around his neck, he found his footing, standing, turning them around, and laying her gently in the center of the bed.

She was breathtaking. Large, round breasts, their pert brown peaks begging to be suckled. Her wide, rounded hips were spread, welcoming him back into her warmth, while the brown and pink folds of her slick opening clenched, glistening with want as he positioned himself between her legs, carefully stroking himself.

She was everything he needed. A slight niggle in the back of his mind tried to warn him, tried to remind him that opening himself up to her was a danger he didn't need. But before the thought could take root, he watched her slide two fingers in her mouth, coating them and slipping them between her swollen folds, rubbing the pink nub protruding there. With each flicker of her fingers over her slick flesh, conscious thought became impossible, and his body went on automatic.

He slid into her opening, loving the sight of her fingers playing in her pussy while he moved in and out of her. He leaned over, bracing his arms on either side of her shoulders to give himself more leverage and stealing another kiss as her moans grew louder and she spilled over into bliss.

He chased her orgasm, slamming into her while her climax crested, and her slick walls grabbed him, demanding he succumb to the need he'd fought since this began.

He tried to fight it, tried to remember that before he'd met her, he used to be a man in control of his own body. But then she licked the carved edge of his jaw and whispered in his ear, "Jackson, please," and he was lost.

He couldn't explain it. Nothing about her being in his world beyond her case made sense to him. But as her words traveled through his ears and into his heart, his sac tightened, hitching up higher and higher as his orgasm pulled every drop of his remaining power and released it in the searing first jet of come that ripped through him, tearing a deep howl that climbed from his chest, out through his throat, and into the air.

When his climax ebbed and his lungs and heart fought to regulate his breathing and pulse, he understood two things. The first: because he wasn't twenty anymore, he would need to sleep long and hard before he could do that again, and second: he would definitely do that again.

―――――――――――

Jackson held Aja as tightly as he could without crushing her. His need to have her skin against his should make him uncomfortable as hell. But instead of discomfort, he felt at ease, soothed in a way one only felt when they were safe. Considering his line of work and the problematic relationships he'd had with women, he couldn't honestly remember a moment when he felt so certain there wasn't a threat around the corner.

"I need this."

Aja looked up at him with confusion in his eyes. That was when he realized he'd spoken aloud.

"Need what?"

He noted the absence of panic in him as he prepared to answer her. Yet another piece of proof Aja had gotten under his skin. "Us."

"I'm not sure I follow what you're talking about, Jackson."

Join the club 'cause I sure as hell don't get it either.

"Aja, I know I said I wanted to just have fun, to see where this thing between us went. But I don't think I was being honest with you or myself."

He felt her tense against him, and he realized this was all about to go sideways if he couldn't manage to get his foot out his mouth.

"If you've changed your mind about this, Jackson, you can say it."

He saw what looked like sadness dulling her eyes and etching lines into her brow. But even when she thought she was being rejected, she never cowered. Instead, she faced it head on.

"I've changed my mind, but not in the way you think," he said. She squinted up at him, trying to decipher what he meant. "I don't want casual, Aja. Being with you tonight, doing something as mundane as having dinner in my apartment and making love to you in my bed, it feels right."

She giggled and let her hand slide beneath the cover until she was cupping him, stirring interest anew in his sleeping cock.

"Of course it feels right. My sex is awesome."

She said it so matter-of-factly, all he could do was give in to the happy chuckle sitting in his chest.

"I completely agree with that statement, Counselor. But that's not what I was talking about. I want more of this, Aja. Not just the occasional date and one-off. I want to be with you."

He could see the moment the realization of what he was saying began to seep in. She retreated out of his embrace and pulled herself against the headboard. He followed suit, needing to make sure they were on equal footing. He needed her to understand they were equals in this decision. This was about what they both wanted, not just his feelings.

"Jackson, I'm enjoying what's happening between us. But I don't know if I'm where you are just yet."

He laced his fingers between hers, needing to reassure her and himself too. "I get that. I completely respect that, and I'm not asking you to declare your undying love for me. I just want you to be open to us becoming more. Can you do that? Let me prove to you I'm the only man you'll ever need in your life."

She dropped her eyes, letting them fall to their joined hands. He couldn't tell from her body language what she was thinking. And if he was honest, her silence was beginning to worry him. But no matter what her decision, he promised himself he'd respect it.

"Jackson, I don't know if I'm as certain as you we can make this work. We live ninety minutes away from each other. We're both so busy with our jobs… How can we do this?"

"Do you want this to work?" he asked.

She looked up at him through her thick lashes. "I do."

He scanned her face, looking for hesitancy, but he couldn't find any. That discovery eased the tension he hadn't even realized he was holding in his chest.

"Then if you want this to work, we will make it work. All I'm asking for is the chance. Will you give me that?"

A slow smile blossomed on her face, and the full apples of her cheeks glowed with a warm blush. "You make it hard for a girl to say no, Ranger." She let her hand slide down his firm chest, her nails raking against his nipple and sending an instant jolt of desire straight to his dick.

He grabbed her hand and brought it to his mouth for a quick kiss. "You're avoiding the question, Counselor. But just so you know, if you keep that up, your ability to answer me won't be the only thing that's hard around here."

"Promises, promises."

"Aja?" Her playful smile tugged at his heart, and he had to fight himself to keep from pulling her beneath him right then and there. "What's your answer?"

She pulled her bottom lip between her teeth. On anyone else, it would've just been an expression of contemplation. But on her, it was a turn-on. His blood ran hot at the thought of what new way she'd find to put those luscious lips to work.

"If you want me, Ranger, I'm yours. But please understand, I'm gonna need us to take this slow." She cupped his face, allowing her thumb to stroke the stubble of his beard, both comforting him and arousing him at the same time. "I wasn't secretly searching for a relationship when you walked into my life, Jackson. I've got a lot on my plate with the ranch and Pathways. But I'd be lying if I said the idea of having you all to myself doesn't appeal to me in an instinctive way. If you can handle us taking this painfully slow, I can agree to committing to a relationship with you."

He wasn't sure who leaned in first, but the moment those words crossed her lips, his mouth was pressed against hers. Aja Everett had agreed to have him. As far as he was concerned, there was nothing better in the world. And as they sank back into the mattress, he was determined to prove his gratitude and excitement with every lick, touch, and moan he could offer. Not just for her benefit, although making sure she was satisfied in bed was always a top priority for him. No, this was a reverent celebration for him, a mark of the moment his heart had finally thawed all the way through, and it was beating hard and strong for only one woman: Aja.

Chapter 35

Aja made it as far as the edge of Jackson's bed before he tucked his strong arm around her waist, pulling her back against the solid wall of his chest. "Where are you trying to escape to? I have plans for you that don't involve either of us getting out of this bed."

A knowing smile spread across Aja's lips. If they were anything like the plans he'd had for her last night, Aja was certain she'd enjoy them. "As tempting as that sounds, I have to get back to the ranch."

Jackson raised his head, placing a quick peck on her cheek. "Because of Seneca and Brooklyn?"

"Yes, but not in the way I think you mean. They're not on house arrest. They're not bound to the ranch. They can come and go as they please as long as they show up for work every day."

He wagged his eyebrows in an over-the-top lecherous way, then nuzzled the delicate skin where her neck and shoulder met. He swiped the tip of his tongue across it, making the nerves come alive. "Then stay."

Boy, did she ever want to. She loved her ranch, but waking up next to this man with his natural body heat acting as the best blanket was placing a close second to starting the day appreciating the beauty of her land.

"I really can't. I'm supposed to take Aunt Jo shopping today for the anniversary party we're having next Saturday. She won't hear of ordering the groceries online the way I do. She wants to squeeze the produce herself."

Jackson's hand slid from her waist, up the soft cushion of her abdomen until his large palm was cupping and kneading the tender flesh of her breasts. "I completely agree with the sentiment."

"You're not making this easy, Ranger."

"I thought you liked it hard."

"So not what I meant."

He placed a delicate kiss on her shoulder, meant more to soothe than arouse. But that kiss, coupled with the way his fingers were stroking her nipples, started the first flames of desire in her belly. It wouldn't take much until she was ready for an encore performance of last night.

"What kind of anniversary party?"

"We're celebrating Seneca and Brooklyn successfully completing one year of the Pathways program. One more year, and they'll both have paid their debt to society and will have the ability to go out into the world if they choose to. I still have a long to-do list. If I leave it to Aunt Jo, she'll shop and cook for half the county."

He placed another kiss on her shoulder, moving his hand down between her breasts until he was tightening his arm around her waist again. "That might not be such a bad idea. How are things with the town since Bennett's confession and incarceration?"

She ran light fingers atop his, loving the protective cocoon he was providing her. "On the few occasions we've had to go into town since all the craziness ended, people have been quite apologetic. Apparently Eli did his level best to keep anyone from helping us."

He tugged on her shoulder, and she turned around until they were facing each other. "I know you might have intended for this event to be more intimate. But maybe inviting some of the townspeople could help smooth things over."

She ran her fingers lightly over her scalp and wondered if there ever would be an opportune moment to come together with the people Eli kept under his thumb.

"You're right," she responded. "I know, but…I honestly want to make this meaningful for the two of them. I'm not blaming anyone in town for what Eli did, but having them there, knowing they were his victims too, might make it awkward."

He gave her an easy smile, his dark-brown eyes gleaming with amusement. "You're really excited about this, aren't you?"

"Yeah. Everyone deserves a second chance to get things right. These ladies are working hard to start over. I'm happy to help facilitate that."

She let her hand slide to the side of his face, smooth brown skin giving way to a dark, groomed beard that tickled the delicate skin of her palm. She smiled again, trying to ignore the swell of emotion in her heart that seemed to grow with abandon whenever she was in his presence. "If they can make this work, anyone can. It means there's hope for us all to work through our issues and find something better for ourselves."

His eyes narrowed, and she could see the question forming in their dark depths. Too raw to defend herself against any query his mind was thinking up and too afraid that she'd have to tell him why she needed to cling to that hope of a better tomorrow, she popped a quick kiss on his lips and headed for his bathroom. "Gotta go."

She leaned behind the closed bathroom door and took a steadying breath. Redemption was around the corner for her wards, and for her. Jackson had asked to be the man in her life last night. A fact she was still processing. But she refused to analyze this to death through the lens of her guilt. No, she would accept this chance at joy, even if she didn't quite deserve it at this moment.

Old guilt tried to horn its way in on the fragile happiness trying to blossom inside her. But she refused to let it have its way. Instead, she just reminded herself that if she could hold on for a little bit longer, she too might pay the debt that weighed so heavily on her soul.

And maybe then she wouldn't feel like there was an oven timer ticking on every good thing that came into her life. She wouldn't lie to herself any longer, pretending she could take or leave Jackson's company. She wanted him, for more than the two nights they'd spent in each other's arms. And she would give anything to be worthy of him.

You're almost there, Aja. You're almost there.

———————

Jackson pulled up to the front of the main house and cut the engine of his truck. "We're here." He didn't hide the disappointment in his voice. If she would've allowed it, he'd have kept her hidden in the cove of his apartment for as long as it took to satisfy his ravenous need for her. She hadn't allowed it—for good reason—but it still made him ache to return to reality so soon after experiencing the fantasy of Aja Everett in his bed.

He reached over the console and picked up her hand, kissing the back before lacing his fingers through hers. "When can I see you again?"

He marveled at the open mischief swirling in the depths of her dark eyes. "I'm impressed, Ranger. No waiting three days before calling to show interest; you're making up your own rules to this dating game."

"I'm too old." His chuckle sparked one of her own.

"I know that's right. Forty is knocking on my door."

"Forty is past the knocking stage. It's moved in and has its feet up on my couch. But I'm not here to play games. I told you, Aja. I know what I want. When can I see you again?"

She squeezed their linked fingers and smiled. "Please don't take this as a blow-off, but I really will be busy setting up for the dinner party this week. But I'd love it if you'd attend the celebration."

"You sure they'd want me there? It's not like we're the best of friends. Brooklyn did little more than growl at me while I was here."

"Brooklyn's charm is an acquired taste. I'm sure Seneca would love it, though. My aunt and uncle will be there, and even the Sullivans are coming."

That was a surprise. He hadn't heard her mention Taylor Sullivan or his family since he'd dropped her off after Taylor's confession and release. "I'm surprised you'd invite him."

"I didn't. The guests of honor did. They were given a second chance. They wanted to extend one to Taylor too. He's actually working out an unofficial community service on the ranch. He comes over before and after school to take care of the horses and helps out running errands. He wants to give back after causing so much trouble."

Jackson shook his head, amazed again by her ability to forgive and give people the opportunity to change, to take a new path. "Glad he's trying to turn himself around and make amends, but I can't say I'm not worried you'll trust the wrong person one day and end up hurt."

She looked out the windshield and took a deep breath as if she needed to fortify herself. "There's always a risk in trusting someone. But there's always something to gain too. Like if I hadn't trusted my uncle and finally stopped fighting him to bring in you and your men, we might never have caught Eli in his dirt. Someone might've been seriously hurt, and I never would've had the chance to meet you. Considering how everything turned out, I'd say the gain far outweighed the risk."

She lifted their hands and mimicked his early movements by placing a gentle kiss on his knuckles. The touch was featherlight, but it was powerful, connecting him to her on an elemental level. His heart, his mind, and his soul all relaxing, letting go of everything except her in that moment. "Come celebrate with us, Ranger.

I'd bet even a surly lawman like yourself could learn the benefits of trusting someone every now and again."

He didn't need to attend a party for that. No, he was learning that lesson slowly, with each passing moment he spent in her presence. She'd started as just a case. She'd ended up being much more important than that. If he weren't careful, she might wind up being the person to break beyond all his barriers. And as he promised to be there, he realized there was no question about it. Aja Everett was well on her way to teaching him to trust.

Chapter 36

Aja rummaged through her closet, trying to find something to wear. She was a woman who'd walked the red carpet at Hollywood events on more than one occasion, but she couldn't figure out for the life of her what to put on for a simple dinner party happening in her dining room.

In all fairness, she hadn't dressed herself for those celebrity events. She'd had designers she'd paid hefty sums to create custom looks for her. But standing here trying to decide between a sweater dress and an everyday midi dressed up with a pair of platform stiletto pumps, she longed for the days when her stylist waved a magic wand and made her fabulous with little effort on Aja's part.

The midi dress won out. She prayed she hadn't spent so much time in work boots that she didn't know how to walk in what used to be her signature footwear.

She glimpsed herself in front of the mirror and wondered why she was so concerned with her wardrobe. She wasn't standing before the court; the press and their unforgiving cameras weren't surrounding her. She wasn't about to step out on the red carpet. Why was she having such a hard time tonight?

"Jackson." The smile his name brought to her lips didn't

surprise her. He was an attractive man, and he'd spent the last week showering her with his time and attention via calls and text messages, so of course his name made her smile.

She slid the dress over her head and turned back and forth as she stood in front of the mirror. The dress was cute, but she'd need shapewear to get the look she wanted, and no one had time for that today.

She pulled off the dress and foraged in her closet once more. Her fingers touched a leather corset with light boning she hadn't worn in the time she'd been here. She grabbed a short, black skirt with a slight flare and a white, long-sleeved button-down shirt, and in a blur of limbs, she managed to get everything on.

She held the red corset in her hand, wondering if it was too much for the event. After she zipped its front and looked at herself in the mirror, she didn't care if it was too much or not. Her girls were sitting high and pretty, and her waist was snatched, and she felt almost like a super heroine in the entire getup.

"One thing missing, though." She found another pair of knee-high boots. When you were a petite woman with thick calves and thighs, boots that comfortably fit above the knee were a rare find. So when she came across them at Torrid, she bought them in as many styles and colors as she could find.

These were black like the pair she'd worn last week on her date with Jackson. But instead of stiletto heels, these were wedges. They gave her the same height, with added comfort—a bonus for all the walking she was sure she'd be doing as the host of this shindig.

She sat at her vanity, making a few touch-ups to her earlier applied makeup and piling her long, tiny braids on the top of her head in a messy but cute bun. She clipped some gold-cuff hair accessories onto several of the braids to add a little more pizazz to the style and then reached for a set of large, thin hoops for her ears.

Satisfied with her reflection, she couldn't help but sing the opening lyrics to LL Cool J's "Around the Way Girl." Spending so much time in the corporate world, followed by her work on the ranch, didn't allow for her to tap into her Brooklyn swagger often. Seeing that woman smiling back at her in the mirror gave Aja a jolt of excitement.

Yeah, she was eager to see what Jackson's reaction to her outfit would be. But above all, she was happy to see the resurgence of this long-lost side of herself. The woman who stared back at her was carefree and looked forward to life.

Aja stood and released a long sigh. Her shoulders loose with relief, she headed for the door and paused for a second when another realization dropped into her consciousness—whatever awaited her on the other side of this moment, she was ready to move beyond her past. Seneca and Brooklyn had reinvented themselves, and it was time for her to do the same.

Jackson stood on the front porch, ready to knock on the door, when he heard a vehicle coming up the road. He recognized Colton's large pickup truck and waited for him to make his way out of it and up onto the porch.

Jackson extended his hand, and Colton moved two small gift bags from his right hand to his left to accept it.

"I didn't know you got an invite. Is Storm coming too?"

Colton shook his head. "I don't think so. When I spoke to him about it, he said he was spending some time in Mexico with his mother."

That wasn't strange. Of the three of them, even with the same workload as Jackson and Colton, Storm always seemed to make time for a personal life, for his family. Jackson often envied him that ability. Turning the job off in his head might've been nice every now and again.

"I wasn't aware you and Aja kept contact after her case."

The corners of Colton's mouth curled into a sinister smile. "Jealous much, Dean?"

Jackson didn't know if it was jealousy causing his body to tense at the idea of Aja spending time with another man the way she did with him. But he knew he didn't like that the possibility existed.

"Aja didn't invite me. Seneca did."

Jackson opened his mouth to ask more about the invitation, but Colton knocked on the door, and all too soon, he heard footsteps nearing. He tabled the questions pinging around inside his head for another time and prepared himself to greet Aja.

When she opened the door, he realized he needed more than a few seconds to get himself together. She was stunning. Her hair was piled high atop her head with soft tendrils framing her heart-shaped face and the glint of what looked like gold metal pieces wrapped around a braid or two in different positions. He'd seen them before on women with locs or braids. But on Aja, they somehow appeared regal, a statement of her magnificence, not just something to decorate her hair.

He squeezed his hand into a fist to keep from reaching out and running his palm down the length of her skirt until he could feel that sultry brown swatch of skin exposed at the edge of the fabric. She'd put together an outfit that was fun, fashionable, and sexy as hell, and it made him question how long he would have to wait before everyone left and he could have her all to himself.

He cleared his throat, offering her an easy smile as he finally lifted his eyes up to hers.

She gave him a quick once-over, then looked away from him and focused on Colton. His comrade smiled at her and leaned down to place a quick peck on her cheek. "Thanks for letting Seneca invite me. I don't think I've had a decent meal since we left here."

"Go on and get you something to eat then. There are cock-tails and appetizers set out on the back porch. Aunt Jo put some pulled-pork bruschetta on the table a few minutes ago. That usually goes quick, so I wouldn't tarry."

She opened the door wider, stepping aside to let him in.

"I don't think I know what bruschetta is, but if it's got barbecue sauce on it, I'll eat it," Colton told her.

Jackson shook his head as he watched Colton make his way down the hall toward the kitchen. "Please excuse my uncultured colleague."

Aja waved her hand. "Trust me, Aunt Jo didn't know what the hell bruschetta was either until she saw it on what she calls 'one of them fancy cooking shows.'"

Jackson stepped inside and pushed the door closed, letting his eyes walk up and down her body, then back again, landing on her high-set breasts. "You look edible in that outfit. Was it all for my benefit?"

Her smile brightened as she shook her head. "No. It's for me. If I don't feel like butter in a hot skillet when I look at myself, how will anyone else see me that way?"

He took a few steadying breaths, attempting to push his need for her down. "I'm wearing slacks. Not the best material for concealing arousal. How about you stop trying to make me embarrass myself in public?"

She winked at him and then walked down the hall. He could swear there was an extra swivel in her wide, round hips as she placed each foot in front of the other. He groaned as quietly as he could; even her walk was irresistible.

By the time they stepped out onto the back porch, Jackson had gathered a little self-control and pushed his wayward thoughts to the back of his mind. There was always later, and he intended to make use of any time he could steal when the party was over.

He stood in front of the doorway, scanning the small group gathered on the back porch and the immediate clearing beyond the back of the house.

He recognized many in the group. He'd broken bread with most of them right here on the ranch, including Mat Ryan, who was currently beckoning Aja to meet him on the far side of the porch.

His stomach roiled slightly as Aja excused herself and headed toward Mat. Each step she took toward the man was a reminder Jackson needed to get his emotions in check where Aja and this man were concerned. With Eli Bennett in jail for his crimes against Aja, Jackson couldn't use Aja's safety as an excuse any longer. It was time to fess up: the only reason Mat was still a problem for him was because Aja seemed to care for the man. And if he were being honest, Jackson didn't want her caring for anyone else but him in that respect.

Get it together, Jackson. Even as she's standing in front of him, he's looking across the yard in Brooklyn's direction. There's nothing going on between Aja and him. You're just a jealous fool.

Contrite over his juvenile attitude toward Mat, he went back to panning the group and noted a few people he didn't recognize. They were probably guests of guests. He was about to glance in Aja's direction again when he heard someone calling his name.

"Jackson, it's good to see you again."

He found Aja's uncle, Judge Henry, walking toward him. The judge pulled Jackson into an empty corner of the porch, looking around to make certain no one was near. "I wanted to thank you for all the help you gave my niece. I know from experience that Aja can be obstinate when she believes she's right about something."

"Turns out she was right. She didn't need to listen to me; I needed to listen to her. The true hero turned out to be my father and his security equipment. If we hadn't caught an intruder on camera, we would never have gotten the goods on Bennett."

"I'm still glad you were here." The judge cleared his throat, looking away as if he needed a moment to gather himself. "She's so much like her mother, my late sister. She's headstrong, independent, never wants to ask for help, and will take care of everyone around her but herself. She's so strong, so able, sometimes her aunt and I forget that she needs looking after. I would never have forgiven myself if Bennett had harmed her."

Jackson stilled himself against the shiver that ran through him. The thought of what could've happened during her attack still scraped against his insides, making his heart race with tension.

"I know what you mean. If I hadn't been in the house…" He couldn't finish the sentence, didn't even want to complete the thought. Not then, and definitely not now when they were connecting, discovering what could be between them.

"I've seen the way you look at her."

Jackson forced himself to focus on Judge Henry. "I'm not sure I know what you mean."

"Don't you?" When Jackson didn't answer, the older man laughed and leaned in closer. "My sister Jo tells me you came by to see Aja last week."

Jackson couldn't help the smile that blossomed on his mouth. "Yessuh, I did."

"If I didn't think she'd kill me for trying to give you the what-are-your-intentions talk, I'd certainly grill you about where you think this is headed. But since I'm trying to be more progressive and less meddlesome, I'll just ask that you treat her right. She's carried a lot on her shoulders. It would be nice if she got to have some fun for a change."

"Uncle Ricky, why do you have this man hemmed up in the corner?"

Aja's voice vibrated through Jackson's entire being, pulling at something in his core that instantly responded to its easy lilt. She slid an arm around his waist and nuzzled into his side as she placed her other hand on her hip. "He's here to enjoy himself, Uncle, not to be cross-examined."

Judge Henry placed a sweet kiss on the apple of her cheek and hooked his thumb toward Jackson. "We were chatting, Niece. No inquisitions involved."

She cut her eyes to the side. Not the least bit fooled by her uncle's denial, she wagged a finger at him. "I know you too well, Uncle Ricky."

The man chuckled and threw his hands up in the air, making a show of backing away from the two of them slowly. When he was halfway across the porch, she stepped slightly to the side, dropping her arm from Jackson's waist and putting a respectable distance from them.

"I'm sorry about the full-on PDA. I didn't see any other way that would get him away from you."

There she went again, worrying about everyone around her. Touched by her concern for him but slightly annoyed that she didn't know how he craved her touch by now, Jackson placed his hand low on her waist and pulled her to him so they stood front to front.

"As long as you don't have a problem with it, I don't really care who sees when you touch me."

"Be careful what you say," she answered as she shared a coy smile with him. "You might just give me ideas." He couldn't tell if it was the deep, sultry tone of her voice that made his length twitch or if it was the dirty innuendo that tickled his senses and made lust unfurl deep in the darkest parts of him. Whichever it was, he lost himself in his building need and leaned down to press his lips against hers.

"How long do I have to wait until I can have that skirt of yours hiked up around your waist?"

"It's a buffet-style dinner, so as soon as I make a toast to the honorees, everyone will go inside and fix their own plates, and you and I can find a quiet place to sneak away to."

He kissed her again, this time letting his lips rest against hers a little longer. "Make it happen."

"I'll go get the champagne."

"I'll help."

Between the two of them, they poured champagne for every-one in the small group in record time. He was so uncharacteristically giddy about the idea of touching Aja again that he didn't even mind the knowing smile Colton gave him when Jackson handed him his glass of champagne.

Yeah, he already knew he would receive shit for this by the time the three of them returned to work, but Jackson didn't care. A quick glance over his shoulder and the gift of Aja's sweet mouth curled up into an inviting smile was all he could focus on. Nothing else mattered.

Which was when Jackson Dean, Texas Ranger, understood how deeply he was in. It became obvious this wasn't just fun anymore when watching her smile from across the yard made his stomach drop. He realized then Aja Everett could do anything with him and he would gladly follow her wherever she led. Because that smile and the way her brown eyes twinkled with that spark of intellect and intrigue had somehow tangled him up in a web he didn't want to break free of.

"You are in so much trouble," Colton whispered. Jackson didn't take his eyes off Aja as he listened to his friend. How could he? She had this ability to draw him in, to hold his attention even when he knew he should place it on other things like his friend and colleague who was giggling like an immature teenaged boy, giving Jackson shit.

"Yeah, I know."

"What do you plan to do to stop it, Jackson?"

Aja gave him a quick wave and disappeared back into the house. He turned around to face Colton, his face muscles still tingling from all the exercise they were getting tonight smiling at Aja. He poured himself a glass of champagne and lifted it in a mock solute to his friend. "Not a damn thing."

"Good evening, everyone. It's almost time to eat the lovely meal my aunt Jo was gracious enough to prepare for us. And if you've ever sat at her table, you know I'm gonna try my best to be brief, because if you have the good sense God gave a goat, you don't miss a meal Aunt Jo cooked."

The dozen or so people gathered on her back porch and the extending deck laughed. A quick glance among the people, and Aja easily found her aunt smiling with pride.

"Two years ago, I had everything a woman could want: money, prestige, and the respect of my colleagues. I mingled in the world of celebrities and dignitaries. Figuratively, I was sitting on top of the world. I had everything at my fingertips, and yet still, I wasn't happy.

"As wonderful as things looked on the outside, life was too busy stripping me of everything that mattered for me to embrace the blessings around me. So Aunt Jo called me and told me to come home."

She stopped for a second to clear her throat. The memory of that call, of the love her aunt extended to her, still made Aja so raw on the inside. "I told her I was born and lived all my life in Brooklyn, New York. She told me that Brooklyn might be where I was born and lived, but home was where family was, and my family was in Texas waiting on me. I knew she was speaking the truth, so I packed up my life and came back to Restoration Ranch with a plan to restore, revive, and renew both this land and my life, determined to find my second chance here.

"Seneca Daniels and Brooklyn Osborn came here with the same intentions. They faced far greater obstacles than I ever could have. But even though the deck has been consistently stacked against them, they took a chance on me and my offer of a new beginning and tapped into the healing power of this land to remake themselves.

"And so tonight it is my honor to celebrate these two women and the journey they've embarked on. Ladies and gentlemen, please raise your glasses for Seneca and Brooklyn, two women who have fought for their own piece of happiness. They're proof second chances work."

The small group cheered, and Aja smiled as she caught sight of the glimmer of unshed tears in Seneca's and Brooklyn's eyes. She motioned for them to come up and speak. Seneca begged off, shaking her head and wiping at her eyes. Brooklyn stepped next to Aja, hugged her tightly, and turned back to their guests. "You want to say something, Brooklyn?"

The woman lifted her half-filled champagne glass toward the crowd and said, "Yeah. Let's eat."

Laughter rose into the air, and Aja shook her head at Brooklyn's quintessential response, then ushered her guests inside the house to the waiting chafing dishes. Folks quickly fell in line, heaping the offerings onto their plates and finding a space to enjoy their selections.

Aja found herself in line, plating enough food for two, when Jackson's strong hand settled on the small of her back. "Our plans still on?"

"Yeah, but if I don't fix plates for us now, it will all be gone. And as excited as I am to sneak away with you, I'm not missing Aunt Jo's steamed cabbage for anyone."

"All right, make it quick."

His impatience made her chuckle. "You're the one who'd better be quick. We only have a few minutes."

His eyes widened with excitement. "More than enough for what I have in mind. Now, let me wrap these plates up and stick them in the fridge. I've got plans for you, Ms. Everett."

He took the plates out of her hands and headed toward the counter next to the fridge, giving her the opportunity to get an eyeful of his muscled body as he walked away. Whatever plans he had in mind for her, Aja knew one thing—she was in so much trouble, and she liked it.

Chapter 37

I SHOULD REALLY BE ASHAMED OF MYSELF.

The thought lingered for a moment in the back of her mind. It was true. She had guests upstairs, two of whom were her aunt and uncle. But instead of being a gracious hostess, she was bent over the top of her aunt's deep freezer with her skirt jacked around her waist, and Jackson slamming inside her dripping body so good it was impossible for her to feel any genuine guilt about her behavior.

"God, I'm almost there." This was the second time she'd uttered those words in the short time they'd been locked away in the basement. The first time Jackson had been on his back while she was riding him, milking every inch of pleasure his smooth length offered her.

Determined to live out his fantasy of bending her over the nearest sturdy object and hiking her skirt over her bare ass, Jackson had taken advantage of her momentary postorgasm weakness, and she found herself holding on to the freezer for purchase while he buried himself so deep, her legs were shaking.

She didn't know if he recognized she was so gone, so lost in the ecstasy he brought her that she could hardly stand on her own two feet. But he paused for a moment and hooked his hand behind her knee, causing it to instinctively bend. He lifted her leg and placed it atop the freezer, then bottomed out inside her again, even deeper than before.

"Come on, woman. Give me what I want, or I swear we'll be here until someone from upstairs comes looking for us."

She bit her lip and moaned as quietly as she could. The way he had every nerve in her body on edge, lit with the blazing fire of her desire, she was tempted to hold out on climaxing for as long as she could. Guests be damned, the way her sex molded to his, the way she burned from the inside out as he touched her in the most intimate places, being discovered by people milling about in her home was a reasonable price for satisfaction.

She fought the orgasm trying to take root. She wasn't ready for this to be over yet. But Jackson must have sensed her refusal to let go because he slid his hand down the pad of her abdomen until his fingers slid between her folds and he caressed her clit with his fingertips.

Whatever restraint she thought she had bled away, and she fell to the power of her climax. It grabbed at every muscle she had, forcing her to bear down to keep from falling to pieces.

"That's it, baby girl. Ride it out." He kept pounding into her, kept her riding the crest of her peak, extending it until it triggered another orgasm, one that made her cry out. He leaned in to her, placing a hand over her mouth, muffling the tortured sounds climbing out of her throat.

He pummeled into her until she was spent and her bones became soft and malleable, unable to hold her up. And when her moan turned into an almost sob, his rhythm faltered. The tip of his cock was wedged so deep inside her, straddling the line between pleasure and pain as his release pulsed into the latex barrier separating them. He grabbed on to her breasts, squeezing them as he buried his mouth in the curve of her neck and smothered the powerful roar his orgasm tore from him.

He dislodged himself and sprawled over the freezer as she did. "I swear to God, the next time we do that, I want nothing between us. If my doctor doesn't send me my damn test results soon, I'm liable to shoot him."

She offered a weak chuckle as a response. It was a task breathing and attempting to concentrate on actual words at the same time. Speaking would've required more mental power than she had at the moment.

Since they'd become an official item last week, they'd come to a decision they wanted no barriers between them. All that remained for them to cross that line were Jackson's test results. Aja's had come in yesterday. She was already on birth control, so as soon as his doctor gave him a clean bill of health, they were ditching the condoms.

It probably should've panicked her. But if she knew anything about Jackson Dean, it was that he was a man of his word. She trusted him, and that was important. But the most remarkable thing was they trusted each other and were taking this step together.

It was a big change for both of them. He was moving beyond his past, and she was finally ready to get over hers too.

It was happening. Slowly but surely, it was happening.

Aja stood on wobbly legs, searching the floor for her panties. "I am not going back upstairs bare-assed, Jackson. You tossed them, you gotta help me find them."

He continued to lie on the top of the deep freezer, giggling like a crazed fool, completely unbothered by her frantic request. Realizing her distress seemed to amuse him further, she pulled her skirt from around her waist and walked the few steps to the basket of folded towels sitting on top of the dryer. She removed two hand towels and threw one at him. "If you won't help me, at least go in the half bath near the back of the stairs and clean up."

He sat up, grabbing the towel in one hand. "Darlin', I can't seem to get mad at the thought of your walking around bare-assed under that skirt."

"Jackson," she called out as she continued searching the floor for her undergarments. "I cannot walk around with no panties on while serving guests food and drinks. My aunt and uncle are upstairs."

"True. But only you and I would know. Having that kind of secret running through my mind every time I looked at you would be better than a slice of your pineapple coconut cake. And you know how I love that."

The sound of his delicious words did more than entice her, they aroused her. She turned around to see the naughty smile gleaming in his dark eyes. Everything in her wanted to give in to his request. *No one would know. Just you and that gorgeous hunk of man.*

"If I were wearing pants, maybe. But not with a miniskirt. If I bend over the wrong way, there goes our secret."

Another flash of mischief lit up his face, leaving Aja wondering what carnal thought was crossing his mind when he huffed as he pushed his hand in his pants pocket.

"I guess you're right," he acquiesced before pulling his hand free of his pocket and tossing her panties at her.

"You had them the whole time?"

He laughed again and headed for the bathroom when she balled up the remaining towel and pulled her arm back as if she were preparing to pitch in a championship baseball game.

When he was out of sight, she let the amusement she was holding in for his benefit bubble to the surface. She looked at the crime scene, a.k.a. the deep freezer, and went to a cabinet where she knew there was a bleach cleaner and sponges.

When Jackson returned from the bathroom, Aja was bent over the freezer, spraying and scrubbing the top with furious circular motions. "You keep scrubbing at that thing that way, and you'll take the paint off it."

"If Aunt Jo finds out your naked ass was sitting on top of her deep freezer, she's gonna take a switch to both our hides. I'm not going out like that."

He shook his head, looking at her as if she were losing her grip with reality. "It was closed, and I'm sure the meat inside is vacuum-sealed in thick plastic. Besides, don't you own the land and the houses built on it? Doesn't that technically make this your deep freezer?"

"You obviously don't understand. She is the matriarch of my family. It doesn't matter that I own the deed; that kitchen and everything that goes in it is hers when she's on the property."

"Are you as territorial as your aunt? It could be fun if you are."

She shook her head and put her hands on her hips. "You can take your chances with her if you want. Me? I'm cleaning it so there are no questions later." When she was done, she tossed the sponge in a nearby trash can, returned the cleaner to its hidden spot in the cabinet, and washed her hands in the mudroom sink. She grabbed the hand towel she'd picked up earlier and headed toward the bathroom. "Oh, don't forget to grab a few bottles of wine from the racks on that wall to the far right. That is what we supposedly came down here for. Right?"

He tipped his imaginary hat and gave her a wide smile and a hearty "Yes, ma'am" before heading to the wine rack. A spark of happiness danced inside her belly, and she wrapped her arms around her middle as she embraced it. Whether it was because of his smile or the way he'd made her lose herself in ecstasy a few moments ago, Aja was content. No matter what happened after this, nothing could rob her of the serenity these shared moments with him in her dark basement had brought.

———

Aja carried an armful of wine bottles carefully in a crate. Did she really think they needed the crate she carried, plus the one Jackson held in his hands? Nope. And the lifted brow Seneca shared with her when she caught sight of their bounty said she thought they'd overdone it too. But this was Aja's story, and she was sticking to it. If her courtroom days had taught her anything, it was that the appearance of propriety was much more important than actually being proper.

Jackson placed his crate down and then reached for hers, placing it on the counter alongside his. "Did you get everything you wanted in the cellar?"

Aja held up a finger, suspending Seneca's shady question while she turned to Jackson. "Would you mind getting me a glass of my special iced tea from the fridge? It's in a thermos that has my name engraved on the front."

"Sure thing." He left the two ladies at the counter together and made his way toward the fridge.

She gave Seneca a conspiratorial smile before she answered. They both might know Aja and Jackson's cover was flimsy, but she would not concede defeat to Seneca's attempt to snoop. "Everything." Her answer was accompanied by a hand on her hip and an easy smile. "I found reds, whites, and even a few blushes in the mix."

"I bet you did." Seneca put a hand on Aja's shoulder. "Girl, I want details."

"People in hell want ice water, too, but you don't see them getting it."

"You are so selfish. First you're making special batches of iced tea for yourself, and now you won't kiss and tell."

"You know folks only want sweet tea here. It's a great drink, but mixing alcohol in it is horrible. Long Island iced teas, on the other hand, mix wonderfully with booze."

Seneca shook her head. "So selfish. Stamping your name on everything, including Jackson. It's like sistah code to share details about a man as fine as him."

"Nah. My mama always told me the best way to lose a man is tell your friends too much about him. Not telling."

Jackson returned with a tall glass of the cocktail. Before he could hand it to Aja, Seneca grabbed the glass and drank it until the cup was tilted in the air. "Maybe that will teach you to share."

Aja shook her head. "Probably not. You'd better hope that drink doesn't put you on your ass later. You know how they sneak up on you."

Seneca let a playful sigh cross her lips and waved a dismissive hand at Aja. "You're the worst. I still love you, though, Boss."

Aja smiled. "Feeling's mutual."

Seneca left them at the counter and wandered off to the back door where Aja could see Colton standing. The two smiled easily at each other, piquing Aja's interest. She turned to Jackson. "Those two seem chummy. You think anything could be going on?"

He glanced at them briefly. "He hasn't mentioned anything. But then again, I didn't talk to him about us either."

"How well do you know him?"

"We've been friends since we were kids. Served a bit in the army together. Colton's the strong, silent type. But he's good people. He knows how to press a damn nerve like no one else's business, but he's still one of the best men I know."

She accepted his endorsement, hooking her finger inside his belt loop and tugging slightly. "You bring a bag with you? I was hoping you'd agree to a sleepover."

"If I spend the night, I can almost guarantee you there won't be much sleeping going on."

"Sounds perfect. You prepared to stay?"

"For as long as you'll have me."

Something shifted. The light playfulness between them was pushed aside, and there was something heavier, more substantial linking them. He wasn't just talking about staying the night. If she read people as well as she thought she did, she was inclined to believe he was talking about them in the bigger sense.

I so want to be right about this.

"My door is always open. Maybe tonight we should take the time to talk about that."

He was about to answer when they heard a loud shout coming from outside the house. Jackson opened the back door and stepped onto the back porch, and she followed. Seneca and Colton were locked in some sort of odd embrace. He was trying to hold on to her, and Seneca seemed to be trying to push him away.

"I told you to leave me alone." Seneca was upset, but there was something off about the situation. Aja had seen her upset before, and this wasn't it. Her face was flushed, but her words were slurred, and she couldn't seem to focus her eyes.

"What the hell is going on out here?"

Colton locked eyes with Aja. "Something's wrong with her. Help me."

Aja was about to tell him she wasn't there to help *him* when Seneca went slack in his arms.

"Seneca," Aja yelled. There was no response.

"I told you, something wasn't right. She started slurring her words when we came outside. I was trying to get her to sit when you found us."

He grabbed Seneca up in his arms effortlessly and took quick steps to get her to the lounge swing at the other end of the porch. He laid her on the chair gently, and Aja rushed to her side. She went to lean over Seneca and Colton pushed her back.

"Give her some room. Let me check her out."

She stood still, unable to move. This was her friend; she had to do something.

"Aja, move!"

Having Colton scream at her made her whole body jump and set off violent shivers all over her body. She felt familiar hands on her shoulders moving her aside. "It'll be all right," Jackson said in a slow, smooth tone. "He knows what he's doing."

Aja blinked, still only processing about half of what was going on around her. Panicked, she stared at Jackson, still trying to figure out how she was supposed to respond to this situation. "Aja, honey," he began, speaking slowly as he moved her out of Colton's way. "Let him take care of her."

She focused on every syllable, matching every step he took until she was clear of Colton and Seneca. Jackson pulled her in to his side. He cradled her in his arm, and the tremors she was sure would knock something loose inside her began to subside.

She watched Colton place two fingers at the base of Seneca's neck and held her breath as she prayed her friend's heart was still beating.

"She's got a pulse but it's thready and weak and her breathing seems labored. Get an ambulance now."

Everything slowed down as Aja watched Jackson pull his phone from his pocket and call for an ambulance. Her mind was racing, but everything around her seemed to be happening at a snail's pace. She shook her head, trying to focus on what Jackson was saying. Even though she could see his lips moving, she couldn't hear any of the words coming from his mouth. The only thing she could hear was the loud thud of her heart. It was beating in time with her panicked thoughts and fears for her still unresponsive friend.

What can I do? What can I do?

Aja closed her eyes, trying to pull herself together. She was useless to Seneca this way. And then, breaking through the silence, she could hear the voice of her late mother repeating something she'd always said when young Aja was worried about her dad being on active duty.

"Good thoughts and a little prayer go a long way, Aja girl."

So Aja did just that. She prayed.

She asked God for all sorts of things, bargaining everything from her wealth to her own eternal soul if help could arrive in time, if Seneca could be well again. But by the time the ambulance arrived and Seneca's reddish-brown complexion had turned to an almost ghostly gray, Aja was terrified her prayers had gone unheard or, worse, ignored.

Chapter 38

JACKSON SAT WITH COLTON IN THE WAITING AREA. THE MAN was tense, his eyes darting back to the open door that led into a busy corridor. "You okay?"

"Are you?"

Jackson let the flippant reply slide. Colton's inner asshole made way more appearances than it should, but somehow Jackson knew this wasn't his usually charming self. No, this was panic. It was clear in the way he couldn't seem to keep still. Even when he was seated, some part of his body was moving in a semifrantic way. Like now: they were in uncomfortable plastic chairs that didn't bend or mold to the human body, and Colton's leg bounced up and down like a jackrabbit.

"What's going on, Colton?"

"You know as much as I do. Why hasn't Aja or Brooklyn or the doctors or someone come back here and let us know anything about how she's doing?"

"They've only been gone a few minutes. I'm sure Aja will let us know as soon as she knows anything."

Jackson placed a firm hand on Colton's shoulder, hoping to offer the man some comfort. It didn't matter how many years you worked in the military or law enforcement; seeing someone literally fall in your arms never got easy. "You did all you could, Colt. If you hadn't been with her, God knows what could've happened. Because you were there, she got the help she needed immediately."

Colton bounced his leg up and down again, but the far-off look in his eyes didn't give Jackson much hope that the man had heard anything he'd said. Colton was too focused on Seneca to care about Jackson.

Concerned about the friend who sat next to him and the young woman who'd collapsed in his arms, Jackson stood and walked to the information desk. He found a young woman sitting there tapping away on computer keys. "Excuse me, I need to find out some information on a patient. Her name is Seneca Daniels. She was brought in unconscious this evening."

"Are you family or next of kin?"

Jackson expected that. "No, ma'am. I'm a friend."

The woman gave him a sympathetic glance. "Sorry, sir, the only thing I can tell you is that the medical team is tending to her and she's stable. Any other information you'll have to get from her or her family."

Jackson tapped the counter and gave her a respectful thank-you before pulling his phone out of his pocket and texting Aja to try to find out more. He'd tried not to bother her while she was in the back with Seneca, but Colton's anxiousness was worrying him. She responded she'd call down to the information desk for him.

Aja called immediately, and the young woman administered visitors' passes. Jackson motioned for Colton to follow him, and within moments, they were walking through the door.

"You used your badge to get in?"

"No. I called Aja. I'm surprised you didn't use yours, though. Especially with how antsy you've been since they brought Seneca in."

"It's in the blazer I left inside my truck at the ranch. I didn't think to get it as I hopped in the ambulance with her."

"No worries, brother. You'll be able to see her soon."

They stopped in front of her room, and Jackson knocked on the door and opened it slowly. Seneca was sleeping in her hospital bed. Almost every time he could remember seeing her, she was smiling or laughing or making everyone around her smile and laugh. But tonight, Aja and Brooklyn hovered over her from opposite sides of the bed, their faces long with sorrow and fear.

As Colton pulled up the rear, Brooklyn stood and walked to the door. "I need some coffee. Anyone else want one?" They all shook their heads. Brooklyn left, closing the door behind her, while Colton took her place on the opposite side of Seneca's bed.

Jackson stood next to Aja, wrapping a comforting arm around her. "How's she doing? Do they know what caused this?"

Aja glanced at the sleeping Seneca before lifting her eyes to him. They were sunken and red from all the crying she'd done since Seneca collapsed, and the sight made every muscle in his body tense with the need to take this pain away from her.

"She was drugged. Someone gave her Rohypnol."

"What?" Colton's voice cut through the quiet hospital room like a sharp knife. "How? She drank soft drinks from sealed cans most of the night, and I don't remember her leaving any of them unattended."

Jackson shook his head. "No, she didn't. I poured a drink for Aja from a thermos in the fridge. Seneca took it and drank it instead."

"But no one knew about that thermos of Long Island iced tea I made but you, me, and Seneca. I never mentioned it to anyone else until I sent you to get it."

Cold fear tightened Jackson's muscles as he made eye contact with Colton across the room, and they both came to the same conclusion. Jackson pulled his phone from his pocket and waited for Jennings to pick up on the other end. "Yeah, Boss."

"I need you and Gleason and anyone else you can round up at Fresh Springs Medical now. I also need you to dispatch a forensics team to Restoration Ranch. You're looking for a silverish chrome-colored forty-ounce camping thermos. It should be on the second shelf from the top inside the fridge. Someone tried to poison Aja Everett tonight."

He ended the call and met Aja's confused expression. "How do you know it wasn't meant for Seneca?"

Jackson shook his head. "Because the thermos had your name on it."

Why were hospitals so cold?

It was a near-constant thought as Aja sat rubbing her arms in the waiting area. Seneca's nurse had put them all out of her room so "the patient" could rest. She was more than a patient—she was Aja's friend, and keeping an eye on her was the only thing that helped Aja keep it together.

The waiting area was a few feet away from Seneca's room, but it didn't matter. Aja's guilt fed off her anxiety, and not being able to see Seneca ramped her anxiety up to almost unbearable levels.

"You cold?"

Aja looked up at Jackson. He was sitting next to her, plastered to her as if they were somehow conjoined. From the moment he'd realized someone spiked her drink, he'd refused to leave her side except for when Gleason and Jennings showed up to take their statements.

"This is my fault."

Jackson wrapped his arm around her, hugging her as tightly as the armrests between them would allow. "The only person at fault is the person who laced your thermos with roofies."

Yeah, they were at fault, too, but Aja was the reason Seneca had been endangered. It wasn't the first time she'd been responsible for harm befalling someone close to her. It seemed this was her destiny, to bring pain and hardship to the ones she cared about, even when she was trying her damnedest to help.

"I thought this was over. Eli Bennett is in prison."

"We both know a man like Eli has the means to still pull strings on the outside while he's locked up. We'll sort this out, Aja. I'm not leaving your side until you're safe for good."

She pulled out of his embrace and walked near the window. The dark Texas sky met her like a mirror to her soul—ink black and cold, consuming all the surrounding light. The absence of light sparked fear of the monsters that lurked under its cover. She couldn't see who was coming after her, and as long as she didn't know who Eli's henchman was, she and everyone close to her were in danger.

"You should go." She remained positioned in front of the window like a sentinel waiting for the day to bring reinforcements and aid.

"I'm not going anywhere."

"People around me get hurt, Jackson. You signed up for fun, not to be my permanent bodyguard."

He wrapped his arms around her shoulders and pulled her against him. Any other day, the comfort he offered would have been received with gratitude. And although she was grateful he cared enough to want to comfort her, she couldn't allow herself to be weak enough to accept it. Not when being near her was becoming a prescription for trouble.

"That is the literal thing I signed on to be when I first landed on your doorstep."

"My case is over."

"Apparently not. Even if it were, I'd still be with you. I'd hoped you'd figured this out when I asked you to let me be the man in your life."

She turned around in his embrace to face him, needing to see the truth of his words in his eyes, because her ears did not want to believe the steady, sure cadence of his voice. "I also remembered telling you how busy my life was. If you thought Pathways was gonna put a crimp in our alone time, I'm sure an attempted poisoning might be a tad too much for even you."

His eyes searched hers, and she had to fight to hold back the unshed tears stinging her eyes. Jackson Dean would be the proverbial cherry on top of the new happiness she'd found for herself on Restoration Ranch. But more and more, especially with Seneca lying in a hospital bed now, Aja had to wonder if she were ever meant to experience any lasting joy.

"If you're asking me if I'm too chickenshit to stand by you, you're wrong. For as long as you'll have me, regardless of how difficult and messy the situation, I want to be the man by your side."

She stepped back, needing to put some distance between them. The light, spicy scent of his cologne coupled with the heat his nearness brought were enveloping her. She was overwhelmed, and being this close to him made it hard for her to think.

"You wouldn't want to be with me if you knew the real me." She was certain of that. A man like him who subscribed to the ideals of truth and justice could never tolerate someone with Aja's particular flaws. "Jackson, I—"

He stepped closer to her and placed a finger of her lips. "Aja, if you're gonna try to push me away, save your breath. You are everything I've ever wanted, and there's nothing I wouldn't do to keep you safe. There's nothing I wouldn't work like hell to see you through. I'm here because there's no place in the world I'd rather be."

She lost her battle with her tears; they spilled from her eyes and slid down her face like fat raindrops on the smooth glass of a window. He pulled her into his arms, cradling her head against his heart, making her need to purge herself of her fear and guilt even more profound.

She plastered herself against him, wrapping her arms around his waist and holding on for everything she was worth. In such a short time, he'd become her anchor, the thing that kept her from drifting off into the sea.

When her shoulders stopped shaking from the sobs that racked her body and her tears stopped flowing, he whispered in her ear, "I'm yours, baby girl. I'm not going anywhere." And just like that, Aja's soul opened, and her heart danced in her chest. Jackson may have been the one to make the offer, to say the words, but her heart was filled to bursting with the invisible link that tethered them.

She should've walked away. People like her—guilt-ridden and condemned in their own minds—didn't get the refuge Jackson was offering her. Once you screwed up, life rarely let you get do-overs. But standing here in this big, beautiful man's arms, Aja knew one thing. Coming to Restoration Ranch may have been the first step on her road to redemption, but Jackson Dean was the last mile. He was living proof she could not only restore herself but rebuild, make herself a new thing.

Doubt tried to crop up, to snuff the small glimmer of hope burning inside her. But Jackson squeezed her tighter, and Aja decided whether she deserved it or not, she would take this opportunity to reach for everything she wanted. And right now, that was Jackson Dean. As far as she was concerned, no matter what this phantom stalker had in mind, she would fight for her people but also herself and enjoy this repose for however long it lasted.

Chapter 39

AJA SMACKED THE PILLOW IN HER HAND TO FLUFF IT.

"You keep abusing my pillows like that, and I will call the law."

Aja stopped midfluff and smiled at Seneca looking at her from the en-suite bathroom door. "I want to make sure you're comfortable. A few days ago, you were passed out in a hospital bed because of me. The least I can do is fluff your pillows now that you're back home."

Seneca walked over to the bed, her gait still slow as her body took its time to recover from the drug she'd ingested. She sat on the edge of the mattress and patted the space next to her, showing Aja she wanted her to sit too. "You didn't do this. This wasn't your fault."

"It was meant for me."

Seneca shifted on the bed, trying to make herself more comfortable. "Yeah, it was meant for you, but it was my fast ass that swiped the drink from Jackson's hand. I put myself in harm's way. Stop blaming yourself."

"You ended up in the hospital."

Seneca shrugged, the pallor of sickness giving way to her usual bright smile. "Yeah, where people waited on me hand and foot and let me sleep all day. Some people would call that a vacation."

An unexpected giggle threatened to bubble up in Aja's chest. She shook her head, scolding herself for succumbing to Seneca's antics. "This isn't funny, Seneca. The amount of Rohypnol you had in your system could've been deadly if people hadn't been around when you collapsed. How can you laugh about this?"

The smile dropped slightly from Seneca's face as she settled her eyes on the floor. "The one thing prison taught me is that sometimes you have to laugh to keep from crying if you want to keep your sanity. Being locked away in a metal box for all those years wasn't fun, Aja. But finding a reason to smile, to laugh even, kept me from doing something drastic like slitting my own wrists. Getting drugged, collapsing, and spending a few days in the hospital isn't exactly how I would've planned to spend my time. But it could've been worse."

She let her hand rest on top of Aja's, its contact bringing the gentle warmth of comfort Aja's raw soul craved. "Instead of me sitting here laughing at my own misfortune, I could be dead. Then who would be here to make you laugh? Brooklyn?" Seneca waved a dismissive hand through the air. "We both know that girl wouldn't know a sense of humor if it bit her on the ass. So I gotta stick around a little longer to keep things light around here."

Aja could feel the tears slipping from her eyes as she thought of losing Seneca. But just as quickly, the painful thought was replaced by genuine laughter. "You're so wrong for that."

"Tell me I'm lying." Seneca waited with a raised brow, staring at Aja, waiting for an answer.

"I can't," Aja replied. "But Brooklyn's strength is a more than admirable substitute." Seneca bumped her shoulder and shared a broad smile. The sight of it lifted Aja's spirits, but it wouldn't erase the guilt layering itself all over her soul. "Seneca, I'm supposed to take care of you and Brooklyn."

Seneca shook her head, placing a caring hand on Aja's knee. "You're supposed to provide us with fair employment. You're supposed to pay us a fair wage for our labor. You're supposed to make sure you report any illegal activity you are aware we're involved in. You are not, however, responsible for us. We're grown women, Aja. We have to be responsible for ourselves."

Aja let Seneca's words settle over her. She was more than aware that Seneca and Brooklyn were grown women, but she'd be lying if she said she didn't feel a sense of obligation to them.

"I promised you a new future. Not imminent danger."

Seneca shook her head slowly again. "No, you promised us the opportunity to build something for ourselves. I am so grateful for all your help. But it's time you let Brooklyn and me take care of ourselves and you focus on taking care of that fine-ass man you should spend more time with. You've spent the last few days holed up with me in a hospital room and then signing on to be my nurse-maid here at my cabin. When are you making time for him?"

At night when I'm too exhausted from work and caring for you, I collapse in bed. He makes love to me until I'm boneless and too tired to worry about all the hell breaking loose in my life. "He's staying at the main house with me. I see him every night."

"Good, now go find him. He needs your attention. I don't."

"You sure?"

Seneca gave Aja her signature full smile that was colored with a light filter of mischief. "I am. Besides, if I get in a bind, Brooklyn is back to being my temporary roommate on the nights that Colton can't be here. I'll just bug her."

"You sound like you're looking forward to that."

Seneca laughed hard. "I most certainly am."

———

Jackson let the strain in his muscles settle as he used the shovel to clean out the stalls. He'd spent part of the morning checking on the construction crew. They were moving ahead of Aja's original schedule. The job would be complete within the next two months.

The news they'd beaten the cold-weather deadline would give Aja something to celebrate. After Seneca was drugged, the ranch had taken on a morose and somber tone. There wasn't much laughter, and Aja seemed determined to work herself to death. The news that her buildings were on the verge of being finished and she could open the ranch as a resort should put a welcomed spark back in her eyes.

He missed that. The way her eyes lit up when she was happy or amused with something. It was the reason he made it a point to take care of her every night when they went to bed. She was emotionally weary when she walked into the bedroom. As if she'd lost all hope that life could be good again.

He didn't know how to help her find her hope. So he held her and cherished her and let her know he was there for her in whatever way she needed until he could figure out something better to do.

He finished up in the stables, brought the horses back in, and stopped to stare at Aja's horse before leaving. "Shadow, what are we going to do about our girl?" When the horse gave his head a wayward bob, Jackson smiled and ran his hand down its long, dark muzzle. The horse tolerated Jackson on most occasions. But today, he seemed to sympathize with him over the woman they both cared about. "I know, boy. I'm worried about her too."

Jackson gave the horse's muzzle one more rub, then headed outside the stables. The first thing he noticed was the group of three people walking toward him. Aja, Colton, and Storm closed the short distance, his men greeting him with a handshake when they were closer.

"Look what the cat dragged in."

"I was wondering when you'd make it out."

"A body can't spend a weekend with su madre in Mexico

without all hell breaking loose here." Storm shook his head, then waved a large envelope in front of Jackson. "We picked up Seneca's medical records before coming here. Gleason and Jennings have already been interviewing the guests from the party."

Aja turned to him, her brow furrowed in confusion. "You didn't know about this?"

Jackson shook his head. "I'm officially on leave for another week. Also, considering the sheriff's mistreatment of your case, I didn't trust him not to muck up Seneca's case too."

"Is our cover still intact?" Colton's question was directed at Aja.

"As far as I know. I never told Seneca and Brooklyn who you three really were. I didn't want to hurt them by revealing my dishonesty. Did you mention anything, Jackson?"

He shook his head. "No. Do you know if your aunt or uncle did?"

"I doubt it, but I'll ask all the same. Why?"

Storm removed his hat and ran fingers through the dark waves atop his head. "We have concerns that this could be Bennett reaching out beyond his cell to control things on the outside. If people think we're ranch hands instead of investigators, it may give us a better chance at figuring this out."

Aja took a deep breath as the signs of emotional fatigue and worry hung heavy on her shoulders. "Come on in. I left my cell at the house, but there's a landline in the stables. I'll call them both to make sure."

Jackson was about to follow the three of them inside the stables when his cell phone vibrated in his back pocket. A quick glance at the screen brought a smile to his face.

"Holden, you must've known I planned to call and cuss you out."

Holden's robust laughter reverberated through the phone. "I take it you found out about my mom and your dad?"

"So you have known along with the rest of my family. I get Kip being an asshole and keeping the info from me. He's my kid brother, so he's supposed to make my life hell. But I expected more from you. You, me, and Colt have been friends more years than I can count. Why wouldn't you tell me?"

"You weren't ready to know." Jackson allowed those words to linger in his subconscious as silence filled the line. "I figured it out around the time things got bad with your ex. I didn't think you'd take it well. And to be honest, as tight as we've been, if you'd said one thing out of place about my mama, I wouldn't have cared about your state of mind. Keeping it to myself kept our friendship intact."

Jackson silently agreed. He couldn't deny how miserable he had been back then. "You're correct. I wasn't in my right mind. It wouldn't have gone well."

"As I live and breathe. Is that Jackson Dean admitting he was a mean cuss, angry at the entire world?"

Jackson couldn't get upset at the ribbing. It was true. "Things were bad for a long time. But they're getting better now. I might not think marriage is an option for me, but your mama and my daddy seem to be happy together. I know Ms. Eames has always been good to us. She's a fine woman, and I wish them the best. So all's well on this end. What's up with you? Anything interesting going on in New York?"

Holden cleared his throat. "Actually, I finally got ahold of some of that information you asked me for about one Aja Everett."

Jackson's gut tightened. "What did you find?"

"Nothing on her specifically. She has no priors. According to her record, she's been a stand-up citizen. Worked her way through school, climbed her way up the legal ladder at her firm, busted her ass getting celebrities and one-percenters off the legal hook for a lot of years."

All of that jibed with what he'd discovered about Aja through his own investigation and through the close nature of their relationship. "So what's the issue?"

"There's a client she had. A Drucilla Everett. According to her death certificate, she and Aja were sisters."

"Death certificate? How'd she die?"

"Official cause of death is blunt-force trauma to the head. I have a few contacts at Brooklyn holding. Apparently there was some kind of dustup between Drucilla and another detainee that led to Drucilla getting her head smashed against a wall."

"Damn."

"I know, but after reading her rap sheet, her manner of death isn't surprising. Unlike Aja, Drucilla never seemed to meet trouble she didn't want to get into. She'd been in and out of court, went to juvie for a few months when she was sixteen. She also did a four-year bid in Rikers as an adult. From the time she was released, any legal trouble she got into, Aja got her out of. It wouldn't be surprising if some of her sister's trouble found a way of messing with Aja's life. If you're still working the case, maybe that might be a new angle to look at."

"Maybe. Thanks for the info. I owe you a beer the next time you're in town."

"I will certainly hold you to that."

Jackson ended the call, processing all the things Holden had shared with him. He'd shared the darkest parts of his life with her. Why hadn't she told him about her sister? Wasn't that what people who were intimate with each other were supposed to do?

"What are you hiding, Aja?"

Chapter 40

AJA WATCHED IN DELIGHT AS SHADOW TOOK THE OFFERED apple she held up to him. "You're such a happy boy, aren't you?" She rubbed his shiny black mane and laughed when he used his head to butt her hand again. "You want another one?" She grabbed another apple and held it in front of him. "You're lucky I like you."

"Any man that grabs your favor is a fortunate man."

She turned to see Jackson walking toward her. "You searching for treats too? Don't worry. I might just have a pineapple coconut cake waiting for you in the fridge."

The smile on his face drooped slightly, and concern tingled somewhere in the back of her mind. "What, you don't like my pineapple coconut cake all of a sudden? Everything okay?"

"I don't really know how to say things any other way than direct. I'd love a slice of your cake, but I don't know if you'll still want to share it with me once you hear what I have to say. Are we alone?"

She placed her hands on her waist and straightened her shoulders, preparing for whatever blow he would land. "Colton and Storm went up to the main house. Speak your piece."

He spread his arms wide. "Tell me about Drucilla."

The floor of her stomach plummeted, making her want to reach for a nearby wood panel to keep herself upright. But she couldn't. To react that way would show weakness, and if Jackson smelled blood in the water, he wouldn't relent until he knew all her secrets.

"Where did you hear that name?"

"Not from you," he answered softly.

She let out a heavy sigh. "I hope you're not suggesting that because we're sleeping together I owe you passage into my past? Because if that's what you're thinking, you're wrong."

He shook his head, keeping his features even and mellow. "I don't think you owe me anything. I'd simply hoped that after everything that's happened, you knew you could trust me."

"Trust you? You call rummaging around in my past an example of trust?"

He held up his hands. "I didn't rummage into your life. After you were attacked, I was desperate to put your assailant behind bars. So I reached out to a friend of mine in the FBI who's a field agent in New York. I thought perhaps there was a disgruntled client in your past who might have been responsible for the attack and the vandalism."

She chuckled. It was a low, heavy sound that had nothing to do with amusement and everything to do with her rising anger. "I don't have any disgruntled clients. I kept rich people out of jail for a long time. My clients loved me, and I've got so much dirt on them, they'd never dare to cross me."

"Yeah, but Drucilla wasn't like your other clients, was she? She wasn't a rich blue blood or shiny star."

The mere mention of her sister's name pulled her back into the black hole that period of her life represented. Her chest tightened, and unshed tears burned her eyes.

"No, she wasn't. Dru was a selfish, self-centered train wreck who did everything in her power to ruin me and her, and I had no choice but to sit by and watch her wreak havoc on both our lives."

Her throat felt tight, regret weighing heavy on her chest. *I'm so*

tired of carrying this, so tired of trying to pretend I'm someone I'm not.
She closed her eyes, resolving it was finally time to come clean. She
pressed her lids as tightly as she could, trying to dam the river of
tears behind them. But just like always, her strength wasn't enough
to fight her guilt. *It's time, Aja.* She blew out a steadying breath
while the hot stream of tears scorched her skin as they descended
her face. "Dru loved trouble. And as a result, it meant she and our
mom butted heads all the time. Mama was a country girl, and the
only way she knew how to keep us on the straight and narrow was
to be strict. The boundaries she set worked for me. But for Dru,
they only seemed to encourage her mischief more.

"She'd get in trouble, Mama would lose it, and I would get
caught in the middle as the mediator. And sometimes, when I just
didn't feel like being put in the middle, I'd cover for Dru so Mama
wouldn't know what she was up to. After a while, I was lying for her
all the time. She was my sister. I was supposed to keep her secrets.
How could I tell on her? But then Dru fell in with the wrong crowd
and ended up in juvie.

"When she came home, I hoped being put away had scared
her straight. But it didn't. She did more and more stupid stuff and
expected me to have her back every time. And just like she knew
I would, I did."

She wiped the fresh stream of tears that came and moved away
from Shadow's stall. Animals could sense pain, and if she kept going,
Shadow would probably kick his stall door down to get to her.

"Things got worse between her and mama too. She even
accused me of kissing up to our mother so she always looked bad
in Mama's eyes. I did everything to get her to understand how foolish she was being, but nothing worked. No matter what I did, even
when I was covering for her—and especially as I accomplished my
academic goals or graduated from law school—she seemed to hate
me more.

"I tried to support her, to encourage her. Especially once our mother died. I'd pay for her to sign up for courses, and she'd take the money and use it on something else. I'd set her up with a job, but she'd never show up. Nothing I said or did could get her to clean up her act. Even though she was an adult by then, she still found the wrong people to be around, still wound up doing shit she had no business doing, and just like before, she wound up in serious trouble. This time, she landed herself in Rikers for four years. And when she came out doing the same shit all over again, I finally washed my hands. I couldn't risk my career to keep trying to save someone that didn't want to be saved."

She began to pace, hoping the back-and-forth motion would somehow push down the panic of all those years that was trying to climb through her chest and into the moment they were sharing.

Her tears started falling faster as the memory of what came next climbed toward the front of her mind. Seeing her distress, Jackson moved closer to her, standing in her path so she couldn't pace anymore. Once she stopped, he lifted the pad of his thumb and wiped away her tears.

"What happened, Aja?"

She swallowed, but the grief was choking her, making it hard to talk. *If you've come this far, you need to go ahead and finish it. Tell the truth and shame the devil.*

"One day, it all came to a head. She got picked up for smoking weed in a park. Thinking back on it, it was something so petty, so small, it wouldn't have taken much to get her out of trouble. But I was in the middle of dealing with a VIP client at the firm. If I left, I would've lost millions for my firm. I couldn't leave. So when she called, I told her she'd have to wait. That my career was literally on the line. She didn't want to hear that. It was a Friday, and she didn't want to get stuck in lockup over the weekend.

"She was being so unreasonable and selfish, and she refused to cut me any slack. So to appease her, I told her I was coming, when I knew wasn't.

"The next day as I prepared to go see her, I got a call from the holding facility saying there'd been an altercation with another detainee, and the result was my sister was dead. It happened two hours before that call. If I'd gotten her out the night before, she would still be alive."

Jackson's hands moved down her shoulders until they were around her waist, pulling her into his warmth and safety. But the guilt was stronger tonight, yelling she wasn't worthy of his comfort. It refused to let her focus on the steady security of his grip. It crowded her thoughts and her heart until she could hardly hear anything but the gloomy, persistent voice inside her head.

"Baby, I wish you would've told me this. Not that you owed it to me. I can't believe you've walked around carrying this for so long by yourself."

"Jackson, you were an unexpected tornado that blew into my life. I was resistant when you arrived, but once you were here, I was so glad."

She turned in his arms, looking up at him, her heart slicing into a million tiny pieces when she witnessed the familiar swell of confusion and despair in his eyes she'd witnessed in so many others over the years.

"You were the first person in a long time who didn't look at me with a mix of pity and disgust. My aunt and uncle love me, but sometimes I can see the weight of loss in their eyes and it kills me. Seneca and Brooklyn always seem to look at me as though I'm broken. As if they can always tell when my guilt is riding high and my sister is haunting my dreams. You didn't look at me like that. And a small, selfish part of me latched onto that and didn't want to let it go.

"I wanted to be someone you desired and respected, not the woman with the tragic past you have to handle with kid gloves."

He shook his head. "I never would have treated you that way. This never would have changed things between us."

She could tell by the way he squeezed her tighter to him, he wanted to believe that. She wanted to lean her head against his chest and believe it too. But the truth was out there now, and neither of them could pretend it hadn't been spoken.

"You are a good man, Jackson. The best I've ever met. You can tolerate a lot of things, but lying isn't one of them. A lie of omission is still a lie. The lawman in you can never look beyond the fact I chose pettiness and professional advancement over family, and it cost Dru her life. I didn't want you to know anything for all the reasons I stated, and this one most of all. I didn't want to fall from the pedestal you placed me on. It felt good for someone to believe in how good I could be, even when I knew guilt sullied my past. Now, it's all ruined because you had to go digging into my yesterdays. I hope it was worth it."

Jackson stood in the middle of the stables, unsure what had just happened. He knew it was something bad, but he hadn't been prepared for it. Even worse, he hadn't been prepared to stop it.

He stood there combing through every moment of their interactions together. Everything she ever said to him focused on comfort and making it through struggles without losing your hold on life. He thought she was talking about hypothetical, metaphorical situations. It never occurred to him she'd been talking about herself.

"Dammit, how has she carried this all this time?"

It was the thought of her towing this trough of emotional baggage that spurred him into action. She'd left him inside the barn, but to him, her exit felt far more permanent than he ever wanted it to be.

He might be an uptight asshole, but he wasn't stupid enough to let the best woman he'd ever known walk out on him without making the slightest attempt to fight for her or what they shared.

He glanced at Shadow in his stall, the horse staring at him, his large eyes casting a disapproving glare in Jackson's direction.

"Any suggestions on how to fix this?" The horse bobbed his head and blew a harsh breath through his nostrils. Jackson was convinced the horse probably had a better suggestion than he could come up with. But since the ornery bastard seemed keen on keeping it to himself, Jackson waved a dismissive hand at the animal and made his way out of the stables and to the main house.

He figured he'd know what to say once he reached the back door. But sadly, he still didn't understand how to fix this, other than to promise her nothing from her past could ever make him lose respect for her.

She was a phenomenal woman who'd suffered through incomprehensible emotional struggles. Instead of losing herself in the vices most people, including himself, fell prey to, she'd invested in others to heal herself. She might not see how beautiful that was, but for damn sure he did. He needed to tell her that, and hopefully that would be enough to convince her they could move forward together.

Losing Aja wasn't an option. He'd had enough taken from him; he couldn't let her end up being just another bad memory in his past.

She thought she was selfish, but Jackson was certain he had more hold on that title than she ever could. He'd allowed his pride to keep him closed off from the world, and it was because of Aja that he could experience anything other than suspicion and detachment.

She was special, and it was his privilege to be with her. He would do whatever it took to make this work.

Resolved and determined, he turned the knob and stepped inside. "Aja, baby, I need you to listen—"

"So y'all are at the 'baby' stage of things?"

Jackson watched Brooklyn standing at the sink washing out a dish.

"We're beyond it."

Brooklyn shut off the water and stared at him, scanning and computing information as she did. "You're really into the boss, aren't you?"

"Honestly, yeah. I don't think I realized how much until a moment ago."

Brooklyn laughed. "When you fucked up? Of course that would be the time you realized how good you had it. Such a damn man."

He walked into the kitchen, standing behind the counter and tapping out an impatient rhythm with his fingers. "Brooklyn, no offense, but I'm not discussing this with you. Where's Aja?"

She watched him through narrowed eyes over her shoulder, grabbing a hand towel to dry her hands, and faced him. "She was headed upstairs, but then I told her Mat called and asked her to meet him at his office. She grabbed her keys and left."

"Dammit."

"Give her time," Brooklyn continued. "Whatever happened, she's not ready to deal with it. That's why she headed to Mat's office. She needed time to process. The boss is smart. Whatever's going on between you two, she'll figure it out. And Mat is great at being a sounding board."

Jackson tilted his head and assessed her for a moment. Brooklyn had a great poker face. He really couldn't read her. "You're speaking from experience?"

"Yeah," she replied, dropping her eyes for just a second before walking over to the fridge. "By the way..." Jackson smiled at her less-than-smooth change of subject. "I just finished having a slice of Aja's pineapple coconut cake," Brooklyn said, "Why don't you sit and have a piece? It will probably improve your mood and give you the chance to calm down before you go rushing off and doing something stupid."

He lifted his hands. "Again, you speaking from experience?"

She shook her head. "Nope, my problem is the opposite. I'm too methodical. I plan everything, even the trouble I get into."

They stared at each other, giving her statement time to marinate. He knew from her rap sheet she'd premeditated the murder of her brother-in-law. That was about as intentional as one could get. But that didn't mean she didn't know what she was talking about. If he chased after Aja right now, especially if she was with Mat, things would not go well.

"Sure. I'll take a slice."

"My name ain't Aja. Ain't nobody in here serving you. You want it, it's in the fridge."

Her pronouncement made him laugh, even though he didn't feel much like laughing. "You know, Aja serving me has nothing to do with me being a man and everything to do with the fact she likes taking care of people. It's embedded in her DNA."

She laughed. "I know that. But I don't suffer from that particular ailment. Get it yourself."

He walked off to the mudroom, washing his face and hands before he reached inside the fridge. When he came back, he noticed the tattoo on Brooklyn's upper right shoulder. He'd never seen it before. Probably because she usually had on a button-down shirt over her racer-back tank. But tonight that shirt was tied around her waist, likely to keep the sleeves out of the way as she washed dishes.

"That's a cool tattoo. What does it say?"

"'Tomorrow isn't written.'"

He pulled out a dessert plate from the overhead cabinet, then opened the fridge, looking for the cake. He put both on the counter as she placed a cake knife and a fork beside the cake container.

"Is there any significance to that? It sounds like there's a story there." He went about slicing off his cake and putting the rest back in the fridge.

"Yeah, it was something I got from Mat. When I first got out of the pen, I didn't really see things working out so well for me, and I was having a pretty bad time adjusting to being on the outside. Yeah, I'm an architect, but after eight years in prison for murder, my degrees don't mean shit. I had little hope I'd be able to rebuild my life to what it was before things took a very dark turn. So even though I'd accepted my placement in the Pathways program, I had no illusions it would work for me.

"Mat had this saying on a poster in his office. Every time I went to his office, he'd point to it and explain that tomorrow, and every tomorrow after that, was a chance for me to make things better. The only person who could stop me from having a better life was me. I liked his explanation of things, so I had it tattooed on my shoulder."

Jackson was impressed with Brooklyn's depiction of Mat as a mentor. The two men might never be friends, but it was obvious he'd been a great support to Brooklyn. *I guess he really isn't all that bad.*

"Mat keeps inspirational quotes on the walls of his office?" he asked. "I guess I could see that about him."

"Yeah, that particular one is in Spanish, though. It says, 'Mañana no está escrito.'"

Jackson was about to shovel the first piece of fluffy cake into his mouth when the memory of the broken bracelet in evidence flashed across his mind. The fork in his hand clattered to the plate in front of him, pulling Brooklyn's attention to him. "What did you say?"

She nailed him with a hard glare. "I said the quote is in Spanish. 'Mañana no está escrito.'"

Jackson jumped up. "Come on. I'm taking you back to your cabin. You will stay there, and call Aunt Jo and tell her to stay in her cabin too."

"What's going on, Jackson?"

He pulled out his phone and dialed Aja's number. When it

went to voicemail, he let out a loud growl before yelling, "Do it, Brooklyn." She must've seen the worry in his eyes, because she didn't question him. Instead, they hurried to his truck in the front driveway as he prayed he wouldn't be too late.

Chapter 41

AJA SAT IN FRONT OF MAT'S OFFICE, TRYING TO GET HERSELF together. She'd expected they would have to meet after Seneca was drugged. But after unloading all her emotional baggage on Jackson, she wasn't in the best mindset to be the helpful, cooperative partner she needed to display whenever she dealt with Mat on Brooklyn and Seneca's behalf.

She rummaged through the arm console in her vehicle for her travel toiletry kit. She pulled the fingernail file out and rested it atop her left thigh to keep it out of her way as she continued digging for the eye drops, facial tissues, and lip gloss she always kept there.

She applied the drops and used a facial tissue to clean herself up, added a little gloss to her lips, and ran her hands through her braids. A quick look in the mirror, and she was satisfied she could fool Mat into believing she was the levelheaded, even-keeled owner of Restoration Ranch he'd come to know and depend on. If he doubted her ability to keep parolees safe, he could prevent her from taking part in Pathways. Where would Seneca and Brooklyn be then?

She stepped out of the car and heard the sound of metal

clinking against the tarred parking lot. She bent down to retrieve her forgotten fingernail file and slipped it into her front pocket before taking the few steps to the strip-mall building and opening the door. It was after five; she was certain the friendly receptionist who usually greeted her when she was here during regular business hours had packed up for the day and headed home.

She walked beyond reception down the narrow hallway until she was standing in front of Mat's door. She tapped it lightly, and the door cracked open.

"Mat? You here?" When she received no response, she looked at her watch to see if she'd somehow mixed up the time. Her watch confirmed she was on time. At least this mix-up wasn't her fault. The mess back at the ranch with Jackson was another matter altogether.

She shook herself, too afraid thoughts of her earlier encounter with him would bring her back to tears. Aja walked into the office. She stopped at the desk, looking for something to write a note on, when skin-prickling cold gave way to a deep shudder.

Looking around to see what had her hackles up, she found Mat standing behind the door, leaning on the wall. "You scared me. What are you doing hiding behind the door?"

He remained behind the door, stretching his arm out until it reached the knob while the other hand remained in his pocket. He slowly walked until the door was closed and his back was resting against it.

Something about this picture made her uncomfortable. Not that she'd never been in a room with a closed door with Mat before, but the way the hairs on the back of her neck were standing up, she knew something was wrong.

"Mat? Maybe we should reschedule."

"I'd love to, but there's no time." He swallowed deeply, the muscles in his throat tugging his Adam's apple up and down as his mouth thinned into a straight line.

"What's going on, Mat? If this isn't about Pathways business, I think it's time I left." She stepped around the back of his desk, trying to make an end run for the door. But then he lifted the hand he'd kept in his pocket and pointed a handgun directly at her.

"Aja, I have tried to protect you, but you make it so hard. You have to listen to me. If I don't get you out of here now, they'll kill you."

———————————

"If you kill us trying to get there, who will save Aja?"

Jackson couldn't take his eyes off the road long enough to spare Storm a glance. His tires ate up the dark road illuminated by the flashing emergency lights on his truck. Unless he wanted to risk their lives, he'd keep his focus in front of him and not on Storm. "If he harms her..."

"We'll get there in time, Boss." Storm's declaration did little to make Jackson feel better. "Don't let yourself think otherwise."

It was too late—his mind had made several trips down the darkest possible outcomes already. But even though his fear told him this would end badly, he couldn't stop himself from trying to get there faster.

If he hadn't pushed her, she would be at home with him instead of in the hands of the man who'd tried to kill her. *Please, don't let me be too late.* "Can you do something useful like find out if Colton got us any backup?"

"He already texted me he did. Gleason and Jennings are in town interviewing folks about Seneca's poisoning. They'll meet us there."

One less thing to worry about. With Colton back at the ranch keeping watch over Aja's aunt and her employees, they still needed more bodies to take this madman down.

Aja's could feel the same paralysis that had locked her in place when the scaffold was falling toward her and when Seneca collapsed. She tried to take a breath, but it was stuck in her chest, burning her lungs.

You can't do this again, Aja. You will die this time.

She swallowed hard, clearing her throat, and forcing her rib cage to expand so she could take in much needed oxygen and clear her brain of its anxious fog.

"Mat, put the gun down and let's talk about this."

Mat squinted at her in confusion, then looked down at his own hand.

"This isn't for you." He shoved the gun into the back of his pants, and some of the tension left her.

See, just keep him talking and you'll get out of this alive.

"I would never hurt you," he declared. "I'm trying to save you. I keep trying to save you, but everyone keeps getting in the way. This is my last chance."

"What are you talking about, Mat?"

He ran a ragged, shaking hand through his hair. His eyes were wide and bright with fear. Whatever was going on, he wasn't faking this. He was panicked about something.

"The night your foreman caught me in the bushes, I was trying to get up the nerve to get you away from Restoration Ranch. Then, at the party, while you were in the basement, I slipped into the kitchen and poured enough roofies in your thermos to knock out a horse. I was certain I could sneak you out of the house unnoticed while the festivities were going on. But Seneca somehow got your drink instead."

Aja's brain tried to digest everything spilling from Mat's mouth in a frantic stream of words. "You poisoned Seneca? Do you realize she could have died?"

He stepped closer to her, remorse bleeding into his face as his silence filled the room. "You have to believe me. It wasn't my intent. I was trying to save you." He shook his head and again stepped closer to her. "I know I'm not making any sense. I promise when we're safe, I'll tell you everything. All you need to know is that I trusted the wrong people, and right now, they think you are the only thing standing between them and a lot of money. I can't protect you any longer."

———————

They pulled in front of Mat's office and quickly and quietly made it inside the building with their weapons drawn as they attempted to get their bearings. Jackson could hear a muffled voice coming from the back of the office, but at this distance, he couldn't understand what was being said. All he knew was it wasn't Aja's voice.

Storm must have recognized the panic Jackson was fighting to keep at bay because he placed a firm hand on his shoulder, his eyes questioning if Jackson had his head in the game or not. "How you wanna do this?"

"Fast and hard," Jackson replied. "We can't see inside that room, but we need to catch him off guard and hope we can get her out of there." The layout of the office didn't offer much in the way of cover. There was a small reception area in the front and a narrow hallway that ran from front to back with a few rooms along the corridor. If they came under fire, things could get dangerous quickly.

They walked carefully along the wall leading to the back offices until they each stood on either side of the closed door.

Jackson used two fingers to signal Storm to kick the door in. With a nod, Storm acknowledged Jackson's directive, and the door gave way the moment his heavy boot made contact with it.

Jackson was the first in the room. "Texas Rangers, put your hands in the air and get down on the floor." He scanned the room quickly and spotted Mat in the center of the room with an arm around Aja's neck and his gun pointed toward the door.

Jackson yelled, "Gun," as Storm tried to enter the room. He pushed him aside just in time for the loud bang of gunfire to fill the air.

Jackson needed to get eyes on Aja. He peeked into the doorway to see Mat still standing behind Aja with his arm around her neck.

"Stay back or I will kill her."

"Mat, you don't need to do this. They're the Texas Rangers. There's no way this ends with you getting away." Aja's voice was steady despite the tears streaming down her face. "If you tell me why you're doing this, I'm sure we can figure this out."

"I'm trying to protect you," Mat screamed. "No one would've been hurt if you'd just let go of that stupid ranch."

"What am I missing, Mat? Why do you need my ranch so badly?"

Jackson locked his gaze on to hers, silently encouraging her to keep Mat talking. As long as he was talking, there was a chance things wouldn't escalate.

Gun still drawn and aimed at Mat, Jackson continued to creep slowly into the room.

"You think you're so smart with all your fancy degrees. But you still couldn't figure out what was going on under your own nose on your own land. You've been pissing off the wrong people since you came to town. I've used up all my goodwill to keep you safe now."

"Mat." Jackson called out his name, trying to keep his focus off Aja. "The only way you're walking out of here is if you put your gun down and let her go."

"Texas Rangers, huh? You're signing your own death warrant. Let me pass."

Mat's focus was on Jackson and Storm just behind him at the doorway. He didn't see Aja slipping her fingers into the front pocket of her jeans or the glint of light striking whatever it was in her hand that she slipped into her closed palm.

Jackson gave her a brief glance to make sure she knew what she was doing. Her eyes never wavered. Whatever she was planning, she was fully committed. And if Jackson knew nothing else, it was that he could trust Aja Everett.

Jackson took a step to the right to keep Mat's eyes on him and give Aja time to do whatever she was planning.

She swung her arm back, connecting with Mat's thigh. Screaming out in pain, he dropped his arm, allowing Aja to escape toward Storm, and grabbed his thigh with his now free hand, pulling his fingers away when they connected with what looked to be a fingernail file.

Mat raised his gun to aim at Aja's back.

"Last warning," Jackson yelled. "Put it down now."

Mat stared at Jackson. At first, the man seemed to concede defeat, his gun arm dropping ever so slightly. But then Jackson saw a spark of defiance flash across the man's eyes, and he knew this was going to end badly.

Mat Ryan lifted his gun arm, and the moment he did, Jackson pulled his trigger. Two loud pops cracked the air as both weapons discharged.

Mat fell instantly to the floor, one dark-red stain saturating the center of his shirt and spreading outward. Jackson kept his gun aimed at him, kicking the man's weapon out of his reach and looking around the room to see if Aja was okay. He didn't see her.

He secured the room, picking up Mat's gun, tucking it in the back of his jeans, before leaning down to check for a pulse. When he couldn't find one, he let out a long sigh of relief and slid into the nearby chair against the wall.

Storm stepped back in the room with his gun drawn. "Clear," Jackson choked out as a burning sensation made him grab his arm.

"You all right, man?"

"Is Aja all right?"

Storm jerked his thumb behind him. "She's outside with Jennings and Gleason."

Jackson grabbed his now-throbbing limb and groaned. "Good," he grunted through clenched teeth. "Then now might be a good time to get a bus in here." He lifted his hand from his arm and watched blood drip from his palm onto the front of his shirt and jeans. "I think I'm hit pretty bad."

Chapter 42

AJA WAS MORE THAN TIRED OF THIS HOSPITAL. IN LESS THAN a week, she'd been here twice waiting for the medical staff to update her on the well-being of someone she cared for.

She paced and tried to self-soothe, reminding herself that Jackson was a strong man, and people survived gunshot wounds to the arm all the time. He was here to get help. But whenever she'd start to calm down, the sterile walls and the acrid scent of antiseptic would remind her that people came to hospitals not only for help but to die.

He can't. He just can't.

The heavy ball of anxiety and devastation that had claimed her when she'd learned of her sister's death grew again, sitting in the middle of her chest. How had she found herself in the same situation twice in one lifetime?

How could she endanger another person she loved after everything that had happened with Drucilla?

That she'd classified Jackson as someone she loved didn't strike her as strange. She'd felt that emotion creeping up on her in small instances throughout their relationship.

Cold settled in her bones as guilt and worry wrapped themselves around her, binding her in a helpless cocoon. What if she never got the chance to tell him how she felt? What if he died never knowing how much she loved him?

The warmth of a hand resting on top of hers pulled her out of the endless loop of pain and heartache. She raised her gaze to find Colton sitting next to her.

"You can't lose it now. He needs you."

He was right. Jackson needed her. But not this version of her. He needed someone strong enough to face her own battles before she could assist him in fighting his.

She pulled out her phone and scrolled back to the text Jackson had sent her. She copied the number of the counselor and pasted it into a new message and started drafting.

> **Aja**: Hi, I'm Aja Everett, a friend of Jackson Dean's. He thought you might be able to help me with some trouble I had not too long ago.

She hit Send and was about to push her phone into her pocket when she felt it vibrate in her hand. Surprised at such a quick response and slightly afraid to read it, she tapped the screen and read the waiting message.

> **Jessica**: Hi, I'm Jessica Muñoz. Jackson mentioned you might be in contact. I'm glad you reached out. Would you like to drop by my office or FaceTime for a chat?
> **Aja**: Yes, I would.

"You okay?"

Aja finished texting the counselor and put her phone away before she looked up to answer Colton. "No, I'm not. And I haven't been for a really long time if I'm honest. But I will be."

He offered her a comforting smile. "This isn't your fault. You know that, right?"

The way her emotions were tumbling around, she wasn't as certain of that fact as she wanted to be. "I wish I'd listened when he tried to warn me about Mat."

Colton squeezed her hand. "Whether you went to Mat tonight or not, this reckoning was coming. Whatever he was mixed up in was always going to spill over onto you. The moment that happened, Jackson would have no choice but to do everything he could to keep you safe."

"Have you heard any word yet from your team? Has anyone figured out what the hell Mat was actually wrapped up in?"

Colton shook his head. "Not a clue. But don't worry. We'll figure it out. We're taking his hard drive and his filing cabinets back to headquarters. It will probably take our cyber team at least a couple of weeks to comb through his digital files."

She rubbed the base of her neck, trying to get rid of the tension pulling at the muscles there. She needed this to be over.

"Don't worry about it. He's dead. He can't hurt you anymore. Let us worry about finding out what he was up to. Meanwhile, you just focus on you and that friend of mine who went and got himself shot."

"Family for Jackson Dean?"

Aja stood without thinking. A man in green scrubs walked over to them. Colton stood and offered the man his hand to shake. After greeting him, Colton flashed his badge. "I'm Ranger Adams. I'm investigating Mr. Dean's shooting. The family hasn't arrived yet, but what can you tell me about his condition?"

The doctor glanced at Colton's badge. "Hello, I'm Doctor Cooper. Mr. Dean's surgery went well. He's a very lucky man. The bullet came close to nicking his axillary artery. A centimeter or two in another direction and he could've bled out. Fortunately, that wasn't the case. We removed the bullet, and he's resting comfortably in recovery. He won't be chopping any wood over the next few weeks, but he should recover with little fanfare."

The knot sitting in Aja's chest slightly loosened, and she could breathe around the obstruction. He would be fine.

"Give us a chance to get him settled in a room, and someone will bring you back to see him shortly. I doubt he'll be able to assist your investigation until the anesthesia wears off, but you're welcome to wait until he's awake."

The tension in her chest continued to subside. She still wouldn't feel better until she saw him, but knowing his prognosis was good took most of the pressure off.

When they were escorted to his room, Colton stepped aside for her to enter. "Aren't you joining me?"

"Trust me, Aja, it ain't my face he'll want to see when he wakes up. I'll wait until Storm gets back from his coffee run."

She walked into the dim room. Slowly stepping closer to the bed, she took in the somber picture of Jackson lying so still against the stark white linens.

"Jackson?" He didn't move, didn't answer. She walked to his right side, too afraid to look at the injured arm on the left. She pulled a nearby chair to his bedside and sat, gently wrapping her fingers around his hand and lifting it to her cheek.

"I'm so sorry I didn't listen to you." The tears she'd been fighting since they'd taken him out of that office building unconscious on a gurney fell unchecked. She didn't care how weak she looked, she couldn't stop them, nor the flood of fear and anxiety she'd tried to keep buried. "This is my fault. And if you never want to see me again because of my stupidity, I will completely understand."

He didn't answer. Except for the rise and fall of his chest as he breathed and the beep of the monitors connected to him, the only sounds in the room were coming from her.

"You saved me. You put yourself between me and that maniac and took the bullet that was meant to kill me. I'm torn between undying gratitude and wanting to wring your damn neck. Why would you do that for me? Why would you risk everything to save someone as hardheaded and unworthy as me?" She held his hand tighter as her shoulders shook and her words became thick sobs.

"I could've lost you," she continued. "You could've died, and I would never have had the chance to tell you how much I love you. I'd never have had the chance to tell you that more than anything, I want to be a woman worthy of your love. I'd never have been able to thank you for saving me."

He groaned, and once she cleared her watery vision with a swipe of her fingers, she saw him move his head toward her voice.

"Ev...ery..."

She stood, running a soothing hand over the top of his head. "Let me go get a nurse." She tried to release his hand, but he tightened his hold on her.

He cleared his throat, opening his eyes, trying his best to focus his sleepy vision on her. "Everything," he whispered. "Did it 'cause you're everything."

Her face still a watery mess, she smiled down at him. "Exactly how much of my confession did you hear?"

"'Nough to hear the woman I love tell me she feels the same."

Tears continued to well up in her eyes. "You deserve so much better than me."

"Not about what I deserve. 'Bout what I want. Want you." He blinked his eyes and cleared his throat as if trying to shake off the remnants of the anesthesia. When he looked at her again, his eyes were more focused. He pulled their joined hands to his mouth and pressed a soft kiss against the back of her hand. Even in a hospital bed, he was always attempting to comfort her. "You're all I need, Aja. You're perfect for me."

"When you say it, I believe it."

He smiled up at her, the dark depths of his eyes shining with happiness, forgiveness, and love. "Then let me spend the rest of my life saying it to you, so neither of us forgets."

"You sure you want to tie yourself to the likes of me? Wherever I go, trouble seems to follow."

His full lips tugged into a wide grin. "Lord if that ain't the truth. But I was made to keep you safe and happy. I'll gladly spend my life protecting you. I love you, Aja."

"I love you too, Jackson. But you'd better make sure this ain't just the anesthesia talking. There are no backsies on this deal. Once you agree to it, the terms are final."

"Then let's seal it with a kiss and make it official."

She brought their mouths together, the warmth of his touch chasing away the chill of guilt and anguish that had cloaked her for so long. The pain of her tumultuous relationship with her sister and the horrible events born of it were still there. But when he touched her, smiled at her, the ache wasn't as profound, and the cut of guilt wasn't as deep. Jackson Dean had come to protect her from physical harm. But in the end, his presence had given her so much more. He'd saved her life, and her heart.

"I do like how you negotiate, Ranger. I do indeed."

The End

Torn between duty and attraction, these Texas Rangers will have to learn to trust love, even when the law tells them not to.

Keep reading for a sneak peek at

COLTON

COMING SOON

Chapter 1

COLTON ADAMS QUICKLY PACKED HIS BAG. HE'D JUST SIGNED off on most of the reports for the Mat Ryan case, and as soon as his colleague Storm Cordero walked himself into Colton's office with the cyber department's wrap-up, Colton could officially stamp this case closed.

Three weeks of sifting through an entire parole office's documents to try to figure out why the hell Ryan had contributed to the aggravated harassment and assault of Aja Everett pushed well past his nonexistent patience for paperwork. As far as they could see, there was no rhyme or reason behind it, and Ryan's partner, Eli Bennett, didn't seem to be in the sharing mood to help lift the fog.

The twinge of a familiar pinch in his gut made Colton stiffen. That was his overactive brain trying to tell him there was something more. He'd felt it since the start of this case all the way to the finish when his supervisor Jackson put a bullet in Mat Ryan, ending the man's life. But with no supporting evidence, all he could do was pack his shit and get his happy hips on the road back to Restoration Ranch.

Persistent vibrating in his back pocket had him pulling out his cell and grinning like a fool when he saw Seneca Daniels' name flash across the screen.

He accepted the call and quickly placed the phone next to his ear. "Evening, pretty lady. To what do I owe the pleasure?"

"Pleasure. I like that word." The sultry tone of her voice climbed through the phone and spilled inside his brain, spreading throughout the rest of his body like a wildfire. "How 'bout you get yourself on over here and we examine it more closely?"

Tension tightened every part of his body, including the flesh pressing uncomfortably behind the metal zipper of his jeans. He groaned in response. "Seneca. You can't talk to me like that when I'm this far away from you and in public."

Her devilish giggle revealed her lack of concern about his current predicament. In fact, he'd say it was a safe bet she was enjoying herself.

"You still in Austin, cowboy? That's too far away for what I have planned for you. What are you doing all the way out there anyway?"

He groaned again. Not just because his need for her had his skin feeling tight with desire. Nope, guilt was running a close second. "I promise, I'll be there as soon as I can. But Sen, as much as I'd like everything the sound of your voice has me wanting, we need to talk."

"I thought only women said that. Are you trying to let me down easy or something?"

"Never," he growled more than spoke. From the day he'd met her, he'd wanted nothing more than to press his body against hers and find out what his name on her lips sounded like while he slid inside of her. But there was only one thing standing in the way of that. He was a Texas Ranger and she didn't know it.

Thinking about revealing this truth to her caused some of his internal heat to dissipate. *How do you tell the woman you've been lusting after for the last eight weeks that everything she knows about you was a lie concocted to help you investigate her?*

"Colt? You still there?"

The sound of his name snapped him out of his thoughts and made him take a deep breath. He was a son-of-a-bitch for a lot of reasons, but hurting Seneca couldn't be one of them.

"Darlin', the one thing you can count on is my desire to get closer to you. There was a lot going on at Restoration that made that difficult. But now, that's all behind us."

"But?" she pressed, and he chuckled. He could picture the raised eyebrow and the no-bullshit slant of her mouth as she said that.

"I just want to be real with you about who I am, Sen. You've been through hell and I never want to add to that. So, as much as I wanna leave here and head straight for your place, how about we meet at the diner on Main Street for dinner, instead? Once we get everything out in the open, I promise I'll take you back home and gladly let you have your way with me if that's what you want."

Her sweet giggle jumped through the phone, lifting his mouth into the broadest grin. "Now that sounds like a plan, cowboy. Hurry up. I'm hungry—for dinner and *you*."

A tap on the door followed by Storm leaning his head in made him mute his phone. "Hargrove wants to see you."

The bottom in his stomach fell. "He say what for?" Storm's usual easygoing face was pulled into tight lines as he shook his head. Whatever this was about, Colton was certain it would do two things: piss him off and fuck up his plans with Seneca.

Colton nodded and Storm closed the door. He unmuted the phone and tried to keep his tone light. "Hey, Sen, I gotta take care of one last thing before I can head out to you." He glanced at his watch quickly before he continued throwing things in his beat-up leather satchel—because he was a cowboy and he refused to carry a briefcase. "I'll meet you at the diner in two hours. That work for you?"

"Sure does. See you then, sweetness."

She disconnected the line and all he could do was shake his head. Whatever Major Hargrove wanted, Colton promised himself one thing: he wasn't about to disappoint that sexy-as-all-hell woman by getting bogged down with Ranger work.

He threw his bag on his shoulder and thanked God in heaven he was only temporary supervisor for his team. Jackson would be back from medical leave in five weeks and it would no longer be Colton's job to report directly to Major Hargrove again.

———————

"You wanted to see me, Major?" Colton could tell shit was about to go sideways when he his supervisor smiled and waved him in. Major Hargrove was a hardass of the highest caliber. He was fair, a man who led by example, and Colton respected his leadership greatly. But even though Hargrove was a tough but fair boss, the man didn't often find reasons to welcome his Rangers into his office with a smile. *What the fuck did I do now?*

"Colton, I know you're about to head out on leave, so thank you for dropping in before you left."

Colton nodded as he sat slowly, waiting for Hargrove to get to the point. "No problem, sir. What can I do for you?"

"How long have you been under my command?"

Colton swallowed, the hair on the back of his neck standing up. When your boss asked you something like, it seemed like a pretty good indication that shit was about to go bad. Colton was a by-the-book kind of Ranger. When his career in the Army disintegrated after he broke the rules, Colton always, always followed regulations to a tee. Whatever this was about, it couldn't have anything to do with him following orders.

"Ten years now." Colton's eyes narrowed into slits as he tried to decipher Hargrove's angle. "Is there something wrong, sir?"

Hargrove shook his head, and walked around his desk, sitting in front of Colton. "Colton, relax. You haven't done anything wrong; you never do. You're one my best field Rangers. You complete every stitch of paperwork you're supposed to. You follow all the regulation that go along with the job. If more of my Rangers followed the rules as well as you, my job would be a breeze."

Colton cocked his head before saying, "Thank you for the compliment, Major. But something tells me you're holding back. If you wanted to know how long I've been working here, you could've looked it up on my personnel file. What's going on?"

Hargrove nodded, one corner of his mouth hitched in a halfway smile. "Fair enough, I'll cut to the chase. You've been a field Ranger for ten years and have never sought to move up in the ranks. Why is that?"

Colton's skin suddenly felt uncomfortably tight on his large, bulky frame. This was not the conversation he wanted to have right now. That was especially true when all he wanted to do was spend his next two weeks off with Seneca. Seneca was fun and light and tempting as the day was long. But thinking about leadership, about his past life...that was as far from fun as ice was from a flame.

"Sir, I'm happy doing my job in the field. Not everyone needs a title to feel fulfilled. Sometimes you just want to do your work and go home."

Hargrove chuckled and crossed his arms over his chest. "You're preaching to the choir on that one, son. There are days I'd go back to the field in a heartbeat. But every time I think about that, I think about how many lives I've impacted by being a leader in the Rangers. You are a born leader, Colton. You may not like it, but you can't run from it. I'd really like to see you move up in the ranks, take on more responsibility."

He took a deep breath and slid his hands down his muscled thighs, trying to dry his palms. "What do you have in mind, Major?"

"Captain Johnston is gonna be retiring in the next six to eight weeks."

"Retiring?" Colton did some mental math and put Johnston somewhere about ten to twelve years older than himself. "He loves this job. He's really considering retiring?"

Hargrove nodded. "Yeah, his daughter just gave birth to his first grandbaby and since then, nothing's more important than spending time with that little one. The problem is, he's currently heading up the new office we're opening up in Spicewood. It's a small, remote town in Hill Country about halfway between Austin and Fresh Springs. I need someone to temporarily head it up until Johnson's permanent replacement is able to take command. Whoever I choose as interim lead needs to be someone I'm sure will follow the rules. I think that's you."

Colton wasn't sure what to say. He'd worked hard to gain the confidence of his superior over the decade he'd been here. One, because he'd desperately needed the job, and two, because he prided himself on always giving 100 percent. Too bad his dedication hadn't paid off during his service in the military.

"Are you sure you want me to replace Johnston. What about Jackson?"

Hargrove took a deep breath and leveled his gaze at Colton, pinning him to the chair. "Your loyalty is admirable. Don't worry, Jackson isn't being overlooked. He's my choice for permanent lead. He has a few more weeks of rehab before he can even be assessed to return to duty, so I need you to go in there now and learn the ropes and hold things down until he gets there."

Colton felt the slight bit of tension in his gut lessen as the major relayed his plan. The idea of leading an entire division on his own dug up long-buried memories he'd spent a lifetime trying to forget.

"Son, I know part of the reason you're so meticulous about following the rules is because the one time you didn't, it got you thrown out of the army on your ass. But, Colton, I don't blame you for that. You were put in an unbelievable situation. Even though what you did was technically wrong, I don't think anyone can blame you for your choices."

That was a lie. Colton could think of one person who blamed him for the choices he'd made that had led to him being tossed out of the service: himself.

"Colton, I want you to take on the post. When Jackson is promoted and installed as Captain, he's gonna need a second to lean on. I've already spoken to him about it; he wants it to be you. Take this assignment as interim commanding officer in Spicewood and you'll get a bump in rank to lieutenant too."

Colton nodded. "I'll think about it. Can I let you know after I come back from leave in two weeks?"

"Sure," Hargrove replied as he walked back around to his desk chair. "You doing anything fun?"

He sure as hell hoped so. "I'm actually going back to Restoration Ranch to make sure Jackson's doing okay." It wasn't a complete lie, but he knew it wasn't the complete truth either.

"Tell that lucky son of a bitch I said hi."

Colton stood and chuckled. "Lucky? The man is recuperating from a gunshot wound."

"Yeah, in the arms of a beautiful woman I hear can cook like angels sing."

"I can tell you from firsthand experience that rumor is based in complete fact. It'll be too late to eat by the time I get there tonight. But I'd be lying if I said I wasn't looking forward to her buttermilk biscuits at breakfast."

Colton extended his hand to Major Hargrove and the man grabbed it, giving it a strong shake. "The job and the promotion is yours if you want it. In the event you do, just keep your head down and follow the rules like you been doing and everything will be fine."

Colton took a deep breath as he tried to ignore the warning bells going off in the back of his mind. But experience taught him his life was never that easy. "Sir, full disclosure, if this is a PR thing, you might not want me taking this on."

Hargrove let his hand slip from Colton's as he searched his face for answers. "I've already told you I'm not concerned about your past. You've done good work for me. That's all that matters."

"Maybe, maybe not. Either way, I think it's probably important I tell you this anyway." He straightened his spine and pulled his shoulders back. He needed his boss to know he wasn't ashamed of anything he was about to say. "I have a personal relationship with Seneca Daniels. I know how some folks in high places are. They might not approve of you promoting a law enforcement agent who has a connection with an ex-con."

Hargrove squinted and shoved his tongue in the side of his cheek before sitting back down in his chair and leaning back as he gave Colton an exasperated look.

"Exactly when did this personal relationship begin?"

Colton swallowed hard, wondering if he was canceling his career or not. "It was after the Restoration Ranch case was initially closed, when we thought Eli Bennett was solely responsible for the vandalism and Aja Everett's attack. It wasn't until nearly a month later when Seneca was poisoned with roofies that we reopened the case."

Hargrove tapped his pen against his metal desktop while keeping his gaze fixed on Colton. His face was hard to read, but Colton would bet by the straight line of his mouth, he wasn't too thrilled.

"Does she know who you really are?"

"Funny thing, I'm on my way to tell her now. I can't lie to her anymore. She needs to know the truth."

Hargrove put the pen down and blew out a long breath. "So, your visit to Restoration isn't entirely about checking in on Jackson, is it?" When Colton shook his head, the major let a slow whistle escape his lips. "Boy, if you don't have the damnedest luck when it comes to personal relationships and work." Colton couldn't help the chuckle that slipped from his lips. Hargrove sure as shit wasn't lying. He'd hoped the last time his two worlds collided would in fact be the last time. But apparently life decided once wasn't enough.

"Colt, you haven't committed any infractions I can reprimand you for. As long as Ms. Daniels remains a law-abiding citizen, and you don't actively abet any potential crimes she may commit, who you sleep with is your business. However, I wouldn't go announcing that to anyone before your promotion takes place. Like I said, keep your head down and do your job, and this process should all go smoothly. See you when you return. Hope you'll have good news for me when you do."

Colton eased out of the room and closed the door. He had a lot to think about over these next two weeks, and standing in the hall staring into space wasn't going to help him with anything.

"First things first, Colton," he mumbled as he finally walked out of the building and headed for his truck. "You'd better pray you can explain things to Seneca well enough that she doesn't slaughter you. Otherwise, you might not live long enough to make this decision about a promotion."

Seneca hung up the phone, immediately noting the huge grin on her face. She sank back into her couch and let her shameless thirst for Colton settle in. Her face muscles were beginning to ache from all the smiling she did whenever she talked to Colton, and quite frankly, she didn't care.

Only a couple of weeks had passed since he'd last visited her on the ranch. But damn if it didn't feel like an eternity. Especially after her unexpected poisoning dashed any hopes they'd had of exploring their mutual attraction.

But with all the danger behind them and the clean bill of health her doctors gave her a couple of days ago at her last checkup, Seneca could not wait to lay her eyes and hands on Colton Adams and his sexy ass.

"Are you done daydreaming about Bo yet?" Seneca's smile slipped as she fixed her gaze on Brooklyn walking into her front door. She gave Brooklyn the usual eye-roll reserved for that specific comparison between Colton and Beauregard "Bo" Duke from the *Dukes of Hazzard*. Besides, Bo was cute, but he didn't have shit on the brooding ranch hand that starred in all of Seneca's naughty dreams as of late.

"You know that's some real offensive shit on so many levels, right?"

Brooklyn shrugged in response then continued as if Seneca hadn't asked anything. "I know you don't officially come back to work for another three days, but just so you know, the Welcome Center is finished and ready to be furnished. I need to know when you want to come in and do your IT thing before I have interior design head in."

Seneca sighed heavily and cut her eyes in a sharp slant at her former cellmate. "Listen, dream crusher, stop trying to make everyone in the world as miserable as you."

Brooklyn laughed as Seneca waved her into the cabin. The tall beauty with the smooth, deep brown skin sat in the nearby recliner and put her heels up on the coffee table.

"I'm not miserable, just honest. Blocking bullshit just saves me grief later. But judging by that goofy-ass smile on your face, I'd say you're all for entertaining whatever that cowboy of yours is slinging your way."

Seneca shrugged. Why deny it? She wasn't the least bit ashamed. "Listen, if that pretty ass man wants to break my dry spell, I am not about to stop him. You should try finding someone to do the same for you. Sexin' is guaranteed to better your mood.

Ask Aja. She certainly was in a better mood after she started getting a little brown sugar on the regular."

"Whatever, chick." Brooklyn stood. "Just tell me when you're going in to do your thing so I can get the Welcome Center finished."

"See?" Seneca could see her glee was rubbing on the last of Brooklyn's patience. "If you got a little lovin', your ass wouldn't be snapping at me about work. After I get some, I promise I'm gonna look out for you and find someone to knock the cobwebs loose for you too."

Brooklyn rewarded her with a low growl that amused Seneca into genuine laughter. "Fine, be that way. I'll handle it Monday. Only a few terminals are going in there; it shouldn't take long."

With a squint and a nod, Brooklyn turned to leave, but stopped in Seneca's doorway. She threw a sly smirk in Seneca's direction. "Even if you're a pain in my ass, if you're happy, so am I. Just watch yourself around him, Sen. Anyone that beautiful and charming is hiding something. It could be a wife or a couple of bodies. Either way, don't get in too deep. You've got a lot to lose, so keep it light."

Momentarily overwhelmed by the slight chink in Brooklyn's armor, Seneca's already good mood soared. "I knew you loved me."

Brooklyn rolled her eyes while simultaneously flipping Seneca the bird. She was impressive like that. Fluent in "Fuck You," she never wasted an opportunity to practice her linguistics.

Seneca blew her friend an exaggerated kiss accompanied with the requisite amount of juvenile smooching sounds. Brooklyn stopped a second and chuckled before she headed through the doorway, until the metal wind chimes signaled her exit out the front door.

It was good to have friends. Even perpetually grumpy ones like Brooklyn.

A quick glance at her phone's clock display spurred her to get up and head for her bedroom. She had to see a man about a good time tonight. Being late just wouldn't do.

Seneca checked her hair and makeup in her rearview mirror for what seemed liked the millionth time. She never fussed over her appearance like this, but tonight was the night and she couldn't help wanting to be extra cute. Her curly, natural hair was free of its usual cornrows. And if the hair gods kept smiling on her, the Texas heat wouldn't destroy her trendy braid out.

She primped for a few minutes more before deciding her cute factor was on point and headed toward the diner. She wasn't far from the entrance when she heard someone call out. "You sure do clean up well."

Her muscles locked and halted her stride as a chill passed across the surface of her skin. She didn't need to turn around to know who was speaking. That voice had terrified her for nearly seven years.

"If I'd known all of this was under your standard issue orange jumpsuit, I might have demanded other perks from you than your computer skills."

Sheriff Leroy Hastings finally stepped around and then in front of her. He let his lecherous gaze slide down the length of her and instantly Seneca wanted a shower.

She fought against her desire to recoil in disgust. *Play it cool, Seneca. Stay calm so he doesn't have a reason to react, a reason to feel threatened, an excuse to take your freedom away.*

"Evening, Sheriff."

His lanky form vibrated with a soundless chuckle. "You look like you've got plans. I remember a time when the only plans you had were the ones I gave you. You remember, don'tcha? Those were the good ole days."

That wasn't exactly how she remembered their time together in the state pen when he was the corrections officer in charge of her cellblock. She didn't refute his delusions. Good sense demanded she remain silent if she wanted to get out of this situation with the least harm.

"Well, I don't want to keep you from whatever's waiting on you in the diner, but while I have you here, might as well say what's on my mind. I've run into a bit of a cashflow problem recently. To help that, I'mma need you to resume our previous agreement."

She shook her head out of reflex as panic flooded her insides, making her body feel two sizes too small. Bad move. She could see anger spark in his eyes. She looked around the dark parking lot for another soul or a way out, but there was none.

"I've done my time. You can't do this to me again. You made me use my hacking skills to steal money for you on the inside. That's not happening ever again."

The nonchalant shrug he offered made her blood run cold. "I wouldn't be so sure of that. I was the law when you were in lockup. Now I'm the law out here. Whatever I say goes. And even your fancy lawyer lady can't do anything about that."

The chimes on the door of the diner rang out into the night air as a patron headed in their direction. Seneca took advantage of the distraction and walked around the sheriff and headed for the door. When her foot touched the bottom step, he called out to her.

"I'll be in touch, Ms. Daniels." He smiled, tipped his hat, then walked back to his cruiser.

His words made the hairs on her arms stand up at attention even after he'd pulled out of the parking lot. He might have sounded benign and businesslike, but Seneca saw through his bullshit for what it was. A threat.

She shook herself and headed inside. That man ruined her life for too many years to give him one moment more of her time than necessary.

She waved at Martha-Jean standing behind the counter. "You want me to set you up right here or you want a booth?"

Seneca glanced around. Save for a man sitting at the other end of the counter, the entire diner was empty. Seneca tipped her head toward the booths behind her. "Is the back booth available? I'm expecting company."

Martha-Jean nodded and grabbed two menus before walking Seneca to her requested booth. "Let me know when you're ready to order."

She smiled and took a relieved breath when she sat down. As much as she enjoyed sitting at the counter and chatting with the wait staff as they worked, tonight she needed this booth. It would give Colton and her more privacy. But more importantly, it would give her a chance to get herself together after her encounter with Hastings.

"He's gone. He can't hurt you anymore. Just focus on tonight."

MOTHER DAVIDSON'S PINEAPPLE COCONUT CAKE

Hey Readers!

Thank you for reading *Jackson*! I hope you enjoyed reading it as much as I did writing it. You'll notice Aja uses the sweet reward of pineapple coconut cake to help Jackson's often surly mood. I know it seems farfetched that a slice of cake could have such a powerful impact. But believe me, this sweet, sinfully decadent confection is tasty enough to turn the biggest sourpuss into a dancing cherub. My family has made this cake for generations, so I know firsthand how amazing it is. My grandmother, Mother Davidson, taught my mom and me how to make this. When my kids get a little older, I'm going to teach them how to make it too. But in the meantime, I'm gonna share this wonderful recipe with you.

Whenever I make this, I can still remember standing at my grandmother's side executing every step as she watched me carefully with a smile. Though our great matriarch passed away eleven years ago, I can still feel the warmth of her smile whenever I make one of her favorite dishes or desserts. And between me and you, I have never felt more loved, cared for, or praised, than when my grandmother smiled at me when we cooked together. I 'clare, there is nothing like cooking with your loved ones to show you what's important in life. And that's a lesson Aja teaches Jackson every time she serves him a slice of this cake.

I could go on forever about those good times in my

grandmother's kitchen and how they keep me happy even all these years later. It's my hope you get a sense of that same evergreen happiness every time Aja walks into her kitchen on Restoration Ranch. And let's face it, with the past year being what it was, there's lots to be upset about. But like Aja, I've come to realize that even in the midst of personal trials, a slice of this cake can be a momentary reprieve from the hard times. Much like me, Aja having lived through personal hardships, uses cooking and baking as therapy. So, when she finds a sexy Ranger who doesn't trust easily, she knows all he needs is a little bit of sweetness and her magic ingredient, love, to get through his hard times.

Well, if you're looking for a little happy, g'on and try my grandmother's pineapple coconut cake, and I defy you to be anything but blissful after eating a slice. Just remember, this is a sweet, high-carb treat. So please make sure you take that into consideration before eating it if you have any dietary or health concerns.

Happy baking!
LaQuette 💋

INGREDIENTS & UTENSILS

*Certain ingredients don't have measurements because we pour until the ancestors tell us to stop. That means sweeten or season to taste.

- 1 to 2 14-ounce bags Baker's Coconut Angel Flakes (sweet-ened)
- 1 can crushed pineapple
- ¼ teaspoon cream of tartar
- Vanilla extract
- ½ cup light corn syrup
- Sugar
- 10 eggs (3 eggs for each box of cake mix, 4 **separated** eggs for the meringue—discard the four remaining yolks and keep the whites in a mixing bowl)
- 2 boxes yellow cake mix
- Maraschino cherries
- ⅓ cup vegetable oil
- Water
- 2 6-inch baking pans
- 2-quart saucepan
- 1-quart saucepan
- Hand mixer
- Strainer
- Small mixing bowl (to capture excess pineapple juice)
- Medium to large mixing bowl for meringue and cake batter

- 1 can Baker's Joy (or any non-stick baking spray with flour or, if you're old school, you can grease your pans with Crisco or vegetable oil, then swish flour around it to coat your pans)

STEPS

Preheat oven to 350°F and coat your pans with floured baking spray or oil and flour.

Mix cake mix according to directions on the box. Usually calls for 1 cup water, 3 eggs, ⅓ cup vegetable oil, and a few splashes of vanilla extract.

Pour 1¾ cups batter in each pan, and bake at 350°F for 22 to 27 minutes or until toothpick or fork inserted in center comes out clean. Remove from oven and let cool completely.

Take small mixing bowl & place strainer inside of it. Pour the can of crushed pineapple into strainer and squeeze out any excess juice into the mixing bowl (save the juice).

Pour enough water to coat the bottom of the 2-quart saucepan. Add strained pineapple, then pour a small amount of the juice into the pan. Over a low heat, mix continuously (if you stop, the sugar will caramelize & burn). Cook down mixture until it has a syrupy consistency. Remove from heat.

Pour enough water to cover the bottom of the 1-quart saucepan (approximately 6 tablespoons). Add ½ cup sugar, ½ cup light corn syrup, ¼ teaspoon cream of tartar. Stir over medium heat until mixture is dissolved, then remove from heat.

Separate 4 egg whites into a mixing bowl (discard the yolks). Beat egg whites with hand mixer, then slowly pour the hot sugar/syrup mixture into the beaten egg whites. Beat mixture again until soft peaks form then set aside.

Place your first layer of cake on a plate or cake dish. If it's not level on the top, cut a little bit off to level it out (you're going to stack the layers, so they need to be as flat as possible).

Get your pineapple mixture and spread evenly atop the first layer. Try to make sure the mixture doesn't spill over the sides of the bottom layer. Once you're done, sit the second layer on top of the bottom layer (your pineapple filling should rest between the two layers). Clean away any excess pineapple filling that may have spilled out of the cake when pressed between both layers.

Once both tiers are layered, get your meringue and spread it evenly on the top and the sides of your cake like frosting (the entire cake should be covered in the meringue).

Get your shredded coconut and sprinkle it generously all over the cake. You'll have to gently hand press on the sides to cover the whole cake.

Garnish with Maraschino cherries. You can gently place them on the top or if you want to get fancy, poke toothpicks through the cherries to secure their placement on top of the cake.

Let chill in the refrigerator for 2–3 hours or until meringue/coconut is stiff (not sliding off the cake).

Acknowledgments

Once again, Brooklyn is in the house! It's taken many people to get me to this point in my career, so indulge me while I share my gratitude to those who have helped me along the way.

To God, from whom all blessings flow, thank you for the gift, the desire, the support, and the opportunity. To Damon, my original romance hero—this does not happen without you. Love you forever. To Sterling and Semaj, and Mason and Mackenzie, my heartbeats, the best parts of me. To the late James and Doris Davidson (Granddaddy and Grandma), for a foundation strong enough to keep me standing all these years later. I miss you both so much. To my mama, Pearl, who blessed me with a flair for the fabulous and dramatic, my sister, Ebony, who keeps me laughing, and my baby brother, Ron, who reminds me I'm super at everything I do. (That's why he's my favorite.) Thank you for consistently pouring your faith into me. To all of my JMC, LIJ, and York people—your love strengthens me.

To Latoya Smith, my agent and fellow Brooklynite, thank you for understanding my vision and working your tail off to help me accomplish it. This is only the beginning. To Mary Altman, thank you for the colorful happiness you bring to our work.

To Sourcebooks and Sourcebooks Casablanca, thank you for the opportunity and the support. I'm so excited to make magic together.

To Lexie Craig, Sarah Davis, and my Rogue Romance and CIMRWA families, thank you for being the most driven and inspiring peers a writer could have. You constantly push me to reach for more in a profession that can sometimes feel too big to handle. Thank you for your wisdom and your guidance. It's all led me to this point.

To Rochelle Alers, Beverly Jenkins, Brenda Jackson, Donna Hill, Sandra Kitt, Nikki Night, Zuri Day, Farrah Rochon, Mary B. Morrison, Sylvia Hubbard, Nina Foxx, Serenity King, Zane, Earl Sewell, Eric Jerome Dickey, Carl Weber, Omar Tyree, and the late Francis Ray and E. Lynn Harris, thank you for creating stories about our people, our culture, our communities, and our love that made a young girl believe she could do the same one day.

To my sistahs who always hold me down: C. Chilove, Adriana Herrera, Harper Miller, Xyla Turner, Siera London, Eve Vaughn, Koko Brown, Blue Saffire, Reese Ryan, Piper Huguley, KM Jackson, Elle Wright, Sherelle Green, Sheryl Lister, L. Penelope, AC Arthur, Laurel Cremant, AM Griffin, Toni Jackson, Seressia Glass, Shyla Colt, Naima Simone, and Xio Axelrod. We are magic, never forget that.

To my readers, whether you're a newcomer or a ride or die, your faith in me and my stories keeps me going. Thank you so much for the loyalty and encouragement. You will never know how much I appreciate your support. Thank you for taking this journey with me.

Keep it sexy,
LaQuette

About the Author

LaQuette writes savvy, sensational, and sexy romance featuring unapologetically diverse and bold characters who celebrate their right to appear on the page.

A native of Brooklyn, NY, she crafts emotionally epic, fantastical tales deeply pigmented by reality's paintbrush. Find her on her website: LaQuette.com, Amazon, Facebook, Twitter (@laquettewrites), Instagram (@la_quette), and via email at LaQuette@LaQuette.com.

Newsletter Sign-up

Hello,

If you're interested in staying current with all the happenings with my writing, previews, and giveaways, sign up for my monthly newsletter at LaQuette.com.

Keep it sexy,
LaQuette 💋